The Pact

No one knows you better than your sister

The Pact

In tennis, as in life, nothing ever goes truly to plan. (Samantha Callahan's faultless astuteness.)

After losing at Wimbledon, I screamed at myself, I raged at Annie. And yes, I yelled at spectators to the point where I was almost jeered off the court. Momentarily, I wondered what it would be like to have eight thousand people booing me instead of a vocal handful. Meanwhile, Annie was a picture of composed calm and accepted the defeat with a *that's too bad.* Her emotional detachment inflamed me further. We were poles apart, handling our stress and loss so differently.

Swallowing the urge to vomit, I made my way towards the women's locker room. I needed a long shower to cool down, but I also needed to have it out with Annie. As I reached the entrance, I saw her outside, laughing with several other players like she hadn't a care in the world. Like we hadn't just suffered a humiliating defeat and been booed off court. I couldn't fathom what was going on with her. Was she truly that unaware?

'Annie, it wasn't just me who played badly out there today,' I said, walking up to the group, the pounding in my head growing stronger with every step.

She turned to face me. 'It was a game, Sam. We lost. Move on. There'll be other games. There are always other games.'

Some of the players tittered, which incensed me further.

'How can you say that? How can you dismiss this like it's no big deal?'

'Because it *is* no big deal. There are more important things in life—'

I slapped her. Right then and there, outside the women's locker room, I slapped my sister across the face.

What They Are Saying About The Pact

"From page one there's no looking back. True to form, Darcy delivers the first of many twists...immediately hooking the reader. *The Pact* explores the beauty of sisterhood, the joys of romance, and the trials and tribulations of finding your place in the world."

—J'Aimee Brooker, reviewer, *AusRom Today*

"In *The Pact,* Darcy explores the rollercoaster of life on the doubles tennis circuit and adds the tension of a sibling relationship. Samantha and Annie's fraught journey encompasses love, triumph, defeat, grief and joy; all the feels—alongside liberal servings of humour, snappy dialogue and insight into the human condition. I raced through this engaging read, cheering not only for the sisters to win on court, but also for them to find peace and happiness in life. Lisa Darcy at her best."

—Andrea Barton, author of *The Godfather of Dance*

"Drama, action, love, lust, twists and turns; it's all here. You certainly won't be disappointed reading *The Pact*."

—Jodi Gibson, author of *Reinventing Emily Brown*, *The Five-Year Plan* and *The Memories We Hide*

"The pro-tennis circuit is used by Darcy to explore the complex lives of sisters and doubles partners, Samantha and Annie Callahan as they struggle with their careers and romantic relationships in the hot-house world of elite sport. I was fully engaged by their attempts and frequent failures to understand each other, which ultimately provide opportunities for growth and acceptance. An exciting, pacey read with great characters, plot and dialogue. Highly recommended."

—Diane Clarke, author of *The Photograph*

"Sprightly...well-crafted and lively...containing sharp insights..."

—*Sydney Morning Herald*

"Enjoy this sharp, snappy lesson in survival and success."

—*Woman's Day*

"This pacy and funny novel is plot driven...and genuinely witty."

—*Sunday Age*

"Darcy does what she does best...intermingles romance and personal crisis."

—*West Australian*

The Pact

No one knows you better than your sister

Lisa Darcy

A Wings ePress, Inc.

Women's Fiction Novel

Wings ePress, Inc.

Edited by: Jeanne Smith
Copy Edited by: Bev Haynes
Executive Editor: Jeanne Smith
Cover Artist: Daniella Levy

Wings ePress Books
www.wingsepress.com

ISBN 979-8-89197-995-6-

Published In the United States Of America

Wings ePress, Inc.
3000 N. Rock Road
Newton, KS 67114

Dedication

To my wonderful dad, who excelled at all sports, especially tennis.

In pro tennis, just as in any memorable film or book, you have your hero, villain, heroine, damsel in distress, rake and, of course, the girl next door. Let me tell you a story...'

—Samantha Callahan

One

Samantha

'Samantha! Annie! Samantha! Annie!'

The crowd grew louder, their chanting faster, more intense. We hadn't even left the locker room.

Heart pumping, I stared at my sister, Annie. 'Ready?'

Her eyes brightened. 'Let's do this.'

This was our moment. We were about to realise our dream of playing in the Australian Open semi-finals, Rod Laver Arena, Melbourne Park. The whole of Australia was on our side, willing us to victory.

Because we were on home soil, the pressure was immense. We needed to block out expectations and focus on our game. We'd worked bloody hard to get here and wanted to lift that winner's trophy. And I knew Annie and I could do it.

Tennis bags slung over our shoulders, we high fived each other and opened the locker room door to flashing cameras.

'Samantha! Annie! Samantha! Annie!'

I itched to get on court and play, but first we had to answer the obligatory pre-match questions. More than a dozen reporters stood in the corridor entrance ten metres ahead of us, microphones poised.

Five metres... walking tall, eyes fixed straight ahead. We had nothing to fear.

Three metres... breathing far from calm, our mantra boomed inside my head: *We are winners.*

Annie and I exchanged a smile, confident we'd go all the way.

One metre... adrenalin pumping, the rush.

Showtime!

Annie's boyfriend, Erik Sørensen, stepped in front of us and clapped his hands at the assembled media.

He cleared his throat. 'Erik comes to stop this,' he said in his thick Scandinavian accent.

I clocked Annie to gauge her reaction—surprised, curious.

'Erik has the announcement,' he continued, full of self-importance. 'To say my bride, Annie, is for me the new koala. It matters not that Annie win tennis, she is Erik's new wife, about to be.'

How dare he? Pissed off didn't begin to explain my feelings. What kind of man proposes to his girlfriend via the media just as she was about to play one of the most important games of her career?

Annie squealed and rushed towards Erik. Everyone yahooed, even a couple of rogue ball girls. Reporters gridlocked the narrow corridor leading to centre court.

'Calm down,' I whispered in Annie's direction, but she wasn't listening.

I turned to our coach and mentor, Bern Devlin, aka Bear. 'What the hell just happened?'

He shrugged. 'Deep breaths, Sam.'

How could I breathe deeply when I was practically hyperventilating?

Veteran reporter Prue Hamilton shoved a microphone under my sister's nose. 'Annie, what do you say?'

I willed Annie to say Erik was being ridiculous, that she'd known the guy less than three weeks. Failing that, I wanted her to keep her mouth closed and say nothing.

'Yes! Yes! Yes!' she shrieked.

Shock was the only thing that stopped me from whacking Annie over the head with my new Spalding racquet. And because I love that racquet.

'Samantha,' someone shouted. 'What do you want to say to your sister?'

All I wanted to say was 'Wipe that stupid grin off your face,' but I looked at the expectant faces and gripped my racquet harder. 'Congratulations, Annie. But right now, we've got a match to win.'

Bear put a calming hand on my shoulder. I shot him a death stare but said nothing.

'You girls okay?'

'Of course,' Annie replied dreamily. 'Bear, can you believe it? Erik's proposal was completely spontaneous. He said when he saw me just now it hit him like a lightning bolt that we should be married.'

'And you?' Bear asked me, his hand still resting on my shoulder.

'I'm fine. I just want to get on with winning this match.' I grabbed Annie's hand and dragged her onto the court, away from Bear, Erik and reporters.

'You can't be serious,' I said after we waved to the crowd and put our bags down on the courtside benches.

'What do you mean?'

'About marrying Erik.'

'We're in love.'

I swallowed before speaking. 'It's been three weeks! You can hardly even understand each other's language, for God's sake.'

'We speak the international language of love. Mum would be so happy, don't you think?'

'Mum? Happy?' I couldn't say any more. Mum would be horrified. She'd want us to focus on the game, the win. Before she left, she'd been the driving force behind my love for tennis, and afterwards I really threw myself into it. Tennis became my saviour – playing, training, strategizing – all to please Mum in the hope she'd return.

I shook off Erik's interruption and Annie's response. This wasn't what tennis was about. Our personal lives were not supposed to overshadow the game.

Our opponents, Jelena Tipsarević and Dragana Lukić, were clearly bewildered too. Statuesque and raven-haired, the Serbians made a formidable team. And it just so happened that Dragana was Erik's ex-girlfriend. Usually, Dragana was sombre, but today she positively beamed for the cameras.

Minutes later, we won the toss and elected to receive. Jelena and Dragana strode to their end of the court grinning like Cheshire cats.

Two

Rod Laver Arena had hit thirty-seven degrees, yet Tennis Australia refused to invoke the Extreme Heat Policy and close the roof. Apparently, the mercury had to rise above thirty-nine before that happened, and even then, it was discretionary. My bet? The official thermometer was fucked. We were delirious, melting in the searing heat.

Annie and I were at 0–40. In other words, losing. Surprise!

Thanks to Jelena's huge serve, she and Dragana snatched the first game. I returned fire, but Annie missed one easy lob after another. Flustered, she kept picking imaginary lint from her left shoulder, a nervous habit she'd developed as an adolescent.

'Annie, focus!' I said, not unkindly, when we swapped ends. 'Talk yourself up.'

'I am. Stop hassling me. It's only a game.'

Only a game? We'd been working towards this moment for years. This was so much more than a game. I struggled to slow my racing pulse, counting to ten. The last thing I needed was to lose control.

At changeovers, Annie dawdled, sometimes arriving after I'd been waiting at the baseline a full minute or more, as if she were in another world, which I guess she was. Erik world.

At twenty-eight minutes, we were down five games to two.

Six minutes later, Dragana and Jelena claimed the first set.

The Serbian women dominated us, barely missing a beat in the second set. It was sweltering, the air still. How could they perform under these heatwave conditions? How could we? My shirt was wet, my skirt too. Dehydrated, no amount of fluid seemed to help. But I was determined not to give in. Annie and I had to win this. For us. For Mum. We were a heartbeat away from the finals.

Annie was barely perspiring, apart from a line of sweat on her upper lip.

My eyes fixed straight ahead as Jelena served to Annie. And—aced her.

My eyes almost popped when Annie clapped Jelena's serve. Annie didn't have a hope of returning it, so I had no right to be angry, but that didn't stop me. *Clapped!* What was she thinking?

As the match wore on, Jelena's serve and forehand proved increasingly difficult for us to return. Aggressive and strong, she slammed the ball hard and low over the net. Her control was astounding. To make matters worse, Dragana had a vicious spin on her serve. The ball jumped at odd angles and was near to impossible to return.

Annie and I were overpowered. Our opponents claimed a crucial break to move 3–0 ahead early in the second set.

They continued to victory in little over an hour.

Three

Zach

Zach Baxter clicked off image after image of Annie and Samantha Callahan after their defeat. As much as it pained him, he had a job to do.

Erik and Annie engaged? He slumped slightly, not wanting to believe the scene unfolding in front of him. Annie was so sweet and so unaware of her beauty, charm and sex appeal. And here she was, leaping into Erik's arms, kissing him, then smooching him some more. Zach hadn't seen a media frenzy like this since Agassi proposed to Stefi.

Some women, Annie included, considered Erik tall, dark and handsome in a Viking kind of way. But to Zach, he was gangly and gaunt with a dirty mud-coloured mullet and a long, hooked snout. As for his personality, Zach recognised a serial flirt when he saw one. But Erik was more than that. Not only was he an egocentric womaniser, he was also calculating. No doubt he'd planned every second of his announcement about how excited he was to marry his 'Aussie koala,' down to his bounding into the air, legs and arms akimbo. Erik had guaranteed that he and Annie would be front-page news at the expense of the Callahan sisters' game. And here Zach was, contributing to the frenzy. But the media wanted photos, and he was a professional. He needed to get the best shots to guarantee a sale.

Zach caught Samantha's eye. Clearly seething, she was nonetheless holding it together. As for the spectators, they seemed to have forgotten the women had lost the semis – they rose from their seats, screaming, foot stamping and cheering.

'We love you, Annie!'

'Marry me, Annie!' someone else shouted.

Four

Samantha

The post-match press conference was one of the most humiliating moments of my life. Not only had we let ourselves down, but we'd disappointed our fans and disappointed Australia. Instead of our ranking pushing single digits, we were sure to slip down into the teens.

'Nothing like an impromptu wedding proposal to stir the masses, hey Annie?' commentator Doug Warren remarked.

Beside him, reporter Prue Hamilton raised her eyebrows. 'It's cute, if a little untimely. Do you think Erik's unexpected proposal hindered your game?'

'It didn't help,' I snapped, battling to compose myself.

'Our opponents were the better players today,' Annie said, full of carefree grace. 'Well done to Dragana and Jelena. They deserved to win.'

'You're obviously disappointed, Samantha,' Doug Warren

commented. 'But we couldn't help noticing Annie applauding a 195 kilometre-per-hour serve from Jelena.'

'She hit an unbelievable serve I couldn't return,' Annie said. 'Why not give her credit?'

'Would this gracious gesture have anything to do with your engagement?'

Annie giggled.

Desperate to cut the interview short, I got up to leave, but reporters bombarded me with questions that had nothing to do with tennis.

'Were you surprised to learn of your sister's engagement?'

'How do you get along with your brother-in-law to be?'

'Do you think the engagement will affect your tennis partnership?'

My answers: 'Surprised but delighted;' 'Fabulously;' 'Not at all.' In truth, I wanted to grab Annie by her scalp and scream, 'Are you fucking insane? How could you do this to your career? To us? To Mum?'

'So where to from here?' Prue asked.

'Straight back to training,' I said, just as Annie replied, 'To kiss my gorgeous fiancé.'

'There'll be other games,' Annie said, when we were finally alone with Bear.

'That's not the point.' I was unable to keep the devastation from my voice. 'We're better players than them. We should have won easily. It was the semis. We wanted to take out the finals.'

'Enough.' Bear pulled us in to a tight huddle. 'Everyone loses. It's a fact. You're not entitled to win. The question is, can you come back from it?'

'Of course,' Annie said. 'Now if you'll excuse me.' She practically skipped away, phone to her ear.

I glared after her.

Bear cocked his head. 'GG, it's over.'

'But—'

'But nothing. Cool down. Breathe.'

'Hmph. Why should I listen to you?'

'Because I'm right.'

'Whatever,' I said, knowing the word infuriated him.

I walked into the locker complex, the neutral colour palette meant to induce serenity fuelling my frustration. Ignoring attendants, players and other coaches, I strode past the treatment, ice bath, and massage areas, towards the showers, desperate to lose myself. I shrugged off my clothes and under the hot streaming water swallowed my disappointment.

~ * ~

When Bear started coaching Annie and me after I'd had a serious professional meltdown three years ago, there'd been a spark between us. At that initial practice session, his presence, his voice, and his humour eased my nerves. We chatted easily, and I actually laughed, something I rarely did on court.

'Oi! Samantha,' he said, 'do you know what to do with those balls in your hand?'

I smiled. 'Yes, I'm quite comfortable with two balls.'

He was talented, smart and cute. Three weeks later, we were in Brisbane for a charity tournament and arrived at the nominated hotel to find only two rooms had been booked: one for Annie and her then boyfriend, Anthony, and one for Bear.

'Did you think I'd be flying back to Sydney?' I asked as we stood at the check-in counter while staff scrambled to find another room. 'Alone?'

'I wasn't thinking,' Bear said, his face breaking into a smile.

Finally, the efficient, smiley receptionist said, 'We're fully booked.'

'Pillows down the middle of the bed,' I told him as we caught the lift to our suite on the fifteenth floor.

'Of course.'

'Let's just pretend we're normal people. Tourists,' he said

after we'd dumped our luggage and were staring out the window at King George Square.

I nodded. 'Room service?'

While waiting for our burgers, I arranged several pillows down the middle of our king-sized bed.

Bear laughed. 'Don't worry. I won't be crossing the line.'

Moments later, we kissed, and I was consumed by a sudden flush of warmth. No buildup. No hesitation from either of us. It was… it was like I'd been bought to life. I was finally awake and breathing. Because of a kiss. A kiss so passionate, so full of promise and ecstasy. In that moment, nothing else mattered except Bear and me. Blissful oblivion. Us. Together.

We jumped apart when Annie knocked at our door.

'Sorry guys, this must be awkward,' she said, looking around and confirming there was only one bed. 'Bear, I'll sleep with Sam. You can batch with Anthony.'

Later that night Bear texted: *Hey Gorgeous Girl. Can't stop thinking about you or that kiss…*

I giggled, lightheaded. That kiss. *Same.*

Drifting off to sleep, I received another text. *GG, I think we should revisit that kiss again soon. You?*

Bear caught up with me the next morning. 'Did you get my text?'

In the harsh sunlight, reality dawned. I hesitated. 'Yes.'

'And?'

And? What was I thinking? Forego my ambition for a shot at romance? Annie and I were bloody lucky to have Bear. He could see our potential and tap into it. And more than anything, I wanted us to be the number one tennis doubles players in the world. Bear was the coach who could make that dream a reality. Nothing was going to stand in our way.

'And I think you're great, Bear but—'

'Don't.'

'You're the best coach I've ever had. I want to be the best tennis player—'

'I can coach and—'

'No. I need you.'

'As your coach?'

'Yes.'

'Nothing else?'

I shook my head.

'GG—'

I pushed him away. 'Don't.'

I shuddered at the memory. What a couple of days. Who knows what might have happened had Annie not interrupted?

Bear was a brilliant coach and I needed him by my side. I couldn't afford to get romantically attached and then have it fall apart. Besides, he deserved more than I could give him. I couldn't commit to anything but tennis, and he knew that. Our romantic attachment was severed before it could develop.

Five

The morning after our loss, the Australian newspapers, rather than berating us for our crushing defeat, were surprisingly generous. Most played up the angle about fostering Australian-Norwegian relations and downplayed our lack of concentration letting the match slip from our grasp.

An unfortunate blip, I read. *Annie and Samantha Callahan will come back bigger and better in the next Grand Slam. Once the excitement of getting engaged wears off, Annie will reclaim her form.*

But the media couldn't ignore the fact that with our semi-final loss, our doubles ranking crashed to eighteen. Especially not Prue Hamilton. *One can only hope Annie Callahan finds her rhythm again soon,* she said in her bitchy comment of the week. *I couldn't stomach sitting through another train wreck like that even if I am being paid.*

'It was *one* lousy match,' Annie said, twirling her blonde hair as she read the letters pages, which in the main were understanding about her excitement but wary about where it would lead.

On talkback radio, while the mood was forgiving, there was the occasional dissenting voice. 'What's she doing getting engaged so young?' Emily from Altona asked. 'Why can't she just live with the man? I'm all for Annie having fun, but this engagement is a major distraction. It can't be good for her game.'

My sentiments exactly, Emily from Altona.

~ * ~

'It's not so bad,' my best friend Violet said when I caught up with her a few days later at a Sydney beachside cafe. We sat at an outside table while her daughters, Ava, seven, and Poppy, nine, jumped over waves.

My eyes narrowed as I tore at my paper napkin. 'It infuriates me that Annie needs a man draped around her neck.'

'A man draped around one's neck isn't such a bad thing.'

I looked up. 'You know what I mean!'

'I do, only too well. You build these enormous walls to protect yourself, determined not to fall in love'—I tried to protest, but Violet talked over me—'Annie's the opposite. She's quick to fall head over heels. She loves being nurtured and cherished.'

'Yuck,' I said. 'What she needs is a decent break to find out who she really is, instead of messing around with every guy who comes along.'

'Samantha!'

'What? She broke up with Anthony barely a month before Erik strolled into her life. Couldn't she have taken some time out before she joined at the hip with a new guy?'

Just thinking about the night Erik and Annie met got my blood boiling. It was New Year's Eve, and Bear had insisted we take a break from burpees, squats and planking. So the three of us went to a tennis party in the penthouse suite of an inner Sydney hotel and basked in the balmy summer evening on the fifty-sixth floor, enjoying brilliant views of the city and harbour. Champagne flowed.

Erik sidled up to me and wrapped his arm around my waist. 'Everyone talks about you, a gold medallist,' he said. 'You and I have excellent music together.'

Way too touchy-feely for my liking, I dismissed him as a sleaze straight away. He obviously wasn't used to knockbacks – the shock on his face was priceless.

Minutes later, I saw Annie talking to him, animated, clearly interested. I assumed that after ten minutes she'd wise up to his shallowness. Boy, was I wrong. From that night forward, the two of them had been inseparable.

I might have put Erik's behaviour on New Year's Eve down to nerves or excessive alcohol if other women on the circuit hadn't filled me in quick-smart. When he wasn't in sleaze mode, Erik was obnoxious and opinionated. I quickly came to dislike everything about him: his irritating habit of speaking about himself in the third person; the way he big-noted himself at every opportunity, and the patronising way he spoke to Annie about tennis, like he knew more about the game than she did.

'Obviously she wanted a man in her life,' Violet said, pulling me back to the present. 'Anyway, what are your plans now you're back in Sydney?'

'To put the misery of our loss behind us and train harder.'

'And Annie?'

'She thinks I'm being a baby.'

'And?'

'Yeah, okay, so I'm still pouting about the loss, but jeez, Yasmine-pink-undies-Le Bluth and Sandi Wren won the doubles final. We beat them at the Olympics five months ago.'

'Hon,' Violet said, rubbing my arm, 'let it go.'

'Yeah, can we go, Mum?' Ava pleaded, swinging her earphones in circles.

Violet checked her watch. 'Soon.'

I looked over to the girls, their legs covered in sand. 'Sorry, Ava, I know I'm being boring, sweetie. What game are you playing?'

Ava held out her iPad. 'Soda Crush, level 658!'

'Wow. A lot of my friends play that game, but I don't know anyone anywhere near that level. You're a champion.'

She smiled and turned back to her game.

'I know I need to get over it,' I whispered to Violet. 'As Annie keeps reminding me, there'll be plenty more tournaments. She's committed to playing in Dubai.'

'That's good,' Violet said. 'When is it? Four weeks?'

'Three, but who's counting?'

~ * ~

I drove home thinking about my conversation with Violet, what was said and what had been left hanging. Violet always worried about Annie and me. Childhood neighbours, Violet was our oldest and closest friend. Three years my senior, she was like a big sister.

After Mum disappeared, Annie and I spent most of our time at Violet's house. Her mother practically force-fed us chocolate cake and strawberries most afternoons after school.

Stopped at traffic lights, I glanced up at a familiar billboard, one of many dotted throughout the country. The photo taken by Zach Baxter, captured Annie and me, arms around each other, racquets held high above our heads, beaming after our win at the recent Olympic Games.

And the byline?

Sisters, Samantha and Annie, our golden girls, bringing out the best in each other at the Australian Open. When you've got it, flaunt it!

I shuddered.

The *golden girls* promoted a lot of merchandise. Our product endorsements made us more income than the games themselves. We didn't earn salaries; we only made money through tennis when we won tournaments. But as an advertising duo, our selling power was supreme. No other Australian sporting siblings came close. Our pact was unbreakable.

It had been that way since Annie and I were signed to promote Stay-Up-Socks as juniors. Then came the international deals endorsing racquets and vitamin water. Those companies had reaped the rewards, especially after we won Olympic gold, and so had we.

But now?

If our relationship fell apart and our tennis partnership faltered, it would be catastrophic for our advertising careers.

Six

Bear and Erik watched Annie and me train at our local gym. Despite overlooking the harbour, it was all about treadmills, stationary bikes and dumbbells.

'We have to work harder to keep up with the younger players,' I said when Annie flagged. 'Courtney Gold's only seventeen, and she made it through to the singles' finals.'

'I know,' Annie said. 'I watched the match with you.'

'Ar-nee, come to Bondi now.' Erik! He'd been sitting on a bench scrolling through his phone. Clearly bored.

I bristled. 'We've still got another couple of hours—'

'It's okay,' Annie said, pressing *stop* on her running machine. 'I'll make it up next time.' She stepped off her treadmill and disappeared with Erik.

I could barely contain my frustration. 'Far out, Bear! Before Erik, Annie was determined, even if she wasn't one hundred per cent focused. Her head's so far out of the game it's holidaying several suburbs away. I need to talk to her about commitment.'

'You need to back off,' Bear said as we gathered our towels, drink bottles, racquets and balls. 'Annie's in love. Let her enjoy the moment.'

I crossed my arms. 'Don't. Have you heard him at our practice sessions? *Ar-nee, I tell you not to play your hand this way*, and then he shows her his forehand grip—which is *wrong!*'

'Yes, it is and I'm going to make sure Annie knows.' He put his arm around me. 'Samantha, you can't fight chemistry. I promise you it won't last.'

I brushed his arm away. 'I can't understand why you're so laidback. Don't you care about her tennis career? She's throwing it away.'

'Of course, I care, GG.'

'Don't call me that.'

'Fine.' He squeezed my shoulder. 'I've seen this kind of thing happen before. If we push too hard, Annie'll walk.'

'She wouldn't dare.'

'Wanna bet? She's in love. I know Annie. If I rant and tell her she's being unprofessional and letting herself down, we'll lose her.'

'So, we do nothing?'

'I'm not saying that, but we need to be strategic. Tactics, Sam. We don't want this blowing up in our faces.'

I glanced skyward. 'I want to shake her. Tell her this relationship is all wrong. It's a disaster waiting to happen.'

'Well, you can't. You'll just come across as the nasty bitter sister, jealous of Annie's new-found happiness.'

'Okay.' I put up my hands. 'As if I'm not already precariously close to winning that title.'

Bear laughed.

'I'm not saying I'd dance on his coffin, but really, I hate the prick.'

'Sam!'

'What? You must have seen the way he sidles up to the young female players. He's in for all he can get. At the after-parties, he makes a beeline for the most attractive woman in the room.'

Bear rubbed his chin.

'He's certainly not wasting his limited English vocabulary on people with penises. And if you think for one moment, he and Annie will get married—'

'Is this about Erik, or are you angry with Annie?' Bear asked. 'She's not spending as much time with you now Erik's on the scene.'

'No! If he was a decent guy, I'd be all for it.'

'Really?'

'Even you have to admit he's an annoying distraction while we're practising.'

'Breathe!' Bear commanded. 'In, out. In, out.'

'I don't want to.'

'You are such an older sister,' Bear said. 'Controlling, logical, determined.'

I glared at him.

'What? You are. Annie's more sociable. God forbid if you were both like you.'

'What's that supposed to mean?'

Bear snorted. 'You'd kill each other.'

~ * ~

Bear tried everything to get the two of us back on track. He chose physical activities like running mini-marathons and triathlons—great bonding for disgruntled, disillusioned, tennis-playing sisters. It was exhausting, but we did it. And we did it together.

One Friday morning when Annie and I turned up at Manly beach expecting another sand session followed by a gruelling fourteen-kilometre run, Bear surprised us by sending us away for the weekend to a luxury spa in the Hunter Valley.

'This is so cool,' I said to Annie in the back of a chauffeur-driven car on the way to our destination. I pointed to the spa menu. 'We can have an herbal volcanic wrap or wait—the Cleopatra body wrap.'

'I'd like to try the hot stone therapy,' Annie said. 'Oh look, they have a spa suite and massages for couples. Erik would love that.'

I let the comment slide. 'This is going to be great, Annie. Just the two of us. We'll have so much fun.'

Soon after we arrived and were coated in a green algae wrap, Annie's phone bleated. The Viking!

Later, in the middle of a steam, she got another text message.

'Why didn't you leave the phone in our room?' I said, disappointed we couldn't manage a couple of hours of pampering without being interrupted.

'I have to reply, Sam. It'd be rude not to.'

Finally, when Erik rang in the middle of our yoga class and complained he was lonely and hungry, Annie scarpered. She didn't even make it through one night. Bear's sisterly bonding exercise? A tragic epic failure.

~ * ~

'Don't you think she's lost her spark, her drive-her Annie-ness?' I asked Bear back in Sydney after the spa debacle.

When he didn't immediately respond, I added, 'She's living for that bloke.'

'It's her choice,' Bear replied. 'How's this for a radical thought—maybe the two of them are actually in love? Maybe they're happy. And maybe, if you let yourself go once in a while, you too could find happiness.'

I held his eyes for perhaps a moment too long before looking away. Best not to think about what might have been.

Unlike Annie, who always had guys hanging around, I was happy on my own. I didn't need a man to define me. I knew who I was: Samantha Callahan, professional tennis player, Olympic gold medalist. It was kind of cool being me. Boyfriends, lovers were a distraction, and for an elite sportsperson, distractions were poison. I was single-minded, resolute and refused to fit in with someone else's life. Obviously, I made compromises when it came to Annie, but that's as far as it went. I loved playing tennis with her. We were partners. Family. Outside of that, I ran my own race.

Rather than confront Annie about Erik and risk making an intolerable situation worse, Bear came up with a strategy. After he'd run through our schedule in the lead-up to Wimbledon—Dubai, Miami, Stuttgart and the French Open—he suggested Annie and Erik take a holiday to 'really get to know each other before you and Samantha play in Dubai in a couple of weeks. How does that sound, Annie?'

He needn't have asked because she was jumping all over him, showering him with kisses. 'It's beyond brilliant. Thank you.' She looked at me. 'And don't worry, Sam, I'll still practice.'

~ * ~

When Annie and Erik left for Thailand, I cried. Bereft. We'd had separate holidays before—she was an avid skier while I favoured the sunny Whitsunday Islands, and she'd gone away with boyfriends before—but this was different. Before, we'd always been sooky about leaving each other and promised to ring or at least text every day. This time, Annie didn't even want me to drive her to the airport.

'I'll stay the night at Erik's and we'll catch a cab from there,' she'd told me. In other words, I'll be fine without you.

After four days, when I found myself watching Doris Day movies over and over—my mother's favourites—I rang Violet and invited her over for dinner. I was getting way too maudlin in the apartment on my own.

'I take it we're having spaghetti,' Violet said when she arrived.

'And salad.' Cooking wasn't my forte. Violet knew that.

Over dinner we talked. 'I know it's unrealistic to expect that Annie and I will still be living together ten years from now, but—'

'Annie's your rock and you miss her.'

Yep. Closing my eyes, I visualised my childhood, the times Annie and I tromped into Mum's walk-in wardrobe, pulled out her dresses, jewellery and shoes, and paraded around the house in them. I could almost see Mum and hear her voice. 'Girls, really? You're so silly sometimes.' And then her eyes would sparkle, and she'd giggle and throw her arms out wide to draw us in for cuddles.

I'll never forget the look on Mum's face when Annie and I got the call offering us places at the Sydney Tennis Academy and how thrilled she was. But not long after, on the eve of my thirteenth birthday, she left. It was coming up to fourteen years.

After her disappearance, Annie and I still went into her wardrobe and stared at her clothes, sometimes for hours at a time, but we never dared put them on. Dad accompanied us to various counsellors and group therapy sessions, but Annie and I stopped going after a couple of months, preferring each other's support rather than struggling to bond with strangers. Dad took to the therapy sessions with a lot more enthusiasm than us; he found it comforting knowing he wasn't alone.

At the time, I tried everything I could think of to make Mum come home. What if I did this—learn piano? What if I did that—achieve excellent school grades? I was driven to craziness desperately trying to think of schemes and behaviours that would bring her back. Nothing worked.

Annie and I threw ourselves into the academy, spending most non-school daylight hours there. Me, to quell my feeling of abandonment, and Annie, to soothe her grief.

Five months after Mum went missing, we came home from practice to find her clothes had gone too. Dad had given them to charity. No discussion, no nothing. Two months later, Dad met

Melissa, whose husband had died six months prior to Mum's disappearance.

With Dad occupied with Melissa, I found myself taking on a parental role with Annie more and more, pushing her to work harder at her game. But I was only a child, not equipped to be more than Annie's big sister and tennis partner, so was way out of my depth when it came to protecting her from life's certain tragedies.

Still, we quickly moved up the rankings to become Australian junior tennis champions. As champions, we increasingly played overseas, but Dad rarely travelled with us. Of course, we had chaperones and met other teenagers on the circuit, but mostly Annie and I relied on each other for companionship and strength. Our sisterly bond. Our pact.

When I was nineteen, Dad encouraged us to invest our earnings in real estate, so together we bought an apartment in Mosman and moved in. It was all the reassurance Dad needed to sell the family home and relocate to Albury with Melissa. Within a couple of years, Melissa had given birth to two sons.

These days, it was near impossible to get Dad to a match. We'd given him and Melissa dozens of passes to the Australian Open, invited them to Wimbledon, Paris, New York. But they never came. He'd practically forgotten he was also a father to two daughters. Or maybe the memories were too painful.

Before Mum disappeared, I'd found her sitting on the edge of the bath, crying. When she saw me, she quickly stood up, dried her eyes, and said she was being silly. Then we made cupcakes and ate them watching her favourite Doris Day and Rock Hudson film, *Send Me No Flowers*. She loved them all—*Lover Come Back*, *Pillow Talk*—and while they made her happy, she always cried at the end, no matter how many times she'd watched them. Back then, Dad said she was sad, but now I understood she'd suffered from depression.

Why did she have to leave? Why couldn't she have hung on for us? Did I do something to drive her away? I asked myself the same questions every day, and I still longed to see her.

My phone beeped, pulling me back into the present. 'Speak of the devil,' I said to Violet.

She winked. 'See, Annie does miss you.'

A flush of warmth rose within. 'She wants me to bring her sunglasses to Dubai.'

I can't believe I left my favourites behind, the text message read in part.

Damn, I'm loving wearing them, mostly at night, I texted back.

Don't go getting all Corey Hart on me, she replied.

Seven

In Dubai, I stared round the elegant and vast hotel lobby with its plush furnishings, fresh flowers, and sunlit atrium. It truly was grand. I felt re-energised, focused. The Australian Open result had been disappointing but that was in the past. I couldn't wait to meet up with Annie. I'd missed her so much. I wanted to hear all about her Thai holiday: the beaches, the food, the culture. I was even prepared to befriend Erik. This was to be our new beginning! Time to concentrate and rediscover the magic. We'd pour all our energy into playing unbeatable tennis at the Dubai Championships.

When I saw her, love surged, the past forgotten. 'Annie!'

She looked up and we waved simultaneously before coming together and hugging.

I stood back. 'You look stunning—even more gorgeous than you did a few weeks ago, if that's possible.'

She beamed. 'I've missed you, Sam. Missed us.'

Relief washed over me. I needed to hear that. We were a team. Three years ago, when I'd almost given in, we'd promised each other never to break up the team. 'Tell me everything you've been up to. I'm dying to know.'

In the hotel café, Annie told me all about her holiday with Erik.

'Bangkok was crazy busy, but the Grand Palace was spectacular. Dazzling. And the Phi Phi Islands.' Annie sighed. 'The beaches. Stunning. We snorkelled and swam with fish through coral reefs. Then there were the private bays. Erik and I—'

'Yeah, I get it.'

She giggled. 'As for the food...'

'Sounds amazing,' I said, when she finally drew breath.

'Oh, Samantha, it was. Just magic.' She gave me a quizzical stare. Was my smile slipping? She placed her hand over mine. 'I'm not doing this to hurt you. The truth is, I feel totally powerless to stop myself. It's like I've been hit by some irresistible force and can't pull back. Sometimes it really frightens me. What if Erik gets bored? What if we break up? I'll never cope.'

I'd never heard Annie sound so smitten. 'Annie, you've just told me about your incredible holiday together. Erik's in love with you. He won't leave.'

She wasn't listening. 'It's like I'm under some weird spell, but you know what? I don't ever want to be released from it.'

Great!

'It's unbelievable to think I didn't know him two months ago. And now we're getting married!'

I glanced at her left hand, fourth finger. Naked. I'd hoped the marriage idea had faded. But perhaps they'd simply decided against buying a ring. Or maybe Erik had no money for one.

'So, you and Erik have made...' the words almost got stuck in my throat '...wedding plans?'

'No, but he'd like us to be married in Norway.'

I gasped.

'Obviously, Sydney works better for me,' Annie went on. 'Maybe we can do both. A low-key ceremony in Norway followed by another one in Sydney. It all depends on our tennis commitments.'

'And Erik's work commitments?' I said pointedly. No one seemed to know what Erik did. He used to be a low-grade tennis player, but what now? A professional tennis groupie?

Annie blinked, then glanced at her watch. 'I'd better get going. Erik will be wondering where I am.'

'Of course,' I said, avoiding eye contact. 'Go to him. I'm glad he makes you happy.'

She smiled. 'Thank you, darling. One day you'll find your Erik, too. See you tomorrow on court.' She blew me a kiss and skipped into the elevator.

~ * ~

True to her word, Annie was at the venue on time the next morning, along with a handful of spectators, players, coaches and staff. I spotted Zach in the stands taking photos and waved. We were outdoors and it was hot and sunny, but I was ready.

After a brisk warm-up with our hitting partners, Annie and I got stuck into a game. As we hadn't played together for a couple of weeks, Bear stood on the sideline and pointed out how we needed to adjust our moves. But while he called out one instruction, Erik stood on the opposite side, telling Annie to do something else.

'Ar-nee, hit low!'

'Ar-nee, step back.'

'Ar-nee, your serve!'

Annie was turning from side to side like one of those freaky clown heads at Luna Park.

When Bear realised what was happening, he stopped the game. 'Mate,' he said to Erik, 'we only have two days to prepare. It's going to work better if the girls have one coach directing them, and that coach is me.'

Erik waved his arms in the air, his eyes darting between Bear and Annie. 'Well?' he said finally, glaring at Annie.

She didn't reply.

'Fine.' He stormed off, mumbling something indecipherable.

'Annie,' Bear said moments later, firm but kind, 'you okay?'

She nodded.

We continued practising, but unfortunately Erik's departure was short-lived. He returned with a Coke Zero and was soon shooting his mouth off, even after Bear asked him again not to interfere.

Fifteen minutes later, Bear halted the session and took Annie aside to discuss the issue.

'Erik knows what he's talking about,' she argued. 'He's a professional.'

I looked across to where he was chatting up several young female players. Professional my arse.

Zach stepped down from the stands and headed towards me, his limp hardly noticeable. Back in the day, he had competed on the circuit against Nadal and Murray, but his knee packed in. After several operations, he couldn't sustain the gruelling pace any longer. He couldn't bear giving up tennis altogether, so he turned his photography hobby into his second career. Taking pictures became his way of working through his depression after his retirement, plus he got to hang out with friends. Zach was now one of a handful of fulltime professional photographers on the circuit.

'I see Annie and Erik are still on the fast-track to everlasting happiness and glory,' he said, stopping beside me.

'You reckon?' My voice was a tad higher than usual.

Zach's mouth twitched. 'Hey, did you hear that Dragana's ranking's gone up since she broke up with Erik?'

I raised my eyebrows. 'Whatever.'

'How about you strike a pose and smile like you've just won gold?' Zach said, framing me through his camera lens.

I did as I was told, and Zach started snapping.

'Always the professional, Sam. Thank you.' He wandered off.

~ * ~

Back in Bear's hotel suite after a boxing workout, Bear, Annie and I sat at his elaborate marble inlaid dining table drinking ice water, eating chicken shawarma sliders and rose macrons, and staring out the floor to ceiling windows celebrating Dubai's spectacular skyline.

Annie whistled. 'I'll never tire of this view.'

'No,' Bear agreed. 'But back to business, which is working out the ground rules for your first-round match.'

We'd drawn Dragana Lukić and Jelena Tipsarević, the two Serbians who'd bundled us out of the semis at the Australian Open less than six weeks ago.

On Bear's computer, we watched footage of them playing.

'You can beat them,' he encouraged.

I watched as Jelena faulted on her first serve. 'Now there's an eighty-three per cent chance she'll double fault.'

Annie smiled as Jelena served wide.

'As for Dragana, she likes sharp short points, not rallies, so if we can engage her in a rally, chances are she'll tire and we'll win the point,' I said.

'Exactly,' Bear agreed.

'Remember, Erik knows Dragana's weaknesses,' Annie said. 'They were together for four years.'

'Does it worry you that we're playing his ex-girlfriend?' I asked.

'Why should it? Erik loves me.' Although she said the words with certainty, I caught a flicker of unease in Annie's eyes.

'So, what has Erik said about Dragana?' I asked her.

'She's lazy—'

'Doesn't like long rallies, like I said.'

'See, if you and Erik could work together...'

That was so not going to happen, but I didn't want to pick a fight. 'I still think we'll be at a psychological disadvantage.'

'Rubbish,' Annie said. 'And you talk about me not playing with confidence.'

'Ladies,' Bear said, pulling us in for a group hug, 'let's keep our focus on the game, okay?'

Eight

Zach

Zach watched Annie and Samantha walk out onto the hard court for their match against Dragana and Jelena. While Samantha looked tense, Annie appeared calm, but then again, she was an expert at the poker face. Today, she was the epitome of cool, dressed in her usual white. She'd told him once that all white kept her focused. He remembered a charity breast cancer match in Vegas when Samantha had persuaded Annie to wear a pink bandana, which was a Sam idiosyncrasy.

Annie giggled. 'Really?' Still, she tied it round her head, and looked uncomfortable the entire match.

Samantha seemed to play in whatever clothing was closest on the day, but she always wore a bandana around her forehead. A tribute to her mother, a reminder that her mum was always with her. Never forgotten. Depending on Sam's mood, it might be purple, yellow, red or black. Today, it was red. She was obviously feeling feisty.

Zach saw Dragana mouth something to Annie. He raised his camera and focused his zoom lens on her face.

'Annie, do you not think Erik has a small dick?'

Zach grinned. Dragana was on fire. He concentrated on Annie, who continued smiling, unfazed. That's right, he thought, let it go. Zach had been on the receiving end of verbal abuse plenty of times during his playing career, a dirty strategy some players used to unnerve their opposition. If you let it get to you, it could really mess with your game. Once those words were rolling around your head, choking became an all too real probability.

Thankfully, Dragana's jibes didn't seem to affect Annie. The Callahan sisters were winning. They even high-fived each other a couple of times during the match, inflaming Dragana further.

'Annie, Erik will never love you the way he loves me. His heart belongs to me.'

Dragana's taunts seemed to inspire Annie to fight even harder. Her shots were stronger and faster than Zach had seen from her in a long time. He watched as the women took a break after winning the first set 6–4. Samantha appeared anxious and hot, sweat trickling down her cheeks. Annie sat, sipping her water, looking cool even in the wretched heat.

Zach glanced over to Erik. Amazingly, he'd sat quietly the entire match. Even when the sisters cruised to a 6–4, 6–3 victory, his reaction was subdued.

At the net, Samantha and Annie glowed, but Dragana barely acknowledged them as they shook hands.

Zach caught up with the Callahans as they entered the media room. 'Great match, ladies,' he said, wrapping his arms around their shoulders. 'I got some excellent shots. Annie, you were on fire.'

Erik seemed to have found his voice again and soon got stuck into Annie for not spending enough time at the net. 'You should 'ave net-'overed, Ar-nee, like I tell you.'

That said it all. Annie was not a confident 'net hoverer.' Whenever she was at the net, she looked like she was stuck in cement or chained to the net pole. No one wanted Annie hovering unless it was absolutely essential. Zach couldn't understand why Annie didn't tell Erik to back off.

After the press interview, Zach hopped into a taxi and headed off to Patsy Newcombe's photo shoot at Zabeel Palace.

The thought of being inside a royal Dubai palace intrigued him, but not as much as Patsy, who was an up-and-coming American model he'd met on the flight from Sydney. So, what if she was only twenty? Or was she nineteen? She was pretty, sexy and no slouch when it came to satisfying him in the bedroom—or the shower, for that matter.

He stared out of the taxi window, enthralled by the frantic building activity. Dubai was fascinating in a Disneyland kind of way. The taxi stopped at traffic lights, giving Zach a clear view of a building site. A sea of migrant workers slaved in the heat with no proper scaffolding and zero safety gear. *How were they allowed to work like that?* Zach asked the cab driver to pull over and wait while he took some action shots.

Forty minutes later, he was standing in lush green gardens surrounded by strutting, glamourous peacocks and women. Although not allowed inside the building—the palace was off limits—he was directed towards a grand marquee.

Zach glanced round the predominantly golden interior, complete with exquisite Arabian furnishings and beautiful people, all laughing, all with perfectly straight white teeth and silky hair, radiating health and wealth. A stark contrast to the workers on the building site.

Patsy appeared by his side, wearing a full-length emerald evening gown with diamonds glittering in her ears and around her neck.

'You look incredible,' Zach said, taking her in his arms.

'You're not too bad yourself,' she purred.

As they locked lips, Zach knew he was the envy of every guy in the tent. Still, his mind flashed back to Annie on court that afternoon, tall, lean, tanned and cool.

Nine

Samantha

Before our second-round match, Bear showed me a clipping from Prue Hamilton's most recent press release.

'Thank goodness the Callahans won what most commentators would describe as a grudge match against Serbians Dragana Lukić and Jelena Tipsarević.'

I raised my eyebrows. 'She got that right.'

Bear nodded. 'Keep reading.'

'No doubt the Aussies were out for blood. They certainly extracted it—but can they beat Tammy Keyes and Mary Beattie in the second round? Here's hoping.'

I smiled. 'I have a great feeling about this match. We're going to slaughter them.'

Prue's next line read, *'One final thought: could Annie's fiancé, Erik Sørensen, be stepping up as her new coach? It certainly looks that way.'*

'What?' My voice increased in pitch.

Bear tweaked my shoulder. 'It's under control, Sami. All under control.'

At the warm-up, Bear instructed Annie and me to stick with what we knew best. 'Tammy and Mary are unseeded, but they're also Irish,' he said with a wink. 'You never know what they'll get up to. Good luck out there. Remember, Annie, hit long and hard. Hug the baseline.'

In a flash, Erik grabbed her arm. 'No, Ar-nee, you must net-'over.'

'Erik! Enough.' Bear was not impressed.

Neither was I. Don't listen to him, don't talk to him and definitely don't do what he tells you, I silently implored Annie as we slammed balls during our warm-up. But what did she do? As soon as the match started, she net-hovered. Worse, from the very first game, she didn't even look ahead at Tammy, she kept glancing back to me at the baseline. WTF! You don't turn to see what your partner's doing. We'd mastered these basic skills as seven-year-olds. She wasn't the confident sportswoman who'd played in the first round.

Meanwhile, Erik gesticulated and shouted from the sideline. Moments later, an umpire cautioned him, and he sat down.

Annie began picking at imaginary lint on her left shoulder before every point. She seemed confused, her play increasingly erratic. She had no rhythm, and I couldn't predict her moves.

I tried to balance our game, but it was disastrous. We'd both end up at the net, then both at the baseline—balls slipped through—we weren't in sync at all.

The more points we lost, the more pressure we put on ourselves to win, the worse we played. Annie even started running backwards from the net. Again, what the hell was she thinking? I cursed under my breath. On court, the last thing you want to do is undermine your partner's confidence. But I didn't need to. Annie was doing a great job of that all by herself.

When she looked at Erik for the hundredth time, then at me, I couldn't help myself. 'Annie. Look. Straight. Ahead. Focus.'

During the next point, she sent the ball flying over the net. So far so good. But instead of watching as Mary slammed it straight back at her, Annie's eyes drifted to Erik as if to ask, 'How did I do?'

Our opponents won the point and the game. We played so badly we almost lost the match to unseeded players. I say almost because we clawed our way to a 7–6, 6–4 victory. I'm not saying I carried the game—Annie pulled just enough brilliant moves out of her arse to bring the match home—but it was touch and go.

As we left the court, Erik began lecturing her in front of everyone. 'You do not play well.'

I was furious. 'Shut up, Erik. You have no idea what you're talking about.'

'Samantha!' Annie said, before turning to Erik. 'I'll do better next time, honey.'

'Are you kidding me?' I was ready to fight, but Bear pulled me away.

'Face facts,' I said to Bear after I'd showered and cooled down. 'We were absolute crap out there today.'

'Maybe, but you still won. You survived round two.'

'Just.'

'A win is a win. You should be celebrating.'

'How can I when I know—'

'Shush,' he said, taking my hand. 'You and Annie are great players. I can only guide her the best I can. If she takes my advice, well and good. But right now, she's only listening to Erik.'

'Great. She's playing one game, and I'm playing another. Have you seen the latest rankings?'

Of course, he had. We'd slipped a further four points to twenty-two. If we didn't win this tournament, we'd slip even lower. I was on the *Titanic*, sliding slowly into the frigid water. There were no lifeboats left, and I was either going to have to swim to shore or drown. And we all know how it turned out for those aboard the *Titanic* who didn't make it to the lifeboats.

~ * ~

In the third round, we faced off against Netta Mathieu and Lucia Landry. Putting aside yesterday's close game, I aced Netta straight up. Then I served to Lucia and nailed it again. Meanwhile, Annie's feet bounced on air as she pounded the opposition with her dazzling forehand.

'Rotate, strike, recover,' I said to myself, thrilled with her concentration.

When we took the first set 6–4, Annie couldn't wipe the smile from her face. Her ball placement was accurate, her serves low and fast. She was playing like a dream.

Maybe Netta's outfit is distracting her from the game, I thought as she skipped around the court wearing a hot-pink stretch-velvet dress with baby-pink silk piping on the edge of the neckline and straps. Who wears a cocktail dress while playing professional tennis?

Twenty minutes later, the game was over and Annie and I high-fived each other.

At the post-match press conference, before anyone could ask the French women about the match and their loss, Lucia grabbed the microphone and said, 'I am very 'appy to 'ave posed for the May edition of *Playboy* magazine. I am so proud of my body, and I am proud to be the first French tennis player to pose.'

'I didn't see that coming,' Bear whispered.

I tilted my head towards him. 'Netta doesn't look very 'appy about it, though.'

Netta looked like she'd swallowed several sharp daggers. When the reporters asked her opinion on her partner's new venture, her reply was a curt, 'No comment.'

'She's livid,' Annie said. 'I'm guessing Lucia didn't confide in her before the announcement.'

Ten

We'd finally given Prue Hamilton something positive to talk about.

Annie and Samantha Callahan have secured a quarter-finals berth following their surprise win against Frenchwomen Netta Mathieu and Lucia Landry in the third round of the Dubai Championships. One thing's for sure, with a certain someone missing from their box, one half of the Callahan sisters is playing better than she has all year. Let's hope it continues.

I had a similar theory as to why we'd played so well—Erik hadn't come to the pre-game warm-up, and he didn't make it to the match. Without him lurking in the foreground, sighing, raising his eyebrows or waving his hands about, Annie had no distractions. She was one hundred per cent focused on the ball and played like the Annie of old. That meant I could relax as well. Our game flowed and victory was ours.

~ * ~

Entering my hotel suite, my eyes were drawn to the Arabic calligraphy on the walls. I found it calming, juxtaposed to the glittering chandelier above. Though the room relied heavily on marble and gold accents, the patterned rugs and pops of burgundy created a luxurious but comfortable vibe. It wasn't home, but I appreciated my privilege. On the dining table I spied freshly delivered fruit and chocolates, flowers and other gifts.

I scrolled through my messages.

Dad and Melissa congratulating Annie and me on our victory and encouraging us to *keep the Aussie flag flying high.*

Violet's *Hey you! Woo hoo! Congratulations. Rick and I were screaming. Could you hear us? The girls are so excited, they want to take you both to 'show and tell' when you get home! I know you can win the tournament. Love you, Violet xxx*

Her text made me smile, but despite being a winner, I had no one to celebrate with. Annie was off somewhere with Erik, and Bear was having a strategy meeting with a couple of coach friends.

I called Violet and moments later, she was screaming down the phone.

'You're a bloody legend, Sam! What are you?'

'A legend,' I said quietly.

'Shout it out! I am a LEGEND!'

I laughed. 'I hear you. But enough about me. How are you, Rick? The girls?'

Violet whistled. 'Let's see. Rick's mauling me right now. Still a maniac, working ridiculously long hours. Ava's got an ongoing vendetta against celery "crunchy water" and Poppy's slamming doors because she can't find her earphones and we're all eating too loudly.'

'Especially when it comes to crunchy water?'

Violet snorted.

'So, for Poppy's birthday, I should buy her a year's supply of headphones and earplugs?'

'Could you? And a kinder personality.'

'Come on, you love her.'

'As only a mother can. So, listen, how about Lucia's announcement?'

'You should have heard Netta going for her in the locker room. She was furious.'

'Love it. So how do you rate your chances against Cindi and Suzy?' We'd drawn Americans, Cindi Gibson and Suzy Gardner for the quarter-finals.

'Good, if we can keep our heads straight. Actually, I have gossip about them too.'

'Tell me!'

'Well, there's scuttlebutt around the traps that they're together—'

'No!'

'They do seem close and cuddly, but I haven't witnessed any fervent kisses. Rumours are doing the rounds about most players on the women's circuit. How else could we deal with the endless breaks due to rain, delayed flights and traffic snarls?'

'True.' Violet paused. 'How are things with you and Annie? You seemed solid on court. It's the best I've seen you both play for ages.'

'Thanks. We're doing okay. I'm trying to keep my temper under control where Erik's concerned.'

After I said goodbye to Violet, I walked out to the terrace and considered flopping on the daybed. Occasionally it would be nice to have some down time to do regular things like go to the movies, sleep in, read. Or to hang out with Violet and her kids, baking cupcakes and eating icing from the bowl. Instead, I hoicked on my sandshoes and went to the gym. Running a few kilometres would sweep the melancholy away.

Eleven

I was disappointed but not surprised when Erik turned up to our warm-up before the quarter-finals. He clearly wasn't about to miss the opportunity to strut in front of the media. Despite Bear's presence, Erik immediately barked instructions at Annie and kept interrupting our play by whistling, slapping his hands on his thighs or shaking his head.

At the end of the session, Bear asked me whether he should talk to Annie about Erik being a distraction.

'Yes! He's distracting me, too! We won the other day when he wasn't around. If I had my way, I wouldn't let him near Annie during any matches. Or training.'

Bear called her over. 'Annie, if you two go out there and play like you played against Lucia and Netta, you'll easily win this match.'

She rubbed her forehead.

'Try not to let Erik distract you, okay?'

'But, Bear, I love him. I play better when he's there.'

That was so untrue, I almost gagged.

She glared at me. 'You don't know what it's like to be truly in love, Samantha.'

I wanted to smack her. 'You can hardly understand him. How can you say you're in love?'

'You can't decide who to love, Samantha. It's fate. I am in love with Erik. End of story.'

I flicked Bear a glance. 'You *can* decide. I have.'

'Then I feel sorry for you because you're lying to yourself.'

'Time out,' Bear said, stepping between us. 'In thirty minutes, you're playing Suzy and Cindi and you need to win.'

'I know,' I replied. 'But I don't think the message is getting through to Annie.'

'Hey, my game's perfectly fine,' Annie said. 'I'm perfectly fine. Get off my back, both of you. Erik's had a lot of experience, and I'd rather play the game he wants me to play.'

'So, Erik's your coach now, is he?' I said, barely concealing my fury. 'Tell me, Annie, does he have any real understanding of the game? I know he played amateur tennis for six months before becoming Dragana's professional handbag.'

'Take that back,' she demanded.

'I would if it wasn't true, but it is. He's only with you because you're a star. He likes the limelight.'

'Well, you'd better get used to him being around because he's not going anywhere,' Annie snapped. 'And if he does, I'm going with him.' With that, she walked off—presumably to find Erik, who I'd last seen chatting up Courtney Gold.

'Be patient,' Bear advised. 'We'll tough it out together, you'll see.'

But I couldn't let it go. 'He has no technique, no style and we've learnt not to do everything he's telling Annie to do from watching the videos of his ex-girlfriend.'

'And have you noticed?' Bear said. 'Dragana's game has lifted considerably. In the space of four months, she's risen from forty-seven to twenty-one in world rankings, despite losing to you two in the first round here.'

'Have you mentioned that stat to Annie?'

He grimaced. 'No, but it's not just me who's noticed.' He glanced at my tennis bag. 'Black bandana day?'

'Very tempting, but no.' I whipped out a red one.

'All right,' Bear said, 'get out there, tiger, and go for it.' He kissed me lightly on the cheek and left.

I am strong and in control, I repeated over and over in my head as I mentally prepared. I could say the words; now I just needed to believe them.

~ * ~

Minutes before we headed out to do battle with Suzy Gardner and Cindi Gibson, I reminded Annie what we knew about them.

'Suzy's prone to making silly mistakes and foot-faulting. Cindi's a powerful left-hander, but not a confident backhander. Whenever you get the chance, hit to her backhand, okay?'

The sun was beating down, the crowds were attentive and enthusiastic, and the umpires and ball girls and boys were ready for action. Despite our argument earlier, I walked onto the court full of optimism.

The umpire chose Annie to call heads or tails in the coin toss. She called heads. We won and elected to serve.

We were annihilated in less than an hour. Fifty-four minutes to be precise. It all happened so quickly. One minute we were firing aces and hitting powerful lobs; the next minute, it was all over. We were gone: 3–6, 1–6.

I was so distraught I couldn't speak. On autopilot, I shook Cindi's hand, then Suzy's. Annie and I were on the fast train to tennis oblivion. I was days away from being forced off the professional circuit and being reduced to coaching children at some tennis clinic in outback Australia.

'Hey,' Bear said moments later, courtside. 'You played your best. But Cindi and Suzy were better competitors today.'

'I'm so tired of that bloody cliché. It's bullshit, Bear.' I turned to Annie. 'What did I say? Hit to Cindi's backhand. Instead, you hit sissy slow balls to her forehand that a blind three-year-old could return.'

'You don't be speaking to my koala like that,' Erik said, pushing his way into the conversation.

I twirled to face him, angry tears streaming down my cheeks. 'Shut the fuck up, Erik. You're the cause of this. You're the reason we're losing. Why the fuck can't any of you see that? Are you all blind?'

'You do not speak to me or my koala that way,' Erik started.

'Or what?' I screamed. 'I'm not afraid of you, Erik.'

'Samantha, don't,' Bear said, holding up his hand.

Annie pulled Erik back. 'Just stop, both of you.'

He waved her off. 'Ar-nee does not need you,' he yelled at me. 'You need her.'

'What we don't need is you telling us what to do,' I yelled back. 'You can't even play tennis.'

'How dare you!' Erik's face was bright red.

'You're destroying our lives.' I took a deep breath and tried silently counting to ten. I made it to three before exploding again. 'Destroying our fucking lives! You'll pay for this!'

Annie pulled Erik away and, seething, I watched them go. Bear tried to reason with me, but the more he pleaded with me to 'let them be' the angrier I became.

'Am I the only one who can see doom descending?'

Back at the hotel, I ignored my messages from Violet, from Dad, from Zach and even from Bear. I didn't want to talk to anyone. The only person who didn't try to contact me was Annie.

Even the panoramic sea views and welcoming marble bath couldn't distract me. Every quickening heartbeat took me to the verge of a panic attack. My throat was dry and constricted, my left eye twitched. Suffering extreme tiredness and shame, I wanted the ground to swallow me up. Again, I'd let everyone down.

Twelve

Back in Australia, we discovered that the public and media were fickle friends. Bear insisted we stop at a newsagent on the way home to buy the papers, and when I saw the headlines, I demanded he buy all the copies in the shop. I considered driving to every other newsagent in Sydney to purchase all their papers too. Only exhaustion stopped me.

'Do you want me to come inside?' Bear asked as the cab pulled up outside the Mosman apartment I shared with Annie.

'No.' My limbs tingled with fatigue. 'I'm hoping Annie's already here, alone, so we can talk.'

'It might be better to get some rest first. You don't want to say anything you'll regret.'

'Yeah,' I said, glancing at the headline of one of the newspapers. *'Where have the glorious Callahan sisters disappeared?'*

I said goodbye to Bear and unlocked the front door. Home at last. I plonked my bags and the papers on the floor and paced through the lounge room to the French doors that led onto the patio. I looked out at the planter boxes overflowing with red geraniums, the Japanese box hedges and robust cumquat trees. But it was the stunning views of the harbour and over to Clontarf that made my skin tingle and heartbeat race. Home!

I deliberated whether to open the doors and sit outside to collect my thoughts, but lost heart. I needed to face the newspapers first. Five minutes later, the lounge room floor was covered with sheets of black and white.

'Exactly when is the Callahans' holiday going to stop?' Prue Hamilton demanded. *'Has their magnificent winning streak come to an end? It certainly looks that way.'*

'What's happened to our golden girl, Annie Callahan?' the *Daily Telegraph* asked. *'What's this Erik guy doing thinking he can coach our Annie? And why isn't Bear putting him in his place?'*

And Doug Warren's take? *'Are the Callahans still going to be playing the sport this time next year, or even three months from now? Because it seems the more Annie falls in love with Erik, the less she loves playing tennis.'*

Social media comments were worse. Everyone loved us while we were winning, but not so much when we were losing.

'What are we going to do about this?' I said, waving the papers in Annie's face the second she walked through the front door.

I hadn't taken Bear's advice, or even my own and spent time staring at the view. No, in the fifteen minutes I'd been home, I'd become increasingly irate, biting my knuckles to stop screaming expletives. To further my annoyance, Erik strode in behind Annie. I couldn't speak to her on the plane because Erik had been sitting next to her, demanding all her attention. How silly of me to presume she'd come home alone.

'Give me a moment to put down my bags.' Annie disappeared to put her luggage in her bedroom.

Erik glanced at the headlines. 'In Norway, these peoples would not be saying this about Ar-nee,' he said, puffing himself up and staring at Annie as she walked back into the living room. 'You be national treasure.'

'You don't know what you're talking about, Erik,' I said. 'You've got no idea.'

'After we marry, Ar-nee not need you,' he said, holding her tight and nuzzling her neck. 'She'll be big star herself.'

'What? Is that true, Annie? Am I wasting my time?'

'Of course, it is true,' Erik said.

'I was speaking to my sister, if you don't mind,' I snapped, my face reddening.

Erik flapped his oversized hands in the air and stalked off towards the bathroom. Good. Perhaps he'd stay in there long enough to give me a chance to talk to Annie without him interjecting. Couldn't she see what he was doing? Driving a wedge between us, taking control of her game. Of her. Although Annie kept saying she was confident, I didn't buy it. From where I stood, it seemed Erik was always putting her down, making her feel inadequate.

'Did Bear tell you about Dragana?' I asked. Not smart of me, but I needed to say something to get her attention.

'What about her?' Annie entered the kitchen and proceeded to eat Crunchy Nut Corn Flakes straight from the packet.

'We have bowls,' I said.

'Yeah, but only long-life milk,' she said, peering into the fridge. 'No point eating dry cereal from a bowl.'

'Dragana's game seems to be improving,' I persisted. 'Why do you think that might be?'

Annie slammed the fridge door. 'We just beat her. She's not that great.'

'According to the latest world rankings, she's very good.'

'I know where this is leading, Sam, and I'm not interested,

okay?' She pinched the bridge of her nose. 'Erik is my lover, my partner, my best friend.'

On cue, Erik appeared beside her and prodded her arm. 'Tell her,' he said, lips barely moving.

Annie shook her head.

'Tell her.' Erik poked her arm more forcefully.

I straightened my back. 'Tell me what?'

Annie stared at the ground. 'Nothing.'

Erik cleared his throat. 'My Ar-nee has decided to play the singles game.'

My eyes widened in disbelief. 'What?'

'I said—'

'I heard what you said,' I spat at Erik. 'Annie, is this true?'

She couldn't look at me. 'I think it's for the best. As Erik says, I'm not getting any younger.'

I almost laughed. 'You're twenty-five! We have a deal, a pact. We're a team. And, if you've forgotten, we've got endorsement contracts to think about.'

'This is what Ar-nee is doing,' Erik insisted.

'Wait,' I said. 'At least talk to Bear.'

Erik waved his hand dismissively. 'The time for talk is over. Erik has made his decision.'

I glared at Annie. 'Erik has made his decision? Since when—'

'Leave it, Sam,' Annie said, tears threatening. She retreated into her bedroom, Erik following behind.

I texted Bear. *Please get over here. Emergency. No time to explain.*

Several minutes later, Annie reappeared with her presumably repacked suitcase.

'Annie, whatever you're thinking of doing, please don't,' I said.

'I'll see you later.'

'Later when? We need to talk strategy for Wimbledon, get a plan together—'

'Ar-nee and Erik have the plan,' Erik said, holding Annie's hand and smiling triumphantly.

I glared at him. 'Could you butt out for one second?'

Bear knocked and walked in without waiting for an answer. He looked pale and tired. 'You should lock your front door. What's the emergency?' He spied Annie's suitcase. 'What's going on?'

Erik cleared his throat. Again. 'Ar-nee is playing the singles. She does not want this'—he pointed at me—'person interfering.'

'How dare you?' I started.

Bear put up his hands. 'Time out. Annie, what's going on?'

Annie mumbled through tears, 'It's all too much. Me, Samantha, tennis, our relationship. I need a break.'

My pulse raced. I wanted to scream. 'And where does that leave me?'

'It's not forever,' Annie said.

Bear scratched his head. 'I agree you both need a break.'

'What the hell?' I couldn't believe it. 'I thought you were on my side?'

Bear looked at me. 'Everyone calm down. Annie, maybe you should give it a week or two before you make any firm decisions.'

Annie opened her mouth to speak, as Erik cut in. 'We have discussed this.' An angry red rash spread across his neck. 'Ar-nee is playing singles now.'

Annie glanced at him. 'Erik, no more.' Then she turned to leave, pulling Erik with her.

'Annie?' Bear said softly. She turned. 'We'll talk in a few days. Okay?'

Annie nodded, and then, grabbing her suitcase handle and racquet bag, she and Erik strode out the front door.

Bear and I sat in stunned silence a few moments before he finally spoke. 'I told you to get some sleep before you talked to her.'

Thirteen

I spent the next week, between phoning Annie and leaving countless messages, trying to understand what was going on between us. Maybe we did need a break. We'd been playing non-stop for two-and-a-half years—the build-up to the Olympics, the stunning heights we'd achieved, followed by our less than stellar start to the year. Time apart might be just the tonic we needed to re-energise our game. It wouldn't hurt to miss the Stuttgart tournament as long as we made it to the French Open in May and then Wimbledon. Yeah, Annie and I just needed a holiday from the relentless rigours of the tennis circuit.

But as much as I told myself that, I didn't truly believe it.

Mum would have said we needed to throw ourselves into a strict training routine, fine tune our skills and block out all other nonsense. To focus one hundred per cent on our game and our partnership. But Mum wasn't here.

I blinked sad thoughts away. Our goal was to make it to the top five, and then-who knew? If we'd managed to win gold at the Olympics, surely we could reach the world number one doubles tennis ranking. It fleetingly crossed my mind to give the singles competition a try, but I quickly dismissed it.

I reached to answer my ringing mobile. It was Annie. Finally.

She launched straight into her speech without even a hello. 'Samantha, I know you won't agree, but Erik and I feel it's best if I focus on my singles game.'

'I see.'

'Not forever, but—'

'For the foreseeable future?' It was official. Erik had convinced Annie to dump me.

She didn't answer so I went on. 'Leaving aside the fact that we're sisters, what about us being a team and sticking together through thick and thin?'

'You take me for granted,' she said.

'I don't.'

I could hear her sighing. 'Look, it's not terminal, it's just...'

'Just what?'

'You're so controlling, Samantha.'

'I'm the older sister, it's my job. Besides, I thought you liked me taking care of things. I always have, ever since—'

'Mum. I know. But I'm an adult now. You've got to give me space. Sometimes I can barely breathe with you around.'

'Fine.' I hung up.

So that was it. I was no longer in the picture. Annie was going to concentrate on her singles game. The media had put pressure on her in the past to move to singles, but she'd resisted, until now. Until Erik got to her. I was dumbstruck. What did this mean for me? What was I going to do now that Annie no longer wanted me?

The idea of finding another doubles partner sent shivers down my spine. I didn't want to play with anyone else. I couldn't. I could only play with Annie. She knew me. Knew my moves and how I played the game. Annie and I were fiercer competitors together; she guarded my back, I guarded hers. We had someone to confide in and commiserate with when we lost. Most of all, I trusted her.

When you played singles, you were alone. Single and alone. And me playing singles was out of the question. I wasn't good enough. On your own, there was no one to blame but yourself. You hit outside the line, you were out. It was your fault. But when you were part of a team, you took the losses like you took the wins: together.

I curled up on the sofa, wrapping my arms around my knees, and willed myself not to cry. It was no use. The more I resisted, the more the tears flowed. Grief gripped me just like when I finally realised my mum was never coming home.

~ * ~

It was several days before Bear pinned Annie down for a face-to-face meeting to nut out the details. I wasn't invited, but afterwards he came over to debrief me.

'She's determined to play singles until Wimbledon,' he said. 'At least, Erik's determined, and Annie agrees.'

I moved back slightly and covered my ears. 'No! How did it come to this?'

Bear shrugged. 'All I know is that Annie's priority is keeping Erik happy, and Erik will only be happy keeping Annie away from you and me.'

'Where to from here?' I asked, my voice wobbly.

'Annie's agreed to meet us a couple of weeks before Wimbledon to start preparation for the doubles tournament.'

'What about Paris?'

'I'm sorry, GG. It's a no go, I'm afraid.'

I let the GG reference slide. 'But we have to play in the French Open.'

Bear threw his hands in the air. 'Samantha, Annie isn't a child. You can't force her to play.'

'So, what you're saying is that at least we have Wimbledon?'

'At this stage, yes. And providing you get along and play nicely, maybe you can get back to your regular doubles routine after that.' He squeezed my hand. 'It mightn't be such a bad thing. With three months until Wimbledon, why not take the opportunity to play in the singles tournament at Stuttgart?'

Heat flushed my face and neck. 'I can't. You know what I'm like. Playing doubles means I only have half a court to cover.'

'Are you telling me you don't like to run?'

'Be serious,' I said. 'Annie's a better player. When I'm one half of a team, it doesn't matter so much if I miss a ball—Annie can make it up. Every time I think about playing singles, I get fearful and anxious.'

'If there's no fear, there's no will.'

'That's ridiculous. I have a lot of fear and no will.' I knew my weaknesses. I wasn't a confident singles player. I liked being part of a team. 'Do you think I've been holding Annie back? It's no secret she could be a brilliant singles player. Erik's only telling her what she already knows.'

Bear's hand was warm around mine. 'You're not holding her back. Annie's been doing that all by herself. But I do think you need to prepare for a future when she might play singles fulltime.'

'But we're a team.'

'Honey, teams break up. Look at The Beatles, ABBA—'

'Music. Not relevant.'

'Come on, at least try your hand at singles. I'll be there with you. I'm not going anywhere.'

'Ha! You'll leave me soon enough.'

They all did eventually. Mum was a distant memory. Dad's focus had shifted to his new family. And now Annie.

'I'll never leave,' Bear whispered. 'I love you, Samantha—are you listening?'

'What?' I was caught up in my own misery.

He visibly swallowed. 'Doesn't matter. Are you going to put yourself forward for Stuttgart?'

'I don't know.'

'Because you're lazy?'

I threw him a weak smile. 'I'm definitely not lazy. But I can't carry the game on my own. That's Annie's department.'

'That's why the time is right for you both to do your own thing,' Bear reasoned. 'Get out from behind your sister's shadow.'

'I didn't realise I was in her friggin' shadow.'

'My mistake.' Bear wisely let the subject drop.

But it was clear what we were both thinking. If there was ever a right time for me to wriggle away from the sisterly bonds that tied Annie and me together, this was it.

The following day, after much discussion and hand wringing on my part, Bear fed the press some bullshit story about the Callahan sisters wanting to 'flex their singles muscles in readiness for their gruelling doubles schedule at Wimbledon.' I doubted they bought the story, but it was the only one we had.

After the press conference, Bear was upbeat, as usual. 'It'll do you both the world of good.'

I hoped to hell he was right because things were screwed the way they were. But if that's how it had to be, that's how it had to be. Still, I was upset that Annie wouldn't speak to me. Was she so under Erik's control that she had no mind of her own? I couldn't focus on eating, sleeping, training. I needed to see her.

Against Bear's advice, I drove over to Erik's apartment in Surry Hills and waited outside. Finally, Annie came outside arm in arm with him.

I got out of my car and called over to her.

When they both turned to look at me, Annie was shaking.

I rushed over to her. 'Annie?'

She sighed. 'Not now, Samantha.'

'If not now, when? You don't answer my calls, my texts, emails, nothing.'

'Please. Give it a rest.'

'No. I want answers.'

Annie paled and stared up at the sky. She seemed to be chanting some sort of mantra under her breath.

'Leave her,' Erik said, pushing me away. 'You've done enough damage.'

'Me? How can you say that? Before you came along, Annie and I were perfectly happy. You're the one who's caused this, Erik. No one else.'

It seemed like only minutes later that Bear turned up and flew into damage control mode, which in this instance meant removing me from the situation. He offered to drive me home, but I just wanted to be by myself so I could break down in private.

As soon as he'd gone, I realised that alone was the last thing I wanted to be. I got out my phone and called Violet.

Fourteen

At a bar near my apartment, Violet handed me a lemon, lime and bitters. With its blush velvet booths, candy-coloured terrazzo table tops and rose pendant lights, this place always (almost always) makes me smile.

'I've never seen you looking so worn and defeated. At least, not since...'

Mum. I held up my free hand. 'I'm fine.'

Violet rubbed my shoulder and pointed to a booth. 'Sit! Tell me your troubles.'

'You know them. They're plastered all over the papers.'

'It's not that bad.'

'Really?' I grimaced. 'Annie and I aren't playing together in Stuttgart or Paris. How much worse can it get?'

Violet's shoulders sagged. 'Give her time.'

'We don't have the luxury of time. There are younger, more determined players ready to take our places. Not only that, but our advertising deals are tied up with being sisters and partners. We're a double act.'

Violet rested her hand on my arm. 'Come on, Sam. It's not like you to give up.'

I stared at the pink-and-white chequered floor tiles before answering. 'Everyone thinks sports people make truckloads of money. We don't. Yes, when we win, we get money, but if we're not playing together or we're not winning, there's no money and no tennis means no endorsements.'

'But those contracts are solid, aren't they?'

'Only until the one-year anniversary of the Olympics, just after Wimbledon. If Annie and I don't have our act together by then, we can wave goodbye to it all.'

Violet sighed. 'You'll find a way to work through this. Both of you. Then together, you'll be more powerful than before. You're driven, Sami. You never give up. That's what makes you so special.'

'Yeah, Bear says I could fight a tenacious bulldog for a bone. But remember...'

'The panic attacks?' Violet asked gently. 'I remember.'

Four years ago, after a succession of losses, my mental toughness had evaporated, my self-belief at an all-time low. I'd confided to Violet that I was holding Annie back, so I stepped away from the game for several months. Until Bear started coaching me, and I reclaimed my drive and determination.

Then there was the attack just before the Olympics.

'Vi, I feel like it's all about to come crashing down around me again. Right from the early days, everyone said Annie had more natural talent than me. That's just the way it is. She's better off playing singles. I'm a noose around her neck.'

Violet glanced round the bar. 'I'm sure I saw some tiny violins playing a moment ago.'

I smiled. 'Point taken. I'm sorry. That's enough bleating about me. How are you doing?'

Violet took my hand. 'You don't need to pretend. You come across as tough on the outside, but I know you too well, Ms

Callahan. Inside, you're soft. Vulnerable. To be honest, I'm peeved Annie doesn't realize that what she's doing plays into your greatest fears.'

My eyes widened.

'It's true. Right now, you and Annie aren't a team, but like it or not, you've got to suck it up. Get on with your own game.'

Before I could catch it, a flash of anger passed over my face and faded just as quickly.

'As for what's happening with us,' Violet went on, 'the usual. Rick works too hard, the girls are squabbling over who loves Justin Bieber more, and the dog has pink food colouring in his tail.'

I raised my eyebrows. 'LOL. He'd fit in well here.' Then. 'Is Justin Bieber still a thing?'

Violet snorted. 'Definitely.'

'I love your family.' I stared at my empty glass. 'Think I'll switch to vodka. You?'

Violet smiled. 'I'll stick with mineral water. Have to pick the girls up from school.' Then she smiled again. 'Actually, I'm pregnant.'

'Violet!' I fought back tears. 'Congratulations—when?'

She made a face. 'Maybe during the Australian Open?'

'Aussie, Aussie, Aussie?'

'Oi, oi, oi.'

I squealed and mock pinched her arm. 'Why didn't you tell me? Why'd you let me go on about myself for hours?'

'It wasn't hours, exactly.'

'I'm so happy for you and Rick. And the girls.' We stared at each other for a moment before I spoke again. 'How are you feeling? I thought two was your limit?'

'Ha,' Violet said, beaming. 'Two, three, four. Kids are a blessing. To be honest, I'm more concerned about how we're going to cope financially.'

'Seriously?'

'Yes and no. Rick's job is steady, but he works long hours. Much of his income is commission-based, and with another mouth to feed, that commission is going to be even more necessary, which means longer hours and more face time in the office. A vicious circle.'

My cheeks burned. I felt selfish and self-centred.

'But you know Rick,' Violet continued. 'He's ecstatic. "If I had my way, babe, we'd have a whole football team".'

'Go, Rick.'

'Yeah. It's hard not to get caught up in his excitement, even with the morning sickness and swollen ankles.'

'That can't be fun.'

She leant back in her chair and stretched her back, then sat upright again. 'Hon, are you really okay?'

'I guess.' I took a moment. 'I have to be.'

'Not to put a dampener on things, but what will you do if Annie marries Erik and ends up living in Norway or somewhere else in Scandinavia?'

I shuddered. 'That's not part of the bloody plan!'

Violet shrugged. 'Life doesn't always go to plan. Look at Rick and me—we had two babies before I was twenty-two. And now I'm bloody pregnant again.'

I dabbed my eyes. 'But you're both so stable and happy.'

'Yes, but I don't get to travel to all the amazing places you do. And even if Annie does marry Erik, you can keep playing tennis for as long as you want. You've got it all, Samantha. The only person holding you back is you.'

'That's what Bear says. Violet, do you think I'm overly dependent on Annie?' I frowned. 'Maybe I need more counselling.'

'Or maybe you just need to cut yourself some slack! Go out and get pissed. Have fun. Preferably with Bear. He's still in love with you. God knows why.'

'I'll ignore that remark.'

Violet patted her tiny bump. 'Hey, I'm preggers. I can say what I want. Bear is gorgeous and wonderful—the perfect man for you.'

'Shut up.' I sighed. 'I'm a really bad friend, aren't I?'

'Sometimes. And to make up for it, you're going on high-rotation babysitting duty once this beauty is born.'

I groaned.

'Okay, maybe not babysitting, but I'll expect you to be more involved with Ava and Poppy.'

'It's a promise. How will you manage three?'

'Hon, I won't know till I get there. It was never my plan to have all these children, but somehow...'

I laughed. 'It just happened?'

'Something like that. I never expected my life to turn out like this.'

'But now you have a family, and a solid family is worth more than any gold medal or Grand Slam title.'

'You have family too, Sami. You've got Annie, Bear, us...'

'It's not the same, is it?'

'Probably not,' Violet agreed. 'So, tell me your plans?'

'I've got three months before Wimbledon to sort myself out and accept that Erik's going to be a permanent fixture in Annie's life. Then, hopefully, we can put the past to rest and concentrate on tennis. In the meantime, like you said, I need to suck it up, focus on my game and do what Bear suggests: try out for Stuttgart and Paris.'

'Singles?'

My shoulders slumped. 'I don't want to partner with anyone else. Besides, Annie and I are only taking a short break. It's not fair to hook up with someone temporarily.'

'Whatever you think,' Violet said.

'What? You're thinking "don't get your hopes up"?'

'Not at all. It's going to be okay. You know that, right?'

I took my time to respond. 'Yeah, but I hate Erik.' I bowed my head for a moment. 'And you know what? As the days drag on, I find myself starting to hate Annie too.'

My greatest fear was losing Annie the way I'd lost my mother—my fear of abandonment was central to my hard-nosed drive to make certain Annie and I won, that we were an impenetrable force that couldn't be broken. With Erik now well and truly on the scene, I wanted to retreat into the foetal position. The once distant thought he could take Annie away from me forever was fast becoming a reality.

Fifteen

At the end of last year, I'd never have predicted that four months later Annie and I would be where we were now, either professionally or personally. Back then, we couldn't be beaten. We were bloody brilliant. At the Olympics, we blitzed the preliminaries, then the quarter-finals and found ourselves in the playoff for the gold medal. In truth, I thought we'd win silver because although we were pumped, our American opponents, Yasmine Le Bluth and Sandi Wren, were on top of their game and hungry as hell to win. They also had the crowd on their side. No doubt it helped that Yasmine always wore a short dress that just skimmed her underwear. When she served, little was left to the imagination.

But here's how it played out. Amazingly, I was in top form with my smashing volleys, and Annie had a consistent and powerful first serve. While I was all over the net, she hung around the baseline. It was thrilling. I'd never felt so alive, so invigorated.

It was Annie who closed out the match with a lob the

Americans couldn't reach. The roar from the crowd was deafening. It was a wonderful feeling: winning gold for Australia!

Bear and other supporters jumped onto the court to congratulate us. What a moment: Annie and me with broad smiles, flushed cheeks, punching the sky, hugging each other and crying, drinking in the moment. Savouring being Olympic champions.

Back then, Annie and I told each other everything. We had no secrets. That's why we were so successful. We worked together and supported each other—in sync, mind and body—so when we played, we brought out the best in each other.

Now I had to play singles. The thought of it scared me to death, but the reality was, I couldn't afford to give up playing competitively for more than a few weeks. Fitness, focus and staying in the game were paramount.

Before I left for Germany, Annie and I caught up briefly. She looked tired, pale and noticeably thinner, but I said nothing. Even though I wanted to grab her and demand to know what was going on, I also wanted to make peace with her.

'Are you okay?' I asked. 'I've missed you.'

Her gaze wandered momentarily. 'Erik's taking good care of me.'

'Good. He's a major part of your life now, and I want you to be happy,' I said with as much sincerity as I could muster.

She smiled. 'I knew you'd come around. This isn't a permanent break. We might even get to play against each other in Stuttgart. Wouldn't that be exciting?'

I almost choked. I couldn't think of anything worse than competing against Annie. I'd played against her when I was sixteen. She was brilliant. Her opponents would come on to the court thinking she was too laidback to care whether she won or not, and she'd beat them before they hit their stride. I knew better, but it was still tough losing to my younger sister. I didn't need to go through that angst all over again as an adult.

~ * ~

A few days later, I was in Germany, hitting up against Bear. Focus. Whack the ball, win the points. *Thump. Thump.* I hit balls until my joints ached, and when I could no longer raise my arm, I jogged until my legs could barely hold me. I was the leanest and fittest I'd been in years, maybe ever. The only way I could keep my demons at bay was by pushing myself to the limit. Most evenings I barely made it through dinner without falling asleep at the table. Bear tried to distract me by suggesting we take a break and sightsee or relax with a Netflix movie, but I always declined. My only reason for being in Germany was to play tennis.

When I wasn't lifting weights or sprinting, I hiked. I knew the major cities by heart. The best boulangeries in Paris, the best boutiques in London, the best cafés in Manhattan, the best apple strudel in Stuttgart.

'Want company?' Zach asked as I was leaving the hotel to go for a run.

I smiled. 'Maybe. Though I was going to use the time alone to think.'

Zach put his arm around me, and we started walking. 'Don't do that. Let me join you. I have gossip.'

'I'm listening.'

'In Miami, Yasmine Le Bluth got a thousand-dollar fine for wearing her dress too short—'

'About bloody time.'

'But if you've got the legs and bum—'

'Anything else?' I asked.

'Running with the Miami theme, several players, including Cindi Gibson, were docked the same amount for racquet abuse.'

'Why?'

'Before her match, Cindi threw everything out of Suzy's locker and called her a filthy whore. She ripped up photos of the two of them together. Apparently, Suzy's having an affair with Netta Mathieu.'

I raised my eyebrows.

'Really!' he said. 'I heard the rumours—all true and captured on camera.'

'Poor Cindi. It's the pressure. It gets to us all.'

'Here in Stuttgart, Courtney Gold's father was thrown out of the players' lounge an hour ago for abusive behaviour. He was yelling obscenities about overpriced beer.'

After my walk with Zach, I remained restless, my nerves on edge. I walked back to my suite and watched CNN. More talk about the men's matches. I turned it off, put my phone on silent, and settled for a long indulgent bubble bath. I tried to keep my thoughts positive and focus on my upcoming game. Most importantly, I needed to stay calm. Winning tomorrow would see me through to the second round and get me over the psychological hump. It was merely a case of mind over matter.

~ * ~

The power of positive thinking must have worked because I won easily against American Debby Bowden, twentieth seed. Noting that she hugged the baseline, I hit just over the net as often as possible. Debby hated coming forward and it showed. It was a good match. I almost cried happy tears.

Annie won her first round as well. Yay!

Bear brought me a printout of the second-round draws. 'You played well. You could be a damn fine singles player, Sam.'

I examined the printout. There it was, in black and white: if Annie and I both made it through round two, we'd be up against each other in round three. Just the thought of it was enough to bring me to tears and the inevitable despair that followed.

Whether it was the fear of having to play Annie, or the fact that I was a hopeless singles player, I crashed out in the second round to Dragana Lukić, of all people.

In the locker room after the match, where players took ice baths or focussed on short, violent bursts of exercise, or simply tried to isolate in preparation for their next match, Dragana happily and illegally puffed on a menthol cigarette and told me Erik wouldn't stay with Annie. 'He is using her so he can travel the world. I grew tired of him—therefore we break up. Now he uses Annie and pretends to be her coach. I have tried to warn your sister, but she does not listen. Like I am jealous. Ha!'

I didn't like what I was hearing. As much as I hated Erik, I didn't want to see Annie hurt. I wanted her to come to her senses and dump him before he finished with her.

'I bet he has not bought ring,' Dragana added.

I had to admit the no-ring thing wasn't a great sign. On the plus side, maybe it meant the relationship wouldn't last the distance. When Dragana and Erik were engaged, she'd worn a two-carat rock on her left ring finger.

'Mine is in my sock drawer,' she told me.

I had no reason to doubt Dragana. And she was certainly telling the truth when she said Erik liked to steal the limelight. I'd seen him in action. He only ever looked out for number one.

'I am not jealous,' Dragana continued. 'If I want Erik back, I can have him. I tell you the truth. Watch him.'

~ *

'What do you think?' I said to Bear ten minutes later as we paced to the court where Annie was playing, after I'd told him word for word what Dragana had said.

'I'm not surprised.'

'So, what are we going to do about it?'

'Nothing, Samantha. Stay out of it.'

'But what if Annie and Dragana come up against each other in the third round?'

'Dragana's taunts in Dubai didn't affect Annie's game. She played brilliantly.'

'She had me as a buffer then.'

Bear sighed. 'Annie's a grown up. She can look after herself.'

I hated that Bear was so sensible. He was also right. If I ran to Annie with Dragana's alleged insights, she'd cut me off completely. It was better to sit tight.

Bear shot me a look of—something I couldn't quite read. Disappointment maybe?

'What's up?' I asked.

'You.'

'What do you mean?'

'You. I'm thinking about you. Again. Why can't you take some time out for yourself? Think about your own love life for a change?'

I didn't want to have this conversation with Bear. Nervous and edgy couldn't begin to describe how I felt.

'Samantha, you must know how I feel about you, what I want.'

'But—'

'Tennis is your life. I get it. But I'm right here, ready, whenever, if ever you change your mind about giving us a go.'

My hand brushed the side of his cheek. 'I don't want you to stay if it makes you feel awkward,' I said, my voice even and steady. Inside, I was trembling. My heart pounded and my palms grew sticky with sweat. I didn't know what I'd do if ...

'Don't worry. I'm not going to pack my bags and leave,' he said, shaking off my hand. 'I'm fine. Where were we?'

We arrived at a packed court where Annie was in the process of getting flogged by Lucia Landry. I glanced at Bear, taking in his commanding presence, his muscular player's body. Though he was older than me, only a little greying at the temples and the slight wrinkles around his eyes gave it away. He was tanned, tall and handsome. No doubt about it.

'Unfortunately, I don't think there's any danger of Annie and Dragana playing each other this time,' Bear said.

Twenty minutes later, it was all over. I watched as Annie strode over to Erik. He whispered something in her ear, and she looked shocked, then he turned her to the cameras, all smiles. His hold around Annie's shoulders was just a little too tight for my liking.

Sixteen

Zach

Zach was propped up at the bar, sipping beer and swaying to an old Eagles tune. Adele, his latest tennis groupie, was beside him. A looker at 178 centimetres tall, with long strawberry blonde hair, blue eyes, and a deep golden tan, she smelt like summer flowers. And was perfect. Perfect for tonight anyway.

'Tell me all about the famous players you've met,' she said, giggly and starry-eyed.

His hand cupped the back of her neck. 'Met? Don't you mean played?'

She giggled some more.

'There are the ones who need to have sex before every match.' He stopped to watch her reaction—still giggling. 'There's a rumour that a well-known French guy urinates on his opponent's face before meeting up with him on court.'

Adele's eyes widened. 'Really?'

'Well, on a photo of his face. Then there are the more normal players like Samantha Callahan, who always wears a bandana.'

'Wow,' Adele said, snuggling as close as she could into Zach's chest.

Later when Zach was at the bar ordering himself another beer and Adele a gin and diet tonic, he heard a commotion at the door. He hurried over to investigate and found Courtney Gold's father, drunk, yelling and throwing punches at a security guard, who had refused him entry. Zach frowned. Courtney Gold was being hailed as the future of Australian tennis. Pity about her father. After celebrating his daughter's advancement to the finals of the Australian Open, he'd been charged with drunk and disorderly conduct, and here he was again, stopping people entering the club to ask them to take him in with them. When they refused, he yelled obscenities into the air.

Zach took out his iPhone and started clicking. The last couple were priceless—Mr Gold being thrown out of the doorway and onto the footpath. The old guy stumbled, then corrected himself and staggered down the street. Just as well. Zach didn't want to get involved, but he'd have gone to the man's rescue if he'd fallen in the gutter. There was such a thing as human dignity.

On his way back to the bar, Zach spotted Erik Sørensen with his hands all over a woman who definitely wasn't Annie. Zach didn't recognise her, so she probably wasn't a tennis player, but she was pretty, and Erik was giving her his undivided attention. What an arsehole!

Zach pulled out his iPhone and clicked some more photos.

The next morning, after Adele had left, Zach checked through the previous night's shots. He emailed his editor several of Mr Gold, but he held off on the ones of Erik. They'd hold for a rainy day. From now on, Zach would keep a much closer eye on Mr Sørensen.

~ * ~

Zach was sitting outside a café near the courts, enjoying the early morning sunshine, drinking coffee and scrolling through his phone when Annie stopped beside him and kissed his cheek.

'What did I do to earn that?' he asked, cheeks flushing. 'Not that I'm complaining.'

'I need a friend.' She gestured to a nearby chair. 'May I?'

Zach nodded as she pulled the chair in and sat down so close he could smell her fresh citrus fragrance.

She pointed at his plate. 'What are those?'

He laughed. 'Poffers.'

Annie scrunched her nose.

'Little pancakes. Don't tell me you've been in Stuttgart all this time and haven't tasted a poffer?'

Fidgeting, she wrinkled her brow.

'Annie Callahan, you haven't lived.' He waved a hand. 'Please let me introduce you.'

A waiter arrived and Zach ordered her a plate.

'And a latte, please,' Annie added.

'One for me too, thanks.' Zach gazed round. 'Where's Erik?'

Annie rolled her neck. 'Sleeping.'

Zach cocked his head to one side.

She whacked his arm. 'Don't look at me like that.'

He smirked. 'Like what?'

'Erik's good for me.'

Zach winced. 'Whatever you say, Annie.'

'He is, and for my game, too. Why can't people see that? Especially Sami.'

'She's your big sister. She worries about you.'

'But Erik's my knight in shining armour.' She giggled. 'My Viking.'

Zach suppressed a gag. 'Okay.'

The coffee and poffers arrived and Annie took a bite. 'Yum!'

She threw her hands in the air. 'Where have the poffers been all my life?'

He smiled. 'I told you.'

'I'm so happy.' Annie's breath hitched. 'You know what it's like to be in love, Zach.'

Zach remained silent, unsure where the conversation was heading.

'You understand. That's why I can talk to you. I can't talk to Sami because she's never been in love. Instead of supporting us, she's always looking for excuses to pick on him.' Annie exhaled. 'She makes me feel like I've let her down, that I'm not good enough.'

'I'm sure Sam doesn't mean to,' Zach replied diplomatically. 'She's protective of you. She couldn't bear to see you get hurt.'

Annie crossed her arms, one of which had several bruises. 'I can take care of myself.'

'That's what Sam's afraid of. I know you two. Sam's worried about being left alone—'

'That's not my fault. I'm not Mum, or Dad, for that matter, but the constant pressure, her constant pressure. When she's not abusing Erik, she's—'

'Focused on the next tournament.'

'Exactly. It's always about the next tournament and sizing up new competitors. She's relentless.'

Annie had a point. With Samantha, there never was an end. It was always about the next tournament and the one after that. And while Sam thrived on that punishing schedule and was forever projecting and thinking about future tournaments and goals, that wasn't Annie's deal, especially when she was in love. Love took precedence over tennis. Annie was just wired that way. It broke Zach's heart.

'You sure you don't want to speak to her about it?'

Annie looked away. 'The break's doing us both good. The longer we're apart, the longer we'll avoid a confrontation.'

Zach knew that once Annie made up her mind, that was it. No point pushing it. Besides, they were sisters. They'd work it out eventually. Right now, what worried Zach more was Annie's weight loss and the noticeable marks on her left arm.

'Been standing in way of the ball machine?' he said, trying to make light of it.

'Pardon?' Annie looked blank.

Zach pointed. 'The bruises?'

'Oh,' Annie replied, rubbing her forearm. 'Yeah, I guess.'

'Is everything okay?'

'Yeah, I'm all right. It's just that with Sami constantly at me, I worry that Erik might get fed up and leave.'

'What? You?' Zach scratched his head. 'How could he?'

'Thanks, but sometimes he stays out all night and won't tell me where he's been. I'm worried he's bored with me.'

Zach knew exactly where Erik went at night, but it wasn't his place to tell. This was the first real conversation he'd had with Annie since she'd started dating Erik, and he didn't want to spoil it.

'Have you tried talking to him about it?' Zach paused. 'Asking where he goes?'

Annie hesitated. 'He gets angry and starts shouting in Norwegian.'

Zach leant over, steepling his fingers. 'Listen, Annie, he's not... I hate to ask this... but he's not physically hurting you, is he?'

Annie rocked back in her chair away from him. 'No, of course not. How could you say that?'

'Sorry, my mistake.'

'I have enough people hovering around me, Zach. I don't need you too.'

Zach's stomach lurched. 'Point taken.'

She smiled. 'Good. Now, how's your love life?'

'Nothing to tell,' he said, thinking back to his night with Adele. He should call her.

After Annie left, he thought about the Callahan sisters some more. Several years ago, during one of Annie and Zach's heart to hearts, Annie had confided in him about their mother's disappearance. 'I overheard the police talking to Dad the night she went missing—they said she'd committed suicide, thrown herself off a cliff. But they never found Mum's body.'

He'd felt devastated for them both. Since then, it seemed Annie had to come to terms with it, though she craved love and acceptance. Samantha, though, was another story. Maybe without any physical evidence, Samantha couldn't accept her mother's death. He'd watched her work through anger, blame, bargaining and depression—she'd experienced it all. All except acceptance. From Zach's observation, Sam was shrouded in a permanent black mist. And she appeared to be sinking deeper since Erik had entered the picture.

Seventeen

Samantha

Let's face it, tennis means Wimbledon. If you can make it there, the world is yours for the taking because Wimbledon is the tournament by which all others are measured.

A few years back, most chat was about Roger Federer—would he or wouldn't he set a new record of fifteen Grand Slam titles? But this year it was all about Annie and me. Would we team up again? Would our pact survive?

Last year, we only made it as far as the third round. We'd had a difficult draw and were beaten—just—by Yasmine Le Bluth and Sandi Wren. But I didn't get as bent out of shape as I had after losing lesser competitions because we had the Olympics to look forward to. During the week following our loss, Annie and I had concentrated on having fun. We'd gone to see *The Book of Mormon* and *Hamilton*. We ate at fabulous restaurants. And we shopped. Boy, did we shop—in edgy boutiques in Notting Hill and

Shepherd's Bush, then on to Bond Street, Harrods and Kensington High Street. On our last day, a Saturday, we traipsed around the Portobello market. Despite the rain and freezing cold, it was one of the best weeks of my life.

This year, although we were staying at our favourite hotel, smack bang in the middle of the West End, there'd be none of that frivolity. Still, the familiar adrenalin rush from being in London kicked in. Whenever I was here, the same thought occurred to me: why didn't I live here? I loved the city.

'Come on, Bear,' I said. 'Let's go on the Eye thingo again.' I was smiling, happy that we'd arrived a couple of days ahead of schedule so we could enjoy London as tourists before having to face Annie and Erik.

He groaned good-naturedly. 'I can't face the crowds. How about an ice-cream instead?'

I leaned against him as we stood in the queue. 'Chocolate or vanilla?'

'Rum and raisin today, I think.'

I raised my eyebrows.

He smiled. 'What? I can be spontaneous.'

And then he kissed me, in the middle of London on a glorious summer's day. It was slow. It was forceful. It was all-consuming. I reached up on my toes to get closer to him. The kiss was exactly how I remembered it from three years ago. Bliss. Passion. Oblivion. All those feelings of hunger and desire came rushing back.

I tried to stop but he kissed me again, this time even more fervently. It took all my strength to eventually pull away.

'Why?'

'I was being spontaneous. I thought—'

'You thought wrong.' I glared at him, then softened and extended my hand to shake his. 'Friends?'

'Always.' He pushed my hand away and enveloped me in a tight embrace. 'One day, you'll come to your senses and admit—'

I slapped his arm. 'As if.'

'I am very determined, GG.'

We walked in companionable silence alongside the river for several minutes before he spoke again.

'Nervous?'

'What about?' I was still secretly reeling from his touch.

'Seeing Annie tomorrow,' he said, wiping ice-cream from my nose.

I nodded. 'A little.'

Soon enough, Annie and I would be playing on Centre Court. I visualised us walking down the tunnel into the arena, past all the photos of former champions—Ash Barty, Serena Williams, Novak Djokovic, Roger Federer. I almost didn't dare to picture us winning the doubles final, holding the cup aloft, and our winning photo hanging alongside them. But if you didn't dream, didn't project yourself as a winner, how could you hope to become one?

*

'I've missed you so much,' I said to Annie when she finally arrived at the courts for our first practice session. I couldn't believe it had been seven weeks since I'd seen her. 'Looking great. As always.'

She smiled. 'I feel it.'

I was determined to be on my best behaviour so as not to upset her, but I was flustered, didn't know how to keep the conversation going. I really didn't want to talk about Erik or their engagement, though I noticed she still wasn't wearing a ring.

It was a relief when an hour later, we got notification about the first-round draws.

'Great news,' I said, as we scanned the play sheets. 'We're up against Molly Fischer, the singing fool, and Kristy-hopeless-at-the-net Banta. We've beaten them on numerous occasions, and we can do it again.'

Molly irritated the bejesus out of me. She sang all the time—in the locker rooms, in the shower, even on court during warm-ups. And here's the thing: she wasn't a particularly good singer. I'd even go so far as to say she was tuneless, but that didn't stop her.

'They're playing well,' Annie said.

'Yeah, they are, so let's keep Kristy up at the net and get Molly to run around.'

'Exhaust her.'

'Exactly. You know what Americans are like. Boundless enthusiasm and pep.'

Annie's eyes narrowed. 'We'll do whatever it takes.'

'Because...'

She giggled. 'We're warriors not worriers.'

A mantra we hadn't used for a while, but one that was definitely apt.

We put in long training hours, and after only four days, our racquet skills were as sharp as they'd been last year. Gradually, our sisterly bond returned, although I was still cautious around her. It helped that Erik wasn't hanging around. When he wasn't there, Annie concentrated and played smart.

Unfortunately, when Erik did make it to our sessions, Annie got so nervous she missed basic shots, her serves lacked punch and her volleys had no power. Telling Annie she served 'like a box of hammers' wasn't helpful in anybody's language, but she took Erik's advice to heart even when he said things that were totally off the wall.

Annie didn't complain; at least not to me. Maybe it was because she knew my opinion about Erik, or maybe she didn't want to admit that their romance wasn't the fairy tale she'd wished for. Whatever the reason, she kept any negative thoughts about Erik to herself, even when he berated her for being past her prime. On those occasions, I wanted to kill him even more.

The day before our first match, I got my chance. I'd been trying to keep my feelings locked inside, but when he started banging on yet again about Ar-nee's serve and Ar-nee's stance and Ar-nee's failure to play at the net, it was all I could do to control myself until Annie slipped away to the bathroom. Then I exploded.

'Keep your opinions to yourself,' I said through gritted teeth.

Erik's brow wrinkled, and he put his hand up in front of my face. 'Eh?'

'I don't know what Annie sees in you, but I know it's only a matter of time before she wakes up to who you really are. An arrogant aging playboy who's out for all he can get!'

He stared straight ahead, his face devoid of expression. 'Erik does not listen to this.'

'You know what I'm talking about. Dragana told me you have no intention of marrying Annie. I'm watching you, Erik. And you can cut out that third-person bullshit as well.'

'Erik does not listen to this,' he said again, dismissing me with a wave.

'Yeah, well, Annie's not listening to your bogus advice,' I started, then saw Annie heading towards us. 'He's all yours,' I said to her, smiling, and left them to it.

I wished I hadn't mentioned him not marrying Annie. He'd probably rush out and buy her an engagement ring just to spite me.

~ * ~

'Everyone knows the Callahan sisters are great on grass,' Prue Hamilton said at the pre-match press conference.

'Yes, grass is like a second home to us,' Annie replied.

'It's our thing,' I added. 'It's where we learnt to play tennis.'

It was true. I loved playing on lawn, even though clay was a lot more forgiving, and you could slide on it. I loved the colour and the smell of grass.

'You expect to do well at Wimbledon?' Prue asked, smiling benignly.

We had to be careful with Prue. Annie and I weren't her flavour of the month, and I didn't want her bringing up our recent separation. We needed to show the media and our fans that, despite the interruption to our schedule, Annie and I were still committed to the game. Wimbledon was our chance to prove to the world that the Callahan sisters had the drive, enthusiasm and stamina to win.

'Yes, of course,' I answered. 'Annie and I have been tucked away the past few days honing our skills. Now we're ready to take on the world. We're pumped, no doubt about it.'

'A few days isn't much preparation. What was Stuttgart about?' Prue probed.

'It was never our intention to play doubles at that tournament,' I said. 'As Bear mentioned earlier this year, we were scheduled for a break, so we took the opportunity to give our singles game a workout.'

'Treat it like an additional training program?' Prue suggested.

'Exactly.'

'Though that didn't go quite according to plan,' Annie chimed in.

'Could that have had anything to do with your fiancé, Annie?' Prue asked.

Annie blushed. 'Not at all. Now we're in London, things are going great, like Samantha said.'

'So, you two are friends? There are rumours—'

'Of course, we're friends,' I said. 'In sync all the way.'

'Because if you're thinking of playing singles fulltime, Annie—'

Annie clenched her jaw. 'No, of course not.'

'I'm just saying,' Prue went on, 'Australians, Evonne Goolagong and Ash Barty have won...' She paused. 'You could be the next Aussie.'

'Samantha and I are a team,' Annie said firmly.

Prue gave in. 'Okay. And Bear? I heard—'

'Bear looks at our game from every angle,' I said. 'We talk tactics with him, and when we're feeling down, he's the guy who builds us up again.'

'Do you agree, Annie?' Prue asked.

Annie exhaled. 'I'm with Bear one hundred per cent.'

'But I thought Erik—'

'No more questions, thanks,' Bear said, bringing the interview to a close. 'It's time.'

~ * ~

'We can do this,' I said to Annie as we walked towards court number three to take on Molly and Kristy. We were both wearing regulation white; Annie in a simple white dress and me in skirt and polo. A white bandana of course.

'Is this the new number three or the old number two court?'

I laughed. 'New number three, I think. Why doesn't Wimbledon name its courts after famous players?'

'It would be a lot less confusing.'

'I'll say. So, you ready?'

For a split second, Annie looked doubtful.

'Annie, need I remind you of Kalgoorlie?' I shuddered at the memory. Those competitions were tough. Backbreaking. 'Just remember,' I told her, 'Molly's a nervous server, and when Kristy's under pressure, she's hopeless at the net. Also, we're better grass players than them.'

On court, looking up from the manicured lawn, I saw Bear take his seat in the box reserved for our supporters. Annie looked up too, no doubt searching for Erik. I couldn't see him, but guessed he was loitering close by.

I glanced at the ball kids and did a double take. 'Kurt, right?' I recognised him from the year before. Not a bad effort, considering there were over 250 of them picking up over 54,000 balls used during the 679 matches over a thirteen-day period. (My stats recall was above average.)

'Yes, Ms Callahan,' he said, nervously looking over his shoulder before handing me two balls.

'Sorry,' I muttered. Ball kids weren't supposed to have any contact with the players. By talking to Kurt, I'd placed him in an awkward position. According to game rules, he had to stand still and remain silent while on the court, regardless of whatever mayhem was going on around him.

Annie got off to a blistering start. Her first serve was way too powerful for Kristy. A smashing ace.

'What the fuck!' Kristy yelled and was promptly cautioned by the line umpire.

I pumped my fist in the air. 'All right,' I mouthed. 'Way to go, Annie.'

It was pure magic. Annie's forehand and cross-court backhand penetrated Molly's, and we won the first game, then the second and the third. Our opposition was crumbling. In only fourteen minutes, we were up 3–0. Yes, yes, yes! The Callahan sisters were back in top form. Who said anything about a slump? From here on, it was going to be sunshine and rainbows every day.

We won the first set 6–2. Yee-har.

~ * ~

'Annie, we're doing great,' I said, as we waited to return to the court for the second set.

'You think?'

'We've spent over half our lives on grass courts, we can do this. We can win this tournament. It's in the bag.' Then I noticed her whole body trembling. 'Annie?' I said, but she wasn't listening.

I followed her eyeline to the stands. Erik! He was dressed head to toe in white, staring directly at her and wagging his finger.

'Let's get back on,' I said, pushing Annie in front of me onto the court.

Though I could tell Annie was uneasy, she maintained focus and we won the match resoundingly, 6–2, 6–3. We were through to the next round, and I was hopeful we could snag a Wimbledon title.

But a short time later, I saw her face when she was talking to Erik. I knew that expression. It was her resigned 'I'm a failure' face, and when she wore it, it became a self-fulfilling prophecy.

I moved closer to overhear what they were saying.

'Your serve was, how you say, wishy-washy in the last game,' Erik lectured. 'You lose because you not throw the ball high enough.'

'Hey,' I said, wanting to backhand him. 'Annie and I played the best tennis we could, and we won!'

He didn't answer.

'You could say we're two of the top doubles tennis players,' I persevered.

'Congratulations,' Bear said, sweeping into the conversation. 'You won. Bring on the second round.'

'Yeah,' I said, holding him tighter than necessary. I was shaking all over, a combination of relief at winning and fury at Erik's comments.

As we headed into the press room, Annie swayed on her feet and hummed quietly. I was worried about her mental health. Erik's hold over her seemed stronger than merely being in love. It was obsessive, controlling. I really needed to talk to Annie alone to gauge how she was coping and to reassure her that we were doing brilliantly together and that a Wimbledon final was well within our grasp. But right now, that wasn't possible. Erik monitored her every movement.

Eighteen

Zach

Zach was sorting through his non-tennis photos, including some recent shots he'd taken in London, as he listened to the radio. Annie and Samantha were playing well but he agreed with the commentator.

Despite surviving their first round against Americans Molly Fischer and Kristy Banta, the Callahans face a tough battle in the second round against another couple of Americans, Debby Bowden and Daisy Coolridge. Bowden and Coolridge had taken less than ninety minutes to thrash their Irish opponents, Mary Beattie and Tammy Keyes, in the first round.

Still, there were tough battles and there were tough battles. Zach stared at the many photos he'd taken, all with a social issues theme. He was trying to select images for a show he'd been invited to take part in. Tina, a photographer mate, had seen several of Zach's Dubai shots and had encouraged him to keep going. So, Zach had, taking photos in Stuttgart and more recently,

London. His Stuttgart shots were mainly street scenes from poorer neighbourhoods. Shirtless kids playing soccer and hitting tennis balls against decrepit brick walls with sticks, bats and the occasional half-strung tennis racquet.

The London ones were almost exclusively of homeless people: an old woman busking, who was probably only thirty; a toothless guy and his dog—the dog looked better fed than his master; a mum with a couple of young kids, who really should have been in school but were scrounging in bins looking for food instead.

Zach was nervous. This was a whole new venture and failure was not an option. He fought back a desire to delve into his emergency packet of cigarettes. It had been over a year since his last. Sure, Zach was used to his photos being seen by the public, but they were mostly tennis focussed. This time he was challenging himself in a different way, and his inner voice boomed with non-stop criticism.

That night at a local bar where tennis players, reporters and groupies hung out, Zach watched Erik and discreetly snapped photos as he flirted with a gorgeous woman, wrapping his muscular arms around her, whispering into her ear and laughing. It reminded Zack of the photos he'd taken of Erik at another bar in Stuttgart. Why couldn't Erik see how lucky he was to have someone like Annie? He should have been with her, not sleazing all over someone who probably wasn't fit to carry Annie's racquet bag.

Sipping his beer, Zach wondered why things had never worked out between him and Annie. He'd had several opportunities, but he'd always been—what was the word? Reluctant? Afraid? Annie was the real deal. If he made a play for her, he'd be in it for the long term and as much as he hated to admit it, part of him always thought the grass might be greener on the other side. Truth be told, he was a tiny bit like Erik.

'What's going on?' Zach asked when the Viking walked over to the bar where he was sitting.

Erik smiled. 'She is old friend.' He pointed to Zach's empty glass. 'Another?'

Zach gave him a thumbs up. 'Sure.' He could see why Samantha didn't trust the guy. He was built, had charm, and worked his accent and smile for all it was worth.

Erik passed him a fresh beer and they clinked glasses.

'To a good night,' Erik said, glancing towards a blonde beauty who was eyeing Zach.

Zach recognised her—the French junior runner-up.

'She is, how you say, hot for you,' Erik said.

'Maybe,' Zach replied, sipping his drink.

'You Aussies say *go for it*, yes?'

Zach laughed. 'Yeah, I guess we do.' Then he checked himself. The girl was probably barely eighteen.

~ * ~

The next morning, Zach watched Annie and Samantha practice. During a break, while Zach guzzled a Red Bull, Sam came over.

'You look like death,' she said.

'Thanks. I feel like it.'

Samantha raised her eyebrows. 'Out partying? Heaven help the women on circuit.' She paused. 'Did you see him?'

'By *him*, I assume you mean Erik?'

'Who else?'

'Yeah, he was there.'

'And?'

'There's such a thing as a gentlemen's agreement.'

Samantha placed her hands on her hips. 'Don't bullshit me. He hasn't shown up today. He may be keeping a low profile here, but I doubt he's keeping a low profile at the clubs.'

'Does Annie still believe he has trouble sleeping, what with all the different time zones.'

Samantha was non-committal. 'She says he jogs late at night, so he doesn't disturb her.'

'Considerate guy.'

'You bet. Apparently, if he's really wide-awake, he goes clubbing to tire himself out. But only rarely.'

'What do you want me to say?' Zach sighed. 'Erik spends his nights hitting the local bars. It's no secret.'

Samantha clicked her tongue. 'What do I do? I want to tell Annie, but I don't want to rock the boat, not now we're together again.'

'Then let it lie, babe. She'll find out soon enough. If she doesn't know already.'

Nineteen

Samantha

I didn't see Annie again until the morning of our second-round match when we met in the locker room to prepare to take on Debby Bowden and Daisy Coolridge. Annie looked nervous and bug-eyed.

'Okay?' I asked.

'I don't know. Sometimes my confidence just—evaporates. Erik says I'm not trying hard enough. I hate disappointing him.' She stopped talking and started humming. I don't think she was aware of it.

I put my hand on her shoulder. 'Annie, stop. I'm your sister. You can talk to me.'

'Thanks, but everything's wonderful. Really.'

'What's with the humming then?'

Annie looked confused. 'What humming?'

I didn't pursue it. 'When we're on court today, we have to block out every stray thought and concentrate on the game. Let's give it our best shot and play hard all the way to the finals. Merciless focus, okay?'

She gave a tired smile. 'Yes, Mum.'

Okay, we weren't on Centre Court, and we didn't have 13,500 people standing and cheering for us. We were on one of the side courts, playing to less than a thousand spectators. But it didn't matter; it was exhilarating. Familiar pains hit my stomach as I waved my racquet in the air and acknowledged the crowd. Bear was right... if I ever stopped feeling those physical pangs of nervous adrenalin, it would be time to retire.

I turned to Annie. 'Think about our win against Molly and Kristy. You played brilliantly. Just channel that memory.'

Annie looked directly above us to where Bear was sitting. There was no sign of Erik. I briefly thought back to my attack on him, then dismissed it. There was no way he'd miss Annie's second match at Wimbledon.

'Remember,' I said when her gaze returned to me, 'Debby hugs the baseline, and Daisy favours her forehand, so hit to her backhand as often as you can.'

We were up four games to three in the first set, when Debby tripped, twisted her ankle and was forced to retire. One minute, Annie was serving and the next, Debby was on the ground howling in pain.

At the press conference, Debby's twisted ankle was like the elephant in the room. She didn't want to talk about it, she told the assembled media. 'If I give it oxygen, it'll be on my mind and affect my game.'

'A bit late for that, don't you think?' Daisy called out, stamping her foot like a petulant five-year-old.

'I'm trying to stay positive,' Debby said.

'Don't bother,' came Daisy's sour reply.

Two hours later, X-rays revealed that Debby had broken seven bones in her foot and was likely to be on crutches for the next four months.

I didn't care that Annie and I had reached the third round through dumb luck. Could I dare hope we'd make it into the second week?

'Nothing can stop you now,' Bear said, positively glowing.

'But Debby—' Annie started.

'But Debby nothing. You'd have won regardless.'

Bear always knew the right thing to say.

'Have you seen Erik?' Annie asked, looking around. 'I haven't seen him since I left our room this morning, and he's not answering his phone.'

'He's probably buying you a congratulatory present,' I said. 'Maybe he's finally forking out for an engagement ring. In the meantime, we're moving up in the world. We've been bumped from locker room B to A. Yay!'

~ * ~

Our next draw was against Czech players Petra Stepanek and Olga Gerski. In addition to working out and swimming, I'd spent the lead-up to the match pinpointing their strengths and weaknesses. Annie and I had never played them, but Bear and I had watched them in action twice, most recently in Dubai. Petra was an all-rounder, good at the net and the baseline; and Olga had a smashing double-handed backhand. Even though they'd only been playing together six months, you'd think they'd been partners for years.

'You can't assume they'll be easy beats,' Bear said during his pre-match pep talk.

'Olga wears contact lenses,' I said. 'Maybe I can accidentally whack her in the eye.'

Bear smiled. 'I wouldn't put it past you.'

'We need to win this match, Annie,' I said as we took to the court half an hour later. 'If we don't, it's the end of Wimbledon for another year.'

'I know that.'

Mentally, I ran over our opponents' strengths and weaknesses again, and repeated my mantra: *Never give up.* Automatically, I reached up to adjust my bandana, but it wasn't there. Somewhere between the locker room and court, I'd lost it. I tried never to let superstition get in the way of my game, but my bandana was part of who I was. It gave me a connection to Mum. Every time I touched my bandana, I silently mouthed 'I love you.' I'd never played a match without one. But it was too late to search for it now; we were on court.

'What's wrong?' Annie asked when she saw me hesitate. 'Where's your bandana?'

'I ...it doesn't matter,' I replied, determined not to let negative thoughts invade my head. Too late! As quickly as I tried to banish them, new ones appeared and I hadn't even hit a ball yet! I'd seen players brought to their knees by negative thinking. And when you were down that low, it took a hell of a lot of strength to drag yourself out of the psychological hole.

Positive thinking, positive thinking, I kept repeating to myself, over and over. It didn't help that Annie took on my superstition.

'We're going to lose,' she whispered in the third game of the opening set as the spectators went wild after I failed to return another of Olga's magnificent lobs.

'Stop. Until we lose that final match point, we can always win.'

But Annie and I needed some luck to swing our way, and moments later, Bear gave it to us. He threw me my white bandana and I fixed it to my head. The crowd cheered. I looked up to the stands and waved, then bowed. I had my lucky bandana back and was feeling mighty fine. We could win this!

'Quiet, please,' the pernickety umpire called out.

Back to business. At every opportunity I tried to jolly Annie along, but I might as well have been talking to a brick wall. After the next lost point, her movements became stilted, her stance hunched, and she went back to brushing non-existent lint from her left shoulder. Short of beating her up—which I considered several times—there wasn't a lot I could do except try to keep her spirits up.

'Annie, you're doing great,' I said desperately. 'Come on, sis. I screwed up. I'm the one making all the mistakes. We can still win this.'

But Annie continued picking at her left shoulder and missing easy shots. At the net, she either botched volleys or watched shots roar past her. I had no idea what was going on inside her head, and consequently, drew a blank when it came to guessing what she would do next. On top of that, I wasted opportunities. It was tough. Neither of us could compete with Olga's backhand and Petra's assured ball placement. We lost the first set.

Sensing imminent failure, the reliable part of our game faltered. I tossed my head back in disgust and slapped myself on the forehead after losing yet another point. Well into the second set, a linesperson called the ball—my ball—out. I was sure it was in. It had to be. We were down two games to five, 30–40. Losing the point would be catastrophic.

Emotionally charged, I rushed up to the umpire, shrieking, 'How could you let him call that out?'

Video replay revealed that the ball was definitely out, and the score became 2–6.

We lost the match in sixty-eight minutes, our Wimbledon dream in tatters. On top of that, I received a warning for intimidating a linesperson.

I screamed at myself, I raged at Annie. And yes, I yelled at spectators to the point where I was almost jeered off the court. Momentarily, I wondered what it would be like to have eight thousand people booing me, instead of a vocal handful. Meanwhile, Annie was a picture of composed calm and accepted the defeat with a 'That's too bad.' Her emotional detachment inflamed me further. We were poles apart, handling our stress and loss so differently.

Petra and Olga raised their arms in triumph and jogged to the net for the obligatory handshake. I was exhausted, my legs almost buckling as I stumbled towards them. I half-heartedly shook their hands, then reluctantly shook the umpire's.

Off court, when Erik pointed his finger at me and said, 'You are holding Ar-nee back,' I lost it.

'Me?' I screamed; my face flushed with fury. 'I'm holding Annie back? How dare you?'

'Enough with this,' Erik shouted. 'All the time you upset my star.'

'Mate,' Bear said. 'It's been a tough day. We all need to chill, regroup, look at ways to improve our game, then focus on the next tournament.'

Erik's jaw was clenched, and veins visibly throbbed in his neck. 'No! You are both bad for Ar-nee. She is not good player now—'

'Are you listening to this?' I said to Annie, who was staring at the ground. 'For God's sake, grow a spine.' My throat was dry and tight. 'Tell him to shut up.'

She looked up at me. 'Mind your own business, Sam.'

'What the hell? This *is* my business.' My eyes watered and my head pounded, throbbing with pain. 'You and I are the business, Annie. Whether you like it or not, we're a team.'

Annie waved her hands in the air and strode away with Erik.

I bent over, coughing, dizzy with nausea.

Bear rubbed my back. 'Are you okay? You don't look good.'

I ignored him and finally stood. 'How can she do that?'

'Sami, you're practically hyperventilating. Take a warm shower and calm down. Maybe you need a few days off.'

I stared at him, my eyes ice. 'I'll tell you when I need time off *if* I need time off. Thanks very much.'

Swallowing the urge to vomit, I made my way towards the women's locker room. I did need a long shower to cool down, but I also needed to have it out with Annie. As I reached the entrance, I saw her outside, laughing with several other players like she hadn't a care in the world. Like we hadn't just suffered a humiliating defeat and been booed off court. I couldn't fathom what was going on with her. Was she truly that unaware?

'Annie, it wasn't just me who played badly out there today,' I said, walking up to the group, the pounding in my head growing stronger with every step.

She turned to face me. 'It was a game. We lost. Move on. There'll be other games. There are always other games.'

Some of the players tittered, which incensed me further.

'How can you say that? How can you dismiss this like it's no big deal?'

'Because it *is* no big deal. There are more important things in life—'

I slapped her. Right then and there, outside the women's locker room, I slapped my sister across the face.

Lucia Landry stepped between us. Yasmine Le Bluth pulled me back.

'How could you do that to your sister?' Lucia demanded.

'What would you know?' I screamed. 'You're just a centrefold.'

Annie didn't say anything. She just rubbed the bright red mark on her cheek where I'd hit her.

I doubled over in pain before letting out a huge sob and standing, confused and dazed. 'What? What have I done? I'm ...I'm so sorry.' And I meant it. I was truly shocked. I didn't know if she'd heard me because a swarm of women descended on her.

'Annie, are you okay?'

'Someone get her some ice.'

'That sister of yours is a monster! You must press charges.'

I couldn't believe what I'd just done to my sister, my best friend. I was imploding. Unable to see clearly, I rushed to the nearest toilet cubicle, locked myself in and vomited, a shaking, miserable mess.

Twenty

After ending the call with Bear, I phoned Violet, knowing she'd have seen the match. 'I ...have you ...'

'Watching it now.'

'The slap?'

'Unfortunately.'

'How bad?' I spluttered through tears.

'On a scale of one to ten? Fifteen. They've added sound effects—a cracking noise as your palm connects with Annie's cheek.'

I let out a strangled sob.

'Have you spoken to Annie?' Violet asked.

'No.'

'The TV cameras are fixed on the locker room entrance, waiting for you guys to come out.'

'That's never going to happen—'

'Sweetie, the sooner the better.'

'Violet, I hit my sister! I didn't see the cameras. How stupid!'

'Hon, you need to say how sorry you are. That it was a moment of madness—'

'It was!'

'Exactly.'

'I *am* so sorry. I can't get the image of Annie's shocked face out of my head. It's awful.'

'It'll pass,' Violet soothed. 'But I have to warn you, on the screen your face is contorted with rage.'

'Still?'

'Sorry, hon, it's playing non-stop. Sports commentators are going wild.'

'And at Wimbledon, London; the birthplace of decorum and civility—'

'Not the birthplace exactly.'

'I think William and Kate were in the audience. Oh my God.'

'Yeah.'

'I was furious. I couldn't control myself. It just happened. On national television.'

'International, I'm afraid.' Violet paused. 'How could you not have seen the cameras?'

I was too busy sobbing to reply.

'It's okay. I can see how quickly it escalated. Clearly you weren't thinking. Commentators are talking over the footage.'

'What are they saying?'

Violet was quiet for a moment. 'Um... "What's happened to our golden girls?" Another one is saying, "It's a bad sign for Australian tennis.".'

'Oh, God!'

'Now Prue Hamilton's chiming in. "With Annie and Samantha Callahan's Wimbledon loss, Australian tennis has become statistically enfeebled. No doubt about it." I'm sorry, Sam. That woman needs a bullet.'

Gulping, I said, 'I wish the ground would open up and swallow me. My life's fucked. You know what's going to happen now? A media free-for-all. They'll whip themselves into a frenzy, falling over themselves to tell the world how Annie and I've had a falling out. And I'll be portrayed as a horrible bitch who bashes her sister.'

'Don't beat yourself up,' Violet said. 'At least wait until you've had a chance to talk to Annie. Maybe it's not as bad as you think.'

'Who are we trying to kid? Everyone thinks I'm a monster.'

'Hang on,' Violet said. 'Bear's making a statement ...he's saying it was "a slight tap due to emotional distress at having lost the match ...An unfortunate misunderstanding, best put behind us".'

I started crying again.

'Have you spoken to him?' Violet asked.

'Yeah, a few minutes ago. He said I can't hide in the toilet forever.' My voice lowered to a whisper. 'He said the sooner Annie and I walk outside together, the sooner we can put it behind us.'

'Wise words.' Violet took a moment. 'Sami, I'm not saying this isn't a difficult situation, but I know Annie. She'll forgive you. It's been a tough six months for both of you. But right now, you need to do as Bear says and harness your strength to face Annie and the media.'

'I can't.'

'Honey, you can, and you will. Promise me you'll apologise and make it better?'

I couldn't speak.

With bile rising in my throat, I hung up. My head was still pounding, not helped by candle scent wafting in from nearby. Flushed and hot, I slumped on the cold floor tiles, then shivered involuntarily.

What Violet said made sense. I needed to face the music, or, rather, face Annie first and then the media. It was going to be hell, but there was no way around it.

Ever since I was little, I'd been getting into this kind of trouble. I had a vivid memory of hitting Annie over the head with my toy guitar when I was six. Mum had been so angry and disappointed she'd cried. 'Don't ever think you're so special that you can hit your baby sister,' she'd yelled at me. 'This is unacceptable behaviour. You're a big girl. Start acting like one.'

It was Mum who'd drummed into us how important family was and how we should always stick together. This had stayed with me after she left. She didn't do a good job of practising what she preached.

'Samantha!' Bear banged on the cubicle door. 'Please come out.'

'I can't,' I said. 'It's too hard.'

'You can and you will. I'm here. Please unlock the door.'

I had to unlock it eventually, but I was terrified about what Annie and the rest of the world would think of me.

'Everyone's watching me on enormous theatre sized TV screens,' I said. 'Violet said they've added sound effects!'

'Please, Sam, sweetheart, I won't leave your side. We'll get through this together. Please.'

Shaking, I unlocked the door and fell into his arms. 'I'm so sorry.'

'I know you are, sweetie,' Bear said, holding me close. 'But you need to tell Annie. She's just outside.'

'With ...everyone?'

Bear's stance softened. 'It's only the locker room. The first step. The sooner you see her, the sooner it'll be over.'

'She must really hate me,' I said. 'Everyone must hate me.'

Bear pulled me close. 'Come on.'

In the locker room, Olga Gerski approached me first and put her hand on my shoulder. She'd taken out her contacts and was wearing oversized thick-lensed glasses. 'Samantha, you cannot please everyone.'

'True,' I sniffed, feeling guilty about my joke about blinding her. 'But I should at least make a token effort.'

Then Petra patted my back. 'If I knew the day would end this badly for you, I would have eased off. Olga and I would still have beaten you, but we wouldn't have gloated so much.'

Who said there was no love in tennis?

I saw Annie and stumbled towards her, arms outstretched. At least we could have a semiprivate reunion here, without all the world's cameras upon us.

'I'm so sorry,' I said. 'I was out of my mind. It was totally my fault.'

Annie accepted my embrace. 'It's no big deal, really.'

'But I slapped you. The whole world thinks I'm a sister abuser.'

'Don't flatter yourself. Tennis isn't as popular as it used to be. Even golf beats us when it comes to television ratings.'

I couldn't understand why she was being so dismissive. 'I never should've hit you. It was inexcusable.'

'Enough. We lost the match, and you were pissed off. Things got out of hand. You've apologised, it's over. As I said before, there'll be other games. We'll survive this.'

I inhaled deeply to steady myself for the attention we were about to receive. 'Should we go outside?'

But Annie wasn't listening. Her eyes were glued to one of the huge screens where Erik was making a press statement.

'Erik went crazy for the girl from koala country,' he was saying. 'But it was too much. So is better this way, when Erik and Ar-nee are broken up.'

'Oh my God, no,' Annie whispered. 'No.'

'It was moment of crazy,' Erik said. 'But her family, her sister—is too much for Erik.' He held up his hand and made a peace sign before stepping down from the podium.

Annie wheeled around to me, her eyes wide and furious. 'This is your fault, Samantha. You forced him to do this. I hate you.'

Bear took her arm. 'Annie, I'm sure he doesn't mean it.'

'What's happening to me?' Annie screamed, shaking off Bear's hand. 'First Samantha hits me and now Erik dumps me, both on live television.'

'I'm so sorry,' I started.

'Don't you dare.' Annie's voice was ice. 'You hated Erik from the outset.'

'Annie, I am truly sorry. For everything.'

'Too little, too late.' She slumped on a nearby lounge. 'He dumped me on television. Why? Why would he do that?' she said, over and over. 'What did you say to him, Samantha? What did you do?'

I stood helpless. I wanted to scream and throw things, but this wasn't about me and my anger. I had to be strong for Annie. Engulfed by guilt, I hoped Erik hadn't made his announcement because of something I'd said or because I'd slapped Annie. Yes, I'd wanted them to break up, but I'd wanted it to be on Annie's terms. It wasn't supposed to end like this, with her so devastated. It wasn't fair.

Eventually, Annie stopped crying, pulled herself off the sofa and went to shower. Although her eyes were bloodshot and her face flushed, she looked calm when we finally left the locker room fifty minutes later. Vulnerable and emotional, but in control. That'd show the bastard.

'You know they'll be waiting,' I said, referring to the media.

Understatement. As soon as Bear opened the door, the way ahead was blocked by reporters.

'Did Erik tell you before he made the announcement?'

'He was your *de facto* coach, wasn't he?'

'What are you going to do now, Annie?'

'No comment,' was all Annie offered, per instructions from Bear. I don't think she even heard what was being asked. She was in a daze, walking and talking on autopilot.

'You never liked Erik, did you, Samantha?' Prue Hamilton said, shoving a microphone under my nose.

'I wouldn't say that—'

'And what do you have to say about slapping your sister?' Prue interrupted. 'Was that the final straw for Erik?'

'I'm sorry. Truly,' I replied.

'But do you think Erik ended the relationship because of you? Because of your constant interference? In his statement, he implied—'

Bear stepped in. 'That's enough for now. Annie and Samantha have had a difficult day.'

'What about your tennis partnership with your sister, Annie? Is this the end of the Callahans?'

'No more questions, please,' Bear said as he ushered us to a waiting car.

Inside, I put my arms around Annie. 'If I could make today disappear, I would.'

She shrugged.

'I'm so sorry,' I said again, holding her tight.

And I was. I hated seeing Annie so distraught, so emotionally at sea. I had nothing to offer her but hugs and empty platitudes. I hated Erik and was glad to see the back of him, but this? She'd given him her heart and he'd thoroughly stomped on it.

Twenty-one

Back in Annie's suite, all of Erik's belongings were gone. I stared at the silver-leaf sleigh bed standing on a hand-woven rug, the sheer curtains blowing softly with the breeze of the overhead fan. Annie had added her own touches to the room: scented candles and photos on the bedside table, her favourite scarves draped over lamps and chairs. The effect was romantic, soft and charming. And heartbreaking.

'You wouldn't even know he'd been here,' she said, choking out the words as tears streamed down her cheeks. She dialled Erik's number for the twentieth time, but the coward had it switched to message bank.

'Do you want me to stay?' I asked.

She held up her hand as if warding me off. 'I'll be fine.'

'Okay, but please don't rush out tonight and find yourself a new boyfriend,' I said without thinking. As soon as the words slipped out of my mouth, I knew I'd said the wrong thing—again.

'Thanks. I feel so much better now,' Annie said, and collapsed on the couch in tears. 'I'm alone and humiliated, but no, Samantha, I'm not going to find another boyfriend. Regardless of what you think, I'm in love with Erik.'

'I'm sorry. I just meant—'

'I know what you meant. I'm not like you, Samantha. I can't shut myself off from the rest of the world. I like human contact. I like being touched and loved. Not like you who can't bear any kind of intimacy.'

'I'm so sorry for hitting you, Annie. This mess is my fault. If we hadn't argued, if I hadn't lost my temper...'

It was like talking to wood. Annie kept her eyes on her iPhone, willing Erik to call. Finally, I left her sobbing in a hot bath, and slunk back to my room feeling like the biggest arse alive.

~ * ~

The next day, the news was all over the radio, television and social media and I couldn't stomach leaving the hotel. Instead, when I wasn't checking on Annie, I kept my room door locked; my overactive mind firmly set on replaying the appalling events; my body heavy with fatigue.

Tennis glamour couple shock split

Australian tennis star Annie Callahan and her handsome Norwegian fiancé, Erik Sørensen, have ended their six-month engagement with Callahan choosing to concentrate on her doubles partnership with sister, Samantha.

Despite their third-round Wimbledon loss, which resulted in Samantha viciously slapping her sister afterwards, their coach, Bern 'Bear' Devlin, says the sisters' partnership is more formidable than ever.

In a prepared statement, Devlin said the split between Sørensen and Annie Callahan was mutual, despite Sørensen holding a solo press conference to announce the demise of the relationship. Annie Callahan did not speak to the media, nor did she return calls.

'This doesn't concern anyone else,' Devlin said. 'The break-up is entirely amicable.'

I answered the phone flatly. 'Hi.'

'What the fuck, Sam?' Violet gulped. 'I've been frantic trying to reach you!'

'I know. I'm sorry,' I said. 'It's a mess. A horrible, devastating mess.'

'How's Annie?' Violet asked. 'I can only begin to imagine.'

I sniffed back tears. 'Barely coping. She looked like death this morning. Didn't sleep at all.' Last time I'd checked, a grief-stricken Annie was slumped in bed with blotchy tear-stained skin, sad tired eyes and unbrushed hair.

'That's understandable.'

'Yeah. She's still in bed, dozing on and off.'

'I don't know what to say, darling. It's so horrible. I've tried phoning her and left messages...'

'She's turned her phone off,' I replied. 'She's terrified of talking to anyone. Just keeps saying "How can I go outside?" It's crazy that she's the one who feels ashamed.'

'Tell her we're all on her side, inadequate as those words are.'

'Thanks. I told her that her fans love her and that we're in this together.'

'And?'

'She just cries, says she's the one who got dumped, the one who's been humiliated beyond belief.'

'Sami, I wish I could be there with you both. I feel so useless.'

'Bear keeps telling me I need to prepare myself in case she decides to quit tennis altogether.'

'Really? You think she might?'

'Yeah.' I paused a moment. 'I wanted Annie to be the one to end it, not him.'

'Has anyone heard from Erik?'

'He seems to have disappeared.'

'Bastard. How could he do this to Annie?'

As much as I hated to admit it, Annie loved Erik, she really did. It didn't matter that they'd known each other only a short time or that they were different nationalities, they shared a connection and passion. At least Annie thought they did. And now their romance was over in the most excruciating and public way. Bad enough a handful of people knowing about your private life, but the world?

Twenty-two

Zach

Zach called Annie repeatedly for more than twenty-four hours without luck. He knocked on her hotel door several times. Nothing. He was desperate to see both Samantha and Annie, but now that the press was hanging out in the lobby, waiting to pounce when Annie showed her face, he didn't think it likely she'd venture beyond her room anytime soon.

'Hey,' he said when Samantha finally called. 'How are you holding up?'

'I'm fine. It's Annie. I can't believe Erik's vanished.'

Zach clicked his tongue. He wanted to bop Erik in the nose. 'He's probably hiding out with some busty blonde. I bet he wasn't expecting the negative media attention. They've really turned on him.'

'Well, for Annie's sake, if he is with another woman, I hope there are no photos.'

Zach thought about all the Erik pics he had on file. 'Yeah. Let's hope not. Are you in your hotel room?'

'Yeah.'

'Good, I'm about to knock on your door.' He hung up just as Samantha opened it.

'So how is Annie? Really?' Zach asked, taking in her tired and drawn appearance.

'Not good,' Samantha said, leading him inside. 'Room service has just delivered more paracetamol, but I think she needs something stronger.'

'Like this?' Zach pulled a bottle of vodka from his satchel.

Samantha smiled. 'Couldn't hurt. Although maybe getting drunk isn't the best idea.'

'Do you think I could go to her room? See her, as a friend.'

'I'm not sure she's up for receiving visitors.'

'I'm not just a visitor, Sam. We're old mates. I know how tough it is when shit hits the fan. Come on, I can take her the painkillers and you can get some rest.'

Samantha nodded and Zach followed her down the hall to Annie's room. 'Okay, but Zach ...take it easy.'

'Sure thing, boss.'

'I mean it,' she said, handing him the paracetamol. 'I'm two doors away if you need me.'

Zach bowed, then knocked at Annie's door when Samantha walked back to her suite.

Annie opened it immediately. 'What took you so long?' she began, then stopped, almost as if seeing him for the first time. 'Zach?' It was definitely a question. 'I was expecting Sam.'

Although the curtains were drawn, making the room almost black, he could see her eyes were red. The dark shadows under them and her hollow expression showed she hadn't slept. 'I know. Don't get angry. I won't stay long. I bought you a present.' He held up the bottle of Grey Goose.

Annie smiled a little. 'Well, you'd better come in, I guess.'

So far, so good. Zach squinted as he strode to the mini bar, pulled out two tumblers and a tray of ice, then poured hefty slugs of vodka.

'Cheers,' Annie said as he handed her a glass. She downed the nip in one mouthful. 'Agh. My throat's on fire.'

'No wonder,' Zach said. 'I'm impressed.' He poured her another two fingers. 'Here you go.'

She grimaced. 'Bottoms up.'

Zach watched as again she drank the liquid in one gulp. She was certainly putting on a brave face, but he could sense her pain underneath. The way she forgot to smile was a dead giveaway.

He pulled the curtains back a little to let in the late afternoon light. 'Do you mind?'

'Please yourself.'

'Annie, I'm really sorry—'

'I don't want to talk about it.' She closed her eyes as if struggling to stay awake.

Zach opened his mouth to reply but quickly closed it. He didn't know what to say and the last thing he wanted was to upset her.

She snapped back to face him. 'What's happening in the world of tennis? There must be some gossip that doesn't concern me—or Erik. You always seem to know everything before it hits Twitter. What have you got for me?'

'Let's see,' Zach said. 'Cindi's got a tell-all interview coming out with *Hello!* magazine in which she spills the beans about her and Suzy. Apparently, Netta's Suzy's special friend now—'

'Like we didn't know that already.'

'But there's more. Suzy's looking to move to Paris permanently with Netta, but Cindi told me Suzy doesn't like cheese and she hates bread, so the French lifestyle will be completely wasted on her.'

'Ha. What else?' She smiled, but to Zach, it looked forced.

'After Courtney Gold lost her match yesterday, her dad assaulted a cameraman. Apparently, he was drunk, again, and smashed the camera lens. It didn't help that Courtney had been fiddling with her garter and it had been caught on camera.'

'That's right, I forgot she wears a blue garter to every match. I wonder if it's the same one?'

Zach laughed. 'She'd have a suitcase full, wouldn't she? Anyway, she went out and got totally wasted. Ended up abusing fans in Piccadilly Circus.'

'Really?' Annie stared at her empty glass and wiped her wet eyes. 'What else?'

Zach didn't have anything else. Annie, along with Samantha and Erik, was everyone's main topic of conversation. He put his arm around her. Annie sighed and rested her head against his shoulder. She may have been exhausted, but she was still exquisite. He couldn't help stroking her hair.

'I guess I'm the laughing-stock of the circuit.'

Zach continued playing with her hair. 'Not at all. Erik's a dickhead for leaving you.'

'Doesn't make it any easier.'

'You're too good for him, Annie.'

She turned to face him. 'Don't say that.'

'You are.' Without thinking, Zach bent to kiss her.

Annie sat up and pushed him away. 'What the hell do you think you're doing? I'm in love with Erik!'

Zach slumped back to the edge of the couch. *He was such an idiot. Why, oh why did he do that?* 'I'm sorry. That was dumb. Really dumb, Annie. Sorry.'

'Erik's in love with me, too,' Annie mumbled through her tears. 'He's just confused right now.'

Zach couldn't believe what he was hearing. How could Annie still love him? 'I'm not so sure about that.'

'Why? What do you mean?'

'I didn't want to say anything,' Zach began, 'but I saw Erik with another woman at a club in Stuttgart.'

'I don't believe you.'

Zach hesitated, furious that Erik had done this to her. But he'd gone too far now not to go all the way. He pulled out his phone and scrolled through photos. 'Look.' He passed her the phone. 'See for yourself.'

Annie stared at the images, tears streaming down her cheeks. She handed back the phone. 'Get out, Zach. Just get out.'

This wasn't what he'd wanted. Zach wanted to be a good friend to Annie, to make her feel better, not cause her more suffering. He should have been holding Annie in his arms and comforting her right now, not getting kicked out of her room.

'Annie, I'm sorry, but I don't want you pining over some guy who clearly doesn't love you.'

'I don't want to talk about it. Please, just leave.'

Closing the door, Zach's parting memory was of Annie sobbing on the couch. He didn't want to leave, but she'd insisted, and now he was standing in the corridor itching to punch out a wall. How could he have got it so wrong?

Twenty-three

Samantha

Twenty-four hours later, Annie still hadn't left her hotel room. Every time I went to see her, I found her lying on her bed, crying. Always crying. I was furious when Zach came to my room straight after seeing Annie and explained what had happened.

'I'm so sorry. I know I've made things much worse,' he said.

'Why did you try and kiss her?'

'It was only her cheek.' He pressed his lips together. 'Yeah, okay. I wasn't thinking.'

'And she really didn't need to see those photos.'

'I thought they'd make her see what a slimy rat Erik really is.'

'She saw that all right, but given her fragile state, it wasn't smart.'

'No. Clearly.'

I just wish he'd shown Annie the photos before Erik dumped her. Then she might have got in first. But now it was too late. Now it just served more ammunition to make Annie feel stupid and humiliated.

Annie hadn't eaten a proper meal since Erik's announcement. I asked if she wanted to come out with Bear and me for dinner, but not surprisingly, she declined.

'I'll order in,' she said.

'Are you sure. Maybe it'd do you good to get out of this room?'

She turned away from me. 'I said no. I want to be alone. I can't face going out, seeing people point at me and whisper. Especially now I know Erik was carrying on with other women.'

I waited a few more minutes while Annie ordered room service, determined she should eat something.

I didn't particularly want to venture out either, but I'd had my fill of eating on my bed, so Bear and I ate at the hotel's Thai restaurant, mostly because I knew it would be a quick meal.

'I feel better being close by,' I said as we were being seated. 'I'll check on her later tonight. I don't think she can take much more.'

Bear scoured the menu. 'Requests? Banana Blossom Salad? Crispy—'

I yawned. 'I really don't care. You decide.'

After Bear ordered and we were eating fish cakes—well, Bear was. I was pushing mine around my plate— he said, 'Seriously, what was Zach thinking, showing her the photos?'

'To shock her, I guess.'

'The press is having a field day. My phone hasn't stopped ringing.'

'They don't have any photos of Erik, do they?'

'No, but it's only a matter of time before someone takes a photo of him at a nightclub.'

I knew Zach hadn't passed the photos he showed Annie on to his editor. He wouldn't do that; he cared about Annie too much.

'This is my fault,' I said. 'I started it with the slap.'

Bear stared at me for a moment, then went back to eating.

'What? You were about to say something.'

He put his cutlery down before speaking. 'Seriously, Sami, you behaved unprofessionally that day: questioning the umpires, being rude to spectators, hitting Annie. If the business with Erik hadn't happened, your behaviour would be the big news story.'

'But—'

'But nothing. It was appalling.'

'Okay! I'm a beast. The press might not be saying much about the slap now, but they'll never forget it. That footage will get wheeled out every time we play.'

We sat in silence until our mains arrived.

Sick to my stomach, I stared at my green chicken curry. 'Say something.'

'What's to say? I agree with you. They're bound to replay it, but hopefully only at Wimbledon, not at every other Grand Slam. Besides, the public will forgive you—'

'Maybe. Do you think there'll be other Grand Slams for Annie and me?'

'I didn't say that.'

'Then what are you saying? You don't think Annie's seriously considering quitting?'

'I really don't know what's going through her head right now, but whatever she decides, it's time for you to concentrate on yourself. You can't be your sister's keeper forever.'

'I'm not—'

'Really? If Annie chooses a different future, you'll be supportive?'

I sat back in my chair. 'Reluctantly, I suppose. We've always done everything together, at least until Erik came into the picture. I was hoping we could go back to how it was before. I wish we'd never gone to that New Year's Eve party.'

'You wish, you wish.' Bear sounded irritated. 'This is your life we're talking about, Samantha. Focus on what you can control, like perhaps your own game.' He looked down at his plate and forked at his sea bass. 'Here,' he said, holding it up. 'Try this.'

'Thanks, but no. And it's not just the game, but if Annie quits, we're going to lose our endorsements.' I looked at my watch. 'I should go and check on her.'

'Of course,' Bear agreed, resignation in his voice. He knew I wasn't ready to cut the umbilical cord to my sister.

After he finished eating, we paid the bill and walked to the lifts.

'Do you think I've pushed our partnership too hard at the expense of other...' I paused, unsure of what I wanted to say.

Bear looked at me. 'What do you mean?'

We exited the lift and paced down the floral-carpeted corridor towards our rooms.

'Annie and me—do you think I pushed too hard to make the tennis partnership work? At the expense of other things?'

I knocked on Annie's door.

'Like?' Bear said, looking confused.

'I don't know. I'm being stupid.' I knocked again, harder this time. 'Why isn't she answering?' I foraged in my bag, searching for the second key to her room.

Bear checked his watch. 'She'll be asleep.'

I opened Annie's door and called her name. No response.

I walked into her bedroom and saw her lying on top of her bed in the same baggy track pants and tee-shirt she'd been wearing for the past two days. Her room service dinner lay untouched on a side table. Something was wrong.

'Annie?' She didn't move or respond.

I leaned over to rouse her, and my foot kicked something on the floor. I bent down to look: an empty vodka bottle and an empty prescription bottle.

'Bear,' I screamed. 'Call an ambulance.'

Twenty-four

Annie was rushed to St Thomas Hospital to have her stomach pumped, and the next couple of hours passed in a terrifying blur.

'I didn't realise,' I sobbed to Bear as we waited for permission to see her. *Why the hell had I left her alone? All I could think of was that she might die. That I might lose her like I'd lost Mum. I couldn't go through it again.*

Finally, the doctor on duty came to talk to us. I wept with relief when she said Annie would make a full physical recovery. Bear placed a firm hand on my shoulder.

'I stress *physical* recovery,' the doctor said. 'How long Annie will take to heal emotionally and psychologically is an entirely different matter. There are excellent treatment clinics—'

'We'll be taking her home to Sydney,' I said, still dazed.

The doctor swallowed before speaking. 'It could have been a lot worse. She's lucky.'

'I didn't appreciate how low she was,' I said, thinking back over the last couple of days. 'Where did she get the pills?'

'The prescription was made out to Erik Sørensen,' he replied evenly.

More reason to hate him, as if I needed one. It was hard to take in what Annie had done. Before Erik, I'd hardly ever seen her cry. She tried so goddamned hard to be positive all the time. Even after what happened to our family, Annie always looked for a silver lining.

'I don't think she wanted to kill herself, Sami,' Bear said, taking my hand. 'But everything got to her—losing the match, Erik, seeing the photos—it was too much.'

'Not to mention me hitting her.' My breath got shorter, my chest tighter. 'I shouldn't have gone out tonight. I should've stayed with her.'

I doubled over, panting. I'd caused this. Shouting at Erik made him decide that being with Annie wasn't worth the effort. My angry outburst had triggered the devastating chain of events leading to Annie's overdose.

'Stop that. It's not your fault.' Bear stared at me. 'Please calm down, or you'll end up in hospital alongside Annie.'

'But it *is* my fault. I should've suspected something, been more in tune with her.'

'How could you have known?' Bear said. 'She's so damn good at hiding her feelings. You both are.'

'If we'd stayed at dinner longer, she could be dead. I knew she was distraught and heartbroken. Of course, I did. But I didn't realise the extent. I didn't think she was suicidal.'

'Sami, you can't keep beating yourself up like this.'

'Suicide.' I said the word slowly and repeated it several times in my head before speaking again. 'This is history repeating. Mum couldn't cope either—'

'Annie will be okay. She'll pull through this and so will you.'

'Excuse me,' Annie's doctor said. 'You can see her now, but she's still very weak and groggy.'

Annie was lying in bed, looking twenty years older and shivering in an off-white hospital gown. Eyes watering, she grasped for my hand. I reached forward to take hers, tears streaming down my cheeks.

'Sorry,' she whispered.

I sat on the bed, careful not to crush her legs and tried not to stare at her swollen lips, jaw and chin, which were dirty black from the charcoal the doctors had used to pump her stomach.

'You had us worried, kiddo,' Bear said.

Annie was crying. 'I didn't mean it.'

'It's okay. Everything will be okay,' I said, stroking her hair. 'How are you feeling?'

'Tired. My throat feels like it's on fire.' She stopped and gulped for air. 'Love? Love – 15, love – 30. Love? There's no *love* in tennis.'

'She's delirious,' I whispered to Bear.

Annie laughed. 'And deuce! What the fuck?'

After a few minutes, Bear left us alone, and I asked Annie why she'd done it. 'Did you really think your life was so pointless and awful?'

'I don't know,' she said, as if she'd been asking herself the same thing. 'I just wanted to sleep, to forget about everything horrible in my life.'

'But Annie,' I said closing my eyes and seeing Mum. 'After everything we've been through?'

'I didn't think. Didn't think through the consequences. I'm so sorry.'

I couldn't imagine how we were going to get through this. Annie was blinking, fighting to stay awake.

'Sleep, darling,' I said. 'You need to rest.'

'I'm numb, Sam.' For a moment I thought she meant physically—a side effect of the drugs—but soon realised she was speaking metaphorically. 'The victories, the defeats... they keep flashing before my eyes. It's overwhelming. I'm continually disappointing you, Bear, the fans.' She clutched her stomach and winced. 'I'm so sorry for fucking everything up.'

'Shh. You haven't fucked up anything.' I patted her arm, then glanced at my watch. It was after two a.m. 'We'll have plenty of time to talk in the morning.'

'I didn't mean it,' she repeated. 'I didn't want to'—the word got stuck in her throat—'die.'

'Of course, you didn't.'

'Vodka, sleeping pills, having my stomach pumped ...it's so ordinary.'

'I can assure you, Annie, it wasn't ordinary. It was very real and frightening. Promise me you'll never do anything like that again?'

Annie dropped her head. 'I'm so embarrassed and ashamed, Sami. I promise you I'll never do this again. You have my word.'

~ * ~

By the time Bear came back, Annie was asleep and looking peaceful.

'Hey,' he said, kissing my head softly before handing over a bottle of water. 'How are you both doing?'

'Fine. She's sleeping now.'

'And you?'

'I'll be okay.'

'I've arranged for a fold-out bed to be brought for you.'

'Thanks, I hadn't even thought...' I took a moment, holding back more tears. 'Thank you.'

'I can stay with you if you like?'

I squeezed him so he couldn't see me cry. Finally, I pulled away. 'It's fine. You go. You're going to need all the sleep you can snatch before yet another story about the Callahans hits the headlines.'

His forehead wrinkled. 'Unfortunately, I think you're right.'

After Bear left, I lay on the fold-out bed and stared up into the darkness, too wired for sleep. I wasn't about to leave Annie on her own ever again. I was mad with myself that I hadn't seen this coming, and with the anger came mind-numbing guilt. Then I thought about Mum. If only I could have saved her, maybe our lives would have turned out differently. Silent tears fell as I dozed uncomfortably on the squeaky mattress springs.

The next morning, I was hovering over Annie when she opened an eye. I backed away. 'Too close?'

'The heavy breathing was a giveaway,' she croaked.

I walked down the hall to a kitchenette to make her a cup of tea. By the time I returned, she was propped up in bed, looking downcast. I sat on the bed beside her.

'You tried to warn me about Erik,' she said, 'but I didn't listen. Now look at me.'

I chewed the inside of my cheek, guilt gnawing at me. 'About that–'

'I don't need another lecture, Samantha. You were right. I was wrong. Let's leave it at that.'

'I wasn't going to say that–'

'Whatever. It's over, all of it. I'm quitting tennis.'

'What?'

'You heard. When you know, you know.'

'But you can't quit!'

'I can't hack the pressure.' She closed her eyes and yawned. Opening them she said, 'I don't have the merciless focus that you do.'

'Annie, I know you're tired and fed up. Take a month off and rest.'

'You're not listening. I want to stop. Give up. Ash Barty was the world's number one tennis player, and she quit because she wanted to pursue her dreams outside of tennis. I want to do the same. It's time for me to move on too.' She held her head in her hands. 'Besides, I humiliate you every time I walk out onto the court. Even when we do win, we can't enjoy the victory because it's always about the next big game. We can't live in the present because we're too busy chasing the next title, the next trophy.'

'If this is about Erik—'

'You're not listening to me. It's not about him.' She yawned again. 'I'm tired. I'm twenty-five, but I feel sixty. My life is so strict and regimented. Practice here, play there. I'm not my own person. I feel like I'm always letting someone down. Perhaps if I'd spent more time with Erik—'

'Annie, he only wanted to be with you because you're a famous tennis star.'

Her eyes filled with tears again. 'I've lost count of the number of times I've phoned and left messages for him. I've texted and emailed as well. No response. I can't believe he'd be that cruel and heartless.' She glared at me. 'If only you'd been nicer to him!'

'You're right,' I agreed, trying to regulate my breathing. This wasn't the time to bring up details about my final conversation with Erik. 'I'm sorry. I was trying to protect you.'

'I thought he loved me.' She stared down at her hands. 'I guess not buying me an engagement ring was a dead giveaway, huh?'

'He might come back,' I said, knowing it was the last thing I'd like to happen.

She wiped tears from her eyes. 'He won't. Anyway, I've made up my mind. I'm quitting. I want to leave now while I still have some dignity. I don't want to become an old has-been.'

'But'—I tensed—'your body's not hurting.'

'My body *is* hurting. Especially now.' She smiled weakly. 'I'm exhausted. Anyway, even if my body isn't hurting, my heart is.'

I swallowed before speaking. 'Only a few months ago, you were the tenth-ranked tennis player in the world. You're resilient. You'll bounce back.'

'Don't you get it?' Annie growled. 'I'm not resilient. I won't bounce back, as you so breezily put it.'

'I'm sorry. Poor choice of words.' I was trying hard to make sense of everything that had happened in a few short days. Annie was emotionally and physically exhausted and I needed to pull back. 'I'll support you no matter what. You need to do what's best for you and your mental health.'

She smiled. 'Thank you. Now, how about instead of worrying about me, you concentrate on your own game? You keep saying you love it, so why don't you get on with it?'

Her words stung. What Annie didn't understand was that I couldn't get on with it without her. We were a team.

Twenty-five

Zach

Zach was eating breakfast in the hotel restaurant when he overheard two waiters talking.

'It was extreme. She went on a bender. The ambo and cops were called.'

'All over some guy?'

The first waiter nodded. 'She was gutted. I thought Aussies were tougher than that, but she's one seriously messed-up chick.'

Doubling over, stomach cramps swamped him. Recovering, Zach pulled out his phone and called Bear.

'Zach, mate,' Bear said. 'Glad you called. I guess you've heard.'

Zach's hands were shaking. 'No. Tell me.'

'Short story. Annie's fine but she overdosed.'

'No!'

'She's in hospital—'

'I have to see her.'

'Talk to Sam. I'm in full damage control right now, trying to organise flights home, dealing with the media. It's a nightmare.'

'If there's anything I can do, call me.'

'Just keep it to yourself, mate. We need to keep a lid on it.'

Zach signed his bill, moved to the lobby and called Samantha.

'Bear just told me,' he said as soon as she answered. 'How is she?'

'Awful.' Samantha's voice was croaky. 'But she'll be okay... I hope.'

'What happened?'

'She overdosed on pills Erik left behind. Sleeping tablets, I think. Washed down with your vodka.'

'My vodka?' Zach's face dropped. 'You mean she drank the whole bottle?'

'I guess, minus what you drank together.'

Zach slumped against a wall, his legs unsteady, shocked at the consequences of his actions. 'This is my fault. Giving her the vodka, showing her photos of Erik ...if I hadn't gone to her room, none of this would have happened.'

'I'm just as guilty. I fought with Erik. I slapped Annie.'

Zach could see media gathering nearby. Looks like news had got out. 'What can I do?' he asked, as he darted out a side exit. 'I want to make things right. Can I see her? Where is she?'

'St Thomas Hospital,' Samantha said. 'You can say a quick hello, maybe even talk some sense into her. Ten minutes ago, she told me she's quitting tennis.'

Zach jumped in a taxi. 'Wait a tick.' He leaned over to the driver. 'St Thomas Hospital, mate.' He spoke into his phone. 'Quitting?'

'I'm devastated, but then when I think about what she's been through in the last few days, how can I blame her?'

'She just needs a rest,' Zach said. 'A holiday.'

'That's what I said, but she's adamant.'

Zach willed the driver to go faster as they approached yet another red light. 'The press have caught wind something's up. They were prowling around the hotel lobby.'

Samantha sighed. 'Yeah. It was a matter of time. I'll be waiting for you out the front when you arrive. Please hurry.'

'Doing my best.' Zach signed off from Samantha just as his text vibrated with a message from Bear.

Flights booked. Ask Sam for hotel keys, hers and Annie's. Meet me there in one hour to pack bags.

Zach and Samantha embraced when he got out of the cab. He showed her Bear's text. 'You okay with this?'

'Yeah. Thanks. I really appreciate it and so will Annie.'

They paced in silence to Annie's room and stepped inside.

Zach gasped. The sleeping person lying in the bed didn't look like Annie. This person was frail. So pale and thin. 'Sam,' he whispered. 'I can't even...'

She squeezed his hand. 'I know.'

He cleared his throat. 'I should get back to the hotel and help Bear. Please let her know I stopped by and how truly sorry I am. For everything.' Zach pecked her cheek. 'Stay strong.'

As he made his way towards the hospital exit, he saw several reporters hanging around.

'Zach, Zach,' yelled one guy he vaguely knew. 'What's going on? Word on the street is that Annie Callahan's overdosed and is in a coma.'

Zach was in no mood to deal with the press. 'You guys are like vultures waiting to feast on your prey. Just piss off.'

'So, it's true then? Annie's topped herself over some second-rate Scandinavian playboy?'

'Say one more word, and I swear I'll knock you to the ground.'

'Whoa!' The reporter stepped back to let Zach through.

'Annie's fine,' he yelled back. 'You mongrels need to find a new dog to whip.'

Zach knew he was being unreasonable. They were only doing their job, like he had been when he'd taken photos of Courtney Gold's father getting thrown out of the club in Stuttgart. Even so, he wanted to punch them.

Bear was waiting in the hotel foyer when Zach arrived. 'You got the keys?'

Zach held up his hand to reveal two white key cards.

Bear cleared Samantha's room, while Zach packed up Annie's belongings. There was a photo of Annie and Samantha on her bedside table, taken after they'd won gold at the Olympics. Both looked ecstatic. Zach picked up the photo and smiled at the memory. He hadn't seen Annie look that happy in a very long time ...well, since last August when she'd won the gold. He wondered if he'd ever be able to make her smile like that.

Twenty-six

Samantha

Bear collected Annie and me from the hospital and drove us straight to Heathrow airport.

'Zach and I packed your bags,' he said. 'I checked you out of the hotel and organised an earlier flight.'

I smiled at him. 'Thank you.'

Bear turned to Annie. 'I've written a statement for the media.'

'Why?' she asked, confused.

'You can't keep secrets these days, you know that. So, to keep the wolves at bay, I've given Zach a prepared statement that he'll release as soon as we board our flight to Sydney.'

'Saying what?' I asked.

'That due to the training she'd put in for Wimbledon, Annie was fatigued and under nervous strain and was prescribed medication that unfortunately caused an adverse reaction, resulting in dizziness and shallow breathing. She'll make a full recovery but needs complete rest and privacy.'

The way Bear explained it, it seemed reasonable. And it was truthful in a roundabout way: Annie had had an adverse reaction to prescribed medication, except it was Erik's medication, and Bear definitely didn't want Erik's name mentioned.

On the plane, we settled in for the long flight home. As we taxied down the runway, Annie started crying.

'I'm never coming back,' she said. 'All I'd ever think about is what happened to me here.'

I rubbed her arm. 'Don't upset yourself. These feelings will pass. The doctor said so.'

'No, they won't. London will be forever tainted for me—the city where Annie Callahan got dumped and overdosed. Too many bad memories.'

She fell asleep a little while later, and I turned to Bear and said, 'I don't know what we'd do without you. I can't believe we made it this far without any reporters trailing us.'

'All part of the service,' he replied.

'You don't have to do this, you know.'

He put his hand over mine. 'Samantha, as long as you and Annie want me, I'll be here, for both of you.'

I could have wept. It meant so much to hear him to say that because we both knew Annie's recovery would take months, not weeks. As for getting her back on a tennis court, we'd need to take a slowly, slowly approach. Even though I thought tennis was what she needed to take her mind off her problems, I doubted Annie would see it that way. Bear was right, as always: Annie had to decide for herself what she wanted to do, without me interfering. The past few days had forced me to realise I couldn't control everything in life. No one could. Sometimes, truly awful things happened, despite all your hard work trying to prevent them. I should have known that.

~ * ~

On our arrival at Sydney airport, Bear did his best to protect us from the media. 'I don't think you'll want to read the newspapers,' he said, as we passed a couple of newsstands in the arrival terminal. 'Or log on to Twitter and the rest.'

But the headlines were impossible to miss: *Olympic champion in suicide bid; Sister watches over sister*. Annie and her private life were out there for the world to read about. I should have stopped her. Should have been more aware about Annie's torment.

I checked my phone and saw several missed calls from Violet. Amidst all the drama, I'd forgotten to keep her in the loop. I was about to call her when the press came directly at us.

A stampede. We were mobbed.

Bear fronted them, pushing us behind him. Reading from the same statement he'd given Zach, he reiterated that the incident had been blown out of proportion. 'Annie had an adverse reaction to prescribed medication. She'll be back playing competitive tennis in no time, but what she needs now is absolute rest and privacy.'

'You think they'll buy it?' I whispered to him, careful that Annie couldn't hear.

Bear grimaced. 'Maybe. Like gossip, when it comes to press statements, it doesn't matter whether it's true, it matters whether it sounds plausible.'

We strode, heads down, to avoid making eye contact with reporters. As we pushed our way through the crowd to our waiting car, the questions came thick and fast.

'Are you denying it was a suicide attempt?'

'We heard Annie took twenty-five pills. Can you confirm that?'

'The doctors in London said it was touch and go.'

'Ignore them, Annie,' Bear said when she started shaking and tearing up.

Three more metres and we made it to the hire car, safe at last.

'How are we going to get through this?' I asked Bear as our driver battled the morning peak-hour traffic.

'We take it one day at a time. Like walking: you put one foot in front of the other and pray to God you don't trip and land on your arse.'

'Now I know how Sisyphus felt,' Annie piped up.

Bear and I remained silent.

'You know, the myth of Sisyphus,' she continued. 'Condemned by the gods for eternity to repeatedly roll a boulder up a hill, only to have it roll down again once it reached the top. That's tennis.'

'I don't understand—'

'Yes, you do,' Annie snapped. 'We play the game, we hit the ball, and win or lose, we repeat the process for forty weeks a year, sometimes more. I've had enough. It's not fun anymore. Hasn't been for some time.'

'Okay,' Bear replied. 'I hear you.' Then he shot me a look as if to say, *whatever you're thinking about saying, don't.*

It wasn't until we were back in our apartment that I could finally breathe. Without thinking, I threw my arms around Bear and kissed his lips.

'What's that about?' he asked, looking shocked.

'To thank you for everything. For looking after Annie, and me. For being there for us when we both really needed you.'

'I've never been so happy to be home,' Annie said, dropping her bags and sinking into her favourite green patterned armchair.

The sun streamed in as I threw back the curtains and opened the sliding doors to the terrace. 'Me too.'

Annie looked up at Bear as if remembering something. 'Why did you tell the reporters I'd be playing tennis again soon? I won't.'

Bear seemed to take in a steeling breath before responding. 'I don't think we need to alert the media about your decision to quit the game just yet. They have enough bones to gnaw on. Besides,' he glanced at me before turning back to Annie, 'you might feel differently in a couple of months.'

~ * ~

After Bear left and Annie had fallen asleep, I called Violet to fill her in.

'Don't say another word,' she told me. 'You sound exhausted. I'll be over in approximately eleven minutes with cheese, coffee and chocolate.'

True to her word, Violet arrived less than fifteen minutes later laden with goodies. Annie was still sleeping, so the two of us sat on the terrace, drinking cappuccinos, and eating Tim Tams. Even though it was winter, the sun was bright, and my plants were thriving, thanks to Violet.

'I've enjoyed escaping to your little slice of paradise when the girls and Rick get too loud ...or just too much,' she confided.

I gulped my coffee. 'You're welcome anytime.'

'How are you holding up?'

'Okay. Worried about Annie, of course. I was terrified she'd die. And now she's saying she wants to quit tennis.' My stomach still lurched every time I thought about it. 'Annie seems determined. What if she really means it?'

Violet hesitated. 'Hon, you have to let her make that decision.'

'Don't you think I know that?' I said, aware I was raising my voice. I softened my tone. 'I'm scared of...'

'What?' Violet asked. 'Being abandoned?'

I teared up. 'When I thought she might die the other night, Vi, I couldn't breathe. All those memories of Mum, our childhood ...I don't know what I'd do.'

Violet took my hand. 'It's not personal, Samantha. Annie needs time to heal, to recover from the breakup.'

'It's not rational, and I know it's selfish, but we've always been together.'

'Yes, you have...' Violet stopped.

I looked up. 'Say whatever it is you're thinking.'

'I don't want to upset you.'

'I've known you all my life, Vi. You can upset me.'

'Sweetie, perhaps it's time for you to explore your lives separately. I know how close you are, but...'

I knew what she was saying. Ever since Mum left, I'd focused on tennis to cope with the pain and to avoid any kind of emotional attachment. I didn't want to let anyone get close for fear of them leaving me like Mum had.

'I'm trying not to smother her, Vi, really. And I'm trying hard to be a good sister. I'm not going to initiate any conversation about tennis, men, travel—in fact, any topics that could be construed as interfering.'

'Good. She needs rest and calm. So do you.' Violet peered at me. 'I think Annie's dramas have affected you more than you realise.'

Tears welled up again. 'I've made our doubles partnership my whole life. If that ends...'

Violet put her arms around me. 'Come on, you're Samantha Callahan! Passionate, powerful, independent. You've been in tough spots before and you will again, but you always pull through.'

Twenty-seven

Those first few days back home, Annie was inundated with flowers and cards from friends and supporters, all wishing her a speedy recovery. Even Jannik Sinner, tennis's new king, sent her a bunch of pink tulips.

Dad sent a bouquet, too, and rang frequently. He even offered to come up to Sydney, but when I asked Annie, she said it wasn't necessary.

'I worry about you both,' Dad said. 'Especially after your mother. I can't believe Annie—'

'I promise we'll come down to Albury once Annie's feeling better.' I knew he was only trying to help, but my priority was getting Annie on an even keel again. I'd worry about our strained relationship with Dad later.

At night, I heard Annie pacing. Then the crying would start, sometimes for hours on end. It took all my strength not to burst into her room and wrap my arms around her. Every morning, when I took her in a cup of tea, she looked wrung out and exhausted. All day she was listless and irritable. I couldn't spark her interest in anything... conversation, food, shopping, television, reading. Nothing worked.

Finally, on our fourth morning home, Annie emerged from her bedroom and moved to the patio, where the brilliant winter sunshine provided just enough warmth to keep her outside.

'This is my favourite spot,' she said, as we sat on matching cane sun loungers, watching the ferries and sailboats bob along the vibrant blue harbour. 'I can see why it's been called the most beautiful natural harbour in the world.'

'Yeah, sometimes I forget to appreciate it,' I said, thrilled to be talking to Annie in natural light. I gestured to the Adirondack chairs. 'Remember when we bought these in Bondi?'

'And the struggle we had to get them back here. You said they'd fit in your car.'

'Okay, so I was mistaken. Do you think you might be up for walk along the foreshore later?'

She smiled. 'We'll see.'

Happy Annie was looking brighter and receptive to talking, I suggested she might like to see a counsellor. 'Just to talk strategies.'

Her smile vanished, and I immediately realised my mistake.

'I don't need a psychologist telling me how I should be feeling,' she said, staring out across the water. 'I need time to come to terms with everything. And I don't need you hovering, either. I just want to know what I did that was so wrong. I loved him.'

I sucked in some air. 'Maybe it wasn't anything you said or did. I spoke to Erik the day before he made his announcement.'

Annie sat up straight and stared at me. 'What about? Did he tell you anything?'

I hesitated. 'No. Annie, I told him he should leave you alone.'

'What? Why would you say that?'

'I was trying to protect you.'

'You think telling him to break up with me via a media circus on live TV was protecting me?'

'Of course not. I just didn't think he was right for you.'

She stood up, glowering, fists clenched. 'Backstabber! It was none of your business, Sam.' I'll never forgive you for this. Never! Why couldn't you stay out of my life?' Her cheeks flushed. 'I'm going back to bed.'

As she stepped back inside, my trembling fingertips found my mouth. She'd dropped several kilos and her emaciated frame was as thin as a gangly thirteen-year-old. 'I really think you should eat first.'

'Why? Will a burger bring Erik back?' She stalked into her bedroom and slammed the door.

~ * ~

The next morning when I went into the kitchen, Annie was sitting at the breakfast table, coffee in hand, looking severely sleep-deprived.

'I'm sorry,' I started.

She cut me off. 'I'm sick of hearing the word *sorry*. Stop it. Anyway, I'm going away. Everything here reminds me of Erik. I need to escape.'

I spied her backpack by the front door. To calm myself and buy time, I made a coffee. 'How about we go and see Dad?' I said brightly, sitting opposite her at the table. 'He's desperate for us to visit. It'll do us good, a complete break.'

'I want to be alone.'

I couldn't leave her alone. What if she tried to harm herself again? I sipped my coffee. 'You need to talk this through with a professional.' Panic sent my voice escalating. 'You've been through a traumatic experience. Several, actually.'

She leant across the table, eyes unblinking. 'Listen to me, Sam. I've made up my mind. There are more important things in the world than winning tennis competitions.'

'Like what?'

'I'm not exactly sure, but I need to find out. We've spent too much time focused on our tennis achievements—and defeats. There's got to be more to life.'

'Where will you go? What will you do?' My voice rose again. 'Are you talking a week? A month?'

'However long it takes. Maybe a year.'

'A year!' My stomach churned. Acid rose in my throat. 'You can't do that ...we're a team. What about our pact?'

'I need to find my own purpose in life.'

'But you can't leave me. Mum—'

'I'm not Mum, Samantha. I'm nothing like her. Besides, it's not forever. I just need some time out.'

'We promised we'd stick together. You're all I've got.'

'That's not my fault.' Annie reached for my hand and held it. 'I need to be by myself.'

'I'm sorry about what I said to Erik.'

'It doesn't matter.'

'But you're a tennis star, a champion.'

'Stop saying that. Tennis doesn't define me. It's not my life. At least not for the foreseeable future. I can't handle any more expectations, especially yours. You blame me for losing the matches at the Australian Open and Wimbledon.'

I couldn't speak. I blamed Erik, but I couldn't say that.

Annie looked at me sadly. 'Yeah, I thought as much. So rather than continuing to disappoint you and the entire Western world, I'd rather retreat into my own world—'

'Once you've had a few decent nights' sleep, you'll feel differently, I promise.'

'Not going to happen. Thirty or more weeks of the year living out of a suitcase in another bland hotel room? I need something more.' She stood and brushed her hands down the sides of her jeans. 'I packed last night and I'm leaving now. I don't know how long I'll be gone.'

This was it. Annie was really walking out the door.

'Wait,' I said, desperately. 'You just said you didn't want to live out of a suitcase anymore.'

She shook her head.

'I'm sorry for how I acted during your engagement to Erik. I should've been more supportive.'

'It doesn't matter now.

Annie wasn't angry. She was calm and rational. Her words sounded reasonable, smart almost. But I knew they weren't. She wasn't thinking straight. She couldn't march out of our apartment in Mosman and make a snap decision to turn left towards the airport or right and head up the north coast. Could she?

'At least think about it a couple more days,' I pleaded.

'That's all I've been doing since I got back from London. I've made up my mind. The sooner I'm on my way—'

I stood and walked close to her. 'I know you need time out. I'm sorry I haven't been a better sister, a better friend to you.'

'You have.' Annie was teary. 'But this is something I need to do.'

'Is there anything I can say to persuade you to stay?'

She held me tightly. 'Afraid not, big sister. I'm leaving Sydney. I need space. Time to just be me, without the pressure of being Annie Callahan, tennis player, gold medallist and overdoser, dumped by Erik Sørensen and slapped by her sister.'

'That's not what people think,' I started. But Annie was right. There'd been yet another story in the paper about her that morning. Not to mention all the conspiracy theories on Twitter.

Annie glared at me. 'Really? Come on.' She glanced at her watch.

'But you'll let me know where you are?'

'I'll send you a postcard. It's not forever.'

'But what about our sponsorship deals? Our contractual obligations?'

Annie wasn't listening. 'I honestly don't know, Sami. All I know is that I'm leaving.'

She was done talking. Then she picked up her backpack and strode through the open door and out of my life.

~ * ~

I was still sitting on the sofa crying when Violet rang half an hour later.

'Sami...'

I sniffed. 'You've seen her?'

'She needs a break—'

'But—'

'Sam, please. She said you wouldn't listen to her, so please listen to me.'

'Okay.' I leaned back on the couch, my head sinking into a cushion.

'For the moment, she's done with tennis...'

'But...'

'But nothing. Annie wants to be left alone to sort her head out in her own time without other pressures.'

'Like?'

'Like you, honey. Treating her like she might keel over at any moment.'

'I'm devastated about what happened. Erik. The overdose. Why wouldn't I be concerned?'

'Sam, Annie doesn't want to talk about it. She said she's talked about it enough. That she wants to move on, but it's impossible when everyone, even strangers, knows everything about her. She feels like she doesn't have a private life anymore.'

'I thought she might die,' I gulped. 'It bought back a lot of painful memories.'

'For you both, I'm sure,' Violet said.

'Maybe she's more like Mum than I realised.'

Violet sighed. 'Please don't say that.'

'You're right.' I said, my voice breaking. I sniffed back tears and tried to compose myself. 'Tell me about you. How's the baby?'

'Yeah, the baby's behaving, growing. Though he does tend to kick a lot at three a.m.'

'He?'

'We don't know. It'd be nice, though. Imagine having three girls? A boy would break it up a bit, not to mention make Rick happy.'

'He'll adore the baby regardless.' Tears glistened. I couldn't keep up the bravado.

'It's okay, hon,' Violet soothed.

'Annie thought she was entering a new phase of her life and now ...now it's all gone. So...'

'So, all I know is that she left in an uber heading for the airport.'

'International?'

'I have no idea, Sam. I asked and she said she'd let me know when she figured it out.'

'And for how long?'

'I asked that too. She said, "as long as it takes." Annie doesn't want to be restricted by timetables and schedules.'

Twenty-eight

Dazed, I wandered into Annie's bedroom hoping to find ...what? The room was neat. Her bed was made. Nothing seemed amiss. Bottles of perfume sat on her dressing table next to her earrings; necklaces hung from a jewellery tree; several brightly coloured scarves were draped over the ends of the dressing table mirror. From the looks of her walk-in wardrobe, she'd taken few clothes. One of her handbags was missing, but most of her shoes remained. My spirits lifted a little. Maybe she *would* only be gone a few days.

Then I remembered: Mum hadn't taken much either.

I couldn't allow myself to believe Annie would disappear for long. Because if I let her go, truly let her go, she'd vanish, just like Mum.

I walked back into the living room and saw Annie's favourite tennis racquet propped against her favourite armchair. That's when I started crying.

I was still sobbing when Bear arrived mid-morning.

'Come on,' he said, taking my hand. 'Let's get you out of here.'

~ * ~

Bear helped me out of his car and into the elevator up to his city apartment on the forty-fifth floor.

'Hasn't changed much,' I said, staring round the open plan living room at the rendered white brick walls, concrete floor, traditional black leather armchairs and sofa I remembered from my last visit ages ago. Few knick-knacks.

'Give me a break. I'm hardly ever here. I like to keep it clean—'

'And sparse.'

'More like modern minimalism.'

Bear handed me a coffee and I sat on the sofa staring through the floor to ceiling windows overlooking Town Hall, watching the city traffic swirl below. So many people. So many vehicles. But I couldn't hear a sound.

When I sipped it, the coffee was stone cold. The front door opened.

'Have you been out?' I asked Bear, surprised.

He made a point of checking his Fitbit. 'Only for the last hour! I'm making you a late lunch, Gorgeous Girl. Duck risotto okay?'

I nodded and went back to staring out the floor to ceiling windows.

'Why don't you shower first?' Bear suggested. 'You might feel better.'

I did as instructed, but was still exhausted when I dried off in the guest room.

'Samantha, I—' Bear stopped when he strolled in and found me naked, underwear and towel in my hand. 'Sorry.' He started backing out.

'Don't be,' I said, wrapping the towel around my torso. I walked up to him, my mind blank, and pressed my lips to his. When I pulled away, confusion lined his face. Then he returned my kiss and I let my towel drop.

'Sweetheart,' he said, as we stumbled our way towards the bed. I silenced him with more kisses.

I yanked at his shirt and within moments he was naked too. All my pent-up longing for him came bursting forth. I'd denied myself for so long, afraid of letting go, but what was the point when everything could so easily be ripped away in a matter of seconds? The last few days had shown me that.

'Gorgeous Girl,' he said, one arm caressing my back, the other supporting my neck as he pulled my head towards him and kissed me deeply, passionately. 'GG.'

I bit my lip, giving way to my desires. All I wanted was to be with him. Bear. Naked. Fucking.

He nipped my earlobes, my neck, my breasts, my nipples.

I was hungry, desperate for more. More of his hands, his tongue, his touch. Bear took my breath away. His tongue licked my breasts, teasing me, then my stomach, playing with me. I felt lost, lost but at home as my body responded to his stroking.

'Yes,' I screamed.

He looked up and smiled. 'Yes what?'

I was in a trance, a dream-like state. Didn't want him to stop. 'Mmm,' was all I could murmur as we kissed some more.

He shifted on top of me, his body covering mine. 'I want you.'

The feeling was mutual. 'You've got me.'

Finally, he was inside of me, his touch intoxicating, all-consuming, as his fingers continued to explore my inner thighs.

Lying in bed afterwards, Bear stroked my hair and covered my face and neck in kisses. 'Hmm ...that was unexpected.'

'Yes ...it was.'

He pulled me in so close I could feel his lips on my neck as he spoke. His touch sent shivers down my spine. 'I've wanted this since our first kiss. And our second.' He drew back and faced me. 'Please don't reject me again. I couldn't take a third time.'

I nestled into his chest. 'I didn't reject you.'

He put his hand under my chin and forced me to look at him. 'Really, Gorgeous Girl? In Brisbane, you emphatically declared you didn't want a romantic relationship with me. And then again in London.'

'I lied.'

'Well, I'm not lying when I say *I love you, Samantha Callahan*. I always have. Always will.'

'I love you, too.' I felt exhausted, relieved, and very much adored. 'I really do, Beautiful Bear.'

We kissed again for what seemed like an eternity.

'So, what now?' I asked.

'Now, Gorgeous Girl, I make that lunch I promised you. I'm starving.'

But Bear didn't leave the bed for another two hours. By the time we actually did eat, it was late in the afternoon, and I was famished.

~ * ~

For the next twenty-four hours, I stayed holed up in Bear's apartment.

'I like your art,' I said, snuggling him in his bed (we'd decamped from the guest bedroom) and staring up at a colourful naïve painting of a beach surrounded by mountains.

'It's called *Country by the Sea*.' He kissed me and grinned. 'Is that your way of apologising for telling me my apartment looks sparse?'

'How about eccentric? Or eclectic? I can't decide.'

~ * ~

When Bear drove me home, I was hopeful that Annie might have returned, but no. I wandered around the flat, teary and lost. Everything reminded me of her. The navy leather sofa we'd both fallen in love with, the books and knick-knacks we'd collected during our travels, even the pepper grinder. Why? Why did she do it? I asked myself over and over. But I knew the answer. I'd pushed her. If only I'd kept my enormous mouth shut, none of this would have happened.

'You can't keep blaming yourself,' Bear told me. 'Everyone except Annie knew the guy was a player.'

'Yeah, but everyone also knows it's always the messenger who gets shot.'

'But really it was Zach.'

'We all played a part.' I ran my fingers through Bear's hair. 'What do I do with all her stuff?'

'It's too soon, Sami. Come back to my place. We'll deal with this later.'

I was too worn-out to argue.

~ * ~

In the weeks after Annie left, I divided my time between Bear's apartment and mine. I couldn't spend more than a couple of nights alone without teetering on the verge of depression.

I knew first-hand about women who simply disappeared when life became too much. They were never heard from again because that was the way they wanted it. I hoped Annie wasn't going to do that. That she wouldn't completely abandon her old self to start a new life away from tennis ...and me. I hoped one day she'd return.

'She needs time to sort herself out,' Violet said one afternoon when we were walking across the Harbour Bridge.

'It's all my fault. It's like I can't breathe. I'm gasping all the time, trying to take in air that's not there.'

'It's not your fault. It's life, and sometimes life is shitty.'

'I don't know what to do. I'm fine for a couple of days, positive and happy, then suddenly it's like a dark cloud descends on me and I get incredibly angry or uncontrollably sad.'

'Honey,' Violet said, taking my hand and squeezing it.

'Every time I'm out, I search for Annie's face in the crowd. I've tried calling and emailing. But yesterday when I called, some guy answered and told me he'd been given the number from

Optus hours before. I couldn't believe it. And emails to her Hotmail address have started bouncing...' I bent over on the verge of hyperventilating. 'It's like she's officially severed contact. I've got no idea how to get in touch with her.' I swallowed some air. 'What if she's lying in a ditch somewhere? What if...'

'Samantha,' Violet said slowly. 'I've received a couple of emails. She's okay.'

'Really? Why didn't you tell me? I keep thinking the reason I haven't heard from Annie is because something bad's happened to her, either by accident or...'

'I'm telling you now,' Violet said. 'She's fine. Travelling. Getting her head together. Annie never meant to hurt you.'

I puffed out an exaggerated sigh. I should have known Annie would keep in touch with Violet. Violet was undemanding. Violet was a mother. Violet was pregnant. But I was also relieved. As long as Annie kept in touch with Vi, everything would be okay. I ground my teeth and blinked back tears.

Part of me was also fuming. 'I can't believe she's doing this to me. To us.'

'Tell me about you and Bear,' Violet said, changing the subject. 'I'm so happy for you both.'

I forced down my irritation. Ever since we were kids, Violet had been adept at diffusing my anger. 'I was a fool for taking so long. He's ...he's wonderful. Incredible.'

Violet grinned. 'True love?'

'I don't want to jinx it, but we're happy. He keeps me sane.' He really did. Bear kept me from losing it whenever I thought about Annie not coming back.

Would my thoughts about the fear of Annie attempting to kill herself again ever leave me? I doubted it. As long as I didn't know where she was and what she was doing, that dread would remain. I didn't wish it upon anyone.

I checked my messages. *GG, seriously in love with you. Not comedically but seriously.*

I smiled. But a wave of panic washed over me when I thought about what I was going to do next. Tennis meant everything to me, but what was my future now that Annie was no longer my partner?

~ * ~

A few days later, I received a postcard from Annie, saying she was trekking through Asia. *Don't worry about me, I'm doing fine.*

Snap! Annie was doing fine! What about me? Was that all I was worth? A couple of lines on a rotten postcard?

I hated her. Hated what she'd put me through. I wanted to throw all her clothes on the floor and stomp on them. Instead, I threw the card in the garbage, retrieved it, threw it back in the bin, and retrieved it again.

That same morning, I received an email that our most lucrative endorsement contracts were not being renewed at the end of the month.

'It's been a difficult decision, but with Annie's recent spate of negative publicity, we feel it's in the company's best interests,' the email read. *'We're not closing the door completely...'*

I sat on the sofa and cried. I had savings but relied on endorsement income to pay for Bear's coaching fees, especially as it would no longer be split between Annie and me.

And the day got even better when Bear received an email from Annie telling him to release a media statement announcing her retirement and urging him to persuade me to compete again. He was relieved to have some solid information as the press had been hounding him since Wimbledon.

'It'll be good to clear things up,' he said when I arrived at his apartment.

'Perfect timing,' I replied, 'if they hadn't already cancelled, our advertising contracts would have ended anyway now we're no longer a team.'

'It'll be okay, Sam. We'll get you playing again, you'll win tournaments. The prize money will pour in.'

'As long you get paid, that's all I really care about.'

'I can coach other players as well as you,' he replied. 'To take the pressure off.'

'I'd prefer to keep you to myself.'

He brushed my cheek. 'I'd prefer that too, but we have to be realistic.'

I didn't like where this was heading, so I ignored him. 'Please don't tell the media Annie's retiring. Say she's taking extended leave.'

'I can do that,' he said, rubbing his chin, 'if you agree to play at the U.S. Open. It'll give you a good run around.'

I did a quick calculation in my head. 'That's three weeks away!'

'Exactly. You've had long enough to mope.'

'I'm not goddamn moping.'

'Good. One more thing. I want you to pair up with Courtney Gold.'

I nearly choked. 'Courtney Gold? You've got to be joking.'

'I know it's hard, but if you don't want to play singles, you have to find a new doubles partner. And, as luck would have it, I've been approached to mentor her.'

'What? This day just keeps on giving. When were you going to tell me?'

Bear checked his Fitbit. 'Right about now! Don't worry, her father will still be her coach. I'll be back-up.'

I wasn't convinced. The thought of being partnered with anyone but Annie was terrifying. I'd been her partner since she was born. It was inconceivable to think anyone could take her place.

'I'd rather quit,' I said.

'Okay,' Bear said. 'But if you change your mind, Courtney wants to add doubles to her repertoire and is looking for a steady partner.'

Although Courtney and I had never competed against each other, I couldn't think of anyone whose playing manner and style was less like Annie's. Courtney was fiery, determined and persistent, and far too cocky about herself and her abilities. In my experience, players like Courtney came and went. They were flash-in-the-pan, limelight-stealers—all bling and manicured nails.

I tossed my head. 'Definitely not.'

'Why? You have similar playing styles and disposition on court.'

'Please,' I said. 'She swaggers around the locker room like she's the greatest player since Serena Williams.'

Courtney was one of those poser types with an exceptional physique. I imagined that before long, she'd be posing for *Playboy*, à la Lucia Landry. As for Courtney's father, he was a walking advertisement for how tennis parents shouldn't behave, hurling abuse at spectators, being thrown out of tournaments.

'Courtney Gold?' I repeated. 'I don't think so.'

~ * ~

As Bear predicted, I continued to mope, but he kept at me, wearing me down. 'Tell me what you love about the game, GG?'

'Playing with Annie.'

He frowned. 'She's not here. What else?'

'The adrenalin rush when you're winning.'

He smiled. 'Good. What else?'

'The knowledge that at any moment the game can change. You can be down forty nil and still win if the ball falls your way.' I thought some more. 'I love that it's a game of incredible skill, yet there's luck involved, too.'

'You miss it, don't you?'

'I guess. It's a hell of a lot of fun until it becomes a heartbreaking chore.'

'Darling,' Bear said, kissing my neck. 'You have to play tennis. It's in your blood. It's your life.'

Tearing up, I pulled his face towards mine. 'You're right.'

The truth is, I wanted to play tennis. I wasn't ready to give up. If playing doubles meant being partnered with Courtney, I'd give it my best shot.

Twenty-nine

Two weeks later, at the end of August, Bear and I checked in to the same Manhattan hotel we'd stayed at when Annie and I had played in New York last year. So much had happened since then, and being there again reminded me that Annie wasn't.

In preparation for the U.S. Open, Courtney and I had several practice sessions together. She always bounced the ball three times before serving, and she religiously wore her blue garter. Neither of us appeared keen to partner the other. It didn't help that Courtney always ran late and appeared permanently hungover. I wondered why Mr Gold wasn't setting Courtney limits. He was a control freak.

We were on one of the practice courts, into our second set and being cheered by at least a hundred spectators chanting our names, when Courtney stopped playing and started fiddling with her garter as soon as Bear left to go to the bathroom.

After a minute or so, I waved my racquet at the crowd, embarrassed. Background voices started yelling. *'C'mon, Court,'* and *'We came here to see some spirited Aussie tennis.'*

Finally, I walked to her side of the net. 'These people are here to see us play.'

Courtney glared at me. 'We're practicing. This isn't a real match.'

'Fair point, but have you stopped think some of those people can't afford to attend and that's why they're here cheering for us now?'

She looked over to the crowd and brandished her racquet, then turned to me. 'Whatever. I'm done. I need a rest day.'

'Courtney, champions train, losers complain.'

She yawned. 'Did you think that one up all by yourself?'

'You can't do this to me or your fans.' I paused. 'What does Daddy say about your nocturnal wanderings?'

'At least he cares,' she shot back.

'What's that supposed to mean?'

'Exactly what I said. At least he cares enough to be here with me.' I thought she was talking about Annie until she said, 'Where's your father?'

Cheap shot. 'What's your story with the garter?'

'It shows off my great pins. Make the most of what you've got, I say. What's *your* story with the bandana?'

I reached up and touched it. Black today. She didn't need to know about my mum. 'Well, right now I want to shove it down—'

Bear walked back on to our court. 'I can't leave you guys alone for ten minutes without you being at each other's throats. Just play the game.'

I did as I was told and the crowd cheered, but our pairing was a disaster. I couldn't stand her smugness. Okay, she had a decent backhand, and her serve was incredibly fast and accurate, but she was one of the biggest pains in the backside I'd ever met.

After she missed an easy lob, I told her she was nothing like Annie.

'So, you keep saying,' she hit back. 'I'm a much better player.'

'You wish,' I yelled, slamming the ball back at her.

'Your sister's moved on,' she shouted. 'You should too. You know why my parents called me Courtney?'

I rolled my eyes. 'No.'

The crowd thought we were bantering. We weren't.

'*Court*ney. I'm destined to be the greatest tennis player on the court. Get it?'

The crowd whooped and clapped.

'I get it. You really are an idiot.'

'Ladies, you have a match in two days,' Bear said wearily. 'Let's keep it civil, hey?'

'That's enough for me,' Courtney said, sauntering off the court.

'She hardly practices,' I told Bear as I towelled down. 'Her Highness is always in a bar, boozing. That's probably where she's off to now.'

'It's called living, Samantha,' Courtney said, stepping into the conversation. 'Try it sometime. I came back to invite you to this happening party tonight, but I won't bother. Have fun, lovebirds.'

I went to protest, but uncharacteristically gave in. She had a point. Until recently, I hadn't been able to focus on tennis, to think about when or if I'd play again. I couldn't concentrate, not knowing where Annie was or what had become of her. But now that I'd received a card and an email, I had to let her go. I was no good to anyone sitting around crying about my sister, who was probably having the time of her life in some exotic foreign land. Annie was okay. And if not okay, at least she was surviving and doing whatever the hell it was she needed to. And so was I. I'd made a promise to Bear that I'd stick with Courtney and that's what I would do. For now.

Thirty

Zach

Zach was eating breakfast at a diner in SoHo, New York, reading the news sites on his phone when he spotted a piece by Prue Hamilton about tennis love matches and whether they could survive.

What's not in question is that Annie Callahan was playing the best tennis of her career, having just won gold at the Olympics, when she met Erik Sørensen. Soon after Sørensen announced their engagement, Callahan's ranking plunged lower than Kim Kardashian's cleavage.

Zach couldn't dispute that.

As for the other Callahan sister, Samantha, aka 'The Slapper,' it's rumoured she's in a relationship with her coach, Bern 'Bear' Devlin. Devlin has repeatedly declined to elaborate. 'Those old rumours?' he said. 'Can't you guys come up with anything better?'

Zach stared at the photo of Annie that accompanied the piece. Where was she? If only he could talk to her, apologise. He still felt so guilty about her overdose. He'd called and emailed, but she hadn't replied. Finally, he'd resorted to writing a letter and slipping it under the front door of the Mosman apartment. He still didn't get a reply, but he knew she'd received the letter. Samantha had told him she'd hand-delivered it to Annie.

The next day she'd left the country.

He thought back to his conversation years ago when Annie had confided in him about Mrs Callahan's suicide. She must have been suffering clinical depression to have done that to her daughters. Still, a flash of anger passed at how deeply her behaviour had scarred the sisters. Annie could have died had Sam not checked on her. A moment of madness, and well, it could have gone either way.

So, as much as he hated that she'd gone away, he understood. Annie was looking after Annie.

He checked his watch. Time to meet Samantha.

~ * ~

At the SoHo Arthouse, Zach directed his friend to the photography exhibition they were there to see. 'Looking good, Sam. What have you been up to?'

She smiled. 'This and that, loving being back in NYC. Just a shame I don't have much time off. I guess you know about Courtney?'

'Your new partner? Yes. Congratulations.'

'Bear's forcing me.'

'As he should.'

'Thank you!' Samantha stretched her arms sideways and exhaled. 'After Bear released the media statement, I expected the attention to die down, but it's escalated. We've been bombarded with questions. Do I know where Annie is? Are we in regular contact? How do I feel about partnering Ms Gold?'

'How do you feel about playing again?'

'Insecure. Like I'm going to fail, slap Courtney or say "fuck." You know, the usual.'

'You could be quite funny if you chose to let go.'

'And you could easily *not* be a man whore if you chose *not* to let yourself go.'

Zach grinned. 'Touché. I'm working on it.'

In fact, since London, Zach hadn't hooked up with anyone. Almost losing Annie had made him realise how deeply he cared for her. Casual sex? Too shallow. At the same time, he knew himself well enough to realise he'd get over it eventually and be back to his old self. He thought about Annie. Would she ever return to her old self? Would she ever return?

They'd stopped in front of a black and white photo of two boxers. One was giving the other a swift uppercut to the chin.

Samantha looked deep in thought. 'Powerful image.'

'Capturing a moment in time. I never thought I could feel as passionately about photography as I do, but there you go.'

Samantha turned to him. 'I get it.'

'Yeah, speaking of passions, any word on Annie?'

'Nope, not since I received a postcard from Asia.'

Zach was trying to read her expression. Had Samantha moved on or was she just putting on a good front? He really couldn't tell.

They shifted further along the exhibition.

'Gotta love Prue's most recent piece,' he ventured.

Samantha snorted. 'She certainly knows how to spin shit.'

Zach raised his eyebrows. 'But the love match is going well?'

Samantha blushed. 'We're hanging out.'

'I see. Which is why you're being so accommodating re Courtney?'

'Bear's sole objective is to get me playing again. To stop me obsessing about Annie.' She turned to him, suddenly serious. 'I love him, Zach.'

'I know you do, babe. Full marks to the Bear. You two belong together—and you need to get back in the game. It's time.' He tweaked her cheeks and immediately regretted it.

'Shut up! That's exactly what Bear said. And about the cheek pinching—'

Zach smiled. 'Sorry. Now, enough about you. Back to me. I'm taking part in a photography exhibition in Sydney in October, and I want you to come and fawn over my fabulous prints.'

Samantha looked suspicious. 'Are they of anyone I know?'

'Actually, not too many. I've been collecting images from Dubai, London, Paris, all over. The show's called *Urban Sprawl.*'

'Sounds fascinating,' she said, taking his arm. 'Count me in.'

Zach grinned. He knew he could rely on Samantha. Outside the gallery, before they said their goodbyes, he'd been on the verge of telling her that Erik and Dragana were back together but changed his mind. He didn't want to ruin the mood. Samantha seemed happy and he didn't want to spoil it. Besides, Zach hadn't recovered from the consequences of last time he told a Callahan something about Erik.

Thirty-one

Samantha

At the pre-match interview, reporters fired the usual questions about my new partnership with Courtney and our upcoming match against Irish women Tammy Keyes and Mary Beattie.

Then Prue turned to Courtney. 'How do you rate your chances?'

Courtney's eyebrows puckered. 'There'll always be tough opponents, players who think they're better than me. But I always find a way to win. Today will be no different.'

One hour later, when Courtney and I were warming up, I started my usual rundown, talking through strategy. 'Tammy's a regular double-faulter. If she doesn't get her first serve in—'

'Would you please stop droning in my ear?' Courtney said, raising her voice. 'They're ranked, what? Ninety? I don't need your psychobabble to fire me up. Let's just get out there and thrash them.'

We won the toss and elected to serve. Courtney was up first. We won the game in three minutes, Courtney firing four aces in a row. Okay, so perhaps she didn't need my pre-match pep talk.

Her playing was flawless, which meant I could concentrate on my game—which I did after a quick scan of the full stands searching for Annie. I couldn't help myself. I knew I wouldn't see her, but that didn't stop me hoping and looking. All I saw was a mass of bright colours, visors and clapping hands. I waved off my doubts and focused.

We won the match 6–2, 6–2.

I was pumped. 'Great game, Court. You were brilliant.'

'You know it,' came her modest reply.

Hideous would be one way to describe how the post-match interview panned out. I was thrilled to have won, but Courtney dismissed the whole event.

'I could have won this match blindfolded with one hand tied behind my back,' she announced to the waiting media.

'Courtney—' I started, but it was no use. She steamrolled her way straight over the top of me.

'If we don't win this tournament, we should both give up. Doubles is a no-brainer. It requires less skill than breathing.' And with an 'I'm off to the pub,' she was gone.

I was dumbfounded. The woman had balls; I'd give her that. But she was also a dickhead. If her mindset didn't improve, our partnership was destined to be brief. I was barely making it onto the court as it was. I didn't need her dismissive attitude as well.

I'd cooled down by the time I moved into the players' lounge, but rubbing the back of my neck, I had an acute desire to flee rather than face everyone again. Last time I'd seen most of these women was after I'd slapped Annie when they'd called me a monster.

'Good to see you back,' Sandi Wren said. 'Looking forward to whipping you into shape in the third round.'

'No, no,' Olga Gerski chimed in, grinning. 'I'll be whipping Ms Callahan in the second.'

I smiled. 'Nice to know I still have friends.'

'Samantha, darling,' Olga purred. She could only purr when she had her contact lenses in. It didn't work so well with her thick glasses. 'We're very glad to have you in the competition, but that dreadful Courtney Gold!'

'She's not as bad as Lucia,' Sandi said. 'Being a *Playboy* bunny has completely gone to her head.'

'I'll say,' Olga said. 'I couldn't believe it yesterday when she threw her racquet after losing to you, Sandi. And she refused to do the post-match interview.'

'A complete diva,' Sandi agreed. 'Got fined five thousand dollars though, so it wasn't all bad news.'

'I've missed you guys,' I said.

'Yeah, I bet. I notice you and the Bear are still smiling,' Olga said.

Sandi's eyes widened. 'The rumours are actually true this time?'

I blushed.

~ * ~

When Courtney didn't turn up to training the next day, I complained to Bear. 'Olga and Petra are hardly easy beats. We need all the practice we can get.'

'It'll be okay,' he soothed. 'Come on, I'll take you shopping.'

I didn't argue. Hitting Saks sounded like a good diversion.

Annie and I had always binge shopped together in the different countries we'd visited. It was one of the activities that bonded us. But since her departure, I hadn't wanted to at all—not without her telling me to go for it or making puking noises when she thought my choice was butt-ugly. There was no one I trusted for a second opinion like Annie. But I was in New York, and I liked the idea of roaming the streets with Bear.

That night, back at the hotel after dinner, he surprised me with a pair of emerald earrings I'd admired in a store window several hours earlier.

'I love them!' I squealed as I put them on. 'And I love you too.' I covered his face in butterfly kisses. 'You make me so happy.'

'You make me happy too, GG, but I should get going. You've got a big day tomorrow.'

'We could just snuggle,' I said.

'You know where snuggling leads...'

I pulled him towards my bedroom.

~ * ~

We were slated for an eleven a.m. match, and I started panicking when Courtney hadn't arrived at the courts by nine-thirty.

By ten o'clock, I was thinking her only possible excuse could be death.

When she sauntered into the pavilion at ten minutes after ten, I was livid. Talk about disrespecting the game!

'Courtney, if I wasn't so committed to this match—'

'You'd what?' Courtney taunted. 'Quit? Slap me? Be my guest.'

Bear's influence must have been working because where once I would have flown into a fury, this time I let the comment slide. I swung round and marched straight onto the court for our warm-up. Courtney followed.

Self-consciously I bit the inside of my lip when Olga and Petra won the toss and elected to receive. It was an unusual tactic.

'Good luck,' I said to Olga before we went to our separate ends.

'Why the fuck are you wishing *her* good luck?' Courtney roared.

I went to reply but she held her racquet in front of my face. 'One more word and I'll break my racquet.'

'Except you won't because that would mean an automatic code violation.'

Courtney was second on the list of people I disliked intensely, but despite her supremely irritating manner, we won our match. Electing to receive in the first game had worked against them.

I was thrilled. Bear was thrilled. Courtney was ...well, Courtney was just Courtney.

As Bear and I moved towards the podium for the post-match interview, I noticed Prue talking to Courtney's father. I nudged Bear. 'What the?'

As we got closer, I tuned into their conversation.

'It looks like Samantha Callahan is finally getting her groove back after Annie's shock departure,' Hamilton enthused. 'Certainly, partnering with Courtney hasn't hurt Samantha's game, given their winning 6–4, 6–4 margin.'

'Courtney is carrying Samantha,' Larry Gold replied. 'I've said right from the start, Courtney shouldn't be wasting her time playing doubles. She should concentrate where it really counts, on the singles matches.'

Prue turned to Courtney. 'Do you agree with your father?'

Courtney frowned. 'I'm happy to help Samantha out until she gets back on her feet.'

I was outraged. Courtney helping me out! Her obese father telling Prue that Courtney was carrying me!

'How dare they?' I said to Bear.

'I agree it's unnecessary—'

'Unnecessary? Why do I have to listen to some overweight pompous prick tell me how I should and shouldn't be playing my game?'

'Why are you wasting your time with this, Courtney?' Larry Gold's chin protruded, his cheeks bright red. 'Concentrate your energy on singles. Don't bother with this rubbish.'

'But we won,' I said, deliberately keeping my voice low and calm, wishing time would speed up. I had to keep it together. I couldn't risk flying off the handle and reminding the press and the public how badly I'd behaved with Annie at Wimbledon.

'Tell someone who cares,' he barked and stormed off.

'A truly charming man,' I said to Courtney.

'He's an arsehole, but he has a point.'

I exhaled several counts before turning and smiling for the cameras.

Thirty-two

By the third round, Courtney and I were barely on grunting terms. And to top things off, we were up against Dragana and Jelena. Jogging on to the court on an unseasonably freezing day, I could barely think straight. I just wanted the match to be over.

Glancing up to the stands I saw Erik in Dragana's box. Stunned, I almost tripped over my feet. Erik couldn't be dating Dragana again, not so soon after publicly dumping Annie. Yet there he was, looking supremely arrogant, like he owned the world.

If I'd hated him when they were engaged, I despised Erik even more now. After he'd humiliated her on live television, he never contacted her to explain himself. He didn't call when Annie overdosed. He'd completely dropped her without so much as a backward glance. Yet here he was, metres from me, signalling to Dragana and making idiotic baby faces. Clearly, he was back in Dragana's box in more ways than one.

Seeing him threw me. My win-at-all-costs mind-set shattered.

'Where's your form?' Dragana asked me at the first changeover.

'Where's your cigarette?' I hit back, hopefully loud enough for Erik to hear.

'Disappeared, along with your sister.'

That hurt. 'She's on holiday, revelling in her freedom.'

'Quiet, please,' the umpire commanded, looking directly at me.

After that, my confidence was shot. Still, I served and volleyed, chipped and charged, rushed the net and went for broke.

Sensing an imminent loss, Courtney bounced her racquet on the court, called the linesman 'visually challenged' and questioned the umpire's decision. Basically, she behaved like a spoilt brat. I should know. I'd done the same. On more than one occasion. So, despite not liking her, I understood her rage. It was tough having to be a grown up all the time.

The chair umpire called her over and officially disciplined her. On top of everything else, I knew we'd get slammed by the critics.

The crowd turned against us and cheered for the Serbians. Their fickle behaviour inflamed Courtney further.

'Come on,' I whispered to her at changeover. 'Keep it together.'

She flicked her skirt up to reveal her blue garter. 'Always,' she replied.

I needed to follow my own advice. Instead of concentrating on our game, I was obsessing about Dragana and Erik, wasting what little energy I had left thinking up evil curses to heap upon them.

In the end, Jelena's brutal forehand overpowered both of us and we got whipped: 3–6; 2–6. Deservedly so. *Why was I putting myself through this torment again?*

Courtney's father was waiting for us off the court, looking ready to spit fire. 'You both played badly.'

I put my hand up despite feeling numb all over. 'I'm in no mood to listen to—'

'Silence!' He exploded. 'You played like an eight-year-old girl.'

'How dare you?' I snapped. 'You interfering nobody!'

Bear grabbed my arm. 'Let's get out of here.'

Heart pounding, I dreaded the post-match interview.

While Dragana and Jelena were being interviewed, I said to Bear, 'I thought Erik was bad, but in hindsight, not understanding him had its advantages. With Courtney's dad, there's absolutely no mistaking what he's saying.'

'Ignore him,' was Bear's advice. 'I do. Courtney's much calmer when he's not loitering. I'll say that much.'

As soon as I stood up on the podium, Prue Hamilton's questions flew. 'Not one of your best efforts, Samantha. Do you think, given the background, Dragana unnerved you?'

'Not at all,' I replied.

'It can't have helped, can it? Especially with Erik Sørensen being here.'

I'd managed to avoid eye contact with Erik so far, but as Prue said his name, my eyes locked with his. It was only a couple of seconds, but enough to bring every horrible memory bubbling to the surface. Aware of my cold and clammy skin, I took deep breaths to calm myself.

'There's been talk of match-fixing,' Prue continued. 'What do you say to the suggestion that you and Courtney lost on purpose?'

Zach had mentioned rumours of match-fixing when I'd seen him the other day, so I wasn't completely shocked by the question. There was a lot of money to be made, especially by players who might be struggling financially.

'Anyone who knows me knows that tennis means everything to me,' I said. 'I'm offended anyone would imply I could be involved in something so disgusting.'

'I'd never do anything to jeopardise my playing future,' Courtney chimed in.

'How are you feeling about today's loss, Courtney?' Prue asked.

'Devastated, of course,' she answered, tears welling. 'This isn't how I planned this match to end.'

In the background, Courtney's father rolled his eyes and cursed.

'Did you really think bouncing your racquet would win you points?' Prue said. 'Or fans, for that matter?'

Courtney looked startled. 'Of course not. I allowed my emotions to get the better of me.'

Bear signalled Prue to end the interview.

'But I haven't finished,' she said to him. 'I still have questions about Samantha and Courtney's partnership, about Annie, about how you and Mr Gold are sharing coaching roles—'

'Thanks,' Bear said, cutting her off. 'We'll leave it there.'

I couldn't wait to get off the podium. I needed to hide out for a while, get my head together to avoid a full-blown panic attack. My heart was racing, sweat streamed from my armpits, and my stomach was cramping.

'You're being a baby about this,' Courtney snapped as I pushed past her.

I took my time getting to the lockers. One step at a time, taking deep breaths. In. Out. In. Out. But I couldn't control my shaking as though I might collapse at any moment.

A few players came up to sympathise when I entered the locker room, but I could hear others talking in low voices.

'Samantha can't concentrate because she's missing Annie.'

'Samantha's lost her sister and her focus.'

'Samantha was always the less talented sister, and Annie dropped out because she couldn't handle the pressure.'

I gritted my teeth and smiled. A few more minutes and I could go back to the hotel room. A few more minutes and I could finally be alone.

I was surprised when Jelena sought me out and apologised for Dragana's on-court behaviour. 'She is very insecure,' she explained. 'Since she has taken Erik back, it is like he has control of her once again. She hardly smiles. Even when she is practising at the court, I do not see the real Dragana. She is a different person. The only time she is happy is when she is away from him in the locker room, sneaking cigarettes.'

I thought back to Dubai, when Dragana had told me she could have Erik back anytime she wanted.

'And her ranking has dropped,' Jelena revealed. 'Not too much yet, but it has fallen since he is back. Dragana says she must marry him, so I shut my mouth and continue best I can.'

Back in my hotel room, I couldn't stop thinking about Dragana and Erik. Seeing Erik made it feel as if Annie's overdose had happened only yesterday. I was overwhelmed by loss and grief all over again.

Annie didn't die, but I'd lost her all the same. Where was she and what was she doing? My head throbbed, imagining Annie broken in a ditch; stoned and standing on a cliff's edge; lying on a bed in a cheap hotel room having collapsed from an overdose ...or worse.

I doubled over in pain. My stomach cramps and shaking were getting worse, not better. I wanted it all to be over.

Thirty-three

Four weeks later, Violet gave birth to a three-point-four-kilo baby girl with huge brown eyes and a mop of curly black hair. And two days after that, they were both in my living room.

'Isn't she just the sweetest?' Violet said, snuggling into her newborn. 'Her smell is an instant reminder of Ava and Poppy when they were tiny.'

I beamed. It seemed so long ago, now. I held her baby's hand, marvelling at her perfect features and satiny skin. Violet was in love with this one as much as she was with her older girls.

'We're truly blessed.' Violet sighed and smiled at the baby, then at me. 'Despite the sleepless nights and inevitable mastitis that lies ahead.'

'Hello, little Hester Grace,' I said softly. Hester was my mother's name, and Grace was Rick's grandmother's name. 'Mum would ...she'd be overwhelmed. She'd also be so proud of you, Vi. Three beautiful girls.'

'Your mum would be proud of you too. Look how far you've come.'

'No, she wouldn't. I let Annie go, for starters. I'm her big sister. I'm supposed to look out for her.'

'She's okay,' Violet said. 'We got a postcard from her two days ago—I forgot to tell you, what with Hester's birth.' She pulled a postcard from her enormous baby bag and gave it to me. The picture showed a dozen brown cows lying on what looked like a busy city street.

I turned over the card, read the words and spoke. 'India, hey? She didn't make it back for Hester's birth. I was hoping...'

~ * ~

I'd promised Bear I'd stick with Courtney until the Australian Open, but as the tournament approached, I grew more and more prickly. It was exactly a year after Annie and I had played our disastrous semi-final match. As if that wasn't enough to undermine my confidence, Bear had started coaching a young, attractive singles player, Katie Durak, which meant he was less available to me. I was thrown by how much I missed his full attention.

'Why take on someone else? First Courtney, now Katie. I need you.'

'As a favour to her parents,' he said, apologetically. 'I couldn't say no. I've known Katie's dad since we were at primary school together.'

I tried to understand. Bear was a professional and needed to earn a living too. Still.

'I see Bear's spending a lot of time with Katie,' Courtney trilled in the lead-up to our first-round match against Kristy Banta and Yasmine Le Bluth. 'I'm coming a distinct third in his attentions, after you, of course.'

She was winding me up, and I tried not to let her taunts get to me but couldn't help over-thinking every word she said. To make matters worse, the subject came up in the locker room when I saw Kristy and Yasmine before the game.

'I don't like your chances of winning,' Kristy crowed. 'I have a new coach, Maggie, and she's fucking brilliant.'

Coach being a euphemism for lover. Kristy's coaches changed every eight to ten months, sometimes more.

'Bear's new protégée's doing well,' Yasmine chimed in. 'But I'm sure the rumours are nothing to worry about, Sam.'

I was ready to explode but kept a plastic smile firmly fixed on my face.

In the first game, Courtney was serving, which was normally a breeze for her, except this time, she was cited twice for foot-faulting. I was furious when she foot-faulted a third time in the second set, and we went on to almost lose the match. Afterwards, my mind flashed back to Prue Hamilton's questions in New York about match-fixing, I accused her of deliberately sabotaging the game.

'Why would I do that?' she snapped.

'I have no idea how your warped mind works!'

Unfortunately, the media got hold of my comment and blew it all out of proportion, writing that we were feuding, our partnership crumbling. Hello! We *were* feuding and the partnership *was* crumbling, but I didn't want to let the world in on our private hell until after the tournament had concluded. Reluctantly, Courtney and I faced the media together and told the assembled throng we couldn't be happier.

'We're thrilled to be playing together in front of an Aussie home crowd,' I said.

'Good to hear,' Prue replied. 'You're not fighting any demons this time around?'

'What kind of demons?' I asked.

'Annie and Erik's engagement?' Prue deadpanned. 'Surely you haven't forgotten?'

I glared at her. 'Given how things turned out, there's really no need for me to comment, is there?'

'Touché!' She smiled. 'How do you rate Courtney as a partner?'

'She's a ten out of ten.'

'So there really is no feud?' Prue probed.

'That's absurd. We're like this,' I said, crossing my fingers to make my point.

'The finger-crossing bit might have been taking it too far,' Bear said after the interview.

'Tell the people what they want to hear—isn't that your motto?'

'I know you're not overly fond of Courtney, but you two could make a formidable team if you tried.'

'I couldn't cope with her dad—and her—on a regular basis. Besides, I'm a one-coach gal.'

My underlying message didn't get through because Bear dragged me off to watch his new protégée play her singles match. He was doing a great job: Katie barely missed a point in her 6–1; 6–1 win. Afterwards, she threw her arms around him... a little too enthusiastically for my liking.

~ * ~

In the next round, Courtney and I were up against rising Spanish stars Carla Hernandez and Lourdes Alvarez. They were enjoying a six-month winning streak, a fast-track to world domination. I tried to discuss tactics with Courtney, but she dismissed me yet again.

'I have my own tactics.'

'When you're playing doubles, you have to make certain allowances,' I reminded her.

'Samantha, take a pill.'

I carried all my worries into the match and was uncomfortable from the outset.

The weather was blazing, melting me on court. Carla was aggressive and powerful, slamming the ball hard and low over the net. Her speed and control were amazing. To make matters worse, Lourdes had a vicious spin on her serve; the ball jumped at odd angles, making it near to impossible to return.

I was close to collapsing. Why hadn't the match been halted? Ball kids were fainting; my sneakers were sticking to the court surface. Melbourne was burning in thirty-eight degree Celsius conditions, and yet we were forced to continue. I was lost, and whenever I looked to the stands for Bear's support, he was talking and laughing with Katie. He couldn't have cared less that I was playing in extreme temperatures in one of the toughest matches I'd ever endured.

'Samantha,' Courtney shouted as we changed ends, 'forget about Bear and focus on the game. He's moved on. So should you.'

'Shut up,' I yelled at her, then turned to the umpire. 'We shouldn't be playing. Why hasn't the Extreme Heat Policy been enacted?'

I was fined by the umpire, who also looked like she was about to faint.

The second round was an unmitigated disaster: we lost 2–6, 1–6.

That was the end of my partnership with Courtney.

Thirty-four

Zach

Zach snapped photos of a shattered Samantha and Courtney at the post-match press conference as Bear announced that the women had decided to go their separate ways. It came as no surprise to Zach; Samantha had been struggling to hold it together with Courtney for months.

Afterwards, he tracked Sam down at the players' lounge, where she was sitting alone.

'Where is everyone?' he asked.

Samantha stared at the ground, tears streaming down her cheeks.

He sat down next to her. 'Everything all right? You've had a rough trot.'

'Tears of relief, truly,' she told him. 'Finally, I can concentrate on playing the game I want to.'

'Really?'

'Really. Despite crashing out, I'm relieved my days partnering Courtney are over. We're completely, one hundred per cent over each other. Shoot me if I ever have anything to do with her again.'

Zach knew she meant it. He'd never thought she'd play doubles again after Annie left. Samantha was great when it came to studying another player as an opponent, but she wasn't open enough to get to know someone else's playing habits—she couldn't trust anyone the way she'd trusted Annie.

'Where does that leave Bear?' Zach asked.

I hesitated. 'Too early to tell. But it wouldn't surprise me if he and Courtney called it quits too, especially as Bear's now coaching Katie Durak.'

'And Katie's playing very well. A talent to watch.'

'Have you heard anything about them?'

'Silly rumours, Sam. You've got no reason to worry. Bear's a good guy. He loves you.'

'I know, but it's hard seeing him take such an interest in her.'

'He's a coach. That's what he does.'

Samantha smiled. 'Yeah, but why does he have to be so damn good at it?'

Zach threw his arm around her shoulders. 'That's the old Samantha I know. So, what happens now?'

'Not sure. When you've got every newspaper, shock jock and current affairs program dissecting the minutiae of your life, it doesn't take much to make you believe you're on the brink of a minor breakdown.' She looked up at him. 'What would you do in my situation?'

Zach hesitated. 'I really don't know.' Then he realised he did. 'Actually, I'd go out there and give the singles circuit a shot. Play to your strengths, Samantha. Find that killer instinct again and go for it.'

'You're right,' she said, sounding unconvinced. 'I know you're right. Bear said much the same. But it's relentless. I don't know how much longer I can keep it up ...the pressure of performing in front of home audiences. Emotionally, I'm not convinced I can go it alone.'

'Put the Open behind you and focus on the next tournament.'

Though he was saying the words Samantha needed to hear, privately Zach wasn't sure. What if her mental demons sabotaged her performance? He pulled her towards him. 'You're one tough chick.'

She gave him a small smile. 'Is that supposed to be a compliment?'

'You've done it before, Sam. As a professional player, you must move on from the losses. A new tournament is a fresh opportunity.'

They talked a while longer, then Samantha said she had to go find Bear. Zach watched as she left the lounge. The past year had really taken its toll. To be honest, Sam had lost so much of her confidence and drive that Zach wondered how long she'd last on the singles track.

Thirty-five

Samantha

I flew home to Sydney the day after my second-round loss but had to wait another ten days before Bear returned.

'Katie did really well, didn't she?' he said for about the tenth time since we'd sat down for our reunion dinner.

I wrinkled my nose. 'I've already agreed with you. If you want to spend the whole time talking about her, why didn't you invite her to dinner?'

Bear looked surprised. 'She reached the quarter-finals.'

'I know, Bear. I know.'

'What's gotten into you?'

'Nothing. It's just hard when everyone's whispering about you and Katie. You looked very cosy together down in Melbourne, that's for sure.'

'Sweetheart, I'm old enough to be her father. Come on.' He took my hand in his. 'Don't be ridiculous. I love you. You're my one and only.'

‘Not when it comes to coaching.’

‘GG, I can coach you and Katie ...though if you really don’t want me to...’

‘I really don’t want you to, but...’

‘But what?’

‘I’m being petty.’

Bear smiled. ‘I get it. Sami, I love you. Coaching Katie isn’t going to change that, no matter how successful she becomes. Okay?’

I didn’t respond.

‘And I’ve got some news you’ll be happy about.’

I raised my eyebrows. ‘Go on.’

‘Courtney and I are parting ways. It’s for the best.’

I squealed. ‘I really love you!’

‘Yeah, yeah. I’m not about to be seduced by your flattery.’

‘Really?’

‘Well, not for at least another fifteen minutes.’ We kissed and I smiled.

‘I’m glad you’re home. I’ve missed you.’

‘Now, what about you? Given that doubles is out for the foreseeable future’—I glared at him, not wanting to hear what he was about to say—‘you’re left with one option. Singles.’

I went to protest, but I didn’t want to let my fans down and I certainly didn’t want to let Bear down. Or myself. If I quit now, I’d be proving the naysayers right. And I’d be letting Annie down too, wherever the hell she was. I didn’t want to give up tennis. I loved the game too much.

‘You have to give it a go,’ he encouraged.

He was right, of course. But my singles game was different to the way I played doubles. It had to be. And this time, my game would be different to the time I’d played singles when Annie and I had taken a break. This time, it was about my future.

I had to put myself out there, alone, confident and in charge.

~ * ~

Two months later, I was in Florida, preparing to play Debby Bowden, my first-round opponent at the Miami Masters. I'd played and beaten Debby before, but it would be much harder this time, given she was American and had the home crowd advantage.

Luckily for me, at the end of the sixth game (I was trailing two games to four) Debby's niggling ankle injury flared up, and during the next game, she slipped and landed awkwardly. She was treated courtside and had her ankle strapped, but only managed to play a further two games before having to forfeit. This meant I immediately progressed to the second round, and although I was sorry for her, I had to take the breaks, literally, when they came my way.

The next day, I reluctantly accepted Bear's invitation to watch Katie in action. Given she'd made it to the Australian Open quarter-finals, I assumed she'd give Sandi Wren a run for her money, which she did, making a confident start, taking a 6–2 lead.

'She's got the moves,' I said to Bear as we watched her take the first game of the second set. 'She looks good. Graceful, fierce. Amazing serve, blasting forehand.'

Bear rubbed his chin. 'All the ingredients for an outstanding player.'

I whacked him on the arm. 'That's enough.'

Katie won her match, and though I wanted an early night, I said yes when invited out for a celebratory dinner. It was quick as both Katie and I had to prepare for our second-round matches, but for the duration of the meal I had to bite back my jealousy.

'All that flirting got a bit much for me,' I confided to Bear later in my hotel room.

'What flirting?' He laughed. 'I've known Katie since she was a baby. It would be way too weird to flirt with her. Besides I only have eyes for you, Gorgeous Girl.'

~ * ~

In the second round, I was up against Carla Hernandez, whom Courtney and I had lost to a couple of months back. Since then, I'd learnt that Carla had a weak single-handed backhand, so my strategy revolved around making sure I hit to her backhand regardless of where I was on the court.

I won 6–3, 6–4.

Through to the third round, injury-free and feeling fit, I was up against Sofia Petrova, who, at only nineteen years old, had stormed through the first two rounds, leaving veterans in her wake, and dropping only four games. Okay, so my matches hadn't gone that well, but I was confident I could handle the youngster. I'd managed Courtney, hadn't I? I could certainly handle Sofia. Besides, my game was improving.

'If you serve well and take care of your service games,' Bear told me in bed one morning, after he'd done a fine job of servicing me, 'the match will go your way.'

'She has a thing about her racquet, doesn't she?'

'Says it gives her the confidence she needs to win,' Bear said, nuzzling my neck.

'It's just a racquet, for God's sake.'

'Maybe it's just a racquet to us,' he said, pulling back, 'but to Sofia, it's her signature, her lucky charm. Like your lucky bandana, or Courtney Gold's blue garter—'

'Okay, enough with the racquet talk. I admire your confidence in me,' I said. 'And now I have to go practice.'

I made a feeble attempt to get out of bed, but he kissed me in a way that made my toes curl.

'Practice on me,' he said, cupping my bare butt in his hands.

I wrapped my arms around his neck and melted into his handsome, naked body. Bear's attention certainly wasn't focused on anyone but me right now. Tennis could wait.

~ * ~

The day of my third-round match, I stupidly read Prue Hamilton's column.

Samantha Callahan, whose court appearances have become increasingly sporadic, will need to play more tournaments, particularly Grand Slams, if she's to lift her world ranking. Currently seeded forty-ninth, Samantha has struggled to regain her form in the months since her sister's departure from professional tennis. Callahan, twenty-eight, has never won a singles title and has not won a doubles title since Doha. Here's hoping she'll make a triumphant return to form in Miami. She's certainly started out that way.

Meanwhile Bern 'Bear' Devlin's other charge, Katie Durak, nine years younger than Callahan, is in smashing form. Definitely one to watch.

Later, at the pre-match interview, when Prue asked what effect the rumour that Bear had more than a professional relationship with Katie Durak was having on me, I almost gasped. I told her it was nonsense, but my insides churned. Silently, I did my deep breathing exercises to quell rising panic.

When that didn't work, I called Violet, hoping the sound of her voice would calm me.

'Shouldn't you be warming up?' she asked.

'Vi, I can't quieten these thoughts about Bear and Katie, the rumours and insinuations... they're killing me.'

'Sami, Bear loves you. He's besotted. You've got to ignore Prue and the rest of them. It's all just noise and hot air. You are Samantha Callahan and you are a champion.'

Violet's pep talk over, I pushed down all negative thoughts and visualised myself winning the match. And it worked for the first two minutes. Although I started confidently against Sofia, a couple of silly mistakes early on proved costly and she took the first match easily, 6–3. Very quickly, I was at a loss, my shoulders slumping, my self-doubt mounting ...it was all I could do to hold serve. I managed it, but with each lost point my attitude became more negative.

First, I double-faulted, then she pounced when I wrong-footed and shanked a lunging volley. Sofia took the match in one hour and twelve minutes: 6–3; 6–2.

I was out of the tournament.

I didn't take in much of the post-match press conference, except for lots of talk about me not being able to make it past the third round in any of the tournaments I'd played. I didn't want that to become a psychological barrier I couldn't break, but then I heard Dragana say, 'Samantha Callahan always chokes in the third round.'

The sick feeling in my stomach and shortness of breath were all too familiar, out of my control. On the podium, I tried to focus, but the room was spinning. A panic attack was looming. I must have closed my eyes because seconds later, Bear was beside me, steadying me before helping me down.

'Let's get you outside,' he said, guiding me through the mass of reporters.

I wanted to tell him it was over, but no words would come out of my mouth. 'I can't,' I eventually whispered.

'Breathe,' he commanded. 'Don't speak, just focus on slow deliberate breaths.'

I steadied myself. 'Bear, please! I can't do this.'

He held me close, no doubt to silence my self-defeating talk.

~ * ~

A week later, back in Sydney, I headed over to Violet's for lunch.

'Hey,' Vi said, opening the door to let me in. 'Welcome to the madhouse. Please save me from my children.'

I smothered Poppy and Ava in cuddles.

'We've missed you so much,' Poppy squealed.

Two minutes later, they started squabbling.

Violet raised her eyebrows. 'See what I mean?'

'They're okay,' I said. 'They remind me of Annie and me when we were their age.'

'Demons,' Violet replied.

Ava poked her tongue out and dragged Poppy into the living room.

'Good,' Violet said when the girls finally disappeared into the TV room, and it was just me with Violet nursing Hester.

'How are you getting along?'

'It's chaos. Absolute bedlam.' But Violet was smiling. 'I wouldn't have it any other way.'

'Yeah. Hearing Poppy and Ava bicker one moment and the next seeing them laughing and giggling, reminds me...' I stared into space a moment before shaking off the dark side. 'Any word?'

'No more than a postcard now and then, which you've seen.'

Tears trickled down my cheeks. 'My nightmares always end with me finding Annie at the bottom of a cliff. I can't take it anymore.'

'Darling,' Violet soothed. 'I can't imagine what it's like—'

'No, you can't. Neither can Bear. But I can.' I could feel my anger rising and pushed it down. 'I don't want to be one of those tragic figures who keep crying over circumstances they can't change. I've tried really hard to stop searching for Annie in the crowd.'

'That's a huge leap forward.'

'I'm sure I still look for her on some subconscious level, but I'm working at keeping my focus squarely on the tennis court.' I glanced at Hester. 'My heart melts every time I see her.'

Violet blinked. 'And?'

'And nothing.' I playfully pushed Violet away. 'I don't want one of my own, if that's what you're getting at. That's one destination I won't be stopping off at for the foreseeable future.'

'So, you and Bear—'

'Are getting on well, despite his involvement with Katie. In fact, he's asked me to move in with him.'

'Ooh,' Violet said, squealing loud enough to wake Hester who'd been peacefully sleeping in her arms. 'That's brilliant. I'm so excited for you both.'

'But...'

'What? Tell me.'

'I'm not ready. Something's holding me back. I can't quite make the emotional leap to give myself to him one hundred per cent.'

'Is it Annie? Katie? What?'

'Honestly? Both probably. He's got ninety per cent of me, but I'm holding out on the last ten. I guess I'm anxious about Bear and Katie. Then there's Annie. She left me. What's to stop Bear from doing the same?'

'For what's it's worth, I think you're crazy. Why don't you pack up your apartment and rent it out? It can't be healthy living with Annie's belongings. You can't heal if you're thinking about her all the time.'

'But—'

'But nothing, Sam. It's time for you to move forward with Bear and take the next step.'

'Maybe. I just need to put my first solo appearance at Wimbledon behind me, then I can move on. Deal?'

Violet smiled. 'Sounds good.'

All in all, I was cautiously optimistic about the direction my life was taking. But I should have known not to get too happy or complacent because that's when things had a habit of going belly-up.

Thirty-six

Almost as soon as we touched down at Heathrow, my positive framework came crashing down. Disorientated and uneasy, I tried to tell myself there was nothing wrong. It was just jetlag. Except it wasn't.

I remembered Annie saying she could never go back to London because of what had happened to her there, and now I understood why. Being here brought all the regret and angst flooding back.

At least Bear had booked a different hotel, the Langham. It was magnificent, romantic and the indoor pool was especially luxurious. Ordinarily, I would have loved staying there, but the emotions I'd kept under wraps for the better part of six months had resurfaced with a vengeance. Self-doubt hammered at me, relentless and unnerving. Early on, my second morning in London, to dispel the misery I went swimming, but instead of the water feeling cathartic, it bought back more memories of Annie.

Outwardly, I was confident and enthusiastic. Bear was ecstatic. But deep down, I was running on false hope. Even jogging in Regents Park, my inner demons pushed to the fore despite me desperately trying to lock them away.

As wretched luck would have it, my first-round match was against Courtney. I knew her game: she could easily beat me with her powerful serves and secure ball placement. The woman had confidence. Since our dramatic split, I'd managed to avoid her, but the thought of playing her here in the first round made me ready to give up before I'd even started. No doubt Prue Hamilton would be in her element, waiting for me to fail so she could rush in with her false condolences, blaming 'the curse of Wimbledon' or whatever freak theory she was going with.

Thank God we were playing on far-flung court eighteen. Jelena Jankovic once had declared that she 'might as well be playing in the parking lot. I almost needed a helicopter to get there,' but I didn't care. I was just pleased to be at Wimbledon and more than happy to be out of the spotlight.

'Remember,' Bear said in his pre match pep talk, 'You're only as good as your mind lets you. It's a tough physical game, but it's just as tough mentally. You can win this, Sami. You know you can.'

Still, when I walked onto the court to shake Courtney's hand in front of over a thousand spectators, I was so nervous I dropped my racquet.

'Easy,' she said, laughing. 'I haven't even begun to demolish you yet.'

Thank you, Courtney. That was all the encouragement I needed to dig my heels in. Minutes ago, I'd wanted to quit, but now I was fired up, ready to take on the world. She served and I walloped the ball straight back across the net. *Take that.*

I hit the ball hard and low, finding corners, to the left, then the right. Courtney didn't like to run; she preferred to stand still and thwack the ball back when it came her way. I used her lethargy to my advantage and was so focused that I was up five games to four before I realized I actually had a chance of winning the first set.

I took the set, then the rain came down. Courtney smiled. This was good news for her, a chance to get her rhythm back, but I needed momentum. The longer I wasn't playing on court, the more time I had to think about my insecurities—like what the hell was I doing here? I was an impostor.

During the time out, I had a shower, retaped my ankles and tried to stay calm by focusing on my mantras and envisaging winning all points against Courtney. I imagined her serving and visualised me whacking the ball back and winning the point. I saw myself smashing volleys, serves and backhands.

A long forty-five minutes later, the clouds disappeared, and the grounds staff uncovered and swept the court. Courtney and I were allowed a five-minute warmup before play resumed.

In the next set, I gritted my teeth, harnessed my mental toughness, and dug deep to see out the tie-break 7–3, sealing the match with a forehand winner down the line. Courtney was absolutely gobsmacked. I'd rarely, if ever, seen her lost for words.

'Congratulations,' she sniffed.

I didn't hit back with a snide remark. Instead, I said, 'Better luck next time,' and watched as she limped off to find her father. I'd heard things hadn't been going well between them this year, what with Courtney's partying and her father trying to mold her into the player he wanted her to be. Everyone had their own issues to deal with. I was just happy to have shaken mine off—at least superficially.

Thirty-seven

That afternoon, I was sitting beside Bear when Katie Durak won her first-round match.

Bear pulled me in close and watched Katie waving to the crowd. 'What a day.'

I snuggled into him but remained nauseous at the thought of Katie and me ever facing one another on court. How would Bear manage that?

I pushed those thoughts down and got on with preparing for my second-round match against Marta Kubot.

Marta was a relative newcomer to the scene who was getting her fair share of press coverage due to her punishing fitness regime. Born in Poland, she'd been pushed by her mother from a very young age, on court every morning by six, even as a pre-schooler. When she was seven, Marta and her mum moved to Florida, where Marta practiced tennis ten hours a day while her mother cleaned rich people's houses sixteen hours a day, seven days a week, to keep the dream alive.

She was steadily moving up through the ranks, but I didn't doubt I'd win. Not that I thought she'd be an easy beat-she was winning more matches than she lost—but I was optimistic. There was no way this teenager was going to beat me.

Meticulously, Bear and I studied Marta's previous games on his computer. She hated playing at the net, preferred the baseline and was a big server.

'You can win this match, GG,' Bear said the night before.

'I know,' I said, acting brave. 'But if I'm to have a fighting chance, I need to sleep.'

'You're kicking me out of your room,' he said with mock horror.

I smiled. 'Afraid so. Tonight is not your lucky night.'

I went to sleep visualising a win against her as I'd done with Courtney, but woke up several hours later sweating, crying and panicking. I'd dreamt I'd found Annie in her hotel room, lying on her bed, the bottle of vodka and pills on the floor. But this time she was dead.

My heart raced. I needed Bear. I rang him, but there was no answer. In my agitated state, I instantly imagined him in Katie's arms, kissing her the same way he kissed me. All too quickly, my panic symptoms returned, and I had to breathe deeply for several minutes to stop myself from losing it completely.

The next morning, after a long shower and massage, I considered myself marginally better—until I spied Annie in the crowds entering the arena. Immediately, I charged after her. Just as I was about to tap her on the shoulder, she turned. It wasn't Annie, just my over-active imagination playing tricks on me.

I barely made it to the locker room toilets before I threw up. All my hard work to get this far, and for what? My dream of becoming a tennis star had become my nightmare. My insides were eating away at me, gnawing, clawing ...forcing myself to move forward, I somehow made it out onto the court.

Marta was serving first. As she prepared, she flicked at her shoulder—the exact mannerism I'd seen Annie do time and time again. I flashed back to last year's Wimbledon: our defeat, Annie's attempted suicide ...suddenly, it became Annie I was facing.

My arms, my legs, and then my whole body seized. I couldn't move. The slightest distraction, like someone waving a fan in front of their face or a kid chewing gum, was enough to make me miss a ball. Not only that, but Marta was a dynamo, hitting the ball so hard and close to the line it was impossible for me to find a steady rhythm. I was my own worst enemy, feeling rushed on every point.

In the fourth game, I hurled myself to the ground to hit the ball and injured my back. I called for medical assistance, and moments later was carried off the court and helped to the medical tent. I had to forfeit the match.

As soon as sanity returned and I realised what had happened, that yet another tournament had ended in failure, I buried my face in my lucky bandana and cried ...and kept crying. Nothing Bear said could console me.

'I've never seen you like this,' he said. 'Let's get you back to the hotel. We'll give the media a miss. I'll deal with them later.'

'I can't believe I'm saying this,' I told him, trembling in his arms, 'but no game is worth this. I don't want to be a champion this badly.'

'We can fix your back,' he said gently. 'You'll be fine in a couple of days.'

'I won't,' I cried. 'It's not just my back. It's everything. The media, the pressure. I can't function. I feel like I'm having a full-blown panic attack. I can't live like this.'

'We'll discuss it when you're feeling better. Now's not the time.'

The throbbing in my chest intensified. 'I know why Annie wanted to quit so badly because I do, too.'

Back at the hotel, I told Bear I wanted to be alone. I wanted to get as far away from all things connected with tennis as possible. I turned off my phone and stayed in my room, crying and eating junk food. Double-coated chocolate Tim Tams were only the beginning.

The next morning, my back still ached. Despite a hot shower, dread overwhelmed me. I turned on the television just in time to see Katie Durak win her match against Sofia Petrova. She ran straight up to where Bear was sitting and hugged him. That was the final straw. I finally understood what Annie meant about not ever being able to enjoy the moment. The jubilation after winning a match was momentary. I was forever thinking about the next game, my next opponent. And when I lost a match, the disappointment lingered far longer than the joy from any win. I remembered how I'd told Annie she couldn't quit because her body didn't hurt. Well, my body did hurt, and I was ready for it to be over. I didn't need to stay in another Four Seasons hotel, or practice hitting a ball for one more hour, let alone ten.

When Bear came to my suite hours later, I told him as much. 'Katie won again. I've been thinking, you should concentrate your efforts on her.'

'Sweetheart,' he said, moving closer. 'Why would I want to do that? What do you mean?'

'I can't go on. I can't face the humiliation of defeat any longer. When I play tennis, I want to win but I can't. I'm done, Bear. I'm going back to Sydney tomorrow.'

'You can't darling. Please stay.'

'What for?'

'For me.'

'You have Katie. My tennis career is over.'

'Are you kidding me? Please, GG. Think about what you're saying. Be reasonable. I can't go back with you. I have commitments.'

'I know. I also know you'd rather stay here with your protégée than come home with me.'

He closed his eyes and rubbed his forehead. 'That's not true. But I have to. I'm her coach.'

'What about me? You're my coach too. Or have you forgotten that?'

'Samantha,' he said, taking my hands, 'I have to stay.'

'And I have to go,' I said, trying not to cry. 'I think it's over between us.'

'Gorgeous Girl, don't say that. You know it's not true.'

'It is. I've made up my mind.'

'It doesn't have to be like this, Sami. Forget about tennis. You and I love each other. We always have. We can still make it work, right?'

'No.'

'I've stood by you, loved you, looked after you. You've always been my number one. What about me? Are you saying you don't love me anymore?'

I couldn't speak.

'You at least owe me this much,' he said. 'Have you fallen out of love with me?'

'No, I just can't—'

'I love you, and I know you feel the same way about me,' he pleaded. 'I won't let you give up on us. Go back to Sydney if you must. Take a few days to recuperate, and when I get back, we'll take it from there.'

As soon as he left, I fell onto my bed, sobbing. Our relationship was over. I didn't want to think about the consequences, about what might happen in an hour, a week or a year after I'd closed the door on this part of my life. All I knew was that Bear and I had come to an end. I'd had enough. I'd lost a mother, a sister and, to all intents and purposes, my father. I had no family left, no one on my side but Bear. And now, for reasons I couldn't fully comprehend, I had shut him out as well.

Thirty-eight

Two days later, after a long, sleepless flight from London, I arrived in Sydney, relieved to be home. But it wasn't home anymore. Before I'd left for London, I'd been spending all my free time at Bear's. The plants on the veranda had survived, thanks to Violet's attention, but the rest of the apartment? Depressing and lonely.

I dropped my bags in my room, too listless to think about unpacking and walked back into the lounge. Framed on the wall were several press clippings, the highlights from Annie and my doubles career, and our Olympic gold medals. There'd be no more Olympic wins—any wins, for that matter. It was all in the past.

I slumped on the sofa and picked up a photo Zach had snapped of Bear and me. Bear was wearing a black tee-shirt and a cheeky grin. His arm was casually draped around my shoulders, and I was looking up at him, hair covering most of my face. I had the widest smile ever. Back then, I thought I'd explode with happiness. I didn't think it was possible to love Bear more than in that moment, but our love kept growing, deepening.

I put the photo down. I couldn't stand the pain of my own jealousy and paranoia. And I couldn't stand the thought of being hurt and abandoned again.

Meanwhile, Bear kept texting. *GG, I adore you. Couldn't love you more. Please don't shut me out of your life.*

But I did. I ignored every phone call, text and email.

For the next week, I stayed holed up in my apartment. I didn't ring Violet, and I ignored her when she phoned me. Finally, on the seventh day, I relented and texted her saying I was fine but needed space.

I also sent Bear an email, telling him that I'd always love him, but I needed time on my own to work through my feelings about Mum and Annie, and what, if anything, I was going to do with my life.

As soon as Bear arrived in Sydney, he came over, but I refused to see him.

'Samantha, you're being silly. Let me in,' he said from the other side of my locked front door. 'Darling, please. I love you.'

There was nothing he could say to change my mind. 'I've seen firsthand how love and romance can destroy a person,' I told him.

'That's crazy. You and I are nothing like Erik and Annie.'

I didn't want Bear to think he might have a second chance with me, that together we could weather this storm. I had to make a clean break.

I shut myself in the bathroom, ignoring his pleas to be let in.

Eventually he left, and I broke down again. I'd resisted a romance with Bear in the beginning because I valued his friendship too much. The way things stood now, not only was I losing my boyfriend, I was also saying goodbye to the second-best friend I'd ever had.

Thirty-nine

The banging on my front door seemed to go on forever, much to the annoyance of my elderly neighbour upstairs, who kept peering over the railing and tut-tutting at me slumped in a chair on the veranda.

Wearing flannelette pyjamas, looking emaciated, with dark rings under my eyes and much too pale skin, I finally walked inside and opened up.

It was Violet, with Hester strapped to her chest in her pouch. 'Samantha, what's happened?'

'I just...' I started crying. 'I give up.'

Inside the apartment, Violet marched into the kitchen and opened the fridge. 'What's this?' She held up a mouldy apple.

Not waiting for an answer, she threw the apple into the sink and strode into my bedroom. The shutters were closed, the bed unmade.

'What have you been doing?' she asked when I caught up with her.

'Sleeping ...or not sleeping. Mostly I stare up at the ceiling, crying.'

Violet hugged me. 'Darling, what are we going to do with you?'

'I don't want you to do anything. I want to be alone.'

'Sweetie, you're not answering phone calls or texts. You're not even emailing.'

'Because I want to be alone. I don't know what else to say to you, Vi.'

Violet pursed her lips. 'Clearly, you're not eating or taking care of yourself. I can't leave you. Come home with me.'

'Haven't you heard a word I've said? I'm not going anywhere. I want to be alone.' I raised my voice for emphasis.

Violet picked up a couple of DVDs from the sofa: *Lover Come Back* and *Pillow Talk*. 'Doris Day? Now you're really scaring me.'

'They were Mum's favourites.'

Violet sighed. 'I know. I watched them with her too.'

I stared out the window towards the harbour. 'Sometimes watching those movies was the only way to get her to smile.'

Violet dropped the DVDs on a side table. 'I'm really worried about you.'

'I'm okay, truly. I know I haven't been talking to anyone, but I promise I'm not going to do anything stupid. Yes, I'm feeling sorry for myself, but I'm not depressed—'

'Really? Are you sure? Because you sound like you're depressed.'

'I'm sure,' I said softening. 'I just need to process everything that's gone wrong. Make plans for a brand-new life.'

'How about you start by packing up Annie's things?' Violet said, heading towards Annie's room.

I stepped in front of her. 'I'd rather you didn't go in there.'

'Why?' Violet swept me aside and pushed the door open. 'I'm lost for words.' Newspaper articles covered every surface.

'I'm sorting through press clippings,' I explained.

'I can see that. Where'd you get them?'

'I save them, you know that.'

'Yes, but I thought you glued them into scrapbooks.'

'There are too many. I'm overwhelmed by all the stuff that's been written about us ...about me. Some of it's vile.' I picked up a clipping. 'Look what they said about Annie's breakdown and her backstabbing sister.' My hand trembled. 'Now I know what Annie was on about. It's an all-consuming beast. I can't leave the apartment.'

Violet took my hand and led me out of Annie's room, closing the door behind us. 'Please, darling, come over to our house. I'll cook you dinner. You can see the girls. They miss you so much.'

'No,' I said, louder than needed. 'I'm fine on my own. I don't want to leave. I feel safe here.'

'Okay, I'll come back tomorrow.'

'Please don't.'

'I have a key, remember?'

~ * ~

For the next four weeks, Violet and Hester came over every few days, bringing me groceries, sushi and fruit. Most of the food went uneaten. My eyes remained hollow, my skin sallow. My personality had completely vanished, except when I was holding Hester; it was hard to stay sad when holding a smiling, gurgling baby.

Still, no matter how much Violet cajoled, I wouldn't see or talk to Bear.

'He's heartbroken,' she said one afternoon when we were talking on the phone.

'Yeah.'

'Right,' she said. 'Time for a proper dose of reality. Remember how you used to invite friends home, hoping your mum would snap out of her depression and sometimes it worked, if only for a few hours?'

'Don't.' I started.

'Your mum would pull herself together and act like a normal, happy mother.'

'Yeah.'

'So, the big girls miss you. We'll all be over soon.'

'What? No! You can't.'

'I'm bringing them over, whether you like it or not.'

'I can't see anyone, not looking like this. I won't answer the door.'

'Then I'll use my key.'

'Violet, I don't believe you.'

'Believe me. We'll bring afternoon tea. You have one hour to tidy up.'

An hour later, Violet knocked on my door. I answered it before my upstairs neighbour had time to complain.

'We missed you so much,' Poppy squealed, squeezing me tight.

'I missed you too,' I whispered.

'Welcome back to the land of the living, honey,' Violet said, laying out a range of cupcakes and slices.

'Thanks for dragging me back.'

'You'd do the same for me.'

When the girls were in the kitchen making drinks, Violet took my hand. 'You look good.'

'I don't, but thanks. There was no way I could let Ava and Poppy see me looking haggard and sad. I looked exactly like Mum not long before she disappeared. I forced myself to shower, dress and clean up. I'm exhausted.'

'The place smells good.'

'Thank Coco Chanel.'

For the next hour, I caught up on Poppy and Ava's news, drank tea and even ate cake. Then, while the girls tidied up and washed dishes in the kitchen, Violet and I moved to the patio.

'I feel okay now, Vi.' I was staring at Hester, gurgling in my arms. 'But there was a moment...'

'Yes?'

'When I thought maybe I could end it, that maybe I was doomed. Destined to repeat history.'

'Please don't say that.'

'I'll be all right. Really, I will. I'm just saying that I can understand how a momentary lapse in rational thinking could spiral a person. I think I understand now why Annie did what she did. Rational thoughts don't come into play when you're feeling so lost and alone.'

'Okay,' Violet said cautiously. 'What happens now?'

'Well,' I cleared my throat. 'I quite like the idea of coaching.'

'That's a fantastic idea. You used to mentor younger players at your tennis club when you first started playing and only gave it up when you got too busy with the pro circuit.'

'Yeah. Maybe I could. I'm thinking about coaching kids. Starting afresh. Kids are so full of life and optimism, hope.'

'Any ideas where to start? Your old club maybe?'

'I haven't given it a lot of thought, but I think I need a clean break. Maybe even interstate. Who knows?'

'I'd be devastated if you moved interstate, but it's promising you're focusing on something new rather than mulling over the past.'

Forty

After that pivotal conversation with Violet, I set about turning my life around, determined to get my act together. It was tough starting again, and I needed something to occupy myself. I'd travelled enough on the tennis circuit, so that didn't interest me. A couple of publishing houses had approached me about writing my autobiography, but I wasn't ready to tell my life story. Maybe in thirty years.

But coaching kids? That could work. Plus, I needed income. My final endorsement royalties had ceased, and I still had bills to pay.

Along with the job interviews came the inevitable grilling about why I was no longer playing professionally. I was reasonably honest but kept my real demons to myself. I hadn't heard a word from Annie, although she sent occasional postcards to Violet; and I hadn't spoken to Bear for months. I still didn't really understand why I'd left him. I loved him, but when he kept texting me, it took me back to that awful place of hopelessness and fear. *Sami, talk to me. I love you. We can work this out.*

No, we couldn't. Why did he keep coming after me? I was cruel, but I couldn't help myself. I wanted to be alone.

When I was offered a three-month contract at Melbourne Girls Grammar starting in the new year, I didn't hesitate.

'Congratulations,' Violet said when I told her. 'You need to get out of Sydney. A fresh start will help put some distance between you and what's happened.'

She was right. 'I'm looking forward to it. 'Anyway, the position's temporary. Three months tops while the regular coach takes maternity leave.'

Clearing out our Sydney apartment was excruciating. I boxed-up Annie's possessions—shoes we'd bought together in London, art books she'd purchased in Paris, scarves, bags, trophies—all headed for storage.

This was me, Samantha Callahan, giving up, admitting defeat, admitting I had no control over any other being in the universe but myself. As much as I tried to be brave, I wondered whether I'd always feel the gaping hole in my world that Annie used to fill. At least nowadays when I cried, I could control my tears and sadness so they didn't lead to a panic attack, but I was still heartbroken.

I wondered what Annie was doing in India, if she was still there, and how she was faring. I hoped she was in a good place emotionally. I'd stopped thinking that she might be dead. I had to believe she was living and enjoying her life. At least now I could understand why she had needed to get away after her overdose, but part of me was angry she'd severed contact.

When I wasn't thinking about Annie, my thoughts turned to Bear. I wasn't completely numb to the fact that what Annie had done to me, I was doing to him. Shutting him out of my life.

Other than Violet, I didn't tell anyone but Dad where I was going. I was surprised when he invited me to spend Christmas with him, Melissa and the boys in Albury.

Christmas Day was difficult. Not only did Dad not mention my mother, but no one talked about Annie. She was like a ghost at the dining table. I kept expecting her to call or turn up. Late in the day, I checked my phone. There were messages from Violet and the girls, also from Bear. I knew I wouldn't return his call. It was still too painful.

Forty-one

In January, I moved into a sunny apartment near St Kilda beach, and soon after, I started coaching part-time at Melbourne Girls Grammar. It was hard in the beginning. The first few weeks, I worried that the girls were bitching behind my back, calling me a loser. In reality, they couldn't have been nicer, though I hadn't figured on them asking so many questions, not just about the game but about all the players on tour. They were eternally fascinated, so at the end of every session, I'd tell them a funny story about one of my ex-competitors.

Six months later, when Wimbledon rolled around again, I was 17,000 kilometres from the strawberries and cream of the All England Club, still teaching primary school tennis. The teacher who'd gone on maternity leave had decided to take the whole year off, and the principal had asked me to stay on. I was thrilled. I loved coaching. When I took the job, it was a diversion and I needed a different life, but now I was hooked. The girls were eager to learn and improve—happy, enthusiastic and full of hope for the future. I got caught up caring for them as individuals rather than as tennis players in need of improvement. They reminded me of what I'd been like at twelve.

The job kept me busy, and I had little time to think about myself, even if I'd wanted to wallow in what could or should have been. I tried not to think about who I used to be, though it was hard when the Grand Slams were on. Sometimes, I wished I were back in the thick of it, playing against the likes of Lucia Landry and Debby Bowden. But those moments were fleeting.

Occasionally, the girls quizzed me. 'Do you think you'll make a comeback, Miss?'

'We'll see,' I'd reply.

The kids usually left it at that, but the parents were harder to deal with. If I could have spent all my time with the girls and not had to interact with parents ...but you can't pick and choose. You take the good with the bad, the laughter with the tears.

The girls played the game because they loved it (or their best friend did) for the pure joy of hitting the ball over the net. That was their accomplishment. They helped me regain some of my love of tennis; it was magic hearing them laugh when they played. Maybe none of them would make it to the Olympics, but they were having fun and so was I.

A year after making the move, I was finally starting to feel good about myself. I had no injuries and had even put on five kilos—mostly due to my obsession with almond croissants—and had an adequate social life based around the school staff and a couple of friends in my apartment block.

I lived frugally. The money I earnt was spent on rent, food and the occasional restaurant meal. I hadn't bought any new clothes in eighteen months except for a tennis dress and tennis shoes. Not that I'd been a clothes horse back in the day, anyway.

Meanwhile, my apartment in Mosman had been rented out and the long-term tenants were happy. It was an easy, stress-free existence.

It helped that I'd been seeing a counsellor. She'd advised me to write down everything I was feeling after Annie left and I broke up with Bear. I'd started writing letters to Annie, telling her what I was up to in Melbourne and about the girls I was coaching. Of course, I never sent them—I didn't have an address. But I wrote pages and stuck them in my desk drawer. Afterwards, I always breathed easier, like I was ready to face whatever obstacles or opportunities lay ahead.

~ * ~

Mid-January, in school holidays, I took my notepad to one of my favourite cafes not far from Rod Laver Arena, where they baked the most amazing almond croissants. Sitting at an outside table in the sunshine, sipping my cappuccino and enjoying the scenery, I had no complaints. Yes, I could have gone to the Whitsundays to escape the hoopla of the forthcoming Australian Open, but Melbourne was my home now. I couldn't leave every time a tennis tournament was being played. I hadn't gone so far as to buy tickets, but I could feel the vibe. Thankfully, I wasn't having heart palpitations. Not yet anyway. Perhaps enough time had passed that I could be impartial. These days, I could even read the sports pages and Prue Hamilton's comment of the day without thinking *what if?*

A couple of guys strode past wearing sports gear and holding racquet bags and my body tensed. Slightly, but it was there. Maybe I should have gone to the Whitsundays, after all.

'I don't believe it! Samantha Callahan.'

I looked up from my coffee into the direct sunlight. 'Zach?'

'How the hell are you?'

I stood and we hugged. 'I'm fine,' I said, immediately self-conscious, crossing my arms to stop my hands from shaking.

He gestured to the spare chair beside me. 'May I?'

We caught up with what the other had been up to: me, moving to Melbourne and teaching tennis at a posh girls school;

him, still on the circuit and still seeing Tina, the photographer I'd met briefly at his first exhibition.

'My first serious adult relationship.' He winked.

'Well done, you. I saw your handiwork in last weekend's papers. The photos of Sinner are brilliant.'

'Keeps me off the streets,' Zach said, as he accepted a coffee and bagel from our waiter. 'I've also been doing a lot more non-tennis photography.'

'I'd love to see them,' I said, remembering the gorgeous photo of Annie he'd given me, which was now packed away in storage with other memorabilia from the apartment.

'Really? I just happen to have a few.' Zach pulled out his camera, switched it on and started clicking through, with me looking on beside him. 'I've been shooting kids at the local skateboard park. Not literally.'

'Wow,' I said, impressed. 'You've got some great aerial action shots.'

'Thanks.' He turned off the camera, set it on the table and picked up his coffee. 'Let's get it over with, shall we? I'm assuming there's still no word from Annie? The last rumour I heard was that she was living in an ashram in India.'

I blinked slowly. 'She could be anywhere, doing anything. But yes, the last postcard Vi received was from India. All I know is that she's not here.' One of Dad's friends knew 'for a fact' that she'd bought a yacht, a Catalina 27, and was sailing around the Greek Islands. That was my favourite scenario.

'You must wonder...'

'All the time. I used to look for her everywhere, hoping ...but these days I try not to dwell on it.'

'Me too.' Zach drained his cup. 'One day she'll turn up and when she does ...well, who knows how we'll all react?'

I heard someone call my name and turned. It was Marta Kubot, the woman who'd annihilated me at Wimbledon in the last match I'd played. She still looked twelve.

'Marta, it's good to see you,' I lied.

'I am glad to find you. You disappeared after we played.'

'Yes, I had a break.'

'And now?'

'Still on a break.'

'Samantha was one of the best,' Zach said. 'Still could be.'

'I remember now,' Marta said. 'You freaked out after your sister quit.'

'I didn't exactly freak out,' I said, my temper rising. 'I'd just had enough of the relentless practice, the uncertainty of the game.'

'Samantha Callahan! What the fig is your story these days?' another voice said with an unmistakable Texan drawl. Kristy Banta.

'Kristy, good to see you again.' I turned to Zach. 'You'd never know the Australian Open was about to start.'

'You know, I freakin' love Australia,' Kristy said. 'The beaches, the weather. Whatever happened to Annie? I hear she's become a wild-haired recluse who surrounds herself with huge tanks of spiders and snakes, and breeds rats and mice to feed them.'

Highly unlikely. Annie hated snakes. The only time she'd ever laid eyes on a live one was as a ten-year-old when Dad took us to a reptile park. She'd had nightmares for weeks after touching the scaly skin of the boa constrictor.

'Didn't she sail off in a boat somewhere?' Marta chimed in.

'I don't think she'd buy a boat,' Zach said, genuinely puzzled. He looked at me. 'Would she?'

'Did you hear?' Kristy said. 'Thanks to last week's win, I'm now ranked sixth in the world.'

Not a bad effort, I thought, mentally pinching myself. The last time I'd competed against Kristy was at the Australian Open two years ago, when Courtney and I had demolished her and Yasmine Le Bluth. Well, maybe not demolished, but we'd won.

'And you?' she continued.

'Coaching.'

'How fantastic. Would I know the player?'

'Probably not.'

I imagined telling Kristy and Marta that I spent my afternoons teaching a bunch of schoolgirls the correct forehand grip.

Marta and Kristy left, and shortly after, an attractive woman with blonde hair and green eyes flounced past. She waved at Zach and walked inside the cafe. Around us, customers stared after her. She was hard not to notice, given that she was approximately five-foot-ten and sporting a citrus green headscarf with orange polka dots.

'Who's that?' I asked Zach.

'Dionne Leon, Scandinavian goddess.'

I hadn't played her, but I'd heard of her. She was competing in junior tournaments when Annie and I were on the circuit.

Zack poked my arm. 'Check out her hands. She moonlights as a model for Rolex back home in Sweden.'

I glanced down at my fingers—the manicure I'd had a couple of days ago was already chipping. I doubted they'd have what it took to become independent models.

'What do you think about mine?' Zach said, holding up his nicotine-stained fingers.

'Your nails are okay,' I said, trying not to get too close. 'A tad yellow. You smoking again?'

'Afraid so.'

I didn't push it. 'So, what's Dionne's story besides having great limbs?'

'You heard about the huge scandal she caused last year in Florida?'

'No. Tell me.'

'She was caught by team officials drinking with line umpires at a Miami nightclub at three in the morning. She had a game the following day.'

'Sounds like a Courtney Gold trick,' I said.

'She was cautioned, but amazingly she won her match, though there were loud whispers that several dubious line calls went her way. Then last week in Adelaide, at the lead-up tournament, she was snapped in the toilets of a two-bit pub with a guy. Some desperado followed them into the women's toilet and poked his camera phone under the cubicle door. Apparently, they weren't doing anything, but unluckily for Dio, she wasn't wearing underwear.'

'And the photos were published?'

'Yeah, blurry and you could argue it wasn't her, but there was no mistaking those hands. Dio's no shrinking violet. Tennis got her where she is, but now she's making a name for herself pursuing other ventures. The game's become almost secondary.'

'So, she'll have a life after tennis?'

'You bet.' Zach stared admiringly as Dionne sauntered out of the cafe holding a jumbo cappuccino.

Of course, she'd have a life after tennis, I thought. She was drop-dead gorgeous. Unlike me, who didn't have the gorgeous face, the gorgeous hands, or the notoriety. But would I want all that? I'd hate to be papped in a public toilet with a guy I'd just met.

'How about the others?' I asked Zach. 'What's happening with Courtney?'

He dragged his gaze away from Dionne. 'She's all washed-up. You heard she raced off and married some guy twice her age?'

'Vaguely. Bet her father was happy about that.'

'It lasted five weeks, and since then, she's been on a downward spiral, drinking, putting on a massive amount of weight.'

'Ouch. That's got to hurt. I feel sorry for her.'

'Self-inflicted, unfortunately.'

'Is Netta still with Suzy Gardner?'

'Oh, that? There was nothing to it. Suzy wanted to break up with Cindi and couldn't find a nice way, so pretended she was on with Netta. Netta was angry with Lucia. You know how it is.'

'And Lucia?'

'These days she plays in exhibition tournaments. She's a major reality star in France, getting her tits out for the world to see.'

'The things you miss when you're out of the loop.'

'Indeed.' Zach checked his watch and stood up. 'Darl, so good to see you. I've missed you. Any chance you'll come to the Open? I can get you tickets.'

'Thanks, but no.'

'Gala party?'

I thought about the dozens of gala parties Annie and I had been to over the years. They were much more Annie's thing than mine, especially the all-singing and dancing extravaganza that kicked off the Australian Open. Like the time Jelena Tipsarević wore blue ten-centimetre heels and a black micro minidress. Annie and I had giggled as she struggled to climb out from the yellow Lamborghini she'd arrived in without showing her underwear. 'At least she's wearing some,' Annie had said.

'Again, no,' I told Zach. 'But thank you.'

I watched him amble down the street, his limp only slightly discernible. He'd reinvented himself after tennis, first with his tennis shots and now his street photography. Maybe there was hope for me, too.

I didn't ask him about Bear, though he was on my mind the entire conversation. No doubt he was in Melbourne, too, coaching Katie Durak and other talented young players.

Forty-two

Back home, I finished my weekly letter to Annie, filling her in on my encounter with Zach. Usually, my letters bordered on dull, but at least this one had a little gossip. I folded the A4 piece of paper, grabbed a plain envelope, stuffed the letter inside and sealed it. I wrote 'Annie 47' in small letters in the right-hand side of the envelope and dropped it in the bottom drawer of my desk. It was practically overflowing with the dozens of letters I'd written since she'd left.

I hated to admit it but seeing Zach had left me feeling raw and grief welled up again. Living in my bubble, teaching tennis to schoolkids, I could forget my old life ever happened, the good and the bad. But seeing Zach and those women had made it all too real. Thinking about Bear, Annie ...I wasn't as resilient as I'd thought. I really didn't want to waltz down memory lane picking at the scab that was once my glorious career.

Nothing lasted forever. Nothing was permanent. One minute I'd been a rising tennis star being feted at all the best parties in New York, playing at Wimbledon ...the next, I was nothing, a has-been. I couldn't help but think, what the hell went wrong? My mental health and stability for one.

To stem the flow of negative thoughts, I put on my sneakers and exercise gear and went for a run along my favourite route...through the Botanical Gardens, across to Luna Park, and then over to the foreshore. Today, the beachfront was looking particularly spectacular. Finally, my head cleared, and positivity and energy returned.

I'd been running for close to forty-five minutes by the time I turned the corner near my apartment. Someone was sitting on the front steps outside my building. At first glance, I could have sworn it was Annie, but I'd made that mistake before.

I slowed to a jog, my eyes widening as I got closer.

It really was her.

I sped up again, only stopping when I was half a metre in front of her, my legs almost buckling.

'Annie?' I whispered her name.

'Hey, stranger. Surprised?'

She stood up and I wrapped my arms around her, then stepped back. 'Annie ...what are you doing here? What...'

I dropped my arms, then hugged her again, afraid to let go lest she disappear. I had so many questions—questions that had been rolling around my head for the better part of two-and-a-half years—but it was impossible to get the words out. I couldn't believe she was standing in front of me on my doorstep. She looked lovely, ethereal. She wasn't wearing make-up and her skin was smooth, ageless. But she was wearing long flowing robes, *beige* robes, and carrying a backpack. And then there were the open toed gladiator sandal things she was wearing on her feet.

'Come in, come in,' I said, tripping over myself as I pulled her inside. 'Tell me, where the bloody hell have you been?'

'Settle down, Sam,' she said calmly. 'I know it must come as a shock.'

No kidding! Of the two of us, Annie had always been the more stylish, but right now she looked like she'd strolled straight off the set of *Little House on the Prairie*.

'I needed to get away,' she said.

'Congratulations, you achieved your goal,' I said, pacing the living room. 'Are you okay? You're not sick, are you?' Fleetingly, it occurred to me that she'd come back because she was dangerously ill, about to drop dead.

'I'm perfectly fine. I just thought it was time.'

'Time for what?'

Annie yawned and took in the room. She flopped down on the sofa and patted it. 'Nice. I'm glad you kept old faithful.'

I sat next to her, still not quite believing she was here. I should have been furious for all the angst she'd caused, but I wasn't. Not yet. I couldn't be, not until I knew she was okay.

'Have you only just arrived back?'

Where was she staying? Did she have a boyfriend? Someone she'd met on her travels? I assumed from her filthy well-worn backpack that she'd done considerable travelling.

'A couple of hours ago. I got your address from Violet and, voilà.'

'Is that all you've got to say?'

Anger rose, so I retreated to the kitchen and made her a chamomile tea. When I walked back into the room, I said, 'Annie, where have you been all this time?'

'I'll tell you everything, but first I need to tell you about the tennis—'

'Speaking of tennis, I ran into Zach today,' I cut in.

Annie raised her eyebrows.

'He's in town for the Open. It starts Monday.'

'I know,' she replied, bleary eyed. 'That's what I need to tell you, Sam. I got a wildcard entry. I'm playing.'

'You're what?' I was on the verge of hyperventilating. I was seeing spots and my breathing was erratic. 'You're—' I struggled to get the words out. '—playing in the Australian Open? In four days?'

'Isn't it incredible? I just found out I've been picked.'

'I don't believe it.' My throat was dry from panicked breaths. 'How? Have you trained? I thought you were done playing professional tennis?' So many questions.

I was furious. Annie playing professional tennis again? She was simply going to pick up from where she'd left off?

As she drank her tea, Annie kept dozing off. It was clear I wasn't going to get any answers. I stood and made up the futon in the spare room, gave her a couple of towels, and a pair of pyjamas and let her be. As long as she didn't run away again, there'd be plenty of time to prod her until she told me everything.

When I poked my head in a short time later, she was asleep. I pulled the blind down and tiptoed out.

~ * ~

I phoned Violet. 'Who does she think she is, waltzing in here after being away for so long?'

'I only found out when she texted me from the Melbourne Airport,' Violet said. 'There was no hint in her last postcard she was coming back.'

'Five minutes after arriving, she tells me she's playing at the Open,' I raged. 'I feel betrayed and cheated.'

'I'm sure she has her reasons, Sami.'

'It's not just that she's playing tennis, it's that she's come back into my life like we saw each other yesterday. How could she leave me for so long without any contact, and then just turn up like that?'

'Well, if you'd let me speak,' Violet said.

I inhaled. 'Yes?'

Violet was quiet a moment. 'Okay, it's bad form.'

'Bad form? It's appalling. I hate her.'

'No you don't. You're in shock.'

~ * ~

Annie slept through the afternoon and into the night. Cocooned in my own bed, I raked over her revelation. She'd always been the calmer one, but there seemed to be this other aura around her now too. It was hard to put my finger on. A sense of deep confidence, maybe? Mental strength? Resilience?

Even though I hated her for the pain she'd caused me, I didn't want to lose Annie again. I wanted to protect her, make sure she was looked after and fed, happy and comfortable. I knew the foods she liked—guacamole, lamb chops and tomatoes—and those she hated—cheese, cauliflower and kiwi fruit. But another part of me wanted to hit her over the head with my sturdy steel frying pan and tie her to the fridge so she'd never leave me again.

Forty-three

The next morning, I was woken by a buzzing, as if swarms of mosquitoes had invaded my bedroom. I pulled the sheet further over my head, but the buzzing persisted. It stopped, and then started agai ...stopped and started. I stuck my head out and glanced at the clock on my bedside table: four-twenty.

I couldn't go back to sleep, so I got up and turned on the light. The noise intensified as I reached for the door handle. The bloody fridge must be having a breakdown. I opened the door and peered into the living room and there was Annie, sitting cross-legged in pale blue pyjamas and chanting.

'Annie?'

She didn't hear me, so with some trepidation, I moved closer. Maybe she was in a demonic trance.

'Annie!' I tapped her on the shoulder.

She opened one eye, then the other and looked up at me, her calm face devoid of expression.

'What are you doing? It's the middle of the night.'

'Meditating.'

'Is that what you call it? I thought the cat was being strangled. And I don't own a cat.'

'Did I wake you? This is the best time. Before the sun rises. A couple of hours of this and I'm good for the day.'

'A couple of hours of what, exactly?'

'Communing with my guru, centring my core, finding my inner peace.'

'I'm tired and in shock. Could we save this chat until daylight, say in four or five hours?'

Annie stared at me as though I were speaking a foreign language, then closed her eyes and quickly opened them again. 'Of course.' She stood up, stretched and retreated into her room.

I spent the next few hours staring into darkness, sleep eluding me. Feeling wretched, I finally ventured into the kitchen at eight a.m.

'Did I disturb you again?' Annie asked brightly.

'No, I was awake.'

'Excellent. I found some peppermint tea. Come and share a pot with me.'

'Thanks, but I think I'll go for coffee this morning, a strong one.'

'I've missed this,' she said, once we were sitting on the sofa with our full mugs.

I wanted to scream– *'If you missed it so much, why the hell didn't you come back or at least tell me where you were?'*

I didn't. Instead, I took a deep breath, exhaled and said, 'So have I. There were many times when I thought we'd never sit like this ever again.' I took a moment to gather my thoughts. 'I know you promised me you'd never harm yourself again, but Annie, imagine being me.'

'I don't know–'

'Please listen. Imagine being in my shoes, never knowing if you were dead or alive, always wondering, worrying.'

Annie fidgeted and rubbed the back of her neck.

'I really want to understand why you stayed away so long.'

'It was a difficult time for me,' she began.

'Really?' I couldn't stop myself. 'I'm your sister.'

'Yeah, and I'm sorry for everything,' she said. 'But after Erik, I needed to leave and try to find myself.'

'You disappear for two-and-a-half years, and then turn up on my doorstep and tell me you're competing in the Australian Open. You say everything's fine, and I'm supposed to be okay with that?'

'Sorry, but everything *is* fine. I was on a personal journey, and I couldn't come back until I'd finished. If I'd spoken to you, I'd have been tempted to come home and abandon my path.'

'What about me? Do you care about my personal journey? And what the hell kind of journey were you on that you couldn't call or text?'

'I wanted to, really. But the longer I went without contacting you, the harder it became. Not to mention that communication's difficult in remote India at the best of times.'

'You were in India?' I didn't want to give her the satisfaction of telling her I knew where she was because of the postcards she'd sent Violet.

'Didn't I mention that?'

'No, you left that part out,' I said sarcastically.

'Well, yes, I was in India mostly.'

I struggled to remain calm. 'What did you do all that time?'

'Meditated, prayed, practiced yoga, read books.'

I tried to remain engaged. If there were two things I couldn't stand, it was meditation and yoga. My brain was too cbaotic to attempt them.

'I had to do it for myself, for my emotional sanity,' Annie went on. 'And I didn't want to be talked out of it. I needed to concentrate on myself, without any more guilt than I already had about leaving you.'

'And now you're done?'

'I think so.'

'What did you do besides meditate?' I asked, keeping my voice even, although I wanted to explode. 'And where did you do it?'

'I found an ashram, checked in for six weeks and stayed over two years.'

'And you meditated and prayed,' I could barely cough out the words, 'all day?'

'Yeah, usually from three-thirty in the morning.'

'Couldn't you escape?'

'It wasn't prison, Samantha. There was a village nearby, but it was hardly exciting. It took all of ten minutes to hike around. It was so tiny... and there were always lots of cows lolling about, particularly in the middle of the road. I'd maybe buy a banana, then walk back to the ashram and do my daily chores—'

'Chores? Like what?'

'Working in the kitchen, scrubbing floors, cleaning bathrooms. Whatever needed doing.'

'And then?'

'I'd meditate some more.'

'For two years you did this?' I was hurt and confused. 'Didn't you miss me?'

'Of course, but like I told you, I needed to get away from everything and everyone.'

As much as I didn't want to admit it, I understood; that's exactly what I'd done. I'd dropped Bear because of my need to get away from him and all the associated connections with tennis.

Still, I plundered on. 'I thought you meant for a couple of weeks or a month.' I stared at the ground, not daring to speak again until my temper was under control. 'Annie, you were gone for two-and-a-half years, and during that time you didn't call me once. Every time I had an unknown call, I wondered whether it was someone ringing to tell me you were dead. Do you understand?'

Annie closed her eyes, her expression pained.

'Look at me. How could you do that? We're sisters. Best friends.'

She opened her eyes. 'I know.'

'So, who did you talk to?'

'Other people at the ashram, visitors, monks ...I was only meant to stay a few weeks, but when my time was up, I wasn't ready to leave. I cried and agonised and cried some more until it became clear to me.'

'What became clear?'

'That I was there for a reason. I started volunteering at a local orphanage, and when I checked my calendar again, another ten months had passed, then another six months.'

'What did you do?'

'At the orphanage? Taught English mostly, helped teach kids about health and hygiene. You should have seen them, Sami. They're so little and were so grateful. Makes me cry just thinking about them. We'd spend afternoons playing games like cricket and tennis. I'd hit balls against a brick wall, have fun with them. It was then I fell back into tennis and started practicing. All the time.

'Some of the older kids were seriously talented, but they have no opportunities. I got caught up in their lives and was able to let go of all the bad stuff that happened back here and the selfish way I'd been living my life. I was helping destitute kids who had no parents to love and look after them.'

I wasn't about to be sucked in. 'And when you weren't looking after orphans, you were praying and meditating?'

'Is that so hard to believe?'

'Yes, actually it is.'

'I prayed for you, Sami.'

My head was about to explode. 'Thanks.'

'Seriously, I did. I thought about you every day.'

'I appreciate that, Annie, but a letter or a quick email? A phone call wouldn't have gone astray. Even a postcard now and then. Because here's the thing: I didn't receive the cosmic messages you were sending me.'

'I sent you a postcard.'

'One. After that, nothing.'

'I'm sorry you felt neglected—'

'Neglected? What about all the worry and angst you put me through?'

'I didn't ask you to worry about me.'

'How could I not? You're my sister. We were a team.'

'We still are a team, Sam. We'll always be a team, but sometimes you've just got to believe.'

'In what?' I wanted to scream. Before she'd run away, Annie didn't chant or pray or commune with her guru. Okay, towards the end she'd hummed, but I'd put it down to nerves—and Erik. But now, I just wanted my sister back the way she was before.

'Sam, I'm truly sorry for what I put you through. I was only thinking about myself, and it was selfish and wrong of me. There were many times I thought I was doing the wrong thing and cried to come home. India's so poor, there are beggars everywhere, but there's a lot of beauty and serenity as well. And the kids were so delightful and loving. I knew I couldn't come back until I'd found what I was looking for.'

'I missed you,' I said, tearing up. 'I had no idea if you'd ever come home. It was the worst time of my life.'

Annie squeezed my hand. 'I know.'

We sat in silence for a few minutes and ate. I accepted that she was sorry, but now she was back from the wilderness and staying with me, all that hurt and betrayal bubbled under the surface.

'So, are you a vegetarian now?' I said in an attempt to lighten the tone.

'Vegan. I don't do dairy.' There was a long pause, then she said, 'Of course I'm not a vegan! I am trying to stick to a mostly vego diet, though.'

I was still too rattled to appreciate the humour. 'What about shopping?'

'I haven't renounced all worldly delights.'

'And what's with getting up at four in the morning? Not even Olympic swimmers get up that early.'

'It's when I'm at one with the universe.'

I held back a snort. 'And?'

Annie cleared her throat. 'Every day, I asked myself what I wanted to do with my life and finally the answer came to me.'

'And?' Getting Annie to talk straight was like pulling teeth.

'Isn't it obvious? I want to play tennis again, to play the best I can. I owe it to myself.

And continue with the chanting while she was at it? I couldn't imagine a more ridiculous pairing: the inner peace of meditation versus the cut-throat competitive bitchiness of tennis.

Annie took herself off for a shower, and twenty minutes later, having washed and tamed her hair, she looked like her old self, dressed in sports shorts and a blue polo.

'I haven't even asked about you,' Annie said. 'Melbourne, hey?'

'Yeah, the move was a bit rash, but I didn't want to stay in our apartment in Sydney. It's rented out to a very nice couple, by the way.'

'Glad to hear it.'

'I was really torn moving interstate away from Violet and her family, but I thought a change of scenery would be good for me, and then I was offered the coaching job at Melbourne Girls Grammar.'

'Because professional tennis...'

'Didn't work out the way I expected.'

'Tell me about Bear. I heard—'

'We got together after you left.'

Annie squealed. 'See, my leaving had some positives. I always knew you two belonged together.'

'We broke up.'

'What happened?'

'Let's see. Long story short: after you left, Bear and I got together. I carried on playing but I'd lost the drive, that killer passion. Bear was patient and tried really hard to keep me focused, but...'

'But?'

'I was tired. My body ached. I bailed. End of story. And when I quit, Bear and I broke up. On the upside, I got to sleep in for the first time in years.'

'Do you keep in touch?'

'Nope.'

'That's it?'

'Pretty much.'

It was all I was willing to give. I didn't want to talk about Bear.

'Wow. I'm really sad it didn't work out,' Annie said.

I waved her words away. 'Tell me about the Open.'

'They're making the announcement tonight at the gala party.'

'You're going?'

'I want to, but I can't go by myself.' She toyed with her empty teacup. 'Will you come?'

I suddenly felt dizzy and rubbed my neck, trying to shift the rising nausea. 'No way. You don't need me holding your hand.'

I was still angry. This was all about Annie. I didn't know why I was so surprised. After all, she was the one who'd dumped me and left the game. And now she'd materialised out of nowhere to hit up with the big league in the Australian Open singles comp. Meanwhile, I was a has-been nothing, who was expected to drop my new life and fit in with hers.

Annie sighed. 'I do, Sam. I really do.'

'Why would I torture myself by returning to a world where humiliation and I were best friends? And I've already told you I'm not in contact with Bear.'

'So, this is about him?'

Of course not.'

'It'll be hard for both of us, which is why we should do it together.'

'No,' I said, checking my Fitbit. It was ten a.m. The party would be underway in less than eight hours.

'Please! I need you, Sami. Can you help me out this one last time?'

I turned on her. 'You dumped me and ran away, and I had to struggle through on my own until I could no longer take it. I'm the laughing stock of the tennis world. There's no way I can face all those people again. I just can't.'

Forty-four

I couldn't sit still in the cab. I kept crossing and uncrossing my arms and checking my lipstick in my hand mirror. My stomach gurgled and bulged. I could see the movement through my black jersey dress, which accentuated my generous thighs way too much and my barely-there breasts not nearly enough. My head ached.

'What's up?' Annie said, looking serene.

'Nervous. Why aren't you?'

'Believe me, I am.'

'I'm dreading it,' I said, fidgeting some more.

'Samantha,' Annie said, 'I'm sorry I left the way I did. I really am.'

I stared down at my nails. Annie was back and I couldn't believe it. Nor could I believe she was about to play in the Australian Open. I didn't want to be here; I dreaded the idea of reliving those painful memories, but in the end, I'd said yes. Annie was my sister, and she needed me.

I reached up and touched my emerald earrings. Tonight, I was going to have to face Netta, Jelena, Lucia...and Bear. The last time I'd seen most of them was at Wimbledon over eighteen long months ago. I couldn't think about them without remembering what a disaster it had been for me. Humiliating. Then I thought about Annie and how she'd quit, how Erik had destroyed her game, her concentration, her desire to win. How many times had I said to her, 'With tennis, you've got to give one hundred and ten per cent, and even then, it's often not enough. You've got to have drive, courage and determination.'

Annie nudged me. 'We're here.'

I looked out at the City Casino and my stomach lurched. I saw several familiar faces—people who'd been whacking balls at me for years—and for a moment, I missed the game, missed the thrill, the rush of playing in front of a home crowd, being on centre court and hearing the roar of the fans. Such conflicting emotions ...I gasped, heading towards a full-scale panic attack.

'Annie, I don't think I can.'

'Breathe,' she told me. 'Breathe.'

I watched as a procession of glamorous women arrived wearing slinky evening gowns that showed off their athletic frames to perfection. By comparison, I looked like I was heading to the local pizza joint. My hair, a messy up-do, was already falling around my ears. I closed my eyes. How could I face these people again? What was I thinking? I was terrified. 'I've...ah...changed my mind. I want to go home.'

The passenger door opened and suddenly Zach's face was centimetres from mine, beaming a mega-watt smile. 'Hey, you!' Then he saw Annie. 'My God, is it really you? Is this really Annie Callahan I see before me?'

We climbed out of the taxi and the three of us clumsily embraced before Zach took our hands and led Annie and me through the casino foyer towards the ballroom. As he stopped to acknowledge friends along the way, I became even more uncomfortable, aware of the growing number of eyes staring at us.

'Annie,' I hissed. 'You okay?'

She smiled.

Vera Zvonareva, the second-seeded Russian said, 'Didn't you used to be—'

'Annie Callahan,' Annie said brightly.

As we entered the ballroom, a stunned silence filled the room, like a scene from a movie when the hero (or villain) appears, all action stops, the music fades, the chatter ceases. Four hundred and fifty pairs of eyes were upon us right now.

Sensing the awkwardness, most people turned away and pretended to return to their animated chatter. They weren't fooling me. I was confident no one would remember what they'd been talking about before Annie arrived. They were all too busy pretending not to listen in, pretending not to notice Annie or care, when in reality every ear and eye in the room was strained towards us, desperately trying to figure out what the hell was going on.

'This was a mistake,' I said, my voice scratchy. 'I think I'm going to be sick.'

'Hey,' Annie replied in a low voice. 'That's not the Samantha Callahan I know. The Samantha I know would eat these people for breakfast. She could face up to anyone on or off the court.'

'Times have changed. I'm not the person I used to be. I shouldn't have come. It's all too much.'

Zach guided us through the thickening crowd. Wherever I looked, I saw life-sized posters of past, present and future tennis stars hung on the numerous pillars and walls. Huge posters featuring Slazenger and Rolex advertisements swayed impressively from the ceiling. The room was filling quickly, and a low-grade buzz vibrated in the air. People like Yasmine Le Bluth and Molly Fischer might have been enemies on the court, but here, it was all laughter and conviviality.

People crowded around Annie, pushing me aside. I was looking wistfully towards the exit when Bear appeared in front of me. With Katie Durak.

'Samantha!' he said, looking truly dumbfounded. 'I didn't expect to see you here tonight.'

'No, I guess not,' I replied.

Katie moved away to talk to some other players, and Bear and I stood together in awkward silence, slyly looking each other up and down. He still had a great physique, as well as a full head of dark wavy hair and healthy tanned skin. He looked good, handsome. Perhaps a few new wrinkles around the eyes, but let's not quibble. Digging my right nails into the palm of my left hand, I gave myself a talking-to. *Pull yourself together.*

'It's good to see you, GG.'

My bottom lip quivered. 'Yeah, you too.' I'd be lying if I said my heart didn't almost explode out of my chest when he called me GG. 'Are you guys together now?' I asked, glancing towards Katie.

Bear looked horrified. 'Of course not. I told you years ago, she's like a niece to me. And for your information, I no longer coach her. She lives in Florida now, but I keep an eye on her at social events for her parents' sake.'

'Oh.'

'What are you doing here? It can't be just to see me, though I'm flattered, of course.'

I almost laughed. There was a reason I'd fallen in love with him all those years ago. 'Your eternal optimism kills me.' That and your great arms, I wanted to add.

'So, why then?'

'Take a look for yourself.'

He turned to see Annie amongst a sea of well-wishers. 'She's back.'

'Sure is.'

'And?'

'Maybe it's better if she tells you herself, if you don't already know.'

Bear shrugged. 'Know what?'

Annie appeared in front of us, and Bear wrapped his arms around her. 'Welcome home. Where have you been hiding all this time?'

'India.'

Bear's expression was priceless. He couldn't have looked more surprised. 'Really?'

'What? For two-and-a-half years?' Zach said, joining us.

Thank God I wasn't the only one astounded by Annie's revelation.

'Mostly,' Annie replied uneasily.

'Well, wherever you've been and whatever you've been doing, it's worked,' Zach said, oozing charm. 'You look great. Can I get a picture of you and Sami together?'

Annie and I held each other awkwardly, and I fixed a fake smile onto my face. I couldn't focus on the conversation, couldn't focus on the photographs on the wall, couldn't even focus on my champagne. Meanwhile, an ever-increasing swarm grew around us.

'Annie, you're back,' Prue Hamilton observed, sticking a microphone under her nose. 'Why did you leave?'

'Don't answer that,' I said, wanting to protect her. The press had played a part in Annie's downfall. They'd loved her at the beginning of her 'fairytale romance' with Erik but had turned on her when her game started slipping.

'It's okay, Sam.' Annie turned back to Prue. 'I'm sorry for the distress and concern I caused,' she said in a calm voice. 'I needed time to sort myself out.'

'So, you're sorted now?' Prue probed.

'Almost,' Annie replied with a smile. Then she turned to Bear. 'I knew you'd be here.'

'Which begs the question,' Prue cut in, 'why exactly *are* you here?'

I took the chance to fade into the background. My heart was palpitating wildly and with it came the urge to vomit.

Annie caught up with me a few minutes later. She was smiling but gripped her hands together.

'This is a bit daunting,' she said, her voice straining. 'I might have overestimated my ability to see the night through.'

I rubbed her arm. 'You'd never know. You've still got a good poker face.'

Just then, the head of Tennis Australia took to the podium and began his welcoming speech. I tuned out and concentrated on a scuff mark on the floor, until I heard him say '...pleased to announce that Annie Callahan has secured a wildcard entry due to Libby Sherrard pulling out because of a fractured ankle.'

The clapping in the ballroom was thunderous. Annie tried to tell me something, but I couldn't hear over the applause.

'This is probably one of the easiest wildcard choices we've ever had to make,' the speaker continued. 'Annie's a former world number ten ranked doubles player and top twenty singles player. Partnering with her sister Samantha, she won a gold medal at the Olympics, and made the quarter-finals of the Roland Garros three years ago. Although she is currently unseeded, with hard work we believe she'll make the top fifty again before long. We know she'll make the most of this opportunity and wish her luck. Congratulations, Annie.'

The room exploded into even louder cheering and clapping.

'I'm really happy for you,' I said before I was swept aside by more well-wishers wanting to touch her. Had these people nothing better to do? It was an open bar for starters. I was stunned, and hurt that this was so public, surprised that the hurt was so raw. I needed a few minutes alone with her but doubted that was possible given the pandemonium.

'You okay?' Bear asked, handing me a fresh champagne.

'I don't know.' Somehow, I pulled myself together. 'What's new with you?' Any lovers I should know about? Babies? Marriage? 'Who do you see making it into the second week of the competition?'

'I'm mentoring Courtney Gold,' he began.

'Again? Courtney I'm-playing-above-my-ideal-weight Gold? Courtney I-only-drink-a-litre-of-Stoli-a-day Gold?'

Bear raised an eyebrow before draining his Carlton Dry. 'Yeah, okay, but Sam, I have to tell you, Courtney also got in as a wildcard entry.'

'What the—'

He raised his hands. 'Don't look at me. I didn't have anything to do with it.'

I couldn't help it. The hurt and humiliation crept up on me and hot tears pricked my eyes. Annie and Courtney!

'You always were good at nurturing lame ducks,' I said, remembering too clearly how he'd tried to fix my game and my heart.

'I would never call you lame, Sam.'

'Thanks, but I had my share of handicaps.'

When Bear turned to talk to Zach, I drifted towards the wall of photographs to buy time to compose myself. As a distraction, I set myself a little test to see if I could pick when and where the photos were taken, including the year, before reading the caption. All the big stars were up there— Sharapova, Swiatek, Djokovic, Alcaraz, as well as newer faces like Katie Durak. There were pictures of players in action, with their arms around competitors, abusing umpires and each other. The photos were hung chronologically, which made checking out the hairstyles and fashions of the time an unexpected bonus—and the captions were incisive and witty. The organisers had done well.

Forty-five

I stopped in front of a photograph of Annie and me in full flight at the Hopman Cup, our first major win with Bear as our coach. My hair was a mass of brown curls – it was a wonder I could see the ball let alone hit it with any accuracy. By contrast, Annie's blonde hair was a straight, sleek bob. She'd certainly given her straightening iron a good workout back then. The caption was a quote by Bear after our win: *The Callahan sisters are stars on the rise. This is a magnificent time for Australian tennis. The Callahans are the dream team: young and dynamic, with energy to burn.*

It had been thrilling. Annie and I knew exactly where we wanted to be—playing great tennis and whipping the competition. A few photos down the line was another shot of Annie and me, taken three years ago at the Australian Open, ninety minutes after Erik had hijacked our pre-match interview and minutes after we'd been soundly clobbered by Dragana and Jelena. Suddenly, I was back there. Annie and I were winning ...then losing. Then losing more. A catastrophe. And bloody hot, even though we were playing on plexi-cushion, not the scorching rubber surfaces of the past. Not that I could blame the heat for our dismal loss. Or the balls fluffing up. No, the blame for that defeat fell squarely at the feet of one Erik Sørensen, with equal shares going to Annie for not concentrating and Bear for introducing them. And me, I guess, for not supporting my sister at the time.

'A match you'd rather forget?' Bear was beside me again.

'Yeah. If only we'd known then what we know now.'

'You did know, didn't you?'

'I wanted Annie to be happy.' I glanced over to where she was standing with her many admirers.

'And she was, for a while.'

'Whatever,' I said, waving my hand in the air. 'It's history.'

I returned to the photo wall, not wanting Bear to see my tears. And if he did, I didn't want to explain them. Talking to him now, it was almost like our romance hadn't happened, as if I'd only imagined it. I was older, he was older; but he still had that unmistakable confidence and I realised how much I admired him, and how much I'd missed him these last eighteen months. Part of me wanted to tell him how sorry I was for pushing him away. But of course, there was no way I was about to do that.

I stared at the photo some more: Annie's golden highlights, her brilliant smile. And there was me beside her, a dark storm cloud—

'Samantha,' Bear said, interrupting my thoughts. 'Are you still coaching at Melbourne Grammar?'

'Where did you hear that?'

'There are no secrets in the tennis world, you know that.'

'True. I really enjoy it. I feel like I've found my calling.'

'Good to hear. I don't suppose you'd be able to help me with something?'

'It depends.'

'Courtney—'

'Yep. Lame duck, weight and drink problem.'

'I wouldn't put it quite like that.'

'No, you probably wouldn't. What about her?'

'Could you talk to her, maybe take her under your wing?'

I glared at him. 'Are you insane? We didn't exactly part on the best of terms. In fact, I'd go so far as to say Courtney hates me.'

'She doesn't hate you.'

'Whatever. Isn't she supposed to be in rehab?'

'It wasn't rehab, it was a health resort to kick-start her return to the top.'

'Really? I heard it was a psych hospital.'

'Utopia is not a psychiatric hospital. It's not for your heroin headcases or...' He took a moment. 'Look, it's for all sorts of people.'

'Yeah, including those who've *accidentally* run over their wives, shot their husbands, or are drinking their way through a couple of litres of vodka a day.'

'I stayed there, GG—after we broke up.'

I flinched.

'And most of the guests were normal, functioning human beings.'

'Just delicately fragile?' I said, recovering quickly. 'Anyway, why do you think she'd listen to me?'

'Because her coach just quit, and it's only three days until the start of the tournament.'

'And she needs all the help she can get?'

'Exactly.'

'What about her father?'

'They haven't spoken in over a year.'

'I'm sorry about that, but in case you haven't noticed, I'm not living the dream. I don't have anything to offer her.'

'Speak of the devil,' Bear said, waving his right arm in the air. 'Courtney, over here. She has what it takes, Samantha. You know that. Please. You remember what it's like to have that potential nurtured—Courtney!' Bear moved slightly to allow Courtney to step in beside him. 'You remember—'

'Samantha Khartoon,' Courtney mumbled as Prue Hamilton joined the group.

I silently cursed Courtney. She knew my name.

Courtney had changed since last time I'd seen her. She'd transformed from sleek and athletic to ...well, I never realised she was so big-boned.

'I didn't always look like this, you know,' Courtney said, when she noticed me giving her the once-over.

'What? Like the Vicar of Dibley?' Prue suggested, in full bitchy work mode.

Sadly for Courtney, tonight she actually looked worse than the vicar. Puffy, bloated, tired. And overweight.

'How was your holiday?' Bear asked her.

'Holiday?' Prue snickered.

Ignoring her, Courtney replied, 'There were loads of marble water features everywhere and calming music played so low you had to strain your ears to hear. And a fuckload of tealights at night.'

Prue wandered off to tête-à-tête with the players who really mattered, the number one, two and three seeds. Not that they wouldn't know her game plan. You had to be naive not to see that Prue dropped you the moment your ranking fell, and then reeled you in again if your ranking climbed.

'Should you be drinking that?' I asked Courtney, pointing to the glass in her hand, which looked suspiciously like it held a vodka and tonic.

She glared at me as if to say, *And who the hell put you in charge of the living?* 'For your information, it's mineral water.' Then she looked at Zach, who was taking pictures of us. 'Bloody hell, stop that,' she implored. 'When you're a sports star you become public property. Complete strangers think they have the right to comment on the way you're living your life—at least the way you're perceived to be living it—and get morally outraged when they think you're too thin, too promiscuous or too fat.'

'Fame has its downsides,' I agreed.

'You'd know,' Courtney replied. 'The media turned on you and Annie when you started racking up the losses.' She frowned. 'And who are these paragons of virtue anyway? Mostly big nobodies who've never done a thing with their lives. Speaking of which, what are you doing with yourself these days, Samantha?'

'This and that,' I said, but Courtney had lost interest and was trying to catch Katie Durak's eye.

'Good luck with that one,' I said to Bear.

'What a night, hey?' he replied, ignoring my comment. 'I'm guessing the last couple of days haven't panned out as you'd expected.'

'Not exactly.'

'Yeah, of all the scenarios you could have imagined, I bet this one didn't rate a mention.'

I glared at him. 'The one where Annie unexpectedly turns up and announces to the world's tennis elite that she's a starter in next week's Australian Open? No, it didn't.'

Bear was staring at me. 'I know you've got a lot going on right now, but could you come down to the courts tomorrow and look at Courtney's game? I'd appreciate it.'

'I'm no good to you or her. Besides, the tournament starts on Monday.' I checked my watch for extra emphasis. 'There's no time. I'm not ready to deal with Annie being back and all that shit.'

'Good,' Bear said, looking me straight in the eyes. 'Because I'd rather you helped me deal with Courtney's shit instead.'

'No.' I turned away.

He reached out and held my upper arm. Annoyingly, his touch gave me shivers—thousands of tiny tingling Bear bumps. 'You're wearing the earrings I bought you.'

'So?'

'So, you still have feelings for me. Otherwise, you wouldn't have worn them, especially not tonight.'

'Are you crazy? I love these earrings. I wear them all the time.'

'To be close to me.'

'You wish!'

Bear let me go. 'Until tomorrow, eleven o'clock?'

Forty-six

'How did you feel when you saw Bear last night?' Annie asked at breakfast the next morning.

'I don't know. The past twenty-four hours have been overwhelming.' It was like the last couple of years had all been a bad dream. My two best friends were suddenly back in my life. At least I'd have some interesting stories for the kids once the new school year started in a few weeks.

'Any chance you could get back together?'

'Doubtful. We didn't have a good break-up. Back then, I didn't want to be around people who reminded me of the game, so I dumped the whole show.'

'Harsh. Bear still loves you.'

'Annie, I have enough angst in my life.'

'Since when has Bear ever caused you angst?' She took my hand. 'I've missed you, Sam. I'm sorry for the hurt I caused, and I'm sorry about you and Bear.'

'Don't be. If you hadn't left, we might never have gotten together in the first place. It's not your fault. I can make my own decisions.' I clapped my hands. 'Let's get a move on.'

She'd talked me into going to the practice courts with her to meet Bear and Courtney, just like she used to talk me into doing things when we were kids. I might have been the driving force behind our doubles career, but Annie was the persuader in other areas of my life.

~ * ~

'How can you drive with all these trams everywhere?' Annie asked as we idled beside one.

'You get used to them. Like I'd eventually get used to cows roaming the streets if I lived in India, I guess.'

'Fill me in about Courtney,' she said.

'I'd rather you filled me in more about you.'

'No time. Spill.'

'Bad-temper, foul mouth, drinks. The usual. She's ranked ninety-nine but she hasn't played well for some time. You've only got to look at her to see she's playing above her ideal weight.'

Inside Albert Park, I stopped the car and grabbed a couple of racquets, two water bottles and a towel from the boot. We walked over to where Bear was standing at the entrance to the courts. Seeing him, my heart skipped a beat. I longed to reach out and touch him, kiss him, hold him in my arms and never let him go.

'Ladies,' he said, smiling broadly. 'Great day for it.'

I shook off my anxiety and got straight to the point. 'Where is she?'

'I assume you're referring to Courtney? Bathroom.'

'Do you need me to go and spy on her?'

'That won't be necessary. I'm right here,' Courtney said, being a pain in the arse as usual. 'Though I don't know why I have to answer to you.' She turned to Annie. 'I remember you. You were a good player until you fell in love and let your game fall apart.'

'Thank you, Courtney,' Bear said, glowering at her.

'Annie's still a great tennis player,' I said. 'She's also a vegetarian who likes to chant at four in the morning.'

Bear raised his eyebrows.

'Are the draws out yet?' Annie asked.

'Yep,' Bear replied. 'You're playing Sandi Wren, which is great because you've played her at least a dozen times before.'

'Years ago,' Annie replied. 'When Sandi's in form, she has a powerful serve and is an excellent all-rounder.'

'Doesn't matter,' I said. 'When she gets nervous, it's like she's got two left feet. All you have to do is make her twitchy, and the game's yours, Annie. It's a great start.'

'Who am I up against?' Courtney asked.

Bear beamed. 'Debby Bowden.'

'You're in luck, Courtney,' I said. 'From what I've heard, Debby's recovering from yet another ankle surgery. You couldn't get an easier start.'

'Thanks for your encouragement. Not.' Courtney sighed. 'Still analysing every player?'

There was an excellent reason why I'd declared I'd never work with Courtney again after our doubles debacle.

'Let's just get on the court and hit up,' Bear said finally.

Annie left to catch up with some other players, and I watched from the sideline as Courtney fired her first shot over the net. 'Not bad,' I said out loud.

They played for approximately five-and-a-half minutes before Courtney's wheezing and complaining began. 'I need water.'

'There are only two days before the competition starts,' Bear coaxed. 'We've only just started. You won't survive the first set if you continue playing this way.'

'How late did you stay out last night?' I called out.

'Who are you? My mother?' Courtney yelled back. 'I said I need water.' She dropped her racquet and headed towards the bubblers.

'Dehydrated?' I inquired, following her.

'Nup. Thirsty.'

'You've had a drink, Courtney,' Bear said, bouncing a ball nearby. 'Let's get back on the court.'

I didn't know Bear was bothering or what I was doing here. What did I care if Courtney had major motivation issues? But what the hell? I pushed further. 'What did you eat for breakfast?'

'Protein shake.'

'Details?'

She pursed her lips. 'Skim milk, banana, honey, egg and protein.'

'What else?' Bear said, interest piqued.

'I might have had a Mars Bar.'

'And I smell cigarettes on your breath,' he added. 'We've talked about this. You need to do whatever it takes to get back on track. The Open starts Monday.'

It'll take more than two days, I thought. Try two months of intense sprinting, boxing and aerobics, at the very least.

'Can't a girl have any privacy?' Courtney whined.

'Not when you're about to play a Grand Slam,' I said. 'This is your chance. Don't blow it for the sake of chocolate and cigarettes. Or vodka, come to think of it.'

'Who said anything about vodka?'

'No one,' Bear chimed in. 'Focus!'

'Hey, I'm rusty,' she replied. 'I've had serious injuries. Had to rest my knee the last two months, so I've put on a bit of weight. Who wouldn't? Plus, I have a thing for cream-filled biscuits.'

'Stop salivating,' Bear said. 'Let's practice your serves.'

When Courtney and Bear resumed hitting, I stepped to the side. There was a spark of the old Courtney buried underneath, but she didn't seem to want it. The only things Courtney wanted were Mars Bars and Rocky Road. If she were a teacher or a plumber, it wouldn't matter, but Courtney was a pro athlete. To compete, she needed to be in peak physical condition.

'I have no idea what I'm doing here,' I shouted across to Bear after Courtney double-faulted into the net.

'Shit,' she screamed and threw her racquet towards him, missing Bear's feet by centimetres.

He picked up her racquet and walked over to me.

'Even my twelve-year-olds never behave this badly.'

'She's terrified of stuffing up,' Bear mused.

'You reckon? You think this is bravado?'

'Absolutely. How do you think she's playing?'

'Her forehand's okay, but the rest? Courtney's playing as a baseliner, which requires fitness and she's anything but fit. She doesn't like to move on the court. She expects to win without moving her feet and that's not going to happen.'

'Thanks,' Courtney said, joining us. 'For your information, I don't particularly want to hang around with a has-been either. In fact, I don't want you on court with me at all.'

'Too bad,' Bear said. 'There's no one else available and you can't do it alone. You'll be eaten alive.'

'Looks like you're stuck with me,' I told her. 'If I choose to stick around.'

'I'm not paying you.'

I laughed. 'That's okay. Bear is.'

Over at the drink machine, I bought a Red Bull. I didn't like the taste, but needed the caffeine hit.

'Come on,' Bear said to me. 'At least see her through the first round.'

I ripped back the pull-ring and took a long gulp. 'She doesn't want me here. I'm wasting my time.'

'You're not wasting your time. I'll have a word to her. Please, Sam. You owe me.'

I stared at him. 'Owe you?'

'Yes, for breaking my heart and all the anguish you put me through. Besides, I miss you.'

I looked away, cheeks burning. I'd hurt him as deeply as Annie had hurt me.

'This way I get to spend a few days with you,' he continued. 'See if there's any of the old Samantha buried deep inside. Who knows? Now that your sister's back—'

I glanced over to where Annie was watching Courtney arguing with herself or her imaginary friend. 'I can't believe Annie did this to me. She's just stormed back into my life as if she never left.'

'Like you've marched back into mine?'

'I haven't marched back into your life, Bear. You asked me to come today.'

He grinned. 'And you came. Thank you.'

'Right.' I swallowed some more of my drink. 'Anyway, let's leave Annie out of this, okay?'

'Actually, that might be difficult. She's hoping you'll be her practice partner. Obviously, you'll get paid—more so if Courtney and Annie make it through their first rounds. What do you say?'

My head ached and queasiness overwhelmed me. What the hell was going on? There was no way I could do that. 'I can't, Bear, it's too hard. All of it. Being back here, Annie playing, me on the sidelines...'

'I know it's tough, but she's your sister—'

'Whose side are you on?'

'I didn't realise there were sides. I'm just saying, give her a chance.'

'So, what, now I have to deal with your shit as well as my own shit?' Courtney blurted, walking into our conversation, licking an ice-cream.

'You shouldn't be eating ice-cream,' I hissed.

'I so want to smash you,' Courtney hissed back.

'You wouldn't have the energy.'

She glared at me as she swallowed the last of her ice cream. 'I understand why Annie ran away. I would too if I had a sister like you.'

'Ladies, please,' Bear said, pulling Courtney away from me.

'I don't think I can do this,' I snapped. 'Help you coach Courtney, I mean, or be Annie's practice partner. I'm not up for it. I've been out of the game too long.'

He stared at me, seeming to look straight into my heart. 'Sami, you have so much to offer. It would be a shame if you walked away again.'

'That's just it, I don't think I have anything to offer. And even if I did, I'm too hot-headed.'

'You're passionate.'

'That's a polite way of putting it.'

'What is it really? What's stopping you?'

I wanted to tell him that the pressure of playing at that top level overrode the pleasure. But now that I'd seen Bear again, I wanted to be around him, talking, laughing, and hanging out. Even though there was a risk of getting hurt again, I couldn't deny the heart flutters or control my eyes, wide and glowing, from being so close to him.

'Let's take it day by day,' I finally said. 'How about we start over, Annie and me hitting up against you and Courtney?'

He shook my hand. 'Deal.'

~ * ~

I had to hand it to Annie. Even though we hadn't hit a ball together in a couple of years, we moved as one. She was dazzling.

'Just like old times,' she said.

'I guess,' I replied grudgingly.

'Shut up and hit the ball,' Courtney called from the other end of the court.

'Incoming,' Bear shouted, acing me.

'That went better than expected,' he said when we took a break.

'Hmm.' I was still in shock. Twenty-four hours ago, I couldn't have imagined this scene. Yet here I was, playing tennis with Annie, Courtney and Bear.

'So how about it?' Bear asked.

'How about what?' I replied, taking a quick peek at his tanned legs. They're not that great, I told myself, but I wasn't sure I believed me.

'Courtney?'

'All right, I'll help. But if she continues with her bitchy ways, I'm out of here.'

'What is this... fifth grade? I'll talk to her.'

Bear strode to where Courtney was sulking the net. I knew when he'd told her the good news because she tossed her head violently from side to side. I turned and went to join Annie.

'What are you eating?' I asked.

Her eyes widened. 'Cornetto. God, I've missed these.'

'Didn't you hear what I said to Courtney about her diet? You can't have ice-cream.'

'I'm not overweight.' She reluctantly threw the remainder in the bin. 'Courtney can really hit the ball well when she tries.'

'Yeah, but can she stick with it? I swear she has the concentration span of a gnat.'

'Oops. There goes her racquet,' Annie said. We watched it bounce along the hard-court surface. 'Sami, I'm sorry I didn't call you. I know all this has come as a bit of a shock—'

'A bit?'

'Okay, a lot, but I promise I didn't do it deliberately.'

She stopped talking when Bear came over, Courtney dragging behind him.

'Courtney's promised to be more considerate and take your advice,' Bear told me.

Courtney rolled her eyes.

I raised my eyebrows. 'Where are you currently rated on the circuit?' I asked her.

'Lucky ninety-nine. Maxwell Smart would be rapt having me as his sidekick.'

I ignored the wisecrack. 'That means there are ninety-eight women on the circuit who are fitter, fiercer—'

'More talented, yeah. I've heard it all before.'

'I wouldn't say they're more talented than you, but I bet they're a hell of a lot more focused. I doubt they're shoving Rocky Road and ice-creams down their throats.' I looked at Annie, then back to Courtney. 'If you want to get past the first round, you've got to put in maximum effort.'

'I don't just want to get through the first round,' Courtney said. 'I expect to win the tournament.'

'Great. I'm sure Aussie winners, Barty, O'Neill, and Goolagong-Cawley will be cheering for you if and when. But you need to make it happen.'

Forty-seven

'You were hard on Courtney,' Annie told me at dinner that night.

I was eating chicken vindaloo, while she ate potato and pea dhal.

'Excuse me? She's got a game in two days. I wasn't hard enough.' To be honest, I didn't give Courtney any hope of getting through the first round, despite her opponent recovering from surgery. One, she was out of condition. Two, her attitude sucked.

Annie regarded me with her piercing green eyes. 'You're still the same. Anything less than maximum effort isn't an option, is it? No excuses.'

'There's no point being on the court if you're not there to win.'

'So you've told me many times.'

I put my hand up. 'Annie, I'm tired. It's been a long day.'

We ate in silence until I spoke. 'Bear said you're after a hitting partner.'

'And?'

I smiled. 'What else am I doing with my life?'

'Thanks. You standing beside me, means everything.'

'You must be very excited.'

'Excited, but terrified as well.'

'At least you're playing.' I hoped I didn't sound bitter.

'Yeah, and I really do want this. It's an amazing opportunity, and I want to give it my best shot. If I make it through the first round, I'll be pleased.'

'That's not the attitude,' I said, feeling impatient. 'You said you've been given an amazing opportunity, so Annie, you have to go out there and play your best, your hardest. Aim to win—not just one game or one set, but the match. And every match until you've won the final.'

'Wow, you really do still have it,' Annie said, taking a sip of water.

'So do you. Would you really be happy just making it to the second round?'

She shrugged.

'As well as the skill, you've got to have the drive and determination, the mental toughness. No excuses, Annie. Forget about everything else when you're competing.'

'I will, and seriously thanks for everything Sam. I know this is an enormous shock. I appreciate you stepping out of your comfort zone.'

I blinked. 'I've been stepping out of my comfort zone for a while. I never thought teaching twelve-year-olds how to hit a ball would be on my life goals list.'

'But you like it?'

'Love it. The girls are great. They keep me grounded.'

'You should invite them along to the Open,' Annie said. 'I could use some kid energy. I miss my lot from the orphanage.' She grinned. 'You and I aren't so different. Seems we've both been using our time away from professional tennis to nurture kids. What do you make of that?'

'I think you're reading too much into my situation.'

But it got me thinking. My girls would love seeing Annie play. First thing tomorrow morning, I'd email the school and set it up for those girls who were spending their summer holidays home in Melbourne.

'How about you?' I asked. 'How are you feeling being back in civilisation?'

'It's a bit different to Delhi, that's for sure.'

'Any boyfriends while you were away?'

'Nah.'

'Do you ever think about Erik?'

Annie flinched. 'Not much now. In the early days, I was consumed by him. I really thought I was in love with him, but maybe I was just in love with the idea of love. I know you won't believe me, but Erik did have his good points, and I think he loved me in the beginning.'

'I know he did, Annie. But I think he loved himself more.'

She laughed. 'Yeah, I figured that out.'

'You'll be okay if you see him?'

She sipped her water. 'I've got to be. I'm serious about making a comeback and I know eventually our paths will cross. I'm at peace with that.'

'Good. That's great,' I said, hoping she was as tough as she was making out.

I didn't tell her that Erik and Dragana were back together again. She didn't need the added pressure. She'd find out soon enough. Besides, I was a coward. I didn't want her to shoot the messenger and destroy our fragile reunion.

Forty-eight

It was the first day of the Australian Open and I'd barely slept. My hands trembled, my throat itched, and my head throbbed. I could barely manage a cup of tea at breakfast, but Annie appeared calm and focused. Dressed in her trademark white ensemble, hair swept into a high ponytail, she looked like she'd never taken a break.

The papers were full of the golden-haired wonder's return. Most were complimentary, though Prue Hamilton's column could be read either way.

The Australian Open women's matches are shaping up to be the year of the veterans with Netta Landry, Yasmine Le Bluth and Sandi Wren all competing, not to mention the return of the prodigal daughter, Annie Callahan.

'Who's she calling a veteran?' Annie said over her second peppermint tea. 'I'm twenty-eight, hardly an old fossil.'

'Prue likes to stir the pot, you know that.'

'She hasn't changed then.'

'Not one bit.'

Annie continued reading Prue's column to me. *'Annie Callahan made light of her earlier troubles, when her fiancé, Erik Sørensen, dumped her at Wimbledon and left her shattered.'*

Annie glared. 'Yeah okay, I was dumped. *"Then there was her overdose, followed by her disappearance from tennis altogether".'*

'Are you okay?' I asked. 'Prue was fishing the other night, and now it's in print.'

Annie cleared her throat. 'It's the truth. It happened. Being in India taught me to accept the things I can't change. One of those things is the past—I can't pretend it never happened even though I spent months wishing I'd never taken those pills.' She went quiet for a moment. 'I still regret it, but guilt and regret won't change anything, so I deal with it every day the best I can.'

I had to give it to Annie: she was a lot braver and more honest than I was. I would have crumbled had I been on the receiving end of Prue's bitchy comments.

I drove us to the stadium with talkback radio on. We listened as veteran Aussie player, Bruce Duncan made some interesting comments. 'There's a reason I've lived in Britain for the past however many years. Australia has the most ruthless, unforgiving and cruel sports media in the world.' No doubt he'd also been on the receiving end of Prue's barbs over the years.

I took the opportunity to call Violet after Annie had gone to the women's locker room to prepare for her match.

'Nervous?' she asked.

'Marginally. It's been an intense couple of days.'

Violet laughed. 'I bet. How are you feeling?'

'Still in shock, I think. And then there's Bear...'

'Yeah. How do you feel about seeing him again?'

'Like I can't breathe. I'm trying not to let it show, Vi, but every time I see him, my heart skips a beat.'

'What would you do if he wanted to get back together?'

I paused to think. 'Part of me would leap at the chance. But what if it all went wrong again? I couldn't handle losing him again. I'd never recover.'

'Honey, sometimes you need to take a leap of faith.'

'I'm definitely not going to push it. And you? How are my favourite girls?'

Violet sighed. 'Where to start? Hester's into everything. Her favourite word is *mine*. Ava's favourite pastime is embarrassing her big sister by telling me Poppy has a boyfriend.'

'I miss them. I miss you and Rick, too.'

'Same here. But Melbourne's where it's at, sweetie. Though at least we're not having a heatwave like you are down there. I feel for Annie and the other competitors. They shouldn't be playing in such extreme conditions.'

'Annie's been living in India,' I said. 'Hopefully, she's adapted to the heat. Any chance you guys can come down?'

'I'm working on it, babe.'

I ended the call as Bear appeared.

'Coffee?' He handed me a cup.

'Sure. I've had three. What's another? Violet says hi. How's Courtney?'

'Haven't spoken to her this morning. Her game's not until three. But last night, she was on edge, nervous. As she should be.'

Annie appeared beside us. 'It's time.'

'Go get 'em,' Bear said.

She grimaced. 'I feel like an impostor. How can I compete with Olga Gerski's backhand and glamazons like Dionne Leon?'

'Hey, you're here now,' I said gently. 'Remember, we're warriors, not worriers.'

'In the words of Samantha Callahan, get out there and kill it,' Bear chimed in.

A couple of people nearby turned around.

'Am I being too loud?' he said. 'Doesn't matter. You know what you need to do, Annie. Wipe everything else from your mind and get out there and win.'

'Kill doesn't come into Annie's vocabulary,' I reminded him. 'She's on a higher level now.'

'Well, if you're not playing to win,' Bear said, patting Annie's shoulder, 'you may as well trade in your racquet now.'

'Keep in mind that Sandi plays an all-round game,' I told Annie. 'She can come to the net and has a powerful serve. Unfortunately, she has no major weaknesses except that she's inexperienced as far as Grand Slams go. Good luck. Oh, and Annie—seriously, you have to really want it. Talk yourself up, okay?'

Annie smiled and tipped her racquet towards me. She was going to need every ounce of luck against twenty-seventh-seeded Sandi Wren, America's great blonde hope.

As Annie bounced towards the court, a couple of reporters stopped her. Rather than rushing past them, Annie stopped. I had to strain my ears to catch what she said.

'I want to apologise to my fans for leaving the way I did,' she started. 'I wasn't coping with my soaring profile and the grind of professional tennis. I was worn out from the relentless travel and punishing training schedules. That, combined with my personal problems... well, at the time, I thought it was better to bow out of public life.'

'What's changed for you?' Doug Warren asked.

'I'm back because I love the game,' Annie replied. 'I went through a period of soul-searching, but I believe I have the mental toughness to succeed. I'm determined.'

'So, you're going to win today?'

'I certainly aim to. And I'd like to dedicate my play today to my family, friends and fans who've stuck by me.'

'She's got the media eating out of her hands,' Bear whispered to me. 'They still love her.'

'Yeah.' I had no doubt Annie meant every word she was saying, but I wasn't confident she could pull it off.

By the time Annie had taken her end, the crowd was roaring. Thank God we were in Australia—the overwhelming majority were cheering for Annie. Of course, there was a group of vocal Americans in the stadium too, cheering loudly for Sandi.

'Look at Sandi's shoes,' I said to Bear. 'They're at least two sizes too big. Clown shoes.'

'Have you been drinking?'

'What? Her shoes are enormous.'

'I've missed you so much.'

'Shut up and watch the game.' My heart pumped wildly. I could imagine how Annie was feeling.

She opened sluggishly. Her serves were haphazard, her volleys misplaced. As a result, she got thoroughly whipped in the first set, going down 2–6.

'Come on, Annie,' I whispered at the start of the second set. 'Give it your all.'

'She has to want it,' Bear whispered back. His phone vibrated, and he glanced down. 'Courtney's here.'

'That's a good start. Did she bring her racquet?'

'I'll pretend I didn't hear that. Just watch your sister and Clown Shoes.'

I willed Annie on as the on-court temperature rose and spectators became increasingly agitated. People moaned and sighed and waved their programs in front of their faces in an effort to cool down. I was sweating too, but desperately wanted to tell them all to shut up. It was the middle of the Australian summer. It was fucking hot. Deal with it.

I was so busy cursing those around me, I hadn't noticed Annie clawing her way back into the match. She was up four games in only fifteen minutes. A few minutes later, she took out the set 6–4.

The third set would be the decider. Annie looked exhausted but so did Sandi. The heat was getting to them both.

Bear tapped his fingers on the railing. 'I'm not sure she's ready for this.'

'Bit late for that now. But she needs to dig deep.' I rubbed my forehead. 'She'll get through.'

And she did it. *Thump. Thump.* In a tiebreaker, Annie won the third set 7–5. While she pumped her fist in the air and smiled up at the crowd, Bear and I jumped up and down on the spot like primary school kids.

'Far out!' Annie said when we finally met up. 'I scraped through.'

I squeezed her. 'You won!'

After congratulating Annie, Bear got down to the serious business of quizzing her about her game and tactics.

'When you were practising overseas,' he started diplomatically, 'were any of your opponents actually better than you?'

Long pause.

'How deep did you have to dig to get through that match with Sandi?' he went on. 'Because these guys aren't amateurs, Annie.'

'What Bear's trying to say,' I butted in, 'is that these women are professional athletes who want to stomp you into the ground, pound you to within an inch of your life and watch as you beg for mercy.'

'All I want to do is play tennis,' Annie said.

'We all want you to play,' Bear agreed. 'That's why we're here. I know I keep repeating myself, but as much as you want to be all zen about this, if you don't have the desire or passion to win every single time you're on court, you may as well pack up and go home now because the kids you're up against are practising ten hours a day to get where you are.'

'Not Courtney, of course,' I chimed in.

'Thank you, Samantha.' Bear glared. 'Maybe not Courtney. Yet. But the others, the Nettas, the Dionnes, the Olgas—they're all desperate to win and will do whatever it takes.'

'Okay!' Annie replied, clearly exhausted.

'Honey, you remember what it's like on the circuit?' I said more gently. 'How demanding and heartbreaking it is?'

'Boy, do I remember,' she said. 'And the days when we lost, remember? The self-flagellation lasted until the next win when we proved our other wins hadn't been flukes.' She looked down. 'And even when we won, the euphoria was fleeting. It was always about the next game, the next challenge the next triumph, the next high. Wow, now I remember why I abandoned all of this in the first place.'

'Okay,' Bear said as he guided her towards the open door of the media room, 'probably not a great attitude for an unseeded player at the Aussie Open. A player who's been given an amazing opportunity, a second chance at winning. Go in there and talk yourself up.'

As soon as we entered the media room, bulbs started flashing and the questions flew thick and fast.

'Are you pleased with your performance?' shouted a reporter from the back of the room.

'It's a good start,' Annie said. 'My aim is to win back the trust of tennis fans and earn their respect after my shocking performance a couple of years back.'

'Are you referring to—' Prue Hamilton started.

'I think everyone knows what Annie's referring to,' Bear said, stepping up beside her.

'How will you go about that, Annie?' a voice from the crowd asked.

'By focusing one hundred per cent on my game and playing great tennis. In the past, there were issues preventing me from being the best tennis player I could be. Those issues have now been sorted. I won't be making the same mistakes in future.'

'Today was unquestionably a breakthrough win,' Prue conceded.

Annie grinned. 'Yes, unbelievable. I served well, got to the net, and the balls flew my way. I'm thrilled to be back.'

'Are you still nursing a broken heart?' Doug Warren asked.

Exactly the question I'd hoped they wouldn't ask. Even though Annie kept telling me how strong she was, how she was 'over Erik,' it might be a different story when it was thrown in her face.

Annie waved her hand. 'That was so long ago and lasted such a short time ...I'm happy to report that my heart is happy and healthy.'

'You're okay about playing Dragana in round four, assuming you both get through the next couple of rounds?' Prue asked.

Annie looked across at me, then back to Prue. 'I hardly see what playing Dragana has to do with Erik.'

'Don't you know?' Prue was downright gleeful. 'Dragana and Erik have been an item almost since the day you two broke up.'

Annie took her time to answer. Bear eyed her carefully. He'd jump in if things got out of hand.

'Well, good luck to them.' Annie's poker face was in place. 'I'm very happy for them both.'

Bear took control of the microphone. 'I'd like to end the interview by saying thank you to all of Annie's fans. We've been inundated with emails, phone calls, tweets and texts wishing her the best.'

'Yes, thanks to everyone,' Annie agreed, a perfect example of composure and grace. Halfway down the podium stairs, she turned back to the assembled scrum. 'I've got some improving to do, but I'll try not to let you down.'

'You were great up there, articulate and sincere,' I said as we walked. And I meant it. Annie was on the comeback trail. As Bear had said to me earlier, the fault of Annie's perceived overdose was not hers but Erik's. She was the heroine, Erik, the villain.

'All good?' I asked.

'Yes, of course. Why wouldn't I be?' came her curt reply. Annie always shut down a conversation if it wasn't going in the direction she wanted, and over the years I'd become accustomed to it.

'Don't let Prue get to you,' Bear said, checking his Fitbit. 'Courtney's game's up in thirty minutes. I'd better get moving.'

'Who am I kidding? I can't do this,' Annie said when we were alone.

'Annie,' I said, trying to remain calm, 'this had better not be about that prick.'

We both knew who I was talking about.

She hesitated. 'Of course not. Well, maybe just a little. I worked so hard to expel him from my mind, to let him go and move forward, and now he's back, and with Dragana again.'

'You don't have to let him back into your life. You're stronger than that.'

'Am I? I spent so many sleepless nights crying about him. About what a fool I'd made of myself, the whole world knowing my business.'

'I wouldn't say the whole world exactly.'

'Close enough. Anyway, I really thought I'd let him go.'

'So, what's the problem? Acknowledge that he's here and still a huge prick and move on. Please, let him go. Your time with Erik is past. Now it's time to allow other people and other experiences to enter your heart.'

'Hey, that's exactly what my yogi said.'

Forty-nine

Courtney and Debby were on court warming up by the time I took my seat next to Bear.

'Did you speak to her?' I asked.

'Briefly.'

'And?'

'She's as ready as she'll ever be.'

'You don't sound hopeful.'

'Oh, I'm hopeful. I've got a lot of hope. In fact, if Courtney wins, how about dinner? You and me?'

Yes, yes, yes. My heart was backflipping. I couldn't think of anything I wanted more. But I couldn't let my guard down, not until I knew for sure that Bear and I were going to make it this time.

'If Courtney wins today, you'll be celebrating by helping her prepare for round two,' I replied.

Bear pulled a face. 'Good point. Raincheck, GG?'

'Shh. They're starting. And stop calling me GG.'

Courtney always bounced the ball three times before serving. Today, it worked in her favour; her serves were powerful and incredibly fast. She aced Debby twice during the first game. The crowd was definitely on Courtney's side as she began racking up the points and won the first set 6–3.

'That's what we want to see,' Bear said.

'Sure is, but I'll tell you, that white dress she's wearing isn't doing her any favours. You can see every bulge.'

'If I'd said that, you'd attack me for being sexist or fat shaming.'

'Exactly. That's why I'm saying it.'

Despite the dress clinging to her in all the wrong places, Courtney glided through the second set 6–2 to win the match. Immediately after winning the last point, she toppled onto her back in relief, before standing up and dancing around the court, blowing kisses to the stunned umpire and the fans, who were on their feet cheering.

'Say what you want about her personally,' Bear said as we stood clapping with the rest of the crowd, 'but on stage, she shines.'

'She's definitely got the mental issue down pat.'

'That's where Annie and she differ.'

'Yeah, Annie needs to toughen up, whereas Courtney just needs to drop a few kilos and she'll be unstoppable.'

'See,' Bear said. 'I told you.'

'Congratulations,' I said to Courtney when she lumbered off court. I was genuinely pleased for her.

'You played well,' Bear said enthusiastically.

'Piece of cake,' she replied. 'I could murder a beer, maybe a few tequilas—'

'No,' Bear said. 'You've just won your first match.'

'Exactly, time to celebrate.'

'Not so fast. You have to stop by Autograph Island, or have you forgotten that part of the deal?'

Inside the tent, queues of face-painted kids screamed to have their timetables and giant tennis balls signed. Annie was already there, and I watched as she patiently signed her name over and over. She looked up and saw us.

'You must have played a great game,' she said to Courtney. 'I could hear the crowd roar every time you hit a winner.'

'It wasn't hard,' Courtney said.

'Hey,' Debby said as she entered the tent. 'I didn't take my chances early in the match, but next time I'll be ready for you.'

Courtney shrugged. 'Promises, promises.'

'There are kids here,' Bear said. 'Watch it.'

Courtney looked at him. 'Do I really need to do this? It'll probably do permanent damage to my hands, being forced to write my name so many times.'

'You do and you will,' Bear said.

When she was settled, he walked over to me. 'Two from two.'

I smiled. 'Looks like it.'

'You could have an amazing career in front of you—Samantha Callahan, super-coach to those who thought their best was behind them. What do you reckon?'

'Yeah ...just no.'

Bear laughed, then turned serious. 'How are things going with Annie? Really? Are you okay with her being here, playing in the Open, signing autographs?'

'I'm happy for her.'

'But...?'

'But part of me wishes I was back out there too, slogging balls in sweltering heat and ninety-five per cent humidity.'

'And signing giant balls in here?'

I glanced over at Annie, then smiled at Bear. 'Yep. Even that.'

We stood watching as Annie and Courtney frantically tried to keep up with the demand for autographs.

'Here's a thought,' I said. 'What happens if the two of them meet up?'

'Why if?' Bear replied. 'It's going to be *when* they meet up.'

'Okay. *When* Courtney and Annie meet up, the two Aussies battling it out, who are you going to be cheering for?'

Bear hesitated.

'It's something to think about,' I said. 'Seriously, the party's got to end sometime.'

'For now, can we just enjoy it?'

I shrugged. He couldn't avoid answering the question forever. And I had a horrible feeling that things could turn ugly if both Annie and Courtney made it through to the third and fourth rounds.

Fifty

That night, while Annie caught up on sleep, I took the opportunity to soak in a hot bath and think about the past few days. It had certainly gone a lot better than I'd expected. It's just that I wasn't sure I could sustain it. What about tomorrow? And the day after? I'd never been good at spontaneity. I liked to know what was going on and where I was headed, so I could plan, organise my schedule, allocate my time. I splashed the warm soapy water over my upper body and arms. How was I going to divide my time between Annie and Courtney? And what about coaching Courtney full stop? Never in my wildest dreams could I have imagined getting involved in her life again. Talk about a wildcard!

My phone rang. Bear.

'Zach's just called. Courtney's drinking at some bar. He's keeping an eye on her until I get there.'

I groaned. 'Do you want me to come?'

Bear stayed silent, and I wondered if he'd heard me.

'Bear?'

'Yeah, it might be better if you came along,' he said. 'I'll pick you up.'

'But you don't know where I live.'

He allowed himself an audible exhalation. 'Oh, Samantha, how you underestimate me.'

Thirty minutes later, we arrived at a seedy-looking bar in the city. Zach was outside waiting for us.

'She's not completely wasted,' he said. 'But there are heaps of people inside taking photos.'

'Thanks, buddy,' Bear said, and marched inside.

Zach caught my arm as I went to follow and gestured to the woman beside him. 'Samantha, you remember my girlfriend, Tina?'

'Of course,' I said. 'I remember your work from Zach's show. You're an amazing photographer.'

She blushed. 'Thanks.'

Inside, I caught up with Bear. Surprise, Courtney was doing shots with Dionne Leon.

'What are you doing?' Bear asked Courtney. 'You should be at your hotel. Asleep. In bed.'

'Once I find myself a man,' Courtney said, laughing and holding her tequila in the air, 'that's exactly where I'll be heading.'

'You're drunk,' I said. 'We're taking you home.'

'What's she doing here?' Courtney asked Bear. 'And I'm not going anywhere. I'm celebrating with my new best friend, Dio. Isn't that right, Dio?'

But Dionne was metres away, surrounded by admirers and gyrating to the music inside her head.

'Imagine the press getting a hold of these two,' Bear said to me.

I pulled a face. 'I know who'd get the rougher treatment. Dionne's gorgeous and fit and Courtney's—'

'Not. I know. That's why we need to get her out of here.'

'Don't you think I at least deserve a tiny victory celebration?' Courtney bleated.

'Yes, after you win the finals.'

Despite her protests, we maneuvered her out of the club and discreetly dragged her to Bear's car.

'You really need to lose weight,' I said as we heaved her into the back seat.

'Whatever, Miss Goody Two Shoes.'

'Well, that's a first,' I said to Bear, climbing into the front. 'I've never been called Goody Two Shoes before.' I peered around. She was already snoring. 'It's only ten o'clock. We can't take her back to the hotel. There'll be too many people about.'

'What's the alternative?'

'I'm really going to regret this, but I guess she can spend the night at my place. I've got a pull-out sofa—'

Bear put his arm around me. 'GG, you do have a heart. Before you have time to reconsider, I'm going to take you up on your generous offer. Thanks.'

Courtney stumbled along, half-asleep, as we led her from the car into my apartment. After propping her on an armchair, Bear and I set about making up the fold-out sofa in the lounge room.

'What's going on?' Annie asked, emerging from her room, groggy from sleep.

'Courtney's had too much to drink,' Bear said, 'so your sister kindly invited her to stay here, far from prying lenses poised to capture her every humiliating moment on film.'

Annie frowned, then silently walked back into her room, closing the door behind her.

When the bed was made up, Bear and I rolled Courtney into it.

'Don't even think about asking me to undress her,' I said as the two of us stared at her snoring form. 'I'll take off her shoes, but she can sleep in her jeans and diamanté tee.'

'Deal.' He turned to me, his tone serious. 'Thanks for this. It goes above and beyond.'

'It's fine,' I said. 'I'll talk to you in the morning.'

After bidding Bear goodnight, I took off Courtney's shoes, placed her in a semi-comfortable position and put a full litre bottle of water beside her. I retrieved a bucket from the laundry and sat that beside her as well. Just in case. Then I climbed into bed, exhausted.

~ * ~

I'd been asleep for what seemed like minutes before I heard the familiar chanting through the wall. Though Annie confined it to her room these days, it was still loud.

I could also hear Courtney moaning from the lounge room. 'Shut up.'

The chanting continued.

'Shut. Up.' This time her delivery was louder, with more pain. 'Would you shut the fuck up?'

I tumbled out of bed and into the lounge.

'What the fuck is that noise?' Courtney cried. 'And what are you doing in my room?'

'Courtney, it's me. Samantha. You're in my apartment.'

She was holding her head.

'Are you listening to me? I said—'

'I heard what you said. What happened to Dionne? What the fuck! Why are you making that God-awful noise?'

'That would be me making that noise,' Annie said, emerging from her bedroom. 'It's called chanting, and I do it every morning when I wake up.'

'Well, not this morning,' Courtney said, flopping back onto her makeshift bed.

'If everyone could just calm down,' I started.

Courtney groaned some more.

'You're not going to throw up, are you?' I said. 'Because there's a bucket—'

'I need a bathroom,' she screamed, lurching forward.

I helped Courtney stand, and pointed. 'Through there.'

Courtney disappeared into the bathroom. Annie promised she'd keep the chanting down to a dull roar and retreated to her room.

Minutes later, Courtney emerged from the bathroom, looking pale. 'Panadol?'

This was going to be a great few days, no doubt about it.

When Bear arrived at ten thirty, Annie had already left for Rod Laver Arena to practice, but Courtney was curled in the fetal position on my sofa.

'So much for our good intentions,' he said, throwing the morning paper down on the table.

I picked it up. Staring back at me was a grainy photo of Courtney, drink in one hand, cigarette dangling from her mouth, clearly the worse for wear. The headline trumpeted: *Too drunk, too fat! This is why Courtney Gold will never be a tennis superstar.*

'Ouch,' I said. 'What can we do about it?'

'Ride it out, the way we do with all these dramas.' He nudged Courtney, but she just groaned. 'Okay, sleeping beauty, time to get up.'

'Later,' she mumbled. 'I'm not playing today.'

Eventually, he got her sitting upright.

'Drink this,' I said, handing her a double strength coffee.

Courtney took a sip and practically spat it out. 'Yuck. I don't do instant.'

By midday, the three of us were at the practice courts. No mean feat considering Courtney's whining.

'Why aren't you getting into Dionne as well?' she grumbled. 'She was with me.'

'Dionne's not our responsibility,' I said, pushing her towards the court where Annie was already playing. 'And she's not the one on the front page of the morning tabloid.'

'At least I was having fun. F.U.N! Do you remember what that's like?'

‘Enough,’ Bear said.

‘Dionne isn’t even into tennis,’ Courtney continued. ‘She’s just using it as a stepping-stone to become a fulltime model.’

‘Good luck to her,’ Bear said, as he opened a new tin of balls. ‘You, on the other hand, are an elite tennis player, so you need to prove it.’

‘We need to look at your racquet preparation and the importance of maintaining proper footwork,’ I chimed in. ‘You can’t keep throwing your racquet around either.’

Courtney stared at me, clearly not giving a damn what I said. ‘My arm’s hurting.’

‘You need to build it up. Rod Laver squeezed squash and tennis balls to develop his forearm.’

She glanced skyward. ‘Whatever.’

‘You’re going to have to concentrate to make it through the next round,’ I said as she fiddled with her racquet strings. ‘Courtney, are you listening to me?’

‘Why should I? You’re a has-been.’

I chose to ignore her pearls of wisdom. ‘Your problem is that you’re way too emotional, too prone to outbursts both on and off the court. I was like that too, and it did me no favours in the long run. You can’t afford to show any emotion. Stay calm, it’ll be to your advantage.’

‘How?’ She was making circles in the gravel with her sandshoes.

‘Because it’ll frustrate your opponent.’ I flashed back to when Annie and I played each other. Her poker face used to irritate the hell out of me. She was a master at stoicism, just like her hero, Chris Evert. ‘If she doesn’t know what you’re thinking or how you’re feeling, she won’t be able to anticipate where you’re going to hit the ball. If you’re emotional, your game will suffer. You’ll end up losing.’

‘Maybe.’

'Look, I can give you some strategies, and we can practice your technique, but the rest is up to you. If you're going to win, you'll need to focus one hundred per cent.'

'Excuse me! I just won my first-round match, you know.'

'I do know. Congratulations. You were quite brilliant. We need to keep that up. How much do you know about Olga Gerski's game?'

'I know I can whip her arse and still have energy at the end for a double cheeseburger and chips.'

What had I let myself in for? Getting through to Courtney was impossible. I gave up and sat in the umpire's chair at the net.

Courtney glared at me, but took to the court, ready to receive Annie's serve.

They played for less than ten minutes before Courtney got bored and started talking. 'I hear you got married, went off the rails, did drugs and disappeared,' she called to Annie.

'I didn't get married or do drugs,' Annie shouted back.

'I got married last year.' Courtney paused. 'Lasted five weeks. So disappointing. Turned out I'd married into the family from hell. After the wedding, I kept thinking, I don't know this man—who is he?'

Annie didn't answer, so Courtney turned to me. 'You been married?'

'No,' I replied. 'How about you concentrate on the game?'

'We'd only been going out three months before Brad proposed,' Courtney continued. 'I thought he was my dream come true. My very own Prince Charming. So what if he was thirty-nine and still lived at home? Maybe if my dad wasn't a complete fuck-job, I'd still be living at home too.'

'The ball, Courtney.'

'When did you meet Brad?' Annie asked, moving forward.

I climbed down from my chair. Why bother? The three of us met at the net.

'About this time last year,' Courtney said.

'And you got engaged when?'

'Just before Wimbledon, married in September.'

'I bet your father was impressed,' I said. If I couldn't beat them, I may as well join in.

'Yeah, especially as I didn't tell him. We stopped talking soon after Brad and I started going out. He only found out I was getting married when some reporter rang him for a comment.'

'What went wrong?' Annie asked.

'Brad's parents—his mother, to be precise. You'd think alarm bells would have gone off, given I only met them after we got engaged. But I was in love with him and ecstatically happy. So happy that I only hesitated slightly when he suggested, or rather insisted, that we move into his parents' home after the wedding.'

'That can't have been very romantic,' Annie said.

'No. My friends thought it sounded weird. His parents picked us up from the airport after our honeymoon and it all turned to shit.'

'How?' I asked, curious despite myself.

'His mother insisted that Brad sat in the front seat next to her because she was driving, while her husband and I sat together in the back.'

Annie and I looked at each other.

'And then when we arrived back at his crazy mother's house, there were two singles in Brad's room instead of a double.'

'Presumably bells were clanging by now?' I asked.

'They were on fire. I couldn't stand it, so I left.' She started walking off the court.

'No, you don't.' I grabbed at her racquet. 'Stay and play, and I'll go in search of a couple of Red Bulls.'

Courtney looked at Annie.

'Come on, just another set,' Annie coaxed.

My ploy worked. For the next forty-five minutes, Annie and Courtney played each other with very few moans and no tantrums from Courtney. Afterwards, we drove to St Kilda beach for a swim.

'Why didn't we do this first up?' Courtney asked. 'I feel so much better.'

'So,' I said, placing my towel beside hers, 'how much do you know about Olga Gerski?'

'Can we talk about this tomorrow?' Courtney yawned. 'I need sleep.'

'Can I trust you to go back to your hotel, eat proper food and get a decent night's sleep?'

'Yeah.'

'And turn up tomorrow, rested, sober and determined to win?'

'Anyone would think I had a problem,' she sniffed.

Fifty-one

The next morning, Annie and I arrived at the arena promptly at nine thirty, and I met up with several of my schoolkids and their parents.

'We're so excited to be here,' one of the mothers enthused.

'We sure are,' her daughter Isabella said. 'Miss, you're so lucky. I keep pinching myself to make sure it's not a dream and that we're really here.'

'And we're seeing Annie Callahan play,' her friend Lucy chimed in.

I smiled. 'I am so glad you could all come. This nice man here,' I gestured to an usher, 'will show you to your seats. Don't forget to cheer loudly for Annie, and then come to Autograph Island afterwards, and I'll get you sorted with caps and posters. Okay?'

They squealed their agreement.

I hurried to the women's locker room to find Courtney. She was stomping about because she'd lost the blue garter she wore on her left thigh every match.

'Surely you have more than one?' I asked.

'That's not the point,' she said, panic in her voice. 'I want my lucky garter.'

I thought of my panic at Wimbledon when I'd gone on court without my bandana. 'Let's retrace your steps.'

Eventually, Courtney remembered she'd worn the garter when she went out with Dionne to celebrate her first-round win. 'But I can't show my face at that club ever again. Although'—she reached for her handbag—'Here! In the phone pocket of my Prada. Thank God.'

'Great. You've got your lucky garter. Now, about Olga's game...'

Courtney glared at me.

'What? I just want to talk to you about how she plays.'

She sighed. 'Right. Go on then.'

'She has a smashing double-handed backhand, so always try to hit to her forehand. She's also an ice maiden, like Annie. Rarely lets her emotions get the better of her—'

'Unlike me.' Courtney laughed.

'Very unlike you. You won't know what she's thinking or where she's going to hit the ball next, so you have to be prepared for anything. Mind you,' I added when I noticed Courtney's bravado starting to crack, 'Olga used to be a real hothead. She regularly abused umpires and threw her racquet around the court.'

'Really?' Courtney said, brightening.

'Yeah. Occasionally her game can be unpredictable. And if her game's unpredictable, she'll blame her contact lenses.'

Courtney raised her eyebrows. 'Whatever. I have no doubt I'll win. I like travelling and fine dining too much to lose.'

She left to warm up, and I turned my attention to Annie. 'Ready for Yasmine?'

She saluted. 'Ready, Captain.'

'Go get 'em, Annie,' Bear said when he caught up with us on the way to Margaret Court Arena.

Annie nodded, looking determined, then entered the throng of well-wishers, leaving Bear and me in her wake.

'Try not to worry about her,' he said, putting his arm around me. 'Her movement's smoother around the court, and her reach at the net should give her the edge over Yasmine.'

'I hope you're right.'

'When have I ever been wrong? Ready to do the mad dash?' He was referring to the fact that Annie and Courtney were playing their matches at the same time.

'Yep. Margaret Court Arena and Show Court Two, here we come.'

Courtney's match started slightly ahead of Annie's, so we settled down to watch her first set against Olga. It was a sloppy start. Courtney seemed tense. Olga kept rubbing her eyes after every point. It didn't stop her taking advantage of a miss-hit by Courtney.

'She needs to relax,' Bear said when she missed an easy lob.

But somewhere around the fifth game, when Courtney was losing 2–3, a change came over her. Instead of looking around the court and getting distracted by the ball kids, she started playing great tennis, focused and feisty. Twenty minutes later, she'd taken the first set 6–3.

From the very first ball of the second set, Courtney pummelled Olga. It was thrilling to watch. She was serving aces, hitting consistently to Olga's forehand, and no matter how hard Olga tried to get her to run, her balls seemed to land effortlessly within Courtney's reach without her having to move more than a couple of steps.

When Courtney won the second set 6–3, she threw both hands into the air and dance-stepped in mini-circles, smiling, laughing, crying.

Along with the rest of the crowd, Bear and I were on our feet cheering. It was exhilarating. The crowd was ecstatic, and Courtney repaid them by blowing kisses into the stands.

'You did it, you did it!' I screamed down to her before turning to Bear. 'We've got to get back to Annie.'

'This is good, very good,' I said to Bear as we darted to Margaret Court Arena and found that Annie was also winning, 4–3. Maybe they'd both win. My head bounced from side to side, watching the action.

The heat was intense, but the crowds at both games were amazing. Possibly an older crowd at Annie's match, but Courtney had certainly pulled the punters as well. Who said tennis wasn't popular anymore?

I looked up to the stands and saw my students waving madly at me. I waved back.

Bear put his arm around me. 'You seem very popular, Ms Callahan?'

'Yes, and if you don't take your arm away this minute, I'll be popular for all the wrong reasons.'

Bear withdrew his arm. 'Spoilsport.'

I glanced back at the girls, but their eyes were focused squarely on Annie.

'Yasmine doesn't seem to have her mind on the game,' Bear said, all coach-like. 'And thank God Annie's taking full advantage of the situation.'

'Yes, she is,' I grinned. Yasmine appeared to be faltering, and she jarred her right foot leading into the second set. She limped to her chair at the change of ends.

'Come on, Annie,' I screamed.

A moment later, Yasmine tripped on court and called for time out. Five minutes later, she forfeited the match. 'Good times.'

Fifty-two

After Annie's victory, I made my way over to my girls from school, who were jumping up and down on their chairs. Their faces were red and their clothes dripping with perspiration, but their smiles couldn't have been wider.

'She won, Miss!' they shouted. 'She won the match.'

'Come on,' I said. 'Let's go and see her.'

I led them downstairs to where Annie was gathering her racquets and towel.

'Annie!' I beamed. 'Well done, you. Here are some of my students I was telling you about.'

The girls, usually so chatty and confident, stood back in awe.

'It's wonderful to meet you all,' Annie said. 'I'm so glad you could watch me play today. Did you have fun?'

'Did we ever,' Peta, the smallest of the group, said.

They fired questions at her, got their tee-shirts and caps signed, and wished her best of luck for the next round.

'We know you can win, Miss,' Lucy said. 'We'll be cheering for you.'

'Remember what it was like at their age?' Annie said as we headed towards the media room. 'Slugging it out on that daggy uneven weed court.'

'Sure do. The best feeling of my life was acing my opponent and winning the game.'

'They're really nice girls,' Annie said. 'Gorgeous.'

I beamed with pride.

~ * ~

Prue Hamilton started on Annie as soon as she sat for the press conference. 'You've had an easy run so far.'

'I'd better get up there,' Bear said quickly.

'No danger of you burning out, is there?' Prue continued. 'When you only play two or three short sets every couple of days?'

'I don't think I'm in danger of burning out whether I play one or three sets a day,' Annie replied. 'This certainly isn't how I wanted to win the match. I hope Yasmine makes a speedy recovery and we meet up again soon.'

Prue changed tack. 'The tennis world saw you at your peak at the Olympics, where you proved yourself a champion. But punters had you pegged as the loser in today's match. Talk us through what happened.'

'Yasmine hurt her foot. She couldn't overcome the injury and withdrew. The outcome could have been very different had she been fit, and we'd played the entire match.'

'I'm sure.' Prue thanked Annie for her time and turned to the camera. 'Can Annie Callahan rise like a phoenix from the ashes to take the tennis world by storm again? We'll find out in round three, where she'll be squaring off against Netta Mathieu.'

It was Courtney's and Olga's turn to be interviewed next. Olga took to the podium first, wearing her thick-lensed glasses.

'I am not happy with my performance today,' she said, 'but that is the nature of the game. You win some, you lose some. My aim is to win more, obviously.'

I don't think she meant to be funny, but the assembled media laughed.

'My contact lenses were causing me trouble,' she went on. 'The reflection from the hard surface put me off my game. I now have eye strain—'

'We do too from looking at those Elton John seventies jobs you've got attached to your eyes,' Zach quipped next to me, camera in hand.

'If you ask me, it's just attention-seeking,' Courtney whispered. 'I bet she can see without them. She's probably just doing it in the hope of getting an eyewear contract. You wait, next time she plays, her fans will all be wearing oversized glasses.'

'Shush.' I nudged her. 'You're up.'

Courtney was on a high, giggling as she danced up to the microphone.

'How are you feeling about your win today?' a reporter asked.

'Fabulous. I played well. I deserved to win.'

'Still wearing your lucky blue garter?' another asked.

'You betcha,' she replied with a wink, before raising her skirt to reveal it.

I stared at Zach as he snapped off several shots. He turned my way, smirked, and went back to taking more photos. Yes, he was there to do a job, but that didn't mean I had to like it.

'You went AWOL the other night. On a bender?' a reporter called from the back.

'I like to have a good time,' she said, as Bear whispered something into her ear.

'Do you think your weight will continue to be an issue?' Prue Hamilton asked.

'That's all for now, folks,' Bear said.

Courtney looked relieved. She'd probably been hoping they'd have the good grace not to mention her size.

'Don't let the press interviews get to you, otherwise it'll do your head in,' I told her as we were leaving the stadium. 'You need a thick skin to make it in women's tennis.'

She frowned. 'How about a cocktail to celebrate?'

'Don't even think about it,' Bear said.

Courtney took a moment. 'At least I made it this far. That's not so bad.'

'I thought you wanted to win?'

She sighed. 'I'm afraid.'

'Afraid of what?' I asked.

'Afraid I can't do this because I'm too fat. There I said it. I'm fat. I'm the fat kid on tour who everyone laughs about.'

'That's not true.'

'It is so. I shouldn't be here. I'm obese. Everybody knows it. I'm like this gigantic whale on court. I try to get the crowd to like me—'

'They love you,' I said.

'Don't patronise me. They think I'm a hideous blubber whale.'

I stood still and caught hold of her arm. 'Courtney, stop it. You're not obese. Okay, you're carrying more weight than is ideal, but we're dealing with it. Focus on your game and training and your weight will disappear, as long as you lay off the chips and ice-cream.'

'But I get hungry.'

'Eat some fruit,' I said, pulling a banana from my bag and handing it to her.

She took it. What happened to the super-bitch from yesterday and the day before, I wondered, watching as she stalked off to watch Katie Durak and Sofia Petrova hit up. She was usually all bluster and bravado. I'd never seen her let her guard down, not even when we'd dissolved our partnership. This under-confident woman surprised me. Had her weight gain affected her that much? Or was it her short-lived marriage? Her dad's theatrics? There was a long list of things that could have triggered a shift in her behaviour. Or perhaps she'd always had this side, but I'd never seen it.

And maybe, just maybe, she really wanted to win. Granted, she'd been saying she wanted to, but now she was in with a real chance. A round-two win was nothing to be sneezed at. As much as Courtney would never admit it, maybe Bear and I were making progress, after all.

'Guess what?' Violet said when I answered my phone. 'We're heading down.'

'Get out. Really?'

'You betcha. All five of us. We want to surprise Annie and see you, of course.'

Amid squeals and laughing, we planned to meet up when they arrived the following day. I hadn't been this happy in a very long time.

Fifty-three

Zach

Back at the hotel, Zach lay awake in bed. Tina had fallen asleep after sex, but he was too restless after a full-on day. He was as thrilled for Annie as the rest of the press. They were all Team Annie, wanting the wildcard to win. Zach's cynical side knew it would make a damn good story, but he also thought the reporters genuinely wanted Annie to do well. Everybody liked her.

He thought back to the opening night of his first joint exhibition with Tina over two years ago, back when Tina had invited him to be part of the show. Before the guests arrived, checking his Fitbit and clenching his fists, he looked at his photographs on display.

One that struck him was of a homeless boy, about ten years old, dressed in grey rags, shoeless, feeding a puppy bread. The kid was probably starving, yet he had a wide smile plastered on his face. A photo taken seconds later showed the puppy licking the boy's face as he wrapped his arms around the canine. Zach wasn't sure he'd made the right choices but seeing them all hanging together, the pictures looked amazing—confronting and thought-provoking.

He turned to look at Tina's collection entitled, *Everyday Life at Peak Hour*, which was a mix of businesspeople, bike riders, schoolchildren, taken on different days but always at seven a.m.

'Excited?' Pete, the gallery owner, asked.

'That's one word for it,' Zach said. 'Scared shitless would be two more.'

Pete smiled. 'Don't be. We've had lots of pre-interest, so we're expecting good sales tonight.'

Pete drifted away, and Zach stood in front of a photo he'd taken of Annie on a Parisian street. She was looking at a group of four girls, maybe eight years old, who were rushing out of their schoolyard and laughing. Annie's hair was tousled, her expression pensive. He couldn't take his eyes off her. What had she been thinking at the exact moment he'd captured her?

He reached into his jeans pocket and pulled out a not-for-sale sticker and stuck it at the bottom of the photo. He'd give it to Samantha after the show closed.

People started arriving, including Samantha and Bear, and before long, the gallery was crowded. Everywhere Zach turned, he heard positive comments about the photos. Several sold stickers popped up.

Tina tapped his shoulder. 'Hey, Zach. Looking good. So are your photos.'

Zach beamed. 'This has to be one of the greatest professional buzzes ever. I just wish I could spend more time taking these kinds of shots.'

She linked his arm through his. 'Interested in a joint project?'

He stared at her a moment. 'Why not?' He liked her work, and he liked her. She was a good sort and generous, too. If it hadn't been for her encouragement, he'd never have put together his *Urban Sprawl* series.

As the night wore on, they drank and flirted more. Tina was easy on the eye, had a great laugh and, most of all, shared his passion for photography.

Four hours later, they were in bed together. It was the first time Zach had had sex since Annie's attempted suicide. He was glad it was with Tina. She was a cute, intelligent woman who clearly liked him. To Zach's surprise, he was still with Tina and had never been unfaithful.

Tonight, he lay staring into the darkness until he couldn't stand it another minute. He got up, wrapped a towel around his waist and snuck into the second room he was using as an office. At the desk, he switched on his computer and trawled through all the photos he'd taken of Annie over the years.

There were many, but he remembered them all: where they were taken, how she'd played, the conversations they'd had. In every photo, she was a new variation of stunning, with her long blonde hair, those lean tanned legs that went forever and as for that smile ...Zach could stare at her all day, every day.

He was still sitting there, caught up in the past, when Tina walked in.

'Babe, I got worried when I woke up and you weren't beside me,' she said, glancing at his computer screen.

Zach shut his laptop, but it was too late.

'What the actual fuck are you doing?' Tina spat the words. 'Is that porn?'

Zach was horrified. 'No, of course not.'

'Don't lie to me. I saw naked flesh.'

'Tina, it's not porn. Okay?'

'Well, if it isn't, open your computer and show me.'

Knowing he had no way out, Zach flipped open his laptop monitor. Annie's face popped up.

'Who is she?' Tina asked and then exhaled slowly. 'That's Annie, isn't it?'

'No,' Zach said just as Tina reached for the mouse. 'Tina. Don't.'

He wasn't fast enough. Seconds later, a slideshow of all the photos he'd taken of Annie sprang to life. Annie playing tennis, Annie with Samantha, Annie strolling around Paris, London, Manhattan, Sydney, through to the most recent, taken today, dozens and dozens of them.

'They're all of her,' Tina said quietly. 'All of them.'

'It's not what you think,' Zach said.

'Really? And what do I think?'

He didn't answer.

'Are you obsessed with her? Because the evidence implies...' Her expression was one of resigned sadness and frustration.

Zach shut off his computer and took her in his arms. 'Annie's on the comeback trail. I was looking at the photos because I was thinking she'd make a great human-interest story. She disappears for a couple of years only to re-emerge at the Australian Open. It's a media dream.'

'Are you sure it's purely professional?'

Zach wiped the tears falling down her cheeks. 'I'm sorry.'

Tina pushed back and crossed her arms.

He didn't want to be this man, the bad guy. He had to do something about his Annie fixation ...or let her go forever. But that didn't solve his current problem. 'I'm sorry.'

'Stop saying that. What do you mean?'

'I don't think this is working.' He still didn't know if there was any chance he and Annie would get together, but the time had come to end his relationship with Tina. Even though he liked being with her—she was bright, funny and really loved him—Zach wasn't in love with her. But Annie? Zach was head over heels. 'I don't want to hurt you.'

'Spare me, Zach. I'll make it easy for you. We're finished. It's over. I don't want you to settle for me, and I'm not wasting any more time on a guy who is so clearly in love with someone else.'

More tears leaked from her eyes, but she remained stoic. 'I'll leave tomorrow morning. But tonight, you can sleep in here.'

Zach watched as she headed out the door. Should he get up and run out after her? Beg her forgiveness? What was the point? Tina was a great person, but ...still, he felt bad for hurting her. No wonder he'd let his other liaisons drift along. Breaking up was emotionally painful. In the end, he was left with no one—not Tina and not Annie either.

Fifty-four

Samantha

The great news about making it through round two—in addition to being a contender in round three—was you got better service in the players' lounge, bottles of champagne and baskets of flowers turned up in your hotel room, your laundry got done for free, and there was a huge chance of an upgrade. It was fantastic, if you could get past the incredible muscle fatigue, sore joints, twisted ankles, ice-baths and heartache it took to get there.

'Do you want to move to the Windsor and have your laundry done for free?' I asked Annie as we drove out of the car park after a practice session.

'Why? I do it for free at your place. Besides, I like staying with you. I don't want to be surrounded by other players and the media all day, every day.'

'And I'd miss the chanting.'

Annie grinned. 'I got a call from Nike.'

'And?'

'They want to sponsor me. Days ago, they wouldn't even give me a cap. Now they're all over me, offering me shoes, socks, caps, clothing. Amazing how quickly circumstances change. Hey, where are we going?'

I smiled. 'We're taking a little detour.'

I parked the car at St Kilda beach and we walked along the foreshore which was buzzing with walkers, joggers and rollerbladers.

Immediately, I saw Violet and her family playing on the sand. Annie spotted them straightaway too.

'Hey,' she said, running down to meet them and sweeping Ava and Poppy into her arms. 'I've missed you both so much.'

'We're all together again,' Poppy shouted, dragging Annie over to Violet.

'Oh my.' Annie's eyes were glistening. 'Baby Hester.'

Violet beamed. 'She's not a baby any longer.'

I watched as Hester, tentative at first, allowed Annie to pick her up and be cuddled. Part of me was a little jealous, but I dismissed it. This catch-up wasn't about me. It was about surprising Annie.

'Annie, I can't believe it,' Violet said.

'You can't believe it! What are you all doing here in Melbourne?'

'That's a silly question,' Rick said, moving in to greet Annie. 'We came to see you win the Australian Open.'

'I'm not sure about that.' Annie wiped at rogue tears.

'Well, we are,' Violet said. 'Aren't we, girls?'

They squealed 'yes' in unison.

'And how are you, darling?' Violet said, reaching out for my hand.

I'd been quiet, letting the girls have their time with Annie, happy she was finally meeting Hester.

'How does it feel to be thrust back into the limelight after all this time?' Violet pushed.

I smacked my lips together. 'Surprising, I'll say that much.'

'Sit down, sit down,' Violet said, pulling me down to the blanket on the grass. 'We've brought a picnic, wine, your favourite cheeses, the lot.'

'And chocolate-covered strawberries,' Ava chimed in. 'Yum. And lamingtons!'

'I can't get over Hester,' Annie said, staring at her. 'Or you two girls! You've grown so much, and so gorgeous, the pair of you.'

'I want to get my hair cut, but Mum won't let me,' Ava growled.

'And I want to get my ears pierced, and she won't let me do that either,' Poppy said.

Rick laughed and poured the wine. 'Life's so unfair, isn't it?'

Violet turned to Annie. 'Tell us everything.'

'Not much to tell.'

I snorted and popped a strawberry in my mouth. 'Oh, I think there is.'

Annie glanced at me before speaking. 'As Sami probably told you, I was at an ashram in India most of the time, helping out at an orphanage and trying to make sense of the world and where I fit into it.'

'And?' Violet probed.

'Ultimately I decided I want to play professional tennis.'

Rick raised his glass. 'Definitely the right decision.'

'Thanks.'

'You're a winner, Annie,' I said. 'Nike's just offered you a new wardrobe.'

Ava and Poppy's heads looked up from the lamingtons they were devouring. 'Nike?'

Annie laughed. 'Yes, Nike!'

The girls turned their attention back to cake.

'Truth though,' Annie said. 'I really wanted to win that match yesterday on my own merit, not because Yasmine had to pull out.'

'What are you talking about?' Violet said. 'You're through to the third round. That's an incredible achievement.'

'Maybe I'm just tired.'

'I'm sure Kim Clijsters was tired when she battled Caroline Wozniacki in the finals at Flushing Meadows,' I said. 'But did she give up? No! She was an unseeded player who'd been out of the competition over two years.'

'What about Jennifer Capriati triumphing in 2001 at the Open after nearly a decade in the wilderness?' Violet said.

'Okay, I get it,' Annie said.

Violet sipped her drink thoughtfully. 'Honey, you can go all the way. You must have faith in yourself. Also, you've got secret weapons. Sami and Bear are on your side. How can you possibly lose?'

Annie squinted at me. 'Yeah, thanks, Sam, I couldn't do this without you.'

I didn't get a chance to respond because Ava and Poppy were pulling Annie in all directions. She gave in and joined them as they skipped to the water's edge. I watched the windsurfers and paddleboarders. They made these water sports look so easy.

'So, how's she really doing?' Violet asked as we watched her play with the girls.

I stretched back on the blanket. 'Not sure. I mean, she's amazing to get this far. But I think she's overwhelmed.'

'Fair enough,' Rick said.

'And how are you holding up, Sami?' Violet asked.

'All right. Focussed on the matches. Once the Open's over, there'll be time to take it all in. I think I'm still in shock.'

'And you're okay with Annie playing when you're not?' Violet prodded.

I sat up. 'Honestly, I'm a little jealous. I'm trying not to be, but it's tough when everyone's all over her. But don't get me wrong, I'm glad she's back.'

I watched as Annie continued skipping waves with Ava and Poppy and immediately pictured myself doing the same thing with Bear and our children.

Where had that thought sprung from? I quickly dismissed it.

I knew one thing for sure, though. If I ever did have children, there's no way I'd leave them like Mum had left me.

Fifty-five

'That was a lovely surprise. I can't get over little Hester, and how much Poppy and Ava have grown,' Annie said later that night. We were back at my place, watching the men's tennis on TV—Stan Pasanski against Marcos Anderson.

'They're all so excited for you,' I said, pushing down a spike of jealousy.

Two sets down, Pasanski took his seat and hammered his racquet into the ground.

'Uh-oh,' Annie said.

He retrieved another racquet from his bag and smashed that too.

'Surely he won't do a third,' I said.

But he did. And a fourth.

'And they say I'm highly strung,' Annie said as Pasanski calmly strode back on court with his fifth racquet.

I laughed. 'Madly brilliant.'

The next morning, over orange juice and scrambled eggs, I updated Annie on Netta's game. 'She's in good form, but her clothes are getting wackier by the day. The other night in her match against Lourdes Alvarez, she wore a pink tennis dress with a diamanté neckline, satin-bow waistline and matching headband. Looked like she was promenading on the red carpet, not playing tennis.'

'Keeps the crowd entertained,' Annie mused.

'Rethinking your traditional white?'

'Maybe I should sew on a few sequins or add some ruffles?' She laughed, then looked serious. 'That's the least of my concerns. I'm worried about my fitness. I don't have the stamina of the old days.'

'You're fit enough. Netta's a physical player so you need to get out there and end the rallies early. Go for the shots.'

'Is she still doing double knee-jumps till she can barely stand and lunges carrying twenty-kilo weights on each arm?'

'Yeah, she's a machine—skipping, sprints, you name it.'

'I can't do any of that,' Annie said, staring into her empty teacup.

'Maybe not, but you can play the game. Get your poker face on and don't let her see that you're flustered—ever.'

'But—'

'It's tough, but you have to work through it. When you lose your nerve, you lose your serve, and you can't afford to. It's as simple as that.'

'Am I ever going to compete against someone older than me?' Annie said. 'Where are the players like Jane McLeod? She's seven years older than me.'

'Jane often skips this Grand Slam because it's too hot. But you're right, this year the players are younger.'

'I feel like the nanna of the group.'

'Well, Netta's only a year younger than you, old fossil,' I said good-naturedly. 'And hopefully she'll be too busy fussing over what she's wearing to concentrate.'

Fifty-six

Violet, Rick and the girls were already seated in Annie's box by the time Bear and I took our places. I waved to my school students and their parents, who were sitting several rows back.

'Bear, my man,' Rick said, shaking his hand and slapping his back. 'It's been too long.'

'Indeed,' Bear said, turning to embrace Violet and the girls.

Violet smiled and raised her eyebrows at me.

'Don't,' I mouthed. I needed to focus on Annie's game.

'What are her odds?' Bear asked me once we were settled.

'Shouldn't I be asking you that?' I said, peering around at the growing crowd.

'Still wearing the earrings, I see, GG.'

'I told you the other night, I love them. My feelings for stunning jewellery aren't going to change. And I asked you to stop calling me that.'

Bear's eyes sparkled. 'You're still in love with me, I can tell.'

'What about Courtney?' I asked over the cheers as Annie and Netta entered the arena.

'Nah, I don't think she's in love with me.'

'Ha, ha.'

He smiled. 'Haven't heard from her this morning, but we've still got a few hours before her game.'

'Get a load of Netta's outfit,' I said.

Netta was decked out in a fuchsia cocktail dress with slim bodice, dropped waist and pleated skirt but it didn't seem to affect her game. She was all over Annie from the start, her shots low and powerful.

'C'mon, Annie,' Rick and Violet screamed.

'You can't take her seriously in that ridiculous frou-frou outfit,' I whispered.

'Frou-frou or not, she's getting the shots,' Bear observed as Netta aced Annie yet again to take out the first set 6–3.

But in an amazing turnaround, Annie dropped only two games to win the second set and powered into the third.

My heart pounded as her powerful ground strokes proved too much for Netta, who pranced around like a dancing horse. In the end, Annie sealed the win with a net-cord volley winner, prompting Netta to smash her racquet on the ground and earn a gruff rebuke from the main umpire.

Annie dropped her racquet, a combination of relief and exhaustion. With tears streaming down her face, she headed to the net for a handshake. For a moment it looked like Netta would stride off court without acknowledging Annie, but finally she went up to the net and congratulated her.

'Netta's not impressed,' I said to Bear as we stood and cheered for Annie. Immediately, he pulled me in for an enormous hug. Momentarily stunned by a rush of memory and desire, I finally pulled away.

Shaking, I couldn't quite believe I'd just been in his arms again.

~ * ~

'Why do you think you played so badly today?' Prue Hamilton, subtle as always, asked Netta at the post-match interview.

'I'm better on clay,' Netta said, and she wasn't lying. She'd won the French Open last year. 'But I am not playing badly. I am good. Very good. There is no worry with me.'

The reporters turned their attention to Annie, but Netta tapped on her microphone. 'I would like to mention one thing more. I am thrilled to announce that I'm starting my own clothing line, *Netta*. I'm designing right now, and I'm jumping over the moon about it. This is one of the designs.' She pirouetted on the spot. 'So very cool, *non*? From now on, I will always wear my own designs. I think the public like to see the best athletes dress like superstars.'

'Miuccia Prada will be shaking in her boots,' I whispered to Bear.

'Annie, another great win for you,' Prue Hamilton said, clearly fed up with Netta.

'Netta put up a tough fight. It was an exhausting match,' Annie answered.

'Your sister believes you're close to reclaiming your place among the elite,' Prue went on. 'What do you think?'

'I appreciate Sam's confidence. I hope I don't let her down,' Annie replied, looking straight at me.

'Do you feel you've already let her down, given that you're hitting out on your own?' Prue asked. 'Has Samantha Callahan had to give up her dream for you to realise yours?'

Annie's poker face was back. 'I wouldn't put it like that.'

'Really?' Prue replied. 'Because many do. Can you see yourself playing professional doubles with your sister again?'

'I'm ...I'm not sure,' Annie began, but Bear had stepped up beside her, signalling that the interview was over.

It was the right thing for him to do, but part of me enjoyed seeing Annie being put on the spot. Prue's comment certainly made me think. I didn't have a choice about not playing doubles. Annie hadn't given me an option.

'One more question,' Prue called out. 'No doubt you'll be watching tonight's game between Dragana Lukić and Suzy Gardner with interest?'

I saw Annie flinch at the mention of Dragana's name.

'If Dragana wins her match, she's slated to play you in the fourth round,' Prue went on. 'How do you feel about that?'

'Excited,' Annie replied before hurrying out of the press room.

~ * ~

Bear and I headed over to watch Courtney's game against Dionne. Violet and Rick were already there. Annie had gone for lunch with Zach. I'd heard him ask her after the press conference and wondered if he was still infatuated with her. He seemed happy with Tina, though, so perhaps he just wanted to catch up.

'I saw you raise your eyebrows when I said Annie's interview was over,' Bear said as we took our seats in the sweltering heat.

So, he *was* paying attention to me. 'I was interested in their discussion.'

'Do you really believe you've given up tennis so Annie can be a star on her own? Because if that's the case—'

'No.' I chewed my lip. 'I'm ...I'm just not sure what I want to do with the rest of my life.'

'I guess teaching twelve-year-olds can't be high on your agenda.'

'Why not? I like it. There's no pressure.'

'Hear, hear,' Violet said, who was listening. 'You love coaching the kids, don't you?'

'I do.' Violet was spot on. I loved my students' enthusiasm and innocence. It was a healthy atmosphere to be around.

'Can't be very exciting though,' Bear said.

'Sometimes life's better without the excitement. It's calmer, more predictable.'

'And boring,' Bear said. 'Look where you are now, Samantha. Front and centre at the Australian Open.'

Boring? I'd had enough of his interrogation but didn't want to get upset or start a conversation about me getting back on the circuit. 'Speaking of which, Annie's growing more powerful with each game.'

'So that's the end of our chat about you?'

'Yep, enough about me. Annie's match against Dragana could really throw her.'

'Only Annie can work through her demons. It's up to her.'

'Fair enough, but a loss to Dragana will reinforce Annie's fear that she's missed her chance to win a Grand Slam.'

'She needs to be patient. She's only been back in the country a week.'

He made a valid point.

Dionne made her way onto the court to raucous clapping and cheers. She was immaculately groomed, with flawlessly applied make-up and blow-dried bouncy hair.

'You'd think she was off to a party,' Violet said.

'She probably is, after the match,' I replied. 'Do you reckon she has a stylist following her around?'

'She has to,' Violet replied. 'There's no way hair can flick that way on its own, even if she's blow-drying it herself.'

'I take it you're talking about Dionne,' Rick said knowingly.

Violet and I jiggled our heads in unison.

'She's always perfectly made-up, and on court, she never has a hair out of place,' I mused. 'But she must sweat.'

'It's Australia, the middle of summer,' Bear said. 'Everyone sweats.'

'Not if she's had Botox injected into her armpits,' Violet pondered.

Bear wrapped his arms around us both. 'You girls.'

The seats around us began filling up.

'This is so exciting,' Violet said, taking it all in. 'Annie wins her match this morning, and now we're about to watch Courtney, another underdog. It's thrilling.'

'Let's hope she plays as well as Annie did,' I said.

'Dionne's a seasoned player, isn't she?' Violet asked.

'Yes,' Bear replied. 'But I was talking to her coach and manager this morning, and they're not happy. With all the trouble she's been getting into, one of her more lucrative contracts is in doubt. After the tournament's over, she's been instructed to lie low.'

'Fat chance,' I said.

'Maybe, but yesterday she visited the children's hospital. Tomorrow, she's making a guest appearance at a charity fundraiser.'

I grinned. 'Bet she's happy about that.'

'She's been told to keep out of trouble, lay off the drink, and under no circumstances grope any men, even if they tell her they're single and own a castle in England.'

'See,' I said, watching Dionne through my binoculars, 'it's thirty-four degrees and she hasn't raised a sweat.'

Bear grinned. 'I hope you're not going to provide a running commentary on Dionne's armpits for the entire match.'

'I won't mention the word *sweat* again, but I'll be looking.'

Dionne had a certain arrogance on court, a bravado that often intimidated her opponents. But I knew Courtney was ready for it.

'I'm not intimidated by a freakin' hand model,' she'd told me earlier.

'I thought you two were best friends,' I'd said.

'Not on the court. Out there, it's every woman for herself.'

Courtney was right and sticking with that mantra, won the first set 6-4.

Early in the second set, when Courtney double-faulted and then missed an easy lob, Dionne laughed out loud, earning a rebuke from the main umpire. At the change of ends, when she and Courtney brushed past each other, Dionne waved her hand theatrically in the air.

I saw Courtney say, 'Bite me.'

Dionne, serving at 5–6, 15–30, was called for a foot fault on a second serve, giving Courtney two match points.

'She won!' I screamed. 'Courtney won.'

Dionne, outraged, abused a female line judge and threatened to shove a ball down her throat. It all happened so quickly, I stared at her meltdown in disbelief, along with the rest of the sweaty crowd.

'Yep, it's over,' Bear chortled. 'Dionne's just been handed a penalty, so she's lost the point and the match.'

Bear stared at Courtney. 'Look at her, entering the tournament as a wildcard. Amazing. Goes to show anything's possible in the world of women's tennis.'

Around us, people were jumping up and down, whistling and yahooing.

What a day.

'I really did want to bite her,' Courtney told us later. 'I wanted to rip her from limb to limb. That's when my survival instinct kicked in. There was no way I was going down to her!'

'And it paid off,' Bear said. 'You're through to the fourth round.'

At the post-match interview, No-Sweat Dionne made excuses for her loss. 'I was at a disadvantage from the start. Courtney knows too much about my game—perhaps she's been spying on me. And she wears squeaky sneakers! Whenever I served, she squeaked all over the court to distract me.'

'Where will you go from here?' Prue asked.

'I'm shooting a commercial for Red Bull in Tokyo next month, and I'm scheduled for another ad for Rolex—'

Prue smirked. 'I meant with your tennis career, Dionne.'

'Oh, that. Well, if people keep flying me around the world and letting me enter tournaments, I'll keep playing. It's a blast.'

'Do you think you'll retain your endorsements after today's performance?'

Dionne visibly paled and made a slashing motion across her neck with her right index finger, indicating the interview was over.

We all knew if Dionne kept losing and abusing umpires, she could kiss her Rolex contract goodbye. The big brands only wanted winners representing them. It wasn't good enough to be the second-best, unless you were drop-dead gorgeous and wildly popular. And a good sport. While Dionne was gorgeous, she wasn't overly popular, either with the players or the public, women especially.

Fifty-seven

Zach

Zach was enjoying his lunch with Annie at a funky vegetarian restaurant in the city.

'I've always wanted to eat here,' Annie said, taking in the oriental decor. 'How'd you guess?'

'And bonus points,' Zach said, as he poured the wine. 'It's well away from where the tennis fraternity lunch.'

He was pleased with his choice, though it was fancier than he'd imagined, so it made it a little harder to believe this was a casual invitation.

'What's been happening?' Annie asked.

'Well, without naming names, this morning I saw two of the top seeds abusing each other in the locker room. These guys are notorious for their constant fighting, so the other players, fed up, dragged them into a shower cubicle and turned on the cold water. The two guys who started it are now talking about pressing charges against the others.'

Annie raised her eyebrows. 'But not against each other for assault in the first place?'

Zach grinned. 'They say they're like brothers and that's how brothers treat each other.' Momentarily, he chastised himself for mentioning siblings treating each other badly.

Annie stifled a laugh. 'And people say women's tennis is incestuous.'

'Man, until you've been inside the men's locker room—'

'Don't tempt me. It's been a while since I've been inside a men's locker room!'

Zach was more than a little flustered. Thinking quickly, he changed the subject to her game. 'That was another magnificent win this morning. You're really back in the game.'

'I'd never say this to Samantha, so don't you dare repeat it, but sometimes my inner critic hammers at me and I really need to draw on all the meditation and breathing techniques I learnt in India to silence the negativity.'

He took her hand. 'Annie, don't doubt yourself. You're an incredibly talented athlete.' He paused. 'Take it from me—I know. While I was on the circuit, I was battling demons in my head one hundred per cent of the time. I don't know what you did while you were away, but I know you were dealing with intense issues. It's obvious you've returned more passionate than ever. You're a warrior.'

She smiled. 'Warrior, not worrier, hey?'

Zach checked himself and for the remainder of their lunch played it cool, careful not to gush over Annie and tell her how much he'd missed her these past couple of years. His priority was regaining Annie's trust and friendship; perhaps after that, he could talk to her about his feelings for her.

Annie suddenly pulled away. 'I didn't realise it was so late,' she said, looking at him with her gorgeous green eyes. 'I should get going.'

'Of course.' Now she was about to leave, he couldn't bear not to say anything. Really, what did he have to lose? Better to put it out there. 'Hey,' he said, taking her hand again.

She looked bemused. 'What is it?'

'Nothing. It's just ...I know this is probably bad timing, but then there's probably no good timing, so I'm wondering ...I've always had a huge crush on you ...I was wondering if we could go out?' He exhaled. 'I'm going to stop talking now.'

Annie stared at him for several moments. 'I don't know what to say.'

Zach looked crestfallen.

'You're very sweet, but I need to focus on my tennis right now. I can't let anything distract me—it wouldn't be fair to Bear and Sam. Everything else must go on the backburner. I'm sorry. Besides, I heard you had a lovely girlfriend, so you must be happy, right?'

Zach sighed. 'We broke up. That is, I broke up with her. I was a bit of an arse, to be honest.'

Annie kissed his cheek. 'Nah. You're one of the good guys, Zachie.'

Fifty-eight

Samantha

'Hey,' I said to Annie as we ate our omelettes. 'I just got a text from Vi and Rick wishing you luck today.'

She looked up and smiled. 'I wish they could have stayed longer.'

'Me too.' I scanned the day's Twitter headlines about Annie's fourth round match.

Commentators are calling it the grudge match of the competition, I read. *The history between these two speaks for itself* ...yada, yada ...*Sørensen was Lukić's coach, before he started dating Callahan and soon after announced his engagement to her. After their relationship cooled, Sørensen returned to Lukić and resumed coaching her.*

Annie seemed totally unfazed about her looming match with Dragana, and I wondered whether it had anything to do with

Zach. The last couple of days, she'd reminded me of the carefree sister I used to know, relaxed and at ease.

'So,' I said, doing my best to sound casual, 'how was lunch with Zach?'

'Nice. We talked a bit about Wimbledon, and London. He apologised for showing me the photos and for leaving the vodka in my room.'

'He blamed himself. He was devastated when you—'

'Zach was in no way responsible for what happened. No one was. I'm an adult and I take full responsibility for that time in my life.'

True, but my guilt remained for leaving Annie alone that night when she was clearly depressed. I was also worried how Annie would react to seeing Erik today at the match.

'You okay?' I asked for the hundredth time when we walked into Rod Laver Arena two hours later. 'Remember, you can't afford a lapse in concentration. Dragana will take you down. This match is really going to test you—'

'Don't you think I know that?' She sounded apprehensive.

'Speak of the devil,' I said as Dragana arrived next to us, reeking of cigarette smoke.

'I want to wish you good luck today, Annie,' she said.

'That's very nice,' Annie replied, clearly shocked.

Dragana waved her hand in the air. 'I will win, but I am sure you will be a worthy opponent.'

As she turned to leave, I called after her, 'I won't tell Erik about your habit of smoking in the locker room. I know you're not allowed to.'

Annie sucked in some air.

'What? She was being a bitch.' I squeezed her shoulder. 'Good luck. You're a star, Annie Callahan, and don't ever forget it.'

Several of my students were nearby, waving frantically. I waved back, grateful for the distraction, then left Annie to prepare for the match.

Bear was already seated by the time I made it to Annie's box. 'Been here long?'

He smiled. 'Long enough,' he said, pointing to an empty coffee cup and chip packet.

When Annie and Dragana came out on court, they each turned their head in the same direction—to where Erik was sitting in prime position in Dragana's box. I glanced over to the press box and clocked Zach. He was watching Annie watch Erik.

Annie was down 0–40 in the first game when she looked up into the crowd again. I hoped she wasn't searching for Erik, who was hanging over the edge of the players' box like the boorish oaf he was. She glanced back down the court as Dragana served, but it was too late. In a shocking lapse of concentration, Annie smacked the ball out of bounds.

The crowd sighed with disappointment. 'C'mon, Annie,' a couple of voices boomed.

Annie served, and Dragana slammed the ball back, hitting Annie on the forehead and taking the first set 6–1. Annie looked dazed, but luckily could rest between sets. I willed her to get a grip. She'd hate to go down to Dragana this way. Being fairly beaten, yes, but being hit in the head and forced to retire because of concussion? No.

When Annie walked back onto the court, she looked focused and determined. Whatever concentration techniques she'd learnt in India were paying off. It was as if she'd finally woken up. Maybe the hit had knocked some sense into her.

'Annie! Annie!' The crowd chanted her name, which seemed to resonate with her. 'Annie! Annie!'

It didn't matter how hard Dragana tried, Annie was all over her. Several minutes later, she blasted a 180-kilometres-per-hour ace, winning her fourth straight game in the second set to build a 5–2 lead.

Then Erik appeared at the sideline, coaching Dragana. I couldn't believe it. He spoke in Norwegian for a minute, then said in English, 'You win this, Dragana.'

Luckily, the umpire noticed and warned him.

True to form, Erik replied indignantly, 'Erik does not listen to this.'

The umpire fined him anyway. 'Mr Sørensen, one more indiscretion and you'll be banned from the stadium for the remainder of the tournament.'

The crowd roared.

I laughed, then laughed some more when Annie took the set 6–2.

In the all-important third set, she won the first point with a smashing ace.

'She's got a great rhythm going,' Bear said as we cheered her on.

'And Dragana's looking shaky,' I replied.

'The heat's getting to her. She's not at her best in these tough conditions.'

'Whereas Annie looks full of confidence,' I said as she closed out the third game.

It was Dragana's turn to serve and serve she did, acing Annie four times in a row to take the game.

'That's got to knock her confidence,' I said to Bear. 'C'mon, Annie.'

Play began in the fifth game, and I was nervous. Annie had completely changed tactics. Abandoning the safety of her baseline haven, she charged at the net whenever possible.

'What's she doing?'

Bear was silent.

'Bear!'

'Trust her,' he said calmly. 'For a start, she's shortening points in this wretched heat, but it's also a statement of intent.

Look, Dragana's flustered and so is Erik. Annie's being tactical and confusing them both.'

Erik scowled, clearly at a loss and trying to figure out what Annie was up to.

'Oh my God,' I shouted as she took the game and a 4–1 lead. 'Way to go, Annie!'

She looked up briefly and smiled.

This time, Dragana couldn't ace Annie. Annie had cracked her. For the remaining two games, Dragana looked tired and defeated. Annie took the set and won the match. She was through to the quarter-finals.

~ * ~

At the post-match interview, Annie was upbeat, confident and full of gracious praise for Dragana, Bear and me. 'I also want to thank the fans for their tremendous support,' she added. 'They really spurred me on, especially after that hit to the head.'

'You make it sound like this is the end, when it's only the beginning,' Prue Hamilton remarked.

Annie smiled. 'I can hardly believe that ten days ago I was in India, playing tennis to an audience of cows.'

'Now look at you,' Prue said, 'playing in the quarter-finals. How do you feel about that?'

'Beyond thrilled. To play here in front of the home crowd is truly amazing.'

When it was Dragana's turn, she didn't waste any time getting stuck into the umpire, the crowd and finally, Annie. 'The heat was unbearable. The match should have been postponed. It was deliberate to help Annie have the victory.'

'Many players, including Federer, would say that if you can't deal with the stifling heat, you should throw in the towel,' Prue remarked.

'He is a man,' Dragana sniffed. 'What would he know? Men can say foolish things sometimes.' She took a long sip of her water.

'What's going on?' I whispered to Bear.

'Beats me,' he replied.

Dragana started up again. 'Also, Erik is unfairly targeted. He was not telling me to run to the net or to hit to her backhand–'

'Erik wasn't coaching you?' Prue asked.

'I know that is what you believe, but no, he was not. But because the crowd was so obviously against me, he was encouraging me. He is a supportive fiancé.' She held up her left hand to show off the enormous sparkler from her first engagement to Erik.

'Did you say fiancé?' the assembled press asked.

Erik gasped, clearly taken unaware.

'Yes,' Dragana said. 'And now I have played my final singles match. I am moving to a new phase in my life as Mrs Erik Sørensen.'

Erik looked stricken. He raised his hand as if to say something but dropped it just as quickly. It appeared Dragana's retirement and engagement announcement had come out of the blue for Mr Sørensen. She was playing him at his own game. Clearly, he'd been an excellent teacher.

I looked at Annie. She didn't give anything away.

Dragana continued. 'If I cannot compete against best players in the world and win, I should not be playing. Today, I lost against a marginally mediocre player. Now, immediately, I am planning my marriage. I am very happy.'

~ * ~

Later in the locker room, Dragana chain-smoked while gathering congratulations from all the players.

'Should I say something?' Annie asked.

'Like what? No, Dragana knows exactly what she's doing. She's had long enough to prepare for this moment. Come on, let's see what Courtney's up to.'

Annie and I settled in Courtney's box to watch her take on Marta Kubot, but my mind kept wandering. Dragana's statement about starting a new phase in her life had got me thinking about my own life. The last couple of days had been truly crazy, but they'd also made me realise that my time on court was over. A couple of years ago, I could never have imagined saying that. I used to love playing tennis, and I was only thirty—I could have carried on for another four or more years, with luck and no injuries.

But the more I thought about the last few days, the more I found myself questioning what I wanted from life. What did Samantha Callahan want for her future? What gave me satisfaction? Coaching my girls? Yes, absolutely. I'd had more fun with them these past twelve months than I'd had in years. Being with Isabella, Lucy and the others reminded me how much I'd loved playing tennis when I was a child. And one thing was for sure, despite what Bear or anyone else thought, I wasn't about to let those girls down. Nurturing their young talent was exciting. I enjoyed their enthusiasm, their youthfulness, their spunk.

At the same time, I loved the thrill of being back in the game, being at Rod Laver Arena with the amazing professional players I'd come to regard as friends. I loved teaming up with Annie again. I didn't want to be in the spotlight, that much I'd learnt, but coaching? Yeah, I wanted that. Annie had so much potential. I wanted to see it through with her, really nurture her. I had every confidence she could make it to the top.

'I don't know anything about Marta. Who is she?' Annie asked as Marta served up a startling speedy ace.

'That's right—you weren't around when she destroyed me at Wimbledon in my final match,' I said drily.

'Sorry, I—'

I waved my hand. 'No need. It was a shocking match. I completely lost my nerve, then had a fall and was forced to forfeit. She'd have won, regardless of my injury. I underestimated her ability and overestimated my own. It was one of the most humiliating moments of my life.'

Suddenly Bear was beside me, rubbing my back. 'It was a toughie.'

'When did you get here?' I asked, turning to him.

'About when you said "destroyed".'

'Well, I was.'

'Yeah' He continued rubbing my back.

'I'm so sorry, Sami, for what I put you through,' Annie said.

'Water under the bridge,' I said, focusing on the game so I wouldn't break down. 'Marta hates playing at the net, she prefers the baseline and is a big server. And this will interest you, Annie. Look what she does here.'

The three of us watched as Marta prepared to serve. As if on cue, she picked at imaginary lint on her left shoulder.

'Wow, I thought I was the only one who did that,' Annie mused.

'Exactly,' Bear chimed in. 'Did! Not anymore. I haven't seen you do it since you returned.'

'That was one of the habits I kicked in India. My yogi said that it represented a psychological barrier to my tennis success.'

'He was spot on,' I said.

'Look at her now,' Bear said. Marta seemed to be in pain, clutching her left hip. 'I read this morning she's been taking hip-hop classes as a form of relaxation. Obviously, she's had one too many.'

Within minutes, Marta had retired from the match. With an awkward wave to the stunned crowd, she was helped off court and out of sight.

'She was leading too,' Annie remarked.

'Good news for Courtney,' I said. 'Now you're both through to the quarter-finals.'

'If only Marta'd been injured in the match you played against her, things might have turned out differently,' Annie said, as we left the stadium to find Courtney. 'You might not have quit.'

'No sense rehashing it. My time on the court's over and done with. I'm not going back.' Saying the words out loud, lightness descended, and I smiled because I realised it was completely true, and I was absolutely fine with it.

Fifty-nine

The buzz around the stadium was electric. Not only were Annie and Courtney wildcards, but they'd made it to the quarter-finals. People kept mentioning Belgian, Kim Clijsters, who was the first female wildcard player to win a tennis grand slam with her memorable singles victory at the 2009 U.S. Open. But the Australian Open? No female wildcards had made it this far.

Annie was playing Kristy, while Courtney was up against Molly Fischer. I smiled at Bear. 'I'm happy with those pairings.'

'Indeed.' His hand nudged mine.

I flinched. 'Are you trying to hold my hand?'

'There's been no one since you, GG.'

I gulped. 'Bear, I—'

'Bear, I what? Bear, I love you? Bear, you're the only guy for me. What?'

All of the above, I wanted to scream. He was the only guy for me, but still my head was fighting my heart. 'I'm sorry. It's all too much. You, Annie, tennis...'

'But—'

I turned and took his hand anyway. 'Please don't do this to me now, not when we're surrounded by hundreds of people right outside the players' lounge.'

He smiled. 'Agreed. It's late in the day, we're both exhausted and need to eat. Let's go.'

I pulled my hand away. 'No.'

'No? You owe me more than that, lady. You're coming with me.'

He grabbed my hand again and led me through the crowds and out of the arena to a waiting car. A few minutes later, we were at the Langham.

'You're unusually quiet,' he said as we entered the foyer.

'Stunned,' I replied. 'I really need to get changed if you're forcing me to have dinner with you.'

'No way, Gorgeous Girl. If I let you out of my sight, you'll disappear. It's now or never,' he said, steering me towards the hotel restaurant.

'I feel incredibly underdressed,' I said after we were seated. All around us were perfectly coiffed women with immaculate make-up, blow-dried hair and floaty colourful dresses. 'It's making me uncomfortable.'

He held my gaze. 'Good. You deserve to be. Apple martini?'

I pouted. 'I feel like you've trapped me.'

'I have,' he said, clasping his hands together. 'Sam, I'm going to cut to the chase. I love you. Always have. Always will.'

My throat constricted. Where was that blasted martini? 'Bear, I—'

He put his hand up to stop me. 'Hear me out. Regardless of what happens, you need to know that I love you. It's as simple as that. You broke my heart when you left me, but I understand your reasons. Now, I feel I've been given a second chance, so I'm telling you again.'

I couldn't speak because I was crying. Finally, I said, 'Can we talk about this upstairs? In private?'

He smiled. 'Thought you'd never ask.'

While I composed myself in the bathroom, Bear spoke to the staff. Ten minutes later we were standing in his suite, apple martinis in hand.

'I love you,' he said, kissing my forehead.

I put down my drink and fell into his arms, feeling like I'd finally come home. I'd been resisting him for so long, it was pure relief to finally accept the truth and give in. I never wanted to leave his side again, ever. 'I love you, too.'

'Babe,' he said, after we'd showered each other with kisses and were lying on his bed. 'Before we go any further, I need you to read something.'

I knew from the tone of his voice that whatever it was had the potential to make or break us. He got up and walked out of the room, taking my heart with him.

'I wrote you a letter,' he said, returning with an envelope in his hand. 'I brought it with me because I hoped I'd see you, or at least slip it under your front door.'

My eyes were wet with tears. 'I'm too scared to read it.'

He passed it to me. 'Don't be. I'll give you some privacy. Call me when you're ready.'

I held the envelope in my hands, not wanting to open it, but at the same time desperately wanting to read what was inside. Finally, I tore it apart and smoothed out the sheet of paper covered with his handwriting.

Gorgeous Girl,

You are and always will be my love. I can't imagine the immense pain and sadness you are going through after losing Annie, I can only tell you about the heartbreaking pain I feel every day at losing the woman I love. You and I weren't a careless romp in the park...

I giggled. Romp in the park? What are we? Dogs?

I love you fully, and even though you'll deny it a hundred times over, I know you love me too. At least you did. We were good together, GG. From the moment we met, I knew we'd be together. I can hear you saying, 'No, you didn't'—too right, I thought—*'but I know you're the woman for me. Your passion for tennis, your passion for me. Gorgeous Girl, I want you back.*

If I could have one wish, it would be that you can find peace and have your sister home, you know that. But if I could be so lucky as to have two wishes, my second would be that you'd allow yourself to love me again, so we can be together always.

Samantha, I love and miss you. Why can't you love me back? Why isn't my love enough for you?

I folded his letter, wiped a dozen tears from my eyes and rushed out of the room to find him.

Sixty

I woke early the next morning, feeling disorientated. This wasn't my apartment. Then I turned and saw Bear next to me. My beautiful Bear.

'Hey,' he said, stroking my hair.

I smiled. 'Hey.'

He pulled me in close. 'I love you, GG.'

I relaxed into his embrace.

In a perfect world, I'd have remained curled up against him, skin to skin, but I knew Annie would be wondering where I was. I couldn't let her down on her biggest day of the tournament yet. I kissed his nose. 'I'd love to stay, but...'

'Butt, exactly,' he said, smacking me on my naked bum. 'Get outta here.'

Ten minutes later, I was showered, dressed and on my way back to St Kilda. I unlocked my front door to find Annie at the kitchen bench, crying.

'What's the matter?' I said, rushing to her side, wondering

what disasters might have caused this. Something Erik had done? Zach? Dad? Me?

'Oh, Sami,' she said, before tears engulfed her again.

Now that I was closer, I saw a pile of paper sitting on the bench in front of her—all the letters I'd written while she was away.

'Where did you get those?' I felt queasy, my fingers quickly covering my mouth.

'I found them in your desk drawer. I'm only up to letter nine. I can't read quickly because of my tears.'

I stumbled a little. 'It's all in the past. You don't need to—'

'But I do,' she said, taking my hand and steadying me. 'How can I ever understand your pain if I don't read your letters? And Samantha, let me tell you, there's a hell of a lot of pain here.'

I sat down at the bench next to her. 'I can't remember everything I wrote. I was upset. Now that you're here, it all seems like a dream, like I imagined the last two and a half years.'

'Samantha, I'm so sorry.'

'Annie, I said it's okay.'

'But about Mum...'

I took a sharp breath and closed my eyes. Annie kept talking.

'I know how much you loved her. So did I. She was my mother too. When she disappeared, I was devastated, but I accepted she was never coming home. She committed suicide.'

I gasped, feeling like I'd been kicked in the guts.

'Sami,' she said, reaching out to me, eyes misty. 'It's the truth. She didn't just fall off a cliff. She deliberately—'

'I know,' I said, tears rolling down my cheeks. 'But without physical proof—'

'You hoped. But it was true, Samantha ...she did it. Dad tried to talk to you about it, like he talked to me, but you wouldn't listen. When it came to Mum, you didn't want to hear what either of us had to say.' She wrapped her arms around me. 'I wish it weren't true.'

'I kept hoping she'd turn up on my doorstep or at a tournament. I've always known, deep down, but it was just too painful to let her go.'

'Remember the memorial service Dad dragged us to?' Annie asked.

'I hated him for that.'

'No one could mention Mum without you getting hysterical. After a while, I guess we kind of gave up.'

'I'll never be okay with what happened to her—'

'You have every right to feel that way. But you have to learn to live with it and stop blaming yourself.'

'If I don't hold on to the grief, I'm worried I'll forget her.'

Annie smiled sadly. 'You'll never forget her.'

We sat holding each other for what seemed like hours before, finally, Annie stood. I looked at the kitchen clock. It was after nine, and she needed to be at Rod Laver Arena.

I wiped my eyes. 'I don't understand...' I stopped; my throat full of tears again. 'Why she did it?'

'Maybe she didn't mean to. A split-second decision when she was at a really low point. I never meant to drink all that vodka and take those pills. But I did. I'm so glad you found me—'

'Stop.' I threw my hand up in front of my face. 'I can't go there, not today. I love you, Annie, and I loved Mum more than anyone in the world.'

'I know, Sami. I know.'

'She'd be proud of us, wouldn't she?'

Annie smiled. 'Ecstatic! She'd be taking photos and bragging about us to anyone who'd listen. We'd be sick of the adulation.'

I wiped my face and got up. 'You okay?'

'I think so.'

'Good!' I said, pushing my feelings aside. 'We've got a match to get to, Annie Callahan, one you're going to win. Mum would be elated.'

Sixty-one

Two hours later, Annie was warming up against Kristy Banta, playing for her spot in the semis.

When the first game started, she took my advice and hit close to the net. Her efforts paid off. In the first set and deuce on Annie's serve, 5–4, her backhand caught the tape and inched over. Kristy had backed away and couldn't reach the ball in time, so Annie held on to win the game and the first set 6–4.

Bear turned to me. 'She's toughing it out. She might actually win this.'

I squeezed his hand. 'I think you could be right.'

But we'd spoken too soon. Nothing went Annie's way in the second set. Not only did many of her second serves miss their mark, but Kristy had twigged that Annie was squarely aiming for net play. As a result, Annie faced an astonishing second-set collapse, losing three games to six.

But she overcame that setback to claw her way into the semis with a 6–4 win in the final set, rounding off with a stunning backhand smacked to the baseline corner. Kristy, wrong-footed, had no time to turn and missed the ball, making Annie the winner.

'Oh my God! She's won, she's won!' I shrieked, as Bear and I watched Annie, who was still dancing backwards as the ball landed. Then she doubled over, clearly in shock that she'd won.

I couldn't believe it. My little sister was going to win the Australian Open.

~ * ~

'Annie!' I yelled when she joined us after the match. 'You played brilliantly.'

She smiled. 'I'm in shock.'

'You're a star,' Bear said as he guided her to the media room. 'A real star.'

She took his hand. 'Thanks, Bear. For everything.'

'You betcha,' he said. 'You've made the big time, girl.'

'I'm so proud of you,' I squealed.

'Finally, I found the zone and was able to win the game the way I wanted to,' Annie gushed minutes later to the assembled media.

'I wish I could blame poor umpiring,' Kristy said, fighting back tears. 'Or the distraction of squeaky sneakers, recent knee surgery, or any other number of reasons why I didn't win today. Sure, the heat was a factor, but I'm not going to cry about it. Put simply, Annie Callahan was the better player. She deserved to win.'

~ * ~

We had no time to celebrate with Annie, as crowds of fans were waiting to congratulate her at Autograph Island. Bear helped her navigate the crowds while I took a call from Violet.

'It's incredible!' Violet screamed. 'I'm so proud of Annie. And you, Sam.'

'Me?' I was shocked.

'Yes, you're the one that made all this happen. Annie would never be where she is today without your support and belief in her.'

'I don't—'

'Just accept the compliment, Sami.'

'Well, I want to thank you for all your support over the years too. Annie and I finally talked about Mum.'

'That must have been hard.'

'Yeah, and thanks for letting me come to terms with it in my own time.'

'How are you feeling?'

'Sad, I guess, but I have a sort of closure now and acceptance.' I sighed. 'Bear and I are back together.'

'Oh my God!' Violet shrieked. 'For real?'

'For real.'

'And you're not going to do anything stupid to stuff it up?'

'Excuse me?'

'You know exactly what I mean.'

I smiled. 'Yes, I do, and no, I won't.'

Hanging up to Violet's continued squeals of joy, I found my way over to Courtney and Bear. Her match was about to start.

'Hey,' Courtney said when she saw me. 'My dad wants to watch me play. The Australian Open's one of the few tournaments he isn't banned from. What should I do?'

'Let him,' Bear said.

Courtney looked at me. 'What do you think?'

'Give him one more chance. But if he fucks up again, tell him it's over—for good.' I turned to Bear and grinned. 'Everyone deserves a second chance.'

Courtney started off well, winning the first set against Molly, just. But she was hanging by a thread in the second.

'Come on, Courtney!' Bear and I shouted from the players' box. Courtney's father was nearby, on the edge of his seat. I could see it was taking every scrap of his self-control not to shout out, but he kept his cool.

'She should win this match,' I said to Bear. 'She's a much stronger player than Molly.'

'Stronger, yes, but Molly's fitter, more agile.'

It looked like Courtney's nerve was failing. Twice at 4–4 in the second set, she gambled on the video replay and lost. Then, with one umpire challenge remaining, she resisted questioning two calls that would have gone her way.

'She can't lose like this,' I said.

Miraculously, from somewhere deep within, Courtney pulled out her magic to hang on and win the match.

Afterwards, she told the crowd what they wanted to hear. 'I want the fans to know that I'm committed to the game. My aim is to continue improving my fitness and mental toughness. I can do it, and I know I'm going to beat Carla Hernandez in the semis. Then I'm going to win the finals. Like my hero, Serena Williams, I can be number one in the world if I really put in the effort.'

'It's about time you committed to your fans and your sport,' I said afterwards.

'Yeah, and this time, I'm going to listen to you, Samantha,' she said. 'Not like last time when I was so pig-headed, and we each ended up playing our own game.'

'It probably helps that you'll be competing against Carla,' I said. 'You'll whip her. You've come a long way.'

And she had. My opinion of her had dramatically improved these past few days. Courtney was showing real guts and determination. I was impressed.

If Annie and Courtney both made it through their semis, they'd be up against each other in the finals. The FINALS! It was exciting, thrilling, unbelievable! And I felt just a little bit sick.

~ * ~

'I'm nervous,' I said to Bear when I met him back at my apartment for dinner.

'Why? I'm cooking, aren't I?'

I led him into the kitchen, where all the ingredients for a duck confit risotto sat on the bench.

Bear smiled. 'I guess that answers my question.'

'I haven't eaten this since we broke up,' I told him as he set about creating his signature masterpiece.

'Neither have I.'

I poured two glasses of wine and handed one to Bear.

He took a sip. 'Have you spoken to Zach?'

'Not recently. Why?'

'He's broken up with his girlfriend. I thought they were tight?'

'Yeah. So did I.' I bit down on a smile. 'Annie had lunch with him the other day.'

Bear whooped. 'The plot thickens.'

'So about Annie and Courtney,' I said, taking a large gulp and trying to be sensible, 'they've both discovered this iron determination. It's scary. I'm excited for both, but what if—'

'When,' Bear interrupted, grinning.

'—they meet up in the finals?' I finished.

'Let's worry about that when it happens.'

'God forbid if Courtney broke her leg,' I said, and started laughing like some out-of-control hyena.

Bear gave me a look. 'You do know you're not supposed to be thinking like that?'

'Okay, so what are we going to do?' I said, calming down. 'Now I know how Venus's and Serena's mum feels. I really want them both to win.'

'Think of it this way... if that happens, we're guaranteed a win.'

'And guaranteed a loss.'

'Who says you can't have it both ways?'

I couldn't help laughing.

'It's been a crazy couple of weeks. After this is all over, I'll sit down with Annie and see what she wants to do.'

'And Courtney?'

Bear tipped rice into the pan and started stirring. 'I've been fielding calls. There are some excellent coaches wanting to take her on.'

I put down my glass. 'What are you saying?'

'If I have to make a choice, I'll go with Annie. Only if she wants me, of course. But I can't abandon Courtney. We need to find someone who's willing to dedicate their time to her, so she becomes the athlete she's capable of being.' He paused. 'But let's cross that bridge when we come to it. Tonight is all about the duck!'

'It does looks yummy,' I said.

'And it will be.' He glanced at his Fitbit, 'in about forty minutes.'

'Forty minutes?' I reached to kiss him. 'We might need more time than that.'

Bear smiled, eyes burning. 'Really?' Grabbing my hand, he pulled me into the bedroom and down onto the bed.

'You really are so gorgeous,' he said, after he threw a leg over my thighs and started tracing the contours of my face and neck with his fingers.

I reached up behind his neck and pulled him down on top of me, laughing, then kissing. Deeply. Slowly. Twisting my hair in his hand, tongues entwined, our kissing became more passionate, urgent. Our breathing erratic.

Bear pulled away and stared. 'I love you, Samantha Callahan.' His voice, a raspy whisper. 'I really do.'

Words stuck in my throat. All I could manage was a garbled 'love you, too,' as my eyes misted over.

Two hours later, the risotto was ruined, and we were both starving, but I felt calm and so, so happy. Bear loved me. He wasn't going to leave me like my mother had.

I had to let her go to truly move forward with my life. I owed it to Bear, Annie and myself. I would never understand why she did it, but I now accepted that she wasn't in her right mind at the time. I don't think Mum deliberately abandoned Annie and me, it was more that she wasn't capable of thinking about us when she was suffering chronic depression. I was working towards being at peace with that.

Sixty-two

Zach

At the pre-semis interview, Zach stood beside Samantha, madly clicking off photos as Prue Hamilton took to the stand. He glanced at Annie through his lens. She looked alluring and luminous. Totally cool. He moved the camera away from his face so he could look at her uninterrupted.

Annie saw him, smiled and waved. Shaking off his lovesick feelings, Zach resumed snapping, but it was hard to concentrate.

'Do you think you have an advantage, given your age?' Prue asked Annie's opponent, Sofia Petrova.

'Certainly, that plays a part, but I have seen Annie in action. She will be fierce competition.'

'True,' Prue agreed, 'but given your number fourteen world ranking, I wouldn't like to be betting against you.'

'The nerve!' Samantha whispered to Zach. 'How dare she?'

'I grew up watching Annie play tennis,' Sofia said, 'so it is a dream come true for me to be playing her today.'

'She's young and determined,' Samantha whispered again.

Zach considered adding 'dangerous' but thought better of it.

'Please welcome our Aussie battlers, Annie Callahan and Courtney Gold, and their go-to guy, Bern "Bear" Devlin, to the stage,' Prue said. 'Although Annie and Courtney have never played against each other, that could all change if they both win their semis today.'

The audience erupted in wild applause, and Zach snapped off a few shots as Annie and Courtney took their seats on the podium.

Prue continued. 'Both Annie and Courtney have had their share of heartbreak and failure, and both enter their respective semi-final games today as underdogs. Before this tournament, Annie Callahan had hung up her professional tennis racquet for two-and-a-half years. Meanwhile, Courtney has battled injury, weight problems and alleged addiction.'

'I'll admit I lost my way during the past year,' Courtney said, speaking confidently into her microphone.

Zach had to hand it to her. She didn't appear fazed. He'd have been furious about Prue's niggling.

'You and me both,' Annie agreed.

'It is fair to say,' Bear added, 'that both players have struggled in recent times. But that's all in the past.'

'Exactly,' Prue continued. 'It must tug heavily on your heartstrings, Bear, given that you've recently taken Courtney under your wing, but your loyalty to the Callahan sisters goes way back.'

'Yes, these are unusual circumstances, Prue. Both Courtney and Annie were surprise additions to the tournament, and it's a testament to their tremendous courage and talent that they've made it this far.'

'It's wonderful to be here,' Annie said. 'But I have no expectations about today's match with Sofia. I'm just happy to be playing in the semi-finals in front of my home crowd.'

'As for me,' Courtney said, 'I came into this tournament ranked ninety-nine. I hope that's as low as my ranking goes while I'm playing professional tennis. At the beginning of this tournament, other players and certainly some members of the public warned me not to play, saying it would end in my humiliation. But I wanted to give it a go. If I hadn't tried, I'd always have thought, what if? I didn't consider myself a loser, even if others did. And look at me now, about to play Carla Hernandez in the semis. It's a dream come true.'

'I feel the same as Courtney,' Annie said. 'I had to give it a go. Yes, there are players who are stronger, faster and have more powerful serves than me, but I was willing to take a risk and get amongst it. I still am.'

'And now you've both made it to the semis,' Prue said.

'That's right, and as long as I play my best today, I'll be happy,' Annie said.

'Me too,' Courtney agreed.

'And if both Courtney and Annie win,' Prue stage-whispered to Bear, 'they'll have to play each other next.'

Bear nodded. 'If they both win, what a thrilling women's final we'll have. Bring it on!'

Sixty-three

Samantha

Courtney was up first against Carla Hernandez. Annie's match would follow straight after. Bear had gone off with Courtney to give her a final pep talk.

'I don't think I can watch,' Annie told me.

'Do you want some company?'

'Thanks, but Zach's offered to babysit. I'm going to hit up with him and do my best to keep my nerves under control. I hope Courtney blitzes it out there.'

'Shouldn't Zach be taking photos?'

Annie smiled. 'He's taking a break.'

I beamed. 'Ooh la la. I'll see you before your game.'

By the time I made it to Courtney's box, Bear was already seated.

'How is she?' I asked.

'Pumped,' he replied. 'Ready to put up a good fight.'

I was as nervous as if I'd been the one playing. It seemed like an eternity before the game got underway.

'She's starting aggressively,' Bear said, as Courtney fired a powerful lob past Carla.

'Does Courtney have any other way?'

It was a stomach-churning competition. Courtney got one game up, then Carla caught up. They were evenly matched. But at five games to Carla's four, Courtney double-faulted, and double-faulted again. It was five games all.

The first set was tight, but Carla made a crucial break in the eleventh game. Two stinging returns gave her a 6–5 edge. She closed it out in the next game by forcing Courtney into a net error on set point.

I was devastated for Courtney.

'She's a fighter,' Bear said. 'She'll be okay.'

Annie texted me. She sounded disappointed too.

It's not over, I texted back.

In the second set, Courtney struggled to find her form. She was down two games, and then three. I was in tears twenty minutes later when she lost the set, four games to Carla's six.

'You played brilliantly,' I said when we caught up with her minutes later. But I was still sniffing back sad tears.

'No, I didn't, but you know what—I played okay. I did all right.'

'Yeah, you did,' Bear said, hugging her. 'Next year, you'll be unstoppable.'

'I fought hard, I really did,' Courtney told us. 'But as Andy Roddick said in his loss to Federer at Wimbledon in 2009, "We're human. We're not cyborgs."'

'And thank God for that,' Bear said.

'I kept going. I still lost, but I gave Carla a damn good nudge.'

I couldn't dwell on Courtney's loss. It was Annie's turn next. I found her in the locker room, looking cool and collected as usual.

'I'm so excited for you,' I said, sitting down beside her. 'This is only the beginning. Great things are in store for you, hon.'

'You don't know what it means to hear you say that, Sam. To have you believe in me.'

'I do believe in you. How are you feeling?'

'I'm thrown by Courtney's loss. I thought she'd win.'

'Same, but now's not the time to think about Courtney. You need to focus on your game.'

She smiled. 'I've been meditating, visualising. And it was good hitting up with Zach. I'm as ready as I can be for this match.'

'I know you are.' Yes, she had her work cut out for her, but she was in with a chance. Sofia was good but not unbeatable. 'This is what we've always dreamed of. You've worked for this. You've earned it. Now give it all you've got. I know you can beat Sofia.'

Annie squeezed my hands and turned. I was in tears before she'd even made it onto the court.

I found my way to the box, where Bear was waiting. 'How's Courtney?' I asked.

'She was with her dad when I left her. He was hugging her. She'll recover. Annie?'

'Courtney's loss rattled her.'

'Let's hope she can put it out of her mind for the duration of the game.'

I glanced at my phone to see a text from Violet. *We have all our fingers and toes crossed … I'll have you know that's 100 digits.*

I laughed, and replied, *Thank you.*

Annie and Sofia came on court to roars of applause. Annie was in her trademark white Nike dress and looked fit and healthy, her hair neatly tied up in a ponytail. Sofia was wearing a pale blue form-fitting dress and cap, nothing flashy.

I stared around at the crowd. 'It's so bloody hard. Not only has she got the media focused on her, she's dealing with the public's elevated expectations as well. It's an incredible burden.'

Bear squeezed my hand.

Annie won the toss and elected to serve. I could barely watch. On the other side of the court, I saw several girls from school holding signs that said *Go Annie!* in huge letters. God love them.

Go Annie, indeed. It was a convincing start, no doubt spurred on by the crowd chanting, 'Aussie, Aussie, Aussie, oi, oi, oi!'

When she took the first set in forty-three minutes without going down a break point, I was on a high. This was Annie of old. She was a champion.

But Sofia was a dangerous opponent. Even though she missed chances in the first set, she had a powerful serve, confirmed when she opened the second set with a blinding ace.

Come on, Annie, I willed.

Bear was silent, focusing intently. We didn't speak, though I had my hand firmly planted on his thigh and every few minutes he winced as I dug my nails in.

Sofia, with her big serve and nice touch around the net, tried to deceive Annie with drop shots. They worked. She won the second set 6–4.

It was down to the all-important third set.

Not letting her second-set loss undermine her, Annie powered through the first two games, winning both. I glanced at Bear and smiled. She still looked confident and happy. But that soon changed in the third game as we watched her hit a forehand long.

'Whoops,' I said, slapping Bear's knee.

'You're going to do permanent damage,' he said, rubbing his leg.

While Annie was quick around the court, dashing from baseline to net, Sofia had the edge, using her speed to her advantage and winning several shots with her forehand down the line.

'Come on, babe,' I whispered. 'She's doing great, isn't she, Bear?'

He smiled and squeezed my hand. 'More than great.'

Together with the Aussie crowd, Bear and I were hoping for a miracle. But it wasn't to be. Although Annie played valiantly, drawing on all her reserves of grit and courage, she lost the third set 6–3.

With tears in her eyes, she shook Sofia's hand and thanked the umpires and ball kids. The crowd gave her a standing ovation as she strode to her chair and sat.

'This is too much,' I said to Bear through my tears. 'I wanted her to win.'

'We all did, sweetheart. There'll be other times. Annie's a star.'

The crowd chanted 'An-nie! An-nie!' over and over, until Annie, tears streaming down her cheeks, stood up and waved. Everyone went ballistic, hollering and screaming her name.

'Thank you, thank you,' she shouted and waved some more. Then she looked my way, clapped her racquet and blew me a kiss.

~ * ~

'Congratulations,' I said, squeezing Annie tight when Bear and I finally caught up with her en route to the media room.

'But I didn't win.'

'Yes, you did,' I said. 'You made it to the semis. You're definitely a winner.'

At the press conference, the buzz was all about how well Annie and Courtney had performed. It didn't seem to matter that they hadn't won their individual matches. Australian women's tennis was back in the headlines for all the right reasons.

With Annie and me in Bear's car, we dropped Courtney back to her hotel.

'You did good,' I told her, as she jumped out.

'Thanks.'

'See you at dinner?' Bear added.

Courtney smiled. 'Wouldn't miss it.'

Arriving at my apartment, I was about to get out alongside Annie when she stopped me and said, 'Why don't you stay with Bear for a bit? I have a few things to do.'

I frowned. 'What?' Then I smiled and shut the door. 'Okay, if you insist.' I had everything I needed back at Bear's suite for tonight's dinner.

I watched as she practically skipped up the steps to our apartment entrance.

Now it was just Bear and me. God! Those eyes and that mouth.

'What do you think she's up to?'

'No idea, but I get to spend the next couple of hours with you, GG. That's a win-win in my book.'

'You know I'm crazy about you, don't you?' My hand caressed his thigh, as I leant over to steal a kiss as he negotiated the Melbourne traffic.

'Yes, I do, but if you continue groping me, I'm going to have to pull over.'

'So, we'll save it?'

He beamed, cheeks glowing. 'Oh, yes.'

Sixty-four

Zach

Zach was still at Melbourne Park, taking the final shots for the day, when Annie phoned. He knew his voice sounded high and happy when he answered, but he didn't care.

'Are you busy tonight?' she asked.

He hesitated, not because he was busy but because he was nervous. 'No.'

'Good. Do you want to have dinner with Sam, Bear, Courtney and me?'

'Courtney's included?'

Annie giggled. 'Of course.'

'Sure. Why not?'

'Zach?'

'Yes?'

'I'm sitting in your hotel lobby. How quickly can you make it here?'

Zach didn't need to be told twice. He packed up his camera, said his goodbyes and in fifteen minutes was entering the hotel. He spied Annie sitting on a sofa in the far corner, looking even more gorgeous, if that were possible. Wearing a short navy mini dress and pink strappy sandals, Annie's loose blonde hair shone under the lights. Smiling broadly, she looked the happiest he'd seen her.

'Annie,' he said, waving and moving towards her confidently. Inside he was a mess.

She stood. 'Is there somewhere we can talk?'

He hesitated. 'My suite?'

'Why, Zach, I thought you'd never ask.'

The lift to the tenth floor seemed to take forever; at every level another person stepped in, congratulated Annie and asked for a selfie, which she obliged.

'What's this about?' he said, when finally, they were inside his room.

As Zach turned from shutting the door, she was standing closer than expected, so close he could smell her fresh shampoo and lemony scent and feel the sexual energy between them, or so he hoped.

She walked towards the photos spread out on the nearby table, which he'd taken over the last few weeks in Melbourne. There were teens skating, young boys playing basketball, homeless youths hanging out on street corners, buskers with their dogs.

Zach stepped alongside her, shifting uncomfortably from foot to foot.

'These are amazing.' Annie took his hand and looked at him. 'You're so talented.'

'Thanks.' Zach could feel his face flush.

'I have plans to go back to India.'

'Oh.' Zach's mood immediately deflated. He'd read her all wrong. She was about to fob him off. He stepped back and eased himself into a chair. Annie kept standing.

'Not forever, just a couple of months. I was wondering if you might be interested in coming with me?' She turned back towards the shots on the table. 'To take photos of the children to help with fundraising for a foundation I have in mind to set up?'

Zach stood and grinned. 'Annie, I have no idea what you're talking about, but I'd follow you to the ends of the earth. I'm in one hundred per cent. Yes.'

She leaned in and kissed his lips.

Zach's heart was dancing, and his feet were no longer on the ground.

Sixty-five

Samantha

That evening at dinner, Zach ordered Moët for the table. I looked between him and Annie—they were both glowing.

'Here's to all of us,' Courtney said, and we raised our full glasses.

'What an extraordinary couple of weeks.' I took a sip and leaned back in my chair. 'I'm exhausted.'

Courtney groaned. 'You're exhausted? Ha! Next year, my hard work and mental focus is going to pay off. I'm going to make it to the finals, and so are you, Annie.'

We raised our glasses again.

'Sadly for you, Annie,' Courtney continued, 'I'm going to whip your arse. These last couple of weeks I've lost five kilos. I only have another twenty to go, and I'll be back to my perfect wonderful self. I'll be unbeatable.'

'I'm sure you will be,' Annie said graciously. 'Don't spend all your time working out, though. Remember to make some time for love.'

'Nah, Brad broke my heart. Right now, the only thing I'm committing to is my tennis racquet and treadmill.'

'Your ranking's gone through the roof,' Bear said. 'Fifty-five and rising.'

She grinned. 'Yeah, I'll be top twenty and tiny again within the year. But tonight, I'm going to par-tay.'

Bear grimaced. 'Okay, but please—'

'No taking off my underwear in public. I know. Toodles,' she said, before draining her glass and dancing off towards a group of well-wishers. It looked like most of the tennis circuit had decided to eat at this restaurant tonight.

'So, what happens now?' Prue Hamilton asked me, taking Courtney's vacant chair. 'Is Samantha Callahan going to make a comeback too?'

I hesitated, surprised by her interest. 'No. My professional tennis-playing days are over.'

'You know, Sam, personality counts as much as reputation, and with your knowledge of tennis, you could step straight into a media career.'

I laughed. 'I don't think so.'

'Why not? Just because we don't like each other doesn't mean I wouldn't recommend you for a job. Not that you need my recommendation.'

I frowned. 'You're actually serious?'.

'Yes. What's the problem?' she persisted. 'You're an excellent communicator who calls it like it is, and you're well-liked by the public now the slapping incident is in the past. Your sister's on the comeback trail. It's a no-brainer. Think about it.'

'It's worth considering,' Bear said after Prue left our table.

'Possibly,' I said, reaching for his hand, 'but I need to get my priorities straight.'

'And they are?' Annie asked.

'Making up for lost time with my guy.' I leaned in close to Bear.

He raised his eyebrows. 'And you have a lot of making up to do.'

'I have some news of my own,' Annie said once Bear and I had finished canoodling.

I almost stopped breathing. I couldn't begin to imagine what she was about to say. 'Yes?'

'I want to go back to India.'

Total shock. My world was about to come crashing down again. 'What? To live?'

'No, not at all. But I want to give a little back to the country that helped me so much. I want to sponsor a foundation to support orphans through their education. I've discussed it with Zach, and he's coming with me to help with the initial formation and fundraising.'

I looked at Zach, stunned. He smiled back at me and raised his glass.

'Wow,' I said. 'That's amazing.'

'You don't think it's stupid or silly?'

'Of course not. I think it's wonderful.'

'That's so good, Samantha, because it's something I really want to do.' She took a moment. 'For both of us, together. In Mum's name.'

I choked up remembering Mum and then thought about the girls I coached and how they'd want to contribute.

'Absolutely,' I said. 'I'd be honoured to be involved. A team effort. But Annie, you're not going to take off indefinitely again, are you?'

'My wandering days are over—for now. I'll need to go over there to organise the setup, but Melbourne seems as good a place as any to live and focus on my game.' She took Zach's hand. 'It helps that Zach's going to be with me too.'

'This calls for another bottle or three,' Bear said. 'I couldn't be happier for you both.'

Prue Hamilton took to the podium, microphone in hand.

'I didn't think this was an official dinner,' I whispered to Bear.

'It's not. I just think she's in an uncharacteristically good mood.'

'I slipped her a double vodka,' Zach said with a grin.

'Courtney Gold and Annie Callahan have always had talent,' Prue began merrily. 'But now it appears both women—underdogs from the start of this tournament—have forged an unlikely friendship. A friendship that has led both of them to rediscover their love for tennis and accept the higher level of commitment and mental strength needed to dominate this sport.'

The whole restaurant erupted in applause.

Prue waited till it died down before continuing. 'I look forward to next year's Australian Open tournament when I hope these two magnificent athletes will prove the naysayers wrong by taking each other on in the finals. I'm too young to remember Margaret Court and Evonne Goolagong going head-to-head in the 1971 final, or Kerry Reid's 1977 victory over fellow Aussie Dianne Fromholtz Balestrat, but I won't be missing next year's battle. I can't wait.'

She left the podium to a standing ovation.

'That's a pretty good endorsement from a woman who supposedly can't stand the Callahans,' Bear said.

'It's in the past,' I said, waving my hand. 'Like so many other incidents. It doesn't look like she's going to be leaving the circuit anytime soon, and I know I'm not. So maybe I should give her another chance.'

'And me?'

'I was crazy enough to let you go the first and second times. I'm not about to do it again.'

Bear exhaled. 'Thank God for that.'

'I'll say,' Prue Hamilton said, back again. 'You're a much nicer person with Bear by your side.'

'Thanks, I think. Nice speech, Prue.'

'I can be charming when the moment calls for it.' She winked and left.

I turned to Annie. 'You really were brilliant out there today.'

'Thanks, but I wanted to win.'

'Hey Wildcard! Sometimes it takes longer than two weeks to conquer the world. There's always next time. I can see it now.' I grabbed the pepper grinder as my stand-in microphone.

'It was experience over youth today when Annie Callahan, in a stunning comeback, claimed the Australian Open singles title just twelve days shy of her thirtieth birthday. It was a gruelling racquet-hurling victory over Courtney Gold—only the third time the Australian Open singles final has been played out by two Aussies. In an affectionate nod to her sister and mentor, Annie sported a red headband and dedicated her victory to Samantha who's been by her side since day one.'

Annie laughed. 'I certainly will dedicate it to you if I ever win.'

'You will win,' I told her. 'I'm already thinking ahead: Dubai in a couple of months, then Miami, then—'

'Can't we just enjoy the moment?' she said, wrapping her arms around me. 'In the words of the Beatles, "Let it be".'

'Is that really what I'm supposed to do?' I asked. 'Let things be? Let nature take its course? Let the rivers run free?'

'Try as you might, GG, you can't control everything,' Bear said happily.

'The universe doesn't work like that,' Annie agreed. 'Sometimes you've just got to be. Now, who's up for another champagne?'

Acknowledgements

The Pact is the result of blood, sweat and tears ...many. It's been a long journey and I have many people to thank.

I am grateful to the wonderful team at Wings ePress for believing in Samantha and Annie Callahan's story and bringing it to life in *The Pact*. In particular, I'd like to thank Executive Editor extraordinaire, Jeanne Smith, and marketing guru, Michael Embry.

To Daniella Levy, who developed the fabulous cover design and was ever patient working through various niggles along the way, thank you. I love it!

Thanks to my agent, Michael Cybulski, CEO of New Authors Collective (NAC), for his enthusiastic encouragement and belief in *The Pact*, and my writing in general. To all the team at NAC: Sue Anderson, Bella Ellwood-Clayton, Dennis Fisher, and Laura Fulton, it's wonderful working with you all.

Huge shout out to my dear friend, fellow Wings ePress author, and former editorial head at NAC, Andrea Barton. Thank you is not enough for the countless hours of editing, discussion, invaluable suggestions, and constructive criticism you generously provided to bring the Callahan story to life.

Writing is often a solitary existence, but I have many great friends and writing and book club buddies who have supported me over the years. Thank you in no particular order to: Dr Anita Heiss, Heidi Rexa, Michael Bancks, Allison Tait, Dianne Riminton-Johns, Bozena Gawart, Colleen Barry, Penny Doust, Marty Bowles, Sonya Parer, Jeremy Fisher, Susannah Hardy, Anjanette Fennell, Sarah Bourne, Julia O'Keefe, Mandi Gunsberger, Diane Clarke, Lloyd Christison, Roirda Harper, Deb Stewart-Henderson, Donele Overton, Janette McLeod, Fiona Truskett, Valerie Beattie, Cara Jed, Sarah Hawthorn, Kylie Ladd, and Lee Watsford. I'm sure there are more, but there's always next time!

Thanks to Jackie Claridge-Wood for creating Global Girls Online Book Club. I love being a member of this wonderfully embracing community.

To sporting legends, and fellow Wordle and Waffle competitors, Jane McLeod and Libby Sherrard, tennis stars in their own right, cheers for graciously making cameos in the novel!

Chris Harriott, ten years have flown. Our mutual love of musicals, pasta and wine brought us together. Candy Crush, cat wrangling, and your amazing culinary skills keep us together. Here's to many more years of adventures.

Finally, to my family, especially Josh, Noah and Mia, love and adore you all. Now go forth and create drama so I can write my next book. (Of course, I'll change the names ...)

Meet Lisa Darcy

Lisa Darcy is passionate about writing fiction, typically stories centred around women navigating friendships, careers, romance, and ultimately triumphing over adversity.

With several previously published novels with Allen & Unwin, Australia, her seventh novel, *Lily's Little Flower Shop* was published by Bloodhound Books UK in 2021, followed by *My Big Greek Holiday* and *Should You Keep A Secret?* in 2022.

Lisa is also a creative writing teacher, presents workshops, facilitates writing retreats, and has been on panels at many writers' festivals in Australia and internationally.

Dear reader,

I hope you've enjoyed reading this tale of the lives and careers of two totally different siblings.

Your opinion is valuable to other readers like you, who may be looking for books like mine.

Please consider taking a few minutes to post a review, however brief, on the site where you purchased this book or on the Wings ePress web page.

You may also want to visit my author page at the Wings' website, where you can find all the other books in my series.

Thank you!

Lisa Darcy

Printed in Dunstable, United Kingdom

68345203R00208